Return to Port

By T.S. Dawson

Acknowledgements

I apologize if these acknowledgements are starting to sound the same, but I am nine books in and most of the same team has been with me since the beginning. Its like introducing a rock band I suppose: On edits is Christie DeMasi, Donna Goss and Vickie Goodson, computer formatting and what-not is the wonderful John Bryan, and quasi-psychology expert keeping my mind straight as I write is Jill Rowland Marriott.

Form the phone calls with Christie and Donna about content and plot to the conversation with Vickie about consistent character development and about the plausibility of certain plot points, I am really thankful for your input. Also, to John for teaching me again, how to format and helping me start the next book with the proper format so we don't have to reinvent the wheel at the end of the book again, thank you so much. Lastly, to Jill who reminds me that I can do everything I put my mind to, but I don't have to do it all at once, thank you so much. I so appreciate each and every single one of you for being a part of my tribe and helping to make the books by T.S. Dawson possible.

As always, thank you to all of you have hung in there with me through the last two years. Thank you to those of you who waited patiently, those who have encouraged me to keep writing and those of you who have continued read and to spread the word about my books. You are my marketing team and I really appreciate all that you've done and continue to do for me.

Thank you to the reader for giving your time to my writing. I hope you enjoy this book as well as my others.

Sincerely,

Terri
AKA T.S. Dawson

RETURN TO PORT

Soundtrack

Unlike a movie, with the exception of a couple from the list, these are not songs that should play at certain points in the story. They are songs that inspire me to write, songs that help me bring the characters and what they are feeling to life. Sometimes, you may not think they mean a thing to the story and you could be right. It might just be something that moved me at the time.

I often find covers of songs on YouTube that I like better than the original, so if you go looking for the songs and performers listed and don't find them, try YouTube. If there's ever a song that you feel fits one of my books or characters, please feel free to reach out and share with me.

Will the Circle Be Unbroken	Amos Lee
Far Behind	Candle Box
Doing Life With Me	Eric Church
Every Little Thing	Carly Pearce
Yours	Chris Dickerson
Someone Like You	Adele
Marry Me	Thomas Rhett
Mercy Me	Jocelyn & Chris Arndt
Springsteen	Eric Church
Free/Into the Mystic	Zack Brown Band
Whiter Shade of Pale	Anne Lennox
I Just Really Miss You	Miranda Lambert
Desperado	The Eagles

David smiled at our guests. "It's just a shirt. Nothing to worry about," he said, dabbing the Pinot Noir from his sleeve.

"I'm so sorry," I apologized again, this time laughing at my clumsiness and smiled a toothy smile, so embarrassed. "It just slipped right out of my hand."

I'd waited tables for years in college including fine dining at Port Honor. I'd opened wine bottles and poured almost nightly. Never had I spilled a drop before tonight.

David had had such high hopes for our first dinner party as a married couple, but things happen. I wasn't sure how it happened, but the bottle slipped right out of my fingers and tumbled, almost spraying the red liquid down his right sleeve.

Now the door closed behind James and Allison and no sooner did David turn on his heel, snatch me by my arm just above my elbow, raising me to my toes and escorted me to the coat closet mere feet from the door. It happened so fast and was such a shock that I didn't have time to register what had gone on. Within seconds, I found myself pounding on the inside of the closet door, begging David to let me out as he screamed and kicked at the other side of the door.

"How dare you embarrass me?!!!" he screamed. "Who do you think you are? I'll tell you! You are Mrs. DOCTOR David West and you will behave as such or you will suffer dearly!"

The first night, after the shock wore off, I begged David to let me out. I apologized profusely and begged for his forgiveness. I promised I'd do better, swore I'd never do it again as if I'd committed some grave offense. When those things didn't work, I pounded on the door and did my best to break it down. It was a two foot by two foot space with no room for leverage or to get a running start. I was stuck and feared he'd left me, sure that he'd packed his things and was going to divorce me. When I was

8

certain I was utterly alone, I slumped to the floor and folded myself into a ball, hugged my knees and cried. I cried until morning when he let me out. So happy to be out and to see David still there, I threw my arms around him, but no reciprocating embrace was forthcoming.

"You should get ready for your tennis lessons." He just stiffened and then brushed me away.

"Tennis...lessons?" I slipped off of him, this having been the first I'd heard of such.

"Yes, it's what doctor's wives do."

So much was said in that one sentence, so much that told me not to revisit the night before.

That was the first time I was locked in the closet, but I lost count of how many followed. I was a very bad wife and I was an even worse mother. At first the closet was my torment, but eventually it became my solace.

Chapter 1

May 9, 2010

"Let us bow our heads in prayer," the preacher began.

Unlike the lady for whom we were all gathered here for, I didn't darken the doors of church every time they opened. On rare occasions, I attended Sunday school with my grandparents as a child and I'd attended more funerals than I'd care to remember. I knew it was proper to keep your head down and eyes closed during prayer. And for the most part I did so, but as what looked to be the mayor of Whoville led us in prayer for Jay's mother, I lifted my head and peeped. I took stock of the crowd.

Despite his Christmas red and green sweater vest and matching Rudolph necktie, his spiky hair, cherub cheeks and up turned nose, the preacher could not hold my attention. The words he spoke over Mrs. McDonald's casket, the multiple times he told us how the grave diggers were struggling due to the rain from the past few days, I heard him, but he didn't draw me in. He all but announced they were going to throw her in a mud hole. I heard that, too. He gave more description of the grave site than he provided comfort from the scripture. I heard all of what he said, but could not focus my interest. Selfishly, I'd come with a purpose beyond that of just paying my respects to my college roommate over the death of his mother.

I searched the faces of the crowd as the minister droned on. Every pew was full even the ones in the balcony. I craned my neck to see to the back of the church where men stood, packed in shoulder to shoulder. It appeared that folks from far and wide had turned out to usher Mrs. McDonald into the great beyond and the First Baptist Church of Thomson, Georgia was filled to capacity.

Millie, Gabe and their daughters sat with the family as Millie was as close to Jay as his biological sister.

Millie was one of a handful of people I'd kept in touch with from my days at Georgia College. There was a handful of us who'd become lifelong friends and all of us were here today.

Bowing my head, I did praise Jesus that Millie's Aunt Gayle had remembered me when I entered the church. She and her husband were seated four rows in back of Millie.

"Cara," Gayle waived to me, inviting me to sit with them.

I sat between Gayle and Stella and in back of Daniel and Jerry. Stella had lived across the hall from me when we rented apartments in Millie's building, The Jefferson, while we were in college. Gabe had hired me, Millie, Daniel and Jerry when he was the manager of Port Honor and we all started work within weeks of one another. Initially, Millie and Jay were roommates. They'd been friends since childhood and, when Gabe moved in with Millie, Jay moved downstairs and we became roommates. The whole group had become more than my friends. They were my home away from home and my family.

Also seated near us were a few friends I made over the years while visiting Millie and Gabe at their home in Wrens. Of all of the faces in the congregation, one was missing. It was that of a friend I hadn't seen in over a dozen years other than when I stalked him on Facebook, Andy Sheppard.

As much as I knew you weren't supposed to peep during prayers, I knew funerals weren't exactly the time or place to look forward to seeing someone, but since Millie had phoned with the news two nights ago, I had been looking forward to today. In the midst of casual conversation about the arrangements, I asked Millie who all she thought would be there. Millie named off all of the people sitting near me plus, "Stella, Caroline, Jack, Andy..."

Millie could have stopped at his name because I didn't hear much after that.

Although Jay and Millie had been all of our persons at one time or another, Andy had become my person in the aftermath of the Olympic Park bombing. Andy was one of the bartenders when we all worked at Port Honor. He was my person and, then one day, I said something stupid and he wasn't anymore. I let my low self-esteem get the better of me and he served me his version of: "Frankly, my Dear, I don't give a damn."

At twenty-one, I didn't feel I deserved the way he treated me, but the more years passed, the more I came to realize that I got exactly what I deserved. It was Andy that didn't deserve how I had behaved and I had behaved badly. I owed him a long overdue apology, one more deserving than a paragraph sent through Messenger or a text.

A slight pang of disappointment came over me when I first entered the church and didn't see Andy. Disappointment continued to overtake me as the service drug on and now this prayer and a final look around, I was crushed. I'd dreamed for so long for an excuse to see him and now here it was, but he wasn't here. I felt ashamed of myself for using the death of one of my dearest friends' mother as an opportunity to absolve me from the hurt I'd done to another friend. Maybe I was getting what I deserved again.

Feeling sorry for myself, I dropped my head and closed my eyes just as the preacher reached his conclusion. "Amen."

With the bulk of the congregation's heads still hung low, the pallbearers made their way to the casket and a slightly raspy male voice started to ring out.

"I was standing by the window on a cold and cloudy day..."

It was a familiar Johnny Cash song which I'd heard a hundred times while watching The Grand Ole

Opry with my grandparents, but this was unlike any version I'd ever heard.

"When I saw that hearse come rolling, for to carry my mother away..."

A wail came from the front row and I lifted my head to see Jay's sister, Jolene, breaking with the words of the song. Peter, Jay's partner, put his arm around her to comfort her.

The upbeat tempo in which the song was usually sang was not there.

Beyond Jolene and Peter, I caught sight of who I'd been searching for all day. My head cocked to the side and I was mesmerized. It was as if I was twenty years old all over again. I covered my mouth to hide my awe.

"Will the circle be unbroken by and by Lord, by and by. There's a better home awaiting, in the sky, Lord, in the sky." Andy sang with Millie having joined him on stage for backup.

My heart ached for Jay and his family over the loss of their mother, but the delivery of the words to the song, moved me to my core. The sorrow Andy's voice conveyed was like nothing I'd ever felt from a song before. A trill, the vibration, the drawing of breath and the lonesome drowning wail coming from his lips, made my heart swell and break all at the same time.

"I said to that undertaker, Undertaker please drive slow..."

The pallbearers wheeled the casket down the aisle with the family following behind as Andy drove home the depths of their loss.

"For this lady, you are carrying, Lord I hate to see her go."

Aisle after aisle, people lifted their heads and got to their feet as Mrs. McDonald was rolled by. Heads turned to watch her go, but not me. I was fixed on Andy. The years had been kind and the photos he posted on Facebook didn't do him justice. He was exactly as I remembered him as little more than an over-sized boy, but he was a man now.

Others may have heard the sound of the wheels of the cart the casket sat upon strain as it bogged down in the thick carpet. Some may have become distracted with the creaks coming from the wooden floor beneath the carpet and the trampling footsteps of the pallbearers. They may have heard the shuffling of Jay's father's feet or the small sniffles Jay made as he helped his aging father follow his mother one final time. All of that was just background noise to me.

Millie's voice fell away and the gentleman with the guitar stilled his fingers as did the pianist, leaving Andy to finish acapella. "I went home, home was lonesome since my mother, she was gone. All my brothers, and sisters crying, what a home so sad and alone. Will the circle be unbroken, by and by Lord, by and by."

As Mrs. McDonald made her final exit of the church where she'd first been baptized, married her husband and raised her children, Andy finished, "There's a better home a waiting, in the sky, Lord, in the sky."

There were more verses to the song, but that's where it ended with not a dry eye in the place, not even mine. Had there been an overhead photo of the congregation, I would have been spotted in a search of Where's Waldo with me being Waldo. I was the only person still facing forward when the casket passed through the church entry way.

I struggled to see Andy as he made his way back to his seat. I peered between the heads of Jerry and Daniel in front of me. I twisted to see between them and follow Andy. Andy found a chair beside the pianist, and hidden behind a large potted plant.

No wonder I hadn't seen him.

Overlapping the voice in my head, the Mayor of Whoville reminded us once again, "Even though the rain stopped this morning, there's no way of getting Mrs. McDonald in the... well...uerwhhh..."

He paused, remembering the concept of TMI. He stopped himself and redirected. Twitching and not knowing what else to say, he rattled off, "The family thanks you for coming. There will be no graveside service."

The mayor nearly sprinted from the podium, forgetting to detach his clip-on mic and muttering about being starved and passed his lunch time. The carpet in the church might have been worn, but the sound system seemed just stellar.

Gayle leaned to me and snickered, "Where did they find him?"

"I have no idea," I almost laughed back since I was thinking the same thing.

I thought we were whispering, but Jerry heard us. He turned around and added, "According to Millie, Jay said they struggled to get a minister at all. The head minister of the church had to preach his grandmother's funeral in South Carolina today. The assistant pastor had his wisdom teeth removed two days ago and got dry sockets. They called the preacher at First Baptist in Lincolnton and he has the flu. Millie called the Baptist church in Wrens and he had two funerals already scheduled for today..."

Jerry was clearly more informed than the rest of us and only stopped because Daniel cut him off.

Jerry and Daniel had been together for nearly thirty years. They worked with us at Port Honor all those years ago when we first formed this merry band of friends. Jerry was the gossipy, sassy one and Daniel was the practical, funny one.

"They were about to start calling the AME churches, but Jay's siter wasn't sure how that would go over at the big church in the center of town. You know, it still being the South and all." Daniel said it deadpan, as if he wasn't joking, but we all chuckled a little at the thought.

Jerry took over again, "I guess the whole place would have gone up in flames with a black preacher and four gays up in here." He fanned himself, but looked pleased.

Stella joined in the conversation, "Well, I'm surprised lightening hasn't struck the place already because this mixed girl gave one of the gays a shot of Jack Daniels from her purse."

Jerry and Daniel looked at one another, each questioning the other as to who got the libations.

"Not everything's about the two of you." Stella playfully slapped at the two of them. "I gave it to Jay and I gave the whole flask to Peter. He's going to need it the most."

We had been fairly discrete with our words, but we received scathing looks from the elders who were exiting the aisles near us. Apparently, our bursts of laughter were inappropriate as well.

"I missed y'all!" I gushed, taking the hands of Daniel and Jerry and giving them a squeeze.

The group of us milled around and let the rest of the funeral goers make their way out ahead of us. We lingered back in conversation, catching up since we'd last seen one another. Some of the group had kept in touch more closely, but I drifted in and out over the years. I saw Millie fairly often, especially now that I'd moved back to the area, but the group of us didn't have family dinners as often as we once did. She still hosted Friendsgiving in November each year and I attended when I could.

"We missed you, too." Daniel hugged me. Of the two of them, he was always my favorite.

The space between where we had gathered in the main aisle and the stage cleared and Andy made his way toward us. I struggled not to watch as he approached.

Before I'd been transfixed by his voice. I'd never heard him sing before. I had no idea he could sing or how amazing he was. In addition to internally ogling over his voice at a funeral, my inappropriateness knew no bounds. It made me think of things I'd wanted to do to Eddie Vedder, slow rocking sex, the really good toe-curling kind with a man that knew what he was doing. Andy could have looked like anything thanks to that voice, but he didn't just look like anything.

Now, as he made his way over, I realized that he had never looked better. Whereas Daniel and Jerry, underneath his makeup, were aging like milk, Andy was the cliché. He was indeed aging like a fine wine.

Andy was never pale, but he seemed a little more olive skinned than I remembered. He was never thin, but had gained a bit of weight, filling out more so than just embracing his age like most forty-year-old men do. From the fit of his suit, tight across the chest and not the gut, snug over the biceps, you could tell he still worked out. I had to look away to keep from staring and crying over my missed opportunity all those years ago.

The closer he became on his approach, the more details I noticed about his appearance. I looked, but tried not to. By the time he squeezed in our circle next to Stella, I'd taken stock of the whisps of silver around his temples and the ever so tiny crow's feet coming in at the far corners of his eyes.

I had colored my hair for this occasion, just highlights did the trick. I had my own battle to wage against the gray that started to form in a spot straight above my nose. Each time I faced myself in the mirror I thought if I let this go, I would end up looking like a skunk, but I procrastinated. This was the first time I'd colored my hair since before the bombing in 1996.

Towering between Stella and Daniel, Andy asked, "Did anyone else think he looked like a character from The Grinch?" He motioned back to the minister who, at that point, had ditched his microphone and been stopped by the pianist.

There wasn't a one of us who needed to look to verify who he was talking about and we all cracked up.

"You mean the mayor of Whoville?" I said through my laughter, calling his attention to me.

"Exactly!" Andy replied, looking at me for the first time. His face betrayed him as the recognition set in.

The proximity to Andy made me as nervous as I'd been the first time I met him. I was thirty-five years old and intimidated by a man. I couldn't recall the last time I'd had that feeling.

Stella joined the banter, "Jerry, you didn't tell us how they ended up with him."

We all turned our attention to Jerry.

"He's the minister of music and he volunteered. I think it was his first funeral," Jerry explained.

Gayle giggled, "And he'd never been to one before either?"

Andy raised his voice a few octaves, "It's been raining cats and dogs and the wall of the grave just collapsed in on itself." He shifted back to his normal speaking voice, "Who says that?"

"Thank goodness there's no Yelp page for rating ministers," Stella laughed.

"Mrs. McDonald's funeral was definitely memorable," I added.

"Y'all should have seen Millie! She was just stewing. Y'all couldn't see, but I think if Gabe hadn't had her by the hand, she would have jumped on stage and told that guy where to go. Politely where to go, but she would have definitely thrown him off the stage."

We all knew he was right about Millie. Compared to Millie, I was a wall flower.

Our laughter and banter died down when Jay returned with Millie and Gabe. It didn't seem right to continue joking around in his presence, but the first thing Jay said was, "Did anyone else notice anything odd about... I mean, he wore a Christmas decorated sweater vest. What the Hell?"

Needless to say, the laughter could not be contained.

"I swear, if something happens to me, y'all can decide among yourselves who will speak or just take turns saying something." Jay shook his head in disgust.

A few more minutes passed with us trying to convince Jay that it wasn't so bad.

"I've definitely been to worse," Daniel said, cutting his eyes toward his partner and seeking confirmation. "You know it. Remember Matt..." he snapped his fingers, trying to remember Matt's last name. "Matt, you know..."

"Matt Murphy," Jerry spit out before it left his mind again.

"What made it so bad?" Gayle asked, but no one seemed to hear her.

"Right, the one who never came out to his family." Daniel shook his index finger vigorously in a gesture of agreement and somewhat answering

Shocked, both Andy and I asked at the same time, "Matt Murphy?"

To keep her aunt in the loop, Millie whispered to Gayle that Matt had been a bartender at Port Honor the first year we all worked there.

Jay started to laugh, "That's right neither of you knew either. Ha!"

Andy was the first of the two of us to say anything back. "Are you sure?"

Jay looked to the ceiling and muttered, "Forgive me, Lord, for saying this now," before squarely looking from Andy to me. "I'm more certain he was gay than she will ever be that he was straight."

If Peter had been there, Jay would have never said such a thing.

"I didn't even know he had died," I said through complete bewilderment on all accounts.

"That wasn't the only thing you didn't know," Jerry smirked.

All eyes were on me.

"No, I never..." I tapered off. I had just thought about sex in church a few minutes ago, but thinking about it and talking about it there were two very different things.

"You dated him for a year and never..."

Daniel cut Andy off as I spit out, adamantly, "Never!"

Of all the scenarios I'd played out in my head of conversations I would have with Andy, this was never one of them. Luckily, he wasn't allowed to finish that sentence.

"Neither of you knew and you lived with him. You did seem like a bit," Daniel paused briefly to choose his description and started again with, "closed minded and self-absorbed, back then."

"Anyway, Matt never came out to his parents." Jay politely halted any response from Andy and gave a look to Daniel that suggested he not continue down that stretch of memory lane.

While Daniel took the cue, Jerry was more than happy to continue the story about Matt's funeral. "You should have seen it when the girls showed up."

Jerry added a special emphasis to the word "girls", but Gale questioned, "What girls?"

The rest of us knew what Jerry meant, but he was more than happy to fill Gayle in. "The girls," he winked, "from Back Street."

Andy's face went a little white, likely still wondering how he never knew. I cannot say that I was anything less than slightly shaken.

Knowing Gayle wouldn't have any idea what Back Street was, Jay clarified, "It was a drag bar in Atlanta."

Gayle stopped looking puzzled and covered her mouth with her hand to hide her surprise.

"Yes," Daniel quipped at Gayle. "That's the same expression that came over half the church when they walked in wearing their best."

Jay further described, "Sadly, it was all that you are imagining."

At some point during our banter about Matt, Stella had branched off into a side conversation with Millie, but rejoined us. "When did he die and how?"

I looked on, curious to that answer as well.

"I guess it's been about fifteen years ago," Daniel gave part of the answer.

Stella did the calculations in her head. "So, he was thirty?"

"He was two years older than us," I said to Stella. I did know that much about Matt.

"Still, that's so young," she sighed.

Jolene returned with Peter trailing behind and the conversation about Matt tapered off. I realized then that Peter's job for the day was to keep Jolene occupied so Jay didn't have to deal with her. Jay was level headed and could handle anything, but his sister.

"I guess there's no need in taking these flowers to the grave." She held up her phone at Jay. "They just called and said it will be eight o'clock before they are ready for her."

Exasperated, he asked her, "Well, what do you want to do with them?"

"I don't know," she huffed back, dropping her hands and ringing them together around the phone.

Peter reached an arm around her and Jolene leaned into him and started to cry again.

At that point, Jay headed toward the wide variety of flowers that were still sitting around the vacant spot where the casket had been and Millie followed. "Mama would want anything that could be planted to be planted."

Our circle disbanded, but only Gayle and Noah excused themselves to head home.

"Cara," Jay called to me, "would you mind pulling the cards so we can have them to write thank you notes?"

I had just bent over to fetch my purse from under the pew where I sat, but I popped back up and replied, "Sure."

21

"I'll help you," Andy said as I stepped back into the main aisle of the church where he was waiting.

That wasn't the first time Andy had helped me.

Chapter 2

I awoke with a jolt. Half asleep, my ears were still ringing from the equivalent of a cannon blast and I knew what a cannon blast sounded like from all of the years going with my daddy to his Civil War reenactments. It was a frightening thing that I was never prepared for and I certainly hadn't been prepared for what went on last night.

It was July 28, 1996 and sitting bolt upright in my bed, my heart raced. I struggled to catch my breath as I looked around my bedroom.

It was summer and I'd only had sheets on the bed seeing as my roommate and I couldn't afford to run the air conditioning. It was Milledgeville, Georgia and the one thing we could count on was cockroaches the size small dogs and heat rising, but I didn't know whether I was sweating from the stifling heat or having fought like a cat in my dream.

The top sheet was gone and the fitted one was snatched from the mattress and wadded and wrapped like a toga around me. My pillows were flung to the far sides of the room. From the vivid pictures of the dream that were still fresh in my mind combined with the memories, I'd clearly had a reenactment of my own.

We were dancing to Jack Mack and the Heart Attack. We'd made our way to the stage and we were having the time of our lives. My hands were above my head. I was jumping and swaying with the music. Millie was with me and we were alive, more alive than I'd been in my entire life. Then, there was a deafening blast and things went a little fuzzy.

"Ma'am, ma'am, you have to move.

You have to get back." A lady grabbed at me. I really couldn't see her. Her face was a fog. My mind was a fog. I only knew one thing. I had to find Millie.

"But my friend was injured in the blast and now I can't find her."

"Ma'am," the voice came again, "I am sure your friend is fine, but there is nothing you can do here. You need to move so the professionals can get through."

She pulled at me to get up and I thought I was up, but I felt my legs, just jello below me.

"No! She was not alright! She fell and she had blood... She's hurt and I can't find her! Oh my God! Her name is Millie and you have to help me find her. We have to find her!"

I held on to the lady for support and for fear that she would run. Everyone around us seemed to be running and they weren't running in any particular direction.

"Ma'am, you are going to have to trust that the emergency personnel will find her and get her help. For now, you need to go home."

What she really meant is that we needed to get out of there. She struggled to pull me with her, but I wasn't having any of it.

"Go home? I can't just leave her! Here, I will give you all of these collector pins and all of the money I have on me if you will just help me."

The lady did her best to remain calm. "I don't want your money. It's not safe here we have to go."

I let my eyes wander around my room, again assuring myself that I was home and I was safe. I swatted at my arms, thinking of how the shrapnel felt like bee stings and how my blood trickled, but Millie's ran and covered me. I let my eyes fall to the shirt I was wearing. My pajama shirt was clean, but I could smell the burning in the air and blood.

Flashing back to the dream or the images from the night before, my eyes left my shirt and traveled to my hands. They were laying palms up in my lap, trembling and sore from gripping. I didn't know if they were sore from trying to hold on to Millie and being ripped away from her or what I'd just done to the sheets on my bed. I'd fought to hang on to Millie, even in my dream I'd clearly acted it out.

I smelled that night. I felt that night. I heard that night. People screaming and running over us like a stampede of wild animals. They ran for their lives and one of them had the good sense to drag me with them. I could still feel that woman's arms hooked in mine, pulling me. I don't know who she was, in fact I wasn't even sure it was a woman. In my dream, I couldn't see her face, but she screamed like Little Richard. I couldn't thank or curse her or him if I had wanted.

No one knew whether there might be more bombs so everyone just ran. A wave of people flowed through the streets of Atlanta and when it finally spit me out, I had no idea where I was or how to get back to Millie. I didn't know if there were more bombs either, but what I did know was that I had to find Millie.

More frightening than the blast and more frightening than the screams of terror from the people in the park was the faint word Millie spoke as she went down.

"Cara." Low as a whisper with a plea and shock, it was Millie's voice and she said my name. It was that whisper that woke me up.

The first night wasn't the last and it wasn't even the most vivid. Every night for months I had the same nightmares. I awoke winded, heart racing and to a view of a thrashed bed.

We'd found Millie the morning after the bombing. She'd been rushed to one of the hospitals in Atlanta, but after a while, she was fine. She was actually pregnant as it turned out and her life was moving on. My life was not moving on, at least not in the direction I'd planned.
***

My feet hurt. My back hurt. My head and everything in between that didn't flat out hurt was numb. I'd worked a double shift at Port Honor.

Hocking drinks on the beverage cart all day on the golf course and then waiting tables all night in the clubhouse had taken its toll on me, but I couldn't complain. Since the Olympic Park bombing, my college job at the country club had become the one constant in my life. Port Honor had turned into my home-away-from-home. While I wasn't in class or driving the thirty minutes between Milledgeville and the club, I was at the club.

Saturdays were the busiest and today was a typical Saturday even though it was February. Winters weren't nearly as busy as the other seasons at the golf and country club. It was nearly midnight and my last set of customers, members really, had just left. As soon as they were headed toward the exit through the lobby upstairs, I headed for the bar to cash out.

I was so tired it took me three times to count the money from my apron. I typically kept my tips in one pocket and payments from the guests in another. I was certain I hadn't mixed them, but I was short for my payout and my tips weren't excessive. I was holding my head in my hands with my elbows propped on the bar when Andy came back.

Andy was the bartender on duty that night. In fact, he'd been there all day as well and was probably just as tired and eager to get out of there as I was.

"Kindergarteners could count change more accurately than this," I peered up at him, begging for sympathy.

"How far off are you?" Andy asked.

"Fifteen dollars and, oh Hell, I don't know." I looked down at the pile of money and receipts and then back at him.

I scratched my forehead and then leaned down and rubbed my calf muscle. I sat back up and started the counting again. From the corner of my eye, I noticed Andy taking out his wallet. I was so easily distracted that I lost count and watched him take out a ten and a five and slide them my direction.

"Thanks, but I can't take that." I shook my head. "I can't take your money."

"Take the money. You can pay me back tomorrow. We're both working then too."

I almost cried. I was so tired and, since the bombing, whenever anyone was nice to me, tears sprang up. I couldn't seem to help it. It had been a long, hard six months.

"Thank you," I said, trying not to sound like I felt sorry for myself, but I did. I hated owing anyone, a quality instilled in me by my mother. "I'll pay you back tomorrow."

"And if you don't, that's fine too."

"No, I will pay you back."

Andy shook his head and mumbled under his breath, "Just can't be nice to some people."

"I heard you."

Andy went back to drying the bar glasses as I straightened the money and pushed it to his side of the bar. I'm sure he wanted to go home as badly as I did. Andy had been there all day too and we were the only ones left. Gabe had gone home a couple of hours ago and one of his rules were that no one was left to lock up alone. Jerry and Daniel had been on staff with us that night, but their tables cleared out before mine so I was stuck until Andy was finished.

Andy still had one table left. There were three college age guys seated at a table across the bar room and on the opposite side of the fireplace.

I blew the hair out of my face and did the only thing I felt would speed this process along for the both of us. I scooted off of the stool and started toward the table with a tray in my hand. I figured if I started bussing the table, they would take the hint.

Realizing where I was headed Andy said so only I could hear, "Be nice to the one in blue."

I stopped in my tracks when he said the part about being nice.

"Huh?" I jerked my face back around in his direction.

He motioned for me to come back and I did.

"That's Owen Honor. His family used to own this land this place sits on. Hence the name, Port *Honor*."

"Okay." I wasn't impressed.

I got on with it, marched right over to the table and started plucking up the menagerie of beer mugs and shot glasses that the boys had accumulated. The three were playing cards, poker to be exact. I moved around the table taking the glasses and casually looking at their cards. One had a pair and the other was working on a flush, but the one in blue had nothing other than a good poker face.

He took a drag of his cigarette before placing it on the edge of one of the plates we used to serve bread. I couldn't help but think he could have asked for an ashtray instead of doing that to the plate.

With the same hand, he took a swig from the only highball glass on the table. The glass had the remains of something the color of watered-down caramel. I figured it was whiskey so I'd learned the boy in blue was a smoker and liked hard liquor. Those two things were turn offs for me.

His movements were deliberately casual. He should have taken a card, but he didn't. He knew I'd seen his hand and he locked eyes with me as he pushed the money in front of him to the center of the table. He was bluffing. He knew I knew and for a moment I couldn't help, but smile as we shared that secret. He gave me a wink and I immediately diverted my eyes and went back to collecting the glassware.

His bluff worked. He won the pot and the game was over. Thinking they were done for the night I reached for the last glass, the one he'd nursed before making his move. He'd stood and leaned across the table to rake the pot toward him, but stopped.

With a hand over the top of the glass, he insisted, "Let it be." There was a hesitation before he added, "Please."

"Okay," I agreed, "but we're closing so..."

The two losers held their chairs, but not their tongues.

"We're members and..." One started, but I cut him off.

"Then you should know our hours of operation." I smiled politely.

"It's going to take more than you to kick us out, sweetheart," the other looked me up and down as he spoke.

My skin crawled and a shiver ran over me. That one gave me the creeps. This had been a bad idea. I grabbed the glass despite the winner's objection and went on my way toward the kitchen door.

"Hey," the boy in the blue called out to me, "Since you're closing anyway, how about you play a hand with us?"

I looked over my shoulder and I'd had every intention of giving him daggers, but he said, "Please," again. The light from the fire place danced in his eyes and he was distracting, but I wasn't about to accept.

"You've got five minutes," I said.

I tried not to be obvious, but I gave the boy in the blue another once over. He wasn't especially tall. He was taller than me, but nothing imposing.

The other striking thing about him was that he wasn't just wearing a blue shirt. He had on khakis and they fit like Matthew McConaughey's in the movie A Time To Kill. I'd noticed that about him when he stood and raked in his winnings. Every man should be so lucky as to have their pants fit like that, I thought at the time.

The more I thought about it, the more he resembled Matthew McConaughey in more ways than just the pants. It was the shared hair color and tan, too. Good Heavens, I almost had to fan myself, but I quickly remembered, he smoked and he drank whiskey. Yuck.

I concentrated on the thought of how this had been such a bad idea, but instead the thought that took over was the damn khaki pants. Even when I turned around and continued on with the tray, the image of him was cemented in my brain. When I blinked, he was on the backs of my eyelids.

I was almost to the swinging door that led from the bar to the kitchen when the glasses on the tray bobbled. I tried to recover, get them balanced again, but the tray dipped on one side, a few of the glasses tilted and all bets were off. The whole thing went down with a shattering, clanging racket.

I jumped and closed my eyes. Behind them was no longer the sandy blond-haired boy in his baby blue golf shirt. Flashes of light, stings on my arms and that pleading whisper of my name scattered my thoughts. Everything about me clinched and I stood stark still and counted slowly until everything stopped. I made it to eight and that was a record.

"Shit!" I mumbled under my breath as I opened my eyes and saw the mess at my feet. A pile of glass was still a relief to see instead of the image of Millie, bloodied and lying there.

There wasn't one glass that had survived the fall. I was so tired that the thought of cleaning it up brought me to the brink of tears. Before bending down to start the picking up process, I looked around the bar for Andy. I'd fully expected him to jump into action, but he was nowhere to be found.

I let out a heavy sigh of disgust. "Figures," I said to myself as I squatted down, careful not to let my bare knees touch the carpet.

The uniform the female servers at Port Honor were required to wear consisted of a khaki skirt, white button-down dress shirt, a tie and our shoes of choice. I had on some black Doc Martins. Nothing sexy would do in the way of foot wear when it came to standing on my feet that long. The only touch of sexy to the entire outfit was the length of the skirt.

"The shorter the skirt the higher the tips," our manager, Gabe, was known to say.

30

My skirt was almost indecently short. I didn't fear getting one snippet of glass through the Docs, but the skirt made my knees fair game and an even bigger concern was showing my panties when I bent over. I did my best to keep on my toes as I squatted and keep my back and pelvis straight as not to give the boys a show. No matter how tired I was, I dared not fall to my knees or bend.

There was every imaginable size and shape of broken glass. From stems and bulbs to chards, glass circled me in a five-foot radius. I sat the tray on the floor and planned my attack.

"Here," a voice came from behind me, "let me help you with that."

It was the boy from the card game. I knew they had to have seen what happened. Even if they hadn't seen the actual dropping of the glasses, I had been sure they heard the crashing and breaking. Instinctively, they would have looked to see what happened. I was embarrassed and hadn't bothered to turn to face them. I'd kept a hand behind me, securing my skirt, while I focused on the task. Now, here he was, offering to help me.

"Oh, no. That's okay. I've got it. Thanks anyway." I couldn't look up at him. He might see tears or the depths of my exhaustion.

He didn't listen to me. He stooped down to the floor beside me and started helping.

"I really do have it. I'm fine." I might have been just telling myself that.

"Maybe you should just say 'Thank you'," he said as he put one of the more intact pieces of the doubles glass on the tray.

"Thank you," I replied without looking at him.

The image of his face was returning and now I could smell him, too. Over the faint hit of the cigarette he'd had before, I could smell the fabric softener that lingered on his clothes. Despite a night of drinking and smoking, he still smelled nice, which led to more insecurities on my part. I probably reeked of a brewery, diner service and body odor. I'd been at it for sixteen hours and there's only so much one can expect from deodorant. I'd forgotten to bring more so I could reapply between shifts and that was something I sorely regretted at that moment.

"I'm Owen."

His words hung in the air as I concentrated on picking up the slivers without cutting myself.

"And you are?" he asked when I didn't freely supply my name.

I took my eyes off of the carpet for one moment, made eye contact with him and told him my name. "Cara. I'm Cara."

"Nice to meet you, Cara."

I wasn't interested in boys. I'd settled into a solitary life over the last few months and I was just here to get my education and move on. I had my friends and I'd done the boyfriend thing already and as crazy as it sounded, I realized I wanted more out of life than to be someone's substitute mother.

The conversation Matt and I had when he broke up with me ran through my mind.

"You've changed. You're selfish now!" Matt had told me.

A near-death experience, that's what the psychology professor that the college assigned to me had said Millie and I had. She said we had "PTSD," post-traumatic stress disorder. I knew Millie had it, but I'd never thought I had it. I thought, she'd had the near-death experience, not me. I was fine, only some scrapes and little cuts. The professor said the nightmares were classic signs. She said if I hadn't changed, that would have been the abnormal part of the experience.

So, Matt was right. I had changed. Life was short and I didn't need or want him anymore. He wasn't a bad guy. He was actually too nice. Luckily, Matt graduated at the end of the Fall semester and moved away so I didn't have to see him anymore. Breaking up and having to still see him would have still been an irritation even if I did know it was for the best.

Regardless of me giving up on boys, I hadn't kissed one in nearly three months and I liked kissing boys. Owen's shirt was a classic Polo style golf shirt with short sleeves so Owen's arm brushed against mine as he reached for another piece of the glass. He had faint blonde hair on his arm and it tickled as it slid against mine. In an instance, I was reminded just how very much I missed kissing boys.

I did my best to put the kibosh on the feel of his touch that lingered on my arm and conjure up what a boy that smoked and drank tasted like. That gave my stomach a churn and it worked. My arm was mine again.

"Hey," one of the boys that had been with Owen appeared behind us. "Nice panties."

I cringed and a shiver ran through me.

Owen got to his feet. "Leave her alone, man."

"Yeah, whatever. We're taking off," the prick said. I'm sure a roll of his eyes went with his words.

I didn't think they were in any shape to drive, but who was I to mind their business? They lived in the neighborhood that surrounded the club. I knew that because the two of them were regulars. I'd likely see them again tomorrow morning at brunch. I figured they'd be fine to make it the few blocks home so I didn't say anything.

Owen didn't flinch. "Okay. I'll see you around."

"You don't need a ride?" the greasy haired slick asked, surprised.

"Nah, I've got my car."

"Right." The guy tried to whisper, but I could still hear every word. "If you hadn't called dibs, I'd get a ride from her too."

"Shut up!" Owen gave him a shove.

"Are you guys safe to drive?" Owen, clearly more concerned for them than me, yelled across the bar to the other one who was waiting.

Bringing the tray with me, I got to my feet. I was offended by the notion of giving any of them any sort of ride and added my two cents. "Why don't you go on with them? We're closed."

I turned my back and went through the swinging doors. I found Andy down the hall between the door to the bar and the kitchen. He was in the liquor closet taking an inventory of what booze as left.

"What happened?" Andy shouted.

"I don't need an ass-hat like that knowing my name or anything about me for that matter!" I yelled back before tilting the tray and letting everything slide into the trash can and crash with a fury that rivaled mine.

"Ass-hat? That really is a new one!"

I closed my eyes and gave my back teeth a good grinding. Owen had followed me.

I took a moment before replying and I didn't bother turning around. "And dibs is something kids say when they want to press the elevator buttons!"

"Fair enough," he scooted around in front of me, "but just so you know, I only called dibs on you because that's all those ass-hats, as you put it, would understand. Since you seem so oblivious and in your own head, let me explain it to you. Those two had been ogling you all night. Jason, the leader of the ass-hats, is a world class pervert and he was trained by and even bigger world class pervert. The man you waited on earlier tonight that kept dropping his napkin, the one you picked up three times, Judson Harrell, Sr. Get a clue. Everyone in the dining room saw your panties, sweetheart."

He leaned in and I held firm. Emphasizing the word as he came within inches of my nose, he said it again. "Everyone."

I was appalled, but turned on. That was not a sensation I was supposed to have, but I wanted to kiss him. Of course, I knew better. The words jumped out of my mouth. "You smoke and you drink. You probably taste like the south end of a north bound cow."

34

"You'll never know!" He turned and stormed off.

I kept standing there, holding the tray and flushed.

Owen stopped a few feet from the turn to exit from the kitchen to the dining room. He turned around. "Just so you know that was sweet tea in that glass of mine. I don't drink. Ever. And, I had one cigarette and that was just for..." He stopped. "It doesn't matter. The point is, as for what I taste like, you were never going to find out. You had me judged and ruled that out before you ever met me. Way to go Cara. Have a nice life."

"Andy," Owen called as he headed back toward the liquor closet. "Here's your money."

Andy had heard my entire exchange with Owen. He'd come out of the liquor closet when Owen went past, but stayed out of sight. When Owen left, Andy appeared in front of me when I turned to leave the trashcan at the dish pit.

"You really are a charmer these days, you know?" Andy folded his arms across his chest. He stood almost a foot taller than my five foot four inches. Even with a good ten feet between us, his body language emphasized his size. "I practically handed you the best guy in the county." Andy twisted his mouth and rolled his eyes toward the ceiling. "You don't even know what you've done."

Andy shook his head and proceeded with a stern face. He very much came across as the big brother that was disappointed.

I tried to hold my ground, "I don't see what the big deal is."

"The big deal is you haven't been interested in anything since the bombing. Look at yourself."

Compared to effort I'd put into my appearance before the bombing, I'd let myself go. When I came to college, I'd done a damn fine job of reinventing myself, but what he was looking at now was the real me. Now, dying my hair seemed pointless. This girl had dirty dishwater brown hair and it fell from a natural part in the middle of

35

my head. It was a little past shoulder length and I'd only cut the ends off last week to shed the last of the blonde tips. I cut it myself because I was tired of looking like a two-toned car or something, dark up top and light on the bottom. I didn't wear my blue tinted contacts anymore. Now I wore clear ones and what you saw was what you got, brown.

"I'm so sorry, Andy," I tried to apologize.

"My grandmother always said, 'You can't be nice to some people,' and unfortunately, Cara, you've become one of those people."

I just stood there not knowing what to say or how to defend myself.

"Look, we all know you've had a rough time since the bombing and we understand that, but we miss the old Cara. It's been months and months. I'm not saying you have to be something you're not anymore, but I would like for you to be happy and for you to see the good things that are still coming your way."

I was already starting to feel ashamed of myself when Andy sized me up and then delivered the goods, "And stop being mean!"

The tears started coming and there was nothing I could do to stop them. I turned from Andy in a flash to keep him from seeing how he had affected me.

Andy stepped toward me, turned me gently and then took the tray I was still holding and sat it in the dish pit. He wrapped his arms around me as my water works went all open season.

Andy held me for as long as I cried. He stroked my hair as I buried my face in his chest and just cried.

Finally, my sobs started to wain and Andy eased back. "I'll give you a ride home tonight."

"But my car..." I sniffled.

"It will be safe here and I'll bring you back tomorrow."

It wasn't the time to be petty, but I recalled the last time I rode home with Andy.

"Can I ask you not to..."

I don't know why I thought it would be an insult to ask him, but he smoked a bowl between the clubhouse parking lot and the gate leaving that night. It scared the Hell out of me and I'd prayed the whole way home. I knew nothing about pot so I assumed he was impaired, like drunk driving. I was terrified we were either going to wreck or get pulled over. Neither happened and we made it home fine. I hadn't gotten in the car with him since.

That hadn't been the first night he'd smoked pot in front of me. Last Christmas, when most everyone had gone home for winter break, all of us that worked at Port Honor stayed in Milledgeville to work. One night during the break, Matt called me and invited me over for a cookout they were having. In the background, Andy yelled, "If you don't like nobody smokin' no pot, don't come!"

I thought he was joking because, in my sheltered life, people that looked as good as him didn't do that kind of thing. As far as I knew, clean cut people didn't do drugs. I was wrong. I showed up with homemade chocolate chip cookies. They knew I didn't drink so they bought Sprite for me. To my complete and total surprise, they broke out a bong the size of my leg after dinner.

I didn't want to appear a judgy bitch so I did not jump up and run out. I stayed and acted as cool as I could without partaking.

The third of their friends that offered me a hit was sharply shut down by Andy. "It's not her thing. Got it."

I wasn't asked again, but I wasn't ostracized either. They got high. I beat them at poker and they ate the entire plate of cookies that I brought.

Andy didn't make me spell it out. "I won't touch it. I swear."

"Thank you."

I rode home with Andy that night. Actually, I fell asleep in the car on the ride there and didn't wake up until we pulled in the driveway at The Jefferson and I didn't fully wake up even then. I vaguely remembered Andy carrying me inside, when I started to wake the next morning in my bed. My shoes were off, but the rest of my clothes from the night before were still on. My clothes had been the first thing I'd taken notice of, the second was a slight snuffling noise coming from the corner of the room. I scrubbed the sleep from my eyes and found Andy sleeping in the chair, still wearing his clothes from the night before as well.

Despite being startled to find Andy asleep in the chair in my room, I awoke refreshed, having the first good night's sleep I'd had in months. Sunlight was filling the room, but I wasn't sure if it was 7 a.m. or 9:00. I rubbed my eyes and checked the alarm clock. I hadn't set it the night before and I had overslept. We had overslept.

It was 8:45 and we were scheduled to be at work at 10 a.m. It takes forty-five minutes to get from Milledgeville to Port Honor taking the backroads any other day, but Sunday mornings were the worst. There were little rural churches along the way. One's congregation had abandoned their church so there were no worries of them clogging up the roads, but the others were another matter. I'd made the drive almost every Sunday morning for over a year and knew the three remaining churches were made up of elderly drivers who could barely see over their steering wheels. They drove at a safe snail's pace. We would never make it to work on time and we were the only two scheduled to open aside from Alvin in the kitchen.

"Shit!" I exclaimed, leaping from the bed. Shouting the word "shit" did the trick, but I shouted at Andy too. "Andy, wake up!"

Before I'd said his name, Andy was on his feet, squared, fists drawn and ready to fight any intruder. Assessing the room and only seeing me rushing around, he asked through heavy breathing, "What? What's wrong?"

"We've got to go!" I scrambled past him to my closet and dug feverishly for clean pieces to my uniform.

Andy scanned my room again and saw the clock. He seconded my explicative. "Shit!"

"Right!" I said back, still quite panicked about how we were going to make it on time.

Without explanation, Andy made for the door. I noticed he was leaving.

"Where are you going? You're my ride." I panicked again.

Andy answered as he left, "Home to shower and change. Don't worry. I'll be back in twenty minutes. Be ready and waiting out front."

Twenty minutes later, Andy pulled along the sidewalk in front of the Jefferson. I opened the passenger's side door of the old yellow Mercedes he'd inherited from his grandmother. I hopped in, immediately noticing Andy. Freshly showered and shaved, hair still damp, pressed clothes, and smelling like Coast soap.

Coast was a strong smell that I would recognize anywhere. My grandfather used Coast and he was my favorite person in the world and the slightest hint of it, no matter where I was or what I was doing, it stopped me and recalled memories of him to my mind.

"Good morning, again!" Andy said, as I buckled myself in and he gave it the gas.

"Good morning." I gave him a pursed look.

Noticing the look, Andy questioned, "What?"

"I didn't have time to wash my hair so every time I turn my head I smell last night's pecan crusted trout, but you look all fresh and smell great."

Andy laughed, "I'm sorry, did I hear you correctly?" He cut his eyes from the road to me. "You just said I look great and you smell like fish? Are you feeling okay?"

"Oh just stop it!" I acted as if I was pouting and rolled my eyes.

"No, no, I never thought I'd see the day when you thought I looked good."

"You know what I meant and you still look like an ass."

Chapter 3

Saturday night I slept the best I had in months. Sunday night I slept like shit. Monday and Tuesday nights were not any better than Sunday. The nightmares were back and I was exhausted.

My last class was at 2:00 p.m. and I arrived home at 3:15 to find the red light on the answering machine blinking. I rarely got calls during the day because my family knew I was in class. Jay, on the other hand, got messages from his mother at all hours and so often that I most of the time I didn't bother checking the machine. For whatever reason, I walked over and pressed play.

"Hey. It's Andy calling for Cara. Call me back if you want a ride to work today. I promise I'll behave." Andy then left his number.

I debated calling him back. My car was fine. I decided to call him back and let him know I didn't need a ride. I was tired from the nightmares coming back, but I felt I was fine to drive.

Three rings later and Andy answered.

"Hi." I didn't expect him to recognize my voice but he did. Dispensing with the greetings, I started to explain, "I just..."

Andy cut me off, "I'll pick you up in thirty minutes. I got a call waiting so see you then."

I was initially put out by the notion of him not letting me have a say, but it did not take me long to relish the opportunity to have a nap. I sorely needed a nap.

Andy showed up just as he said he would. I hopped in the passenger's side and again found him freshly showered, smelling great and well rested looking. I was jealous.

Andy took one look at me and commented on my appearance. "Let me guess, not sleeping well again?"

My uniform was pressed and my hair and makeup were on point, but there was only so much my drug store

41

makeup could cover. Expecting it to hide the dark circles under my eyes was asking too much and Andy noticed.

"Apparently the only time I sleep well is with you." As soon as I the words left my lips, I realized I hadn't said that quite the way I should have.

Andy snickered immediately.

"You know I didn't mean it like that."

"Just the other day you told me I was great looking and now you can only sleep with me. I am flattered, but I believe we should sleep together again because I'm just not sure I remember it as well as you."

The whole time he was teasing me, I tried desperately to stop him, repeating, "That's not what I meant," and more forcefully, "You know that's not what I meant."

Andy continued as we drove away from the Jefferson and headed out of Milledgeville. "I doubt you are forgettable so I demand a do-over."

"Not funny," I chided him.

Andy quieted down. We made it from the turn off of Jefferson Street to the turn onto Highway 441 in silence. We still had thirty minutes to go before we arrived at Port Honor when we crossed the bridge over Lake Sinclair and Andy offered, "It's okay if you want to go to sleep. I'll wake you up before we get to the guard gate."

"Thanks." I said before leaning my head back and drifting off.

It seemed I'd only just closed my eyes before Andy woke me up. "Cara," he waited a second for me to respond before adding, "We're here. Wake up."

I rubbed my eyes, careful not to smear my mascara. We were just turning in at the entrance to Port Honor when Andy woke me as I had asked.

As always, Andy said something smart-ass-like, "I couldn't have you drooling on yourself as we pulled up to the guard shack or looking dead. I came close to checking your pulse a time or too. I just figured dead people don't drool."

"Oh ha-ha!"

Andy gave a nod to the guard and rolled right through.

"Why is it I always have to stop, but you give the nod and coast on by?" I asked.

"Because he's a dirty old man," Andy made reference to the sixty something year old gentleman that worked the guard gate on Wednesday nights, "And you're a pretty young girl."

My mind stuck on Andy saying I was a pretty young girl and almost missed the remainder of his statement.

"He'd stop you on the way out if he could figure out how," Andy concluded.

The rest of the night my mind kept circling back to Andy saying I was pretty. It wasn't something that bugged me, but it was almost like a thought that kept goosing me. In the middle of taking Mr. and Mrs. Boudreaux's order the thought crept in. While clearing dishes from the table after Mr. and Mrs. Bay finished their meal, there it was again. I couldn't even look at Andy when I went to the bar to pick up the glasses of wine for Ms. O'Neil and her flavor of the week because the thought was there again.

From the day I met Andy, I thought he was the best-looking guy I'd ever seen. When he smiled, he didn't just light up a room. He snuffed out all other light, put the other lightbulbs to shame. If bulbs had brains they would have thought, "Why bother? We can't compete with him." He glowed when he was amused and even more when he was being mischievous. Dark hair, brown eyes, the most endearing looking dimples and he was so tall, tall enough that I felt as though I looked child-sized when standing next to him. I had an instant crush on him.

I spent the first few days at Port Honor trying not to get caught looking at him. Around day four I was passing through the bar, picking up drinks for one of my tables, and trying not to get caught blushing or sneaking looks at him when he said my name, "Cara."

43

My eyes didn't just turn to him, they darted in his direction half feeling caught and half thrilled that that Greek God remembered my name.

"When ya comin' over?" he asked, smiling that smile.

My mind swirled around, but not round and round, there wasn't time for that before his next statement. I didn't know what he was talking about and stood there in marked confusion.

"Yeah, don't wear no panties."

The day he said that to me all of the men seated at the bar howled with laughter as I just stood there and blinked. I had no idea what to do because slapping his face would have gotten me fired.

The next day, Andy tried his little remark in front of a different crowd at the bar, but before they could laugh, I popped back with the most doe eyed, sincere expression, "Why, will you be wearing them?"

That got more laugher than the day before and I wasn't the one left standing there blinking with nothing to say.

Under my breath as I picked up the drinks my guests had ordered, I said smartly, "Joke's on you today!"

Andy heard me and gave me a half smile and a nod, acknowledging I'd gotten him. The crush was dead and he was a pig.

From then on if he said something chauvinistic, I had a comeback. I still didn't like the remarks and I certainly didn't like having to stoop to that level, but I felt better than if I'd just taken it. Somewhere along the way, it turned into a bit of a comedy routine for entertaining the male patrons of the bar. Andy would say something provocative and I would have some saucy come back. I shot him down time and again and it was a game.

Since the bombing, Andy hadn't been so repulsive when he spoke to me. He had been kind, which initially was just as unnerving as when he was slinging sexist remarks. While everyone else went out of their way to ask how Millie was doing and appeared to have forgotten that I had even been at Centennial Olympic Park with her, Andy didn't. In the first few weeks following the incident, he even stopped by my apartment to check on me. He offered to take some of my shifts if I didn't feel like going to work and, in the past, he had always maintained he was a bartender and waiting tables was beneath him.

Thoughts of Andy's kindnesses and sexist remarks mixed around in my head with him referring to me as a pretty girl. I tried to focus on the few guests that came in that Wednesday night, but it was a struggle to keep my mind straight. Mrs. Macy ordered decaf coffee and I gave her regular. I remembered after I sat the cup down and she took a sip. Mrs. Channel wanted her leftovers boxed up to take home, but I forgot and threw them out. It was one blunder after another until all of the guests had cleared out.

"How did you do tonight?" Andy asked as I took a seat at the bar to cash out.

Again, "He called me pretty," poked my brain.

"Um..." Nervously, I tried to fix my eyes on the wad of money I had pulled from my apron. "Alright, I guess."

"Are you okay?"

"Just exhausted." I covered. I couldn't tell him I'd been flittering around all night absentminded wondering what he meant when he said what he did.

"Well, give me just a few more minutes and I'll be ready to go."

It wasn't long after we got in the car, Andy said, "You can go to sleep if you want."

"And I'll magically wake up tomorrow morning in my same clothes and late for class." I tried to make a joking reference to the last time I fell asleep in his car on the ride home.

"Would you prefer I take your clothes off?" Through the darkness, I could still see the smile he flashed at me.

Double shit, I thought. I had walked right into that one.

"I really would prefer that you aren't nocturnal when I take your clothes off. I'm just not that into the midnight stealth action."

I burst out laughing. This was the first time I'd ever laughed at any of his remarks. Usually, I was so offended, but the way he said it this time, with no benefit for his audience, I found him funny.

"What is the midnight stealth?" I laughed, showing my inexperience as I had never heard of that before.

"Ahhh...." For once, Andy Sheppard was embarrassed. As the headlights from an approaching vehicle shined on his face and I could see he was blushing.

"Come on, what's that mean?" I prodded.

"You seriously don't know?"

"No, but I didn't know what the three-date rule was until you explained that one to me either."

I couldn't see him, but I could feel him tense.

"Are you kidding me?" I laughed again. "You can only talk dirty to me on your terms?"

"Oh, I can talk plenty dirty..." Andy stopped himself abruptly.

Still laughing, "Are you okay?"

"I'm fine," he said sternly and gripped the steering wheel with both hands.

"So, what does it mean," I asked again, not letting up.

With no sense of the usual banter, Andy replied flatly, "It means, throwing it on a woman while she is asleep."

"That's it? You were acting like I'd asked you to fully explain the birds and the bees to me."

"Just go to sleep if you like. I'll get you home safely."

That took the fun out of falling asleep, but I was exhausted and it just came naturally.

Mere seconds seemed to pass and a gentle prodding came with the whisper of my name, "Cara, we're here."

I'm not sure what I thought I was snuggling into, but it wasn't my pillow.

"Cara," the voice came again and this time I popped to attention, realizing I was snuggled into Andy's shoulder. His arm was around me and I had been asleep propped against him. The old Mercedes had a bench seat in the front and no armrest between the driver's side and passenger's side to stop me from falling over onto him.

"Oh, sorry about that," I said, sitting up. "Thanks for the ride."

I started out of the car and so did Andy.

"You don't have to walk me in," I told him as I rubbed my eyes for clarity and yawned.

"I know," he said, but didn't make any attempt to leave.

"Okay, well, goodnight." I turned to go inside and Andy followed. "Thanks again." That was supposed to be the dismissal signal that he could go, but he didn't.

"So I figured, we'd test the theory," he said, reaching around me and opening the front door to The Jefferson.

"What," I yawned, "theory is that?"

"The one that you only sleep good with me."

I giggled and got poked in the brain again by him thinking I was pretty. I tried to straighten up and answer as if I wasn't giddy with exhaustion. "You don't have to do that."

"I don't mind. Plus, it would be for science."

I giggled again.

For three weeks, at Andy's insistence, every time we were scheduled to be at Port Honor together, he drove me to and from work. Once back at my apartment, he slept in the chair. For three nights a week, just his presence seemed to keep away the nightmares. I awoke rested and, unlike the first night, in my pajamas and not my clothes from the night before.

Jay was my roommate at the time, but he had started seeing someone. They met a few weeks after the bombing and within a couple of weeks I was virtually on my own. His stuff was still at our apartment, but he wasn't. Jay popped in for clothes and a few things once or twice a week. Sometimes I ran into him, we had a chance to catch up, and sometimes I just got feelings that he'd been in and out while I wasn't there. Occasionally, he called to check in on me, but for the most part, I was alone in the apartment except on the nights that Andy slept in the chair. I never told Jay about the nightmares and I never told him how awful it was being there by myself.

Wednesday, Saturday and Sunday, Andy slept in the chair. It was a wooden side chair with a minimal amount of gold fabric and even less cushion left in it. I'd inherited it from my grandmother along with her Electrolux vacuum cleaner. I imagined sleeping while trying to ride the Electrolux would have been about as comfortable as the that chair.

Since Jay wasn't around, I figured he wouldn't mind so I moved his recliner from the living room into my room.

"Nice," Andy said when he saw Haverty's finest sitting in the corner of my room on Wednesday night.

"Thanks. I think Jay's still making payments on it so just don't eat or drink anything..."

Andy started laughing. "He financed a recliner?"

"Fancy, huh?"

Andy flopped down in it.

"Whoa, no flopping. Gentle."

"What's that a queen size over there?" Andy motioned toward my bed. "Let me have half of that queen and I'll be plenty gentle."

I giggled, blushed and turned my head. "Don't push it."

Andy settled in and I cut off the light by my bed.

"I swear I'll..."

"Goodnight, Andy."

I laid there in the darkness, curled up on my side. I didn't take what Andy had just said for him being a pig anymore. I took it as friendly teasing.

"Andy?" I leaned up in bed. I could barely see him thanks to the light from the street light outside of my window.

Andy jumped up and I heard every spring and joint in the recliner. "Yeah?" he asked in a pant.

"Thanks," I said.

"For what?"

I could see him propping himself up in the recliner on his elbows so he could see me too.

"For being here," I replied. "I really appreciate it."

Somewhere along the way, maybe it was the third or fourth week, but it was definitely sometime in November when I stopped napping on every ride. When I stopped napping, the conversations began. Somedays the conversations were nothing, but other days we talked about our families, what high school was like, and in general we got to know one another, which seemed strange since we had known one another for going on a year and a half.

Andy was a local. He had grown up around Milledgeville. His parents had divorced when he was four years old and he was the only product of their marriage.

"I can't even remember what it was like when they were married," he'd confided.

I said nothing.

"In fact," Andy added, "I can't even imagine the two of them together.

"Same here, especially since I've never met my real father."

"You've never even met him?"

"Nope."

"And you sound perfectly fine with it."

I may have sounded cavalier, but Andy sounded concerned. I wasn't sure whether he was concerned for me or my father.

"How else am I supposed to sound? He didn't care enough about me to stay in touch so…"

I trailed off, but Andy was quick to point out, "I guess that beats being pulled back and forth and never feeling like you belong in one house or the other. Plus, he didn't die, right?"

"No, I mean, I guess not. Anyway, I didn't have that option so I wouldn't know. It is what it is."

Both of Andy's parents went on to remarry and have more children. One of his half-brothers, a child of his mother's second marriage, worked with us for a little while during the Olympics. It was only temporary. When business died down, he went back to working at the Ace Hardware in Milledgeville.

Andy's mother died when he was six and his younger brother was two. He remembered her, but his brother didn't.

"That's so sad," I told him, referring both to his mother dying, but more so about the fact that his little brother didn't remember her.

"I think he got off kind of easy. Like you said, it is what it is, and he can't miss her as much because he didn't know what it was like to have her. You can't miss what you never knew you had, right?"

"I suppose."

Andy didn't disclose everything in one day. Over time I pieced more of his history together and figured out that when his mother died, his step-mother didn't want him. His father didn't put up a fight so he was only allowed to go to their house under the original custody agreement from his parents' divorce, every other weekend. That's how he ended up bouncing from house to house between his grandmother, his mother's sister and his father's house. In all of his disclosure, he never let on that he felt sorry for himself.

Chapter 4

"Are you working on Easter?" Andy asked on our Wednesday evening drive back after work. Easter was coming up that Sunday.

"Yes," I answered. "What about you?"

"You don't always work on Sundays," Andy pointed out.

"Right, but it's Easter and Gabe said it was all hands on deck so it's you and me and the whole gang I guess."

"Would you like a ride on Sunday?" Andy looked from the road to me.

"No. That's okay. I'm going home after we get off," I explained.

"Oh, yeah, Easter with your family?" he asked.

"Yeah. I'll make it there in time for dinner. I may catch a ride with Millie and Gabe."

"What?" Andy swung his head around toward me, confused, and letting the car drifting into the oncoming lane.

"Hey! Eyes on the road!" I half screamed and pointed, alerting him to the truck we were about to hit head on.

Andy jerked the wheel and the car veered back. I slid in the seat and, despite the seatbelt, I slammed into the passenger's side door from shoulder to hip. The front tire on my side went off the shoulder of the road and Andy over corrected.

"Shit!" I braced against the dash with one hand and the door with the other. I thought we were about to spin, but Andy was calm.

"What's the deal?" he asked while gripping the steering wheel with both hands and trying to straighten it back out.

I couldn't answer until he got control of the car and we were safely back in our lane. My heart was racing and I really thought we were about to wreck and there

51

were more cars coming toward us, more cars at that time of the night than I'd seen on that road in all the time I'd been working at Port Honor.

"Well?" Andy said, unphased.

I was looking behind us to make sure we didn't leave a wreck in our wake as I answered. "My grandparents live in the same little town where Millie is from. Avera, where her Aunt Gayle still lives. You've met her aunt. Anyway, we always have holidays at my grandparents' house so I'm just going to catch a ride with them."

"Oh. Okay." After that Andy was quiet the rest of the ride home. He slept in the recliner, but didn't have a word to say.

I said, "Goodnight," as I cut the lamp off, but Andy just grunted.

When I woke up the next morning, Andy was already gone. Usually, my alarm clock woke the both of us up. I thought it was odd, but shrugged it off, thinking he just had some place he had to be. Maybe he didn't sleep well in the recliner.

Usually, I heard from Andy during the day to confirm we were still on for the ride together. This week Gabe had closed the restaurant on Saturday night to allow him and the kitchen staff extra time to prepare for Easter lunch. I had grown accustomed to Andy's call and our rides together and found myself waiting for him to call to confirm our ride together on Friday night.

The day came and went with no call from Andy and even more significant than the fact that he didn't call was that I noticed.

Millie hosted family dinner on Saturday night and all of the Port Honor gang was there as well as all of the tenants from The Jefferson. Stella and Travis who lived across the hall from me were there. Jay brought his new flavor and it was the first time we'd all had the chance to hang out with Chris, who we all affectionately called

"Flavor" behind his back. Jerry and Daniel drove over from their house on the outskirts of Eatonton.

Since Gabe had closed the clubhouse restaurant that night for extra prep time in the afternoon for Easter dinner, and not the evening dinner service, Alvin was able to join us. He came and he brought a girl, Michaela. Alvin had met Michaela while they were both pumping gas at the Texaco between Port Honor and Reynolds Plantation. Michaela was a tennis pro at one of the other clubs on Lake Oconee. As a child she had played against Venus Williams.

"I would have won," she explained as we all had drinks before dinner, "but my mother forgot my bloomers and I had to play in two pairs of panties, one on top of another. It got in my head and I tanked the game. Now she's got national sponsors and playing grand slams and I've got seventy-year-olds and round robins."

Michaela raised her glass and looked lovingly at Alvin, "Still, I think I'm the one living the dream."

Alvin touched his beer bottle to Michaela's wine glass. They toasted and then shared a little smooch. It was cute and I was a touch jealous.

Until that point, I'd looked for Andy, but hadn't seen him. In fact, I smelled his cologne before I laid eyes on him. The scent floated passed me and I immediately turned my head to find him standing behind me.

"Miss your nap time today?" he teased me even though I hadn't napped much in the car lately.

"Maybe," I replied, never willing to give him the ammunition to tease me further if he knew I might actually like hanging out with him.

"Well, whatever," he shrugged. "I brought you something." He handed me little box of cookies from Ryles Bakery, the yellow ones with the smiles on them. "Happy Easter."

"Thank you so much! I love them!" I came close to throwing my arms around Andy's neck and hugging him, but I thought better of it.

Under his breath Andy said, "I know."

I was puzzled as I couldn't recall telling Andy about my obsession with those cookies, but I must have. Those were my favorite cookies and I always went to Ryles on Fridays after class to treat myself for making it through the week.

Andy sat next to me at dinner. If I'd had any sense at all I would have seen how everyone was paired off even me and Andy, but I was a stupid girl who didn't see past the nose on my own face.

Millie hosted family dinner at least once per month. When we all first moved into The Jefferson she held it once a week, but now with law school and her family life, she had to scale back. She didn't always assign themes for family dinner, but as not to compete with the traditional meals, Millie had assigned a theme around holidays. At Friendsgiving she assigned Chinese and this Easter was Italian.

In between his next bite of Chicken Parmesan, Andy suggested, "I'll give you a ride tomorrow morning so you don't have to go in at the crack of dawn with Millie and Gabe."

I almost jumped at the offer. "Yeah, that'd be great," I said even with my mouth full of food.

The remainder of the night, Andy and I hung together. We actually cleaned the kitchen for Millie. I washed and rinsed the dishes and Andy dried and put away. We closed down the party with an awkward parting when he walked me down stairs to my door.

"Night," I said, turning the key in my door.

"I'll pick you up at 9:00." Andy lingered.

"Okay." I opened the door and the hinges squealed.

"I can probably fix that."

I turned around. "What?"

"The door. You made it cry when you opened it."

I laughed. "Excuse me?"

"The hinges, you didn't hear that?"

54

I shook my head. I guess I had gotten used to it and didn't even notice the noise it made.

Andy brushed me aside and headed into my kitchen.

"What are you doing?" I asked after him.

"I'm going to fix it for you." I could hear him opening the cabinets, but he appeared to have found what he was looking for and came walking back out carrying the pan spray.

"What are you going to do with Pam?"

"Same thing I would do with WD-40, but I'm guessing you don't keep that laying around."

Andy then shut the door, sprayed the hinges and all while I just watched, kind of curious.

"Okay, well, thanks," I said as he handed me the spray.

He put his hands in his pockets and lingered some more, but I didn't think much of it. "Jay's out for the night?"

Being used to having Andy around, I didn't stand on manners for entertaining him and left him standing there while I went to put the spray back in the kitchen.

"Yeah, he's staying at Flavor's house."

"I can stay if you like."

I laughed again. "Is that what you say to all the girls?"

The truth was that I would love for him to stay. I still hadn't recovered from the last round of nightmares and was dog tired.

"Okay, never mind then."

I was already leaving the kitchen when I heard him open the door.

"Wait!" I yelled after him. "I was just kidding."

The next morning, he got up early as usual and headed to his house to get dressed for work and then came back to get me.

Easter lunch at Port Honor was as packed as Thanksgiving has been. Gabe and Alvin pulled out all the stops with a forty-foot, forty item buffet of every Sunday dinner dish one could imagine. There was an 11:00 a.m. seating and a 12:30 p.m. seating. The members were dressed to the nines. Mrs. Macy wore a hot pink hat that needed its own zip code and her husband had on a matching plaid vest that I swear I'd seen on a mall Easter Bunny before. The Bays were in attendance with all of their children and grandchildren which made for my biggest tip of the day. Mr. Bay left me a crisp one-hundred-dollar bill. It was busy, but over before we knew it.

After all of the guests were gone, Gabe allowed us to pick the leftover items from the buffet to take home to share with our families.

"I was taught that you always bring something even when going to visit family," Gabe said, "so pick what you like."

Alvin took the rest of the mashed potatoes. I took the rest of the chocolate cheesecake. Jerry and Daniel took some turkey and dressing. Millie didn't take anything because she cooked all day yesterday to take homemade items to her family. Kimmie took the peach cobbler. There was plenty of items still left to choose from, but Andy didn't take anything more than one to go tray with a little serving of each item. That one act let me know that unlike the rest of us, he was just going home to the little house he rented where he'd live alone since Matt moved away.

I didn't have long to think about it and I didn't know what I'd tell my mother. She'd think he was my boyfriend and there'd be no convincing her otherwise. There'd be tons of questions from the rest of the family, but I knew I'd have to endure it. After all Andy had done for me, I could not imagine letting him spend the evening alone.

Millie was sitting in Gabe's office waiting for us to leave. Gabe and Alvin were packing up the kitchen and Jerry and Daniel were resetting the dining room. I was in charge of vacuuming the buffet room and Andy was in the bar alone, counting the till.

No one was paying me any attention so I headed to the bar.

Andy turned his head at the sound of the glass door and smiled when he saw me.

"Hey," I milled around working up the courage to ask him. "Would your step-mother miss you if you came to dinner with me tonight? I told my mother about you and how you'd been helping me out."

That was a lie. I hadn't told my mother anything about him. I could never tell her a boy had been sleeping in my room. She would curse me and fall over dead.

"Um, I don't have anything to wear." He didn't say no.

"It's come as you are." I waved, unconcerned with his excuse. "I'm going like this." That was another lie. I'd brought clothes to change into, pajamas and had packed to stay the weekend.

"But, weren't you going to..."

"Just say you'll come. We'll eat dinner and then head back to Milledgeville after dinner." I refused to take no for an answer.

"What about Millie and Gabe?"

"What about them?" I asked.

"You were going to go with them."

"And now I'm going with you. I'll go tell Millie now."

Millie looked at me puzzled when I explained Andy was coming with me to Easter.

"Is there something you want to tell me?" she asked.

"No. We're just friends and I don't think he has any place to go today so I invited him to come with me," I explained, seeing no reason for this not to be plausible and as innocent as I said it was.

"Really?" Millie furrowed her face. "You're taking Andy home for Easter?"

"It's not like that."

She hardly heard me, "I mean, I thought I noticed something with you two at dinner last night, but... Well, how long has this been going on?"

"We're just friends," I insisted.

"Are you sure?" she asked, still confused.

"Yes, just friends."

"Okay. You'll tell me if something changes."

"Come on, its Andy we are talking about. Nothing's going to change. I'm not even in the ballpark with him."

Millie's face flashed with concern. "Cara, I think..."

"Millie, it's okay." I cut her off. "It's just dinner and then back home to Milledgeville. I'll see you tomorrow."

Millie relented and bid me, "Happy Easter!"

Turning off of I-20 and headed toward Norwood on the back roads to Avera, I finally confessed. "I didn't tell my mother that you had been helping me out."

"What did you tell her?" Andy raised an eyebrow in my direction.

"Nothing."

"Did you tell her you are bringing someone today?" He inquired further.

"I tried to call, but no one picked up." I braced myself.

"But you haven't told your mother anything about me?" he asked for clarification.

"Well, I couldn't very well tell Louise who recently found the Lord, and I mean vigorously found the Lord, that I had been entertaining a boy in my room three nights a week."

"Let me assure you that what's been going on in your room would never be considered 'entertaining a boy' by any stretch of the imagination,'" Andy laughed almost uncontrollably. "And no one under eighty uses the phrase 'entertaining a boy' anymore."

"Well, she'd think we were fucking vigorously, is that better?"

"As vigorously as she found the Lord?" He laughed. "What's with you and the word vigorously?"

"Oh, shut up!"

"So, what are you going to tell her when you show up with me?" Again, Andy looked my way for something for which I didn't have an answer.

I shrugged. "I don't know."

"She's going to think I'm your boyfriend."

Then I laughed.

"What's so funny about that?" Andy did not laugh.

"I'm not even in the ballpark." I didn't mean to tell him that, but I used the same terminology I'd used with Millie. It just slipped out.

"What?" He asked again with specification, "What makes you think that?"

I didn't believe I was someone Andy would give a second thought to dating. Oh, I knew he'd have sex with me if I said the word, but really dating? No, I wasn't the girl for him and I knew it. Part of that belief came from my low self-esteem and part of it came from thinking that I knew Andy.

"The last girl you dated looked like Gabrielle Reese, the women's volleyball star. Tall as you are, legs for days, long brown hair. Jes, Jessica, Jessie? What was her name?"

"Oh my God, seriously? That girl was dumb as a stick. She was pretty, but dang, she couldn't find her way out of a paper sack. I still don't know how she got into college here."

"Anyway." I rolled my eyes.

I also changed the subject before Andy could say anything else. "That's your turn." I pointed to the street after the Gurley's grocery store.

The rest of the way to Avera, I kept us from circling back around to the topic of the ballpark. We talked about my family and I described who all would probably be there.

We reached Avera city limits sign around 4:30 p.m. Avera was tiny with only one caution light in the center of town. One could count the number of old commercial buildings on one hand. The one gas station hadn't been closed long and the little grocery store probably wouldn't be far behind.

"You'll need to make a left at the caution light," I instructed.

"Okay." Andy put on his blinker even though there wasn't anyone behind us.

"It's the one at the right, on the corner at the four-way stop."

As we cruised down Main Street, Andy spotted the line of cars parked along the street. "How many people did you say were going to be here?"

"Only about fifteen at this time of the day."

"Only fifteen," Andy mocked me. "Are you sure I won't be imposing?"

"What's one more?"

My grandparents' house was not big. It was a basic four room house with a small bathroom. There were two rooms on each side of the house divided down the middle by one long hallway. The front door was at one end of the hall and the back door was at the other. At some point they put an addition on the back that consisted of a bedroom off of the kitchen and a car port off of the back door that ran the rest of the length of the back of the house. The porch ran the entire width of the front. At lunch time there would not have been one space, short of their bedroom, that wasn't occupied by all of my relatives. Now the crowd had dwindled and it was just the ones that lived local that were left.

"Cara, dear." Aunt Gladys barely hugged me before moving on.

"And who do we have here?" she asked, hooking her arm in Andy's.

Every family has that one crazy aunt and mine was no exception. Aunt Gladys wasn't the type to wrap up her cat or a Jell-o mold and give them as Christmas gifts, but she wore a ton of makeup, lied about her age, and was loud with everything from her clothes to her voice. Aunt Gladys was my grandfather's sister and she was in her late sixties. She was the first person I'd ever known to have her boobs done and she single-handedly kept the Estee Lauder counter at J.B. White's in business. Most of all Aunt Gladys was a widow and always on the prowl. We were hardly out of the car when she spotted us from her seat on the porch and made a bee-line for Andy.

"Aunt Gladys, this is Andy Sheppard." I started explaining that he worked with me, but I just gave up as she was already leading him toward the house.

Andy looked over his shoulder, pleading to be rescued already, but I just smiled and retrieved the food from the backseat of his car.

I was only a few seconds behind them, but by the time I made it inside, Aunt Gladys was showing Andy off to my other female relatives, including my mother.

"Look what treat Cara brought home," I overheard Aunt Gladys say as I entered the kitchen.

Andy looked like a deer in the headlights.

Aunt Gladys wasn't the only one overheard making comments. My cousin Grace, who was six months younger than I was, leaned over to her mother and said, dripping with disbelief, "*He* came with Cara?"

Apparently, Grace didn't think I was in the ballpark either.

My mother spotted me, lingering in the doorway. "Cara, Honey, come introduce us to your friend." She crossed the room and took the pans of food and squeezed them in on the kitchen table before hugging me.

"This is Andy Sheppard. We work together at the country club," I told her.

"Andy Sheppard, hum," Mom thought for a moment. "Any relation to the Sheppards who live around here?"

"No, Ma'am," Andy replied politely and all of the ladies in the room looked on with approval.

"Manners and tall, dark and handsome," Aunt Gladys fanned herself, "Cara, if I were ten years younger, I'd give you a run for your money on this one."

Ten years, I thought. More like forty years. I just smiled. "We're just friends."

"Girlie, have I taught you nothing? Friends?" She sized Andy up while my mother fretted over my hair and I looked on completely embarrassed. "Are you," she then whisper-screamed, "Gay?"

Granny, as we called my grandmother, who'd been washing dishes, stopped with her hands still in the water, "Gladys! Enough!"

Andy still stood there in good humor, but starting to blush.

Aunt Gladys was not to be detoured. "Well, all I'm saying is if he ain't, then what's the hold up?"

"Cara's the hold up," Grace snickered. Grace and I were both only children and we had a way of teasing one another like sisters.

"So, Cara," my mother took the high road, "You didn't tell us you were bringing a friend."

"It was a last-minute thing," I explained.

Andy pried himself away from Aunt Gladys to join me and my mother near the door and she flitted over to the homemade candies on the dessert table.

"She took pity on me and invited me," Andy explained. "She's very sweet like that."

"That's my girl, always thinking of others." My mother played with my hair and made me feel like a five-year-old. "I like seeing your natural color."

"Mom!" I protested.

"And no more glow in the dark blue contacts. She has such pretty eyes just the way they are, don't you think?" She posed her question to Andy.

I protested a little stronger, "Mom, seriously!"

"I think they are beautiful," he replied and my insides flipped involuntarily.

"So," my mother looked Andy up and down, while keeping an arm around me, "Not gay?"

Andy smiled and looked at his shoes as his face turned red. "No, Ma'am."

"Okay, just checking," Mom grinned. "I mean, if you are, well that's fine and all..."

"That's enough," I said. "Come on, I'll take you to meet the men folk. They aren't quite as out of their heads as these ladies."

On holidays the women lingered in the kitchen even when not prepping the feast. They compared notes on husbands, children and grandchildren, swapped recipes, reminisced about the good old days and exchanged gossip. We left the ladies to their business of heating up dinner and likely talking about us when they thought we were out of earshot.

The men congregated in the living room. Pops, as we called my grandfather, was holding court from his La-Z-Boy when we walked in. He had the remote gripped in one hand and a stogie in the other.

"Hey! There's my girl!" For seventy years old, he was still spry. He popped right up out of the recliner like a Jack in the Box and in one move he had his arms around me in a bearhug.

The other men in the room kept watching whatever college football game was on the TV and they paid us no attention beyond a few flippant, greetings to acknowledge my presence.

"Hey, Pops!" I said a few octaves higher than normal.

Pops released me. "Let me look at you." He took two steps back. "You get prettier all the time."

63

I just stood there smiling, basking in the glow that Pops heaped on me. I loved it. Although I liked to think I was his favorite, I was almost sure he said the same sweet things to Grace.

Sizing me up, Pops noticed Andy standing behind me. "Sugar Pie, did you bring a friend?"

"Right," my head fluttered, remembering Andy was there. "This is Andy. He works with me at Port Honor."

Andy extended his hand to Pops and they shook.

"That's a firm grip you got there, son." Pops shifted his eyes to me. "I like it."

I smiled bigger, forgetting for a moment that Andy wasn't my guy and there was no reason for me to swell with pride over Pops' approval.

Pops reached over to the table between his chair and Granny's. He picked up a small box and turned back to us.

"Ever had a real Cuban, Andy?" Pops opened the box and offered Andy one of the cigars.

"Oh, no, sir. I don't smoke."

I knew that was a bit of a lie. A vision of the bong flashed before my eyes and I coughed.

Andy cut his eyes at me, but kept the cordial smile plastered across his face.

"Neither do I except on special occasions." Pops held the box out closer to Andy, offering again.

At the holidays, Granny made fudge, divinity, turtles and other homemade candies as treats and Pops bought Cubans.

Andy shook his head and politely declined again. "I won't lie to you, Sir. I've smoked a bit in the past." My eyes grew big as I didn't know where Andy was going with this.

"But," he continued, "I don't think Cara likes it when I do so I'm gonna pass."

"Good answer!" Pops said and he snapped the cigar box shut.

About that time is when Aunt Carmen, my mother's sister, stuck her head in the living room door and announced that dinner was ready.

As we made our way to the kitchen, Pops walked with me. "I think you've got a good one, Cara," he nudged me.

"We're just friends," I insisted.

"Uh, huh," he grunted, holding the door to the kitchen for me and then Andy.

By the end of the evening, there had been a dozen side conversations with statements similar to those Pops made. Everyone was convinced Andy and I were an item, or should be, despite my contradictions. They were so convinced and he'd been such a hit that Granny and Pops invited him back for the July 4th barbecue.

"I don't think I have ever seen so much food short of at a Golden Corral Buffet," Andy remarked on our way back to Milledgeville that night.

"That was only half of what's usually there. Remember they had already eaten once before we got there." I commented.

"I think I ate some of everything." Just outside of Avera city limits sign, Andy unbuttoned his pants.

"What are you doing?" I shrieked.

"Hurting. I ate 'til I hurt myself," he kind of moaned. "Your aunt just kept passing bowls and platters and insisting that I try this and that and, oh my God, I am dying."

"I meant your pants... Did you just unbutton them?"

"Yes! Just pray we don't get pulled over."

I tried not to laugh, but was unsuccessful.

"It's not funny. When your aunt wasn't handing me something, your mother was putting extra helpings on my plate. I don't even like ambrosia and I felt obligated to eat it."

My laughter kept rolling. Everyone in the family knew one serving of Aunt June's ambrosia was the equivalent eating an entire box of Correctol.

"I didn't want to be rude so I kept eating."

"What all did you eat?"

"What didn't I eat? There was turkey, fried chicken, dressing with that egg chipped up gravy stuff, like Thanksgiving food, and..."

"You mean, giblet gravy?"

"I guess. Christ," he exhaled carefully, "I think I ate every vegetable known to man."

"Why didn't you tell them you were full or didn't want anymore?"

"I don't know. I was just trying to be polite and I didn't know who made what so I didn't want to turn down something they made and hurt their feelings."

"You are way nicer than I am."

The drive from Avera back to Milledgeville took us through Sandersville. It was dark and the clouds were covering the moon and stars. The street lights weren't as prevalent on the bypass as they were if we'd taken the route through the town, but I still see the turn we would have taken if we were going to my mother's house.

"Right there," I said, pointing to the road coming up on the right. "I grew up about three miles down there on the left, that's when I wasn't with my grandparents in Avera."

"It's only thirty more minutes to Milledgeville. Why didn't you just live at home and commute?" Andy asked.

"I wanted the full college experience. Plus, if I stayed home, my mother was going to make me pay rent. I figured, if I was going to pay rent, I might as well do it closer to school."

Andy didn't see the point in my reasoning and I took that as an opportunity to asked a question of my own. "You are from Milledgeville, yet you don't live with your family. You rent a place of your own. Did you want the full college experience as well?"

"It wasn't quite like that," he replied, obviously concentrating on the road ahead.

"What was it like?"

During our conversations in the car, Andy usually glanced back and forth between me and the road when talking. Now, he wasn't looking at me at all.

"Even though I didn't go far, I had to go," he noted.

"What does that mean?" I turned in my seat so that my back was against the door and I was sitting facing him.

Between Sandersville and Milledgeville, Andy reminded me of our earlier conversations about how he didn't really have a set place to live when he was growing up.

"As soon as I was old enough to choose who I was going to live with I had enough of flipping back and forth from one family member to the next and all but my grandmother had had enough of me so I decided I'd just stay with her. I was fifteen. When I was eighteen my aunt found my stash of weed. She threatened to put my grandmother in a nursing home unless I moved out. So, I moved out and I've been on my own ever since."

"Wait. Hold on." I couldn't believe what he said. I couldn't believe he'd been completely on his own since he was eighteen and I couldn't imagine one of my aunts threatening my grandmother over me. "Your aunt threatened to put your grandmother in a nursing home unless you moved out? You said you looked after your grandmother and did her shopping and..."

"Yep. I took her to doctor appointments and I drove her home in this car the day we buried my grandfather. That's when I first moved in so she wouldn't be by herself and so I could escape my situation."

"But your aunt would have rather had your grandmother live alone than to just tell you to get rid of the marijuana and stop doing what you were doing? That makes no sense!"

"It is what it is."

"I'm so sorry. I mean, no wonder you were smoking weed or doing most anything else to find an escape."

Andy hit the brakes, fishtailed the back end and nearly brought the car to a stop. I straightened up and started scanning the sides of the road. I thought he was dodging a deer or something, but I was wrong.

"Do not," he said sternly, "ever feel sorry for me!"

Stunned, I muttered, "Okay?"

"I'm serious! I want a lot of things, but I don't want anyone feeling sorry for me, especially you!"

I drew back to the far reaches of the passenger's side of the car. Little else was said until we pulled up in front of The Jefferson.

Andy parked in a spot near the front door, but he made no move to get out. "I had a great time and I love your family. You're really lucky to have them. It's good to be reminded what normal is sometimes."

"Thanks," I said, still wondering what was wrong. "I'm glad you came." I smiled and added, "But we are far from normal."

"Well, thanks for inviting me and I'm just going to go on home." Andy hadn't unbuckled and he made no move to walk me to the door.

He usually came in and stayed. It was kind of our thing without being a *thing*.

"Are you okay? Did I say something wrong?" I worried I'd offended him.

"It's not you. It's me."

"Oh. That does mean it's me. I've heard that line before."

"No seriously. Go try to get some sleep. I'll pick you up Wednesday for work."

"Okay." I didn't want him to go, but I didn't know what to say. I leaned across the car and hugged him.

Andy held on to me and we hugged for longer than we normally did. In all honesty, I didn't want to let him go.

"Thanks for going with me. Happy Easter."

Andy had lived alone since Matt moved out and I didn't want him to go home alone, but what choice did I have? I didn't understand what happened, but I had to let him go.

Chapter 5

It was near midnight and I wasn't asleep. I laid there rehashing the day still trying to make sense of the ride home. I knew I was the only one home in the entire building and normally that would have made me scared to the point that I heard every pop and creak of the old building settling. I would have been on edge and on my last nerve, but thoughts of Andy consumed me.

I'd never had a guy as a best friend, but was that what this was? I didn't know what this was. I had Jay, but that wasn't the same. Jay was like a girlfriend, but not quite. What I had with Andy was nothing like what I had with Millie or Stella or any of my female friends from high school. It didn't need a term or a label, but I just didn't know what it was. But whatever it was, seeing the empty recliner in my room made me miss it.

Two nights in a row, I finally fell asleep well after 2:00 a.m. No nightmares the first night or the second. The first night I didn't dream at all that I remembered. The second night, dreams of Andy filled the night with a jumping around progression, a look, a graze of his hand, and finally the culmination, we were about to kiss when the phone rang and woke me up.

I jerked the phone off the receiver, stunned from the dreams featuring him, frustrated and disappointed that it had been interrupted.

"Hello?" I answered, looking around for my alarm clock. It was still dark out.

"Cara?" It was my mother's voice.

"Mom?" I asked, seeing the clock. It wasn't even 7:00 a.m. yet.

"You need to get dressed and come home." Her voice was shaky and I knew what she sounded like when she was worried. This was it.

"What's wrong?" I sat up in bed. She had my attention and I was definitely awake now.

"Just meet me at home and I will tell you when you get here."

"Tell me now!"

The line was silent other than her breathing.

"Mom! Tell me now!"

My mother broke, her tears spilling through the phone. "Pops had a heart attack. He's... He's... Cara, I don't want you getting on the road upset. I'll come get you."

"What?" I jumped out of bed and started searching for clothes. "I'm on my way!"

"No, promise me you won't drive if you are crying."

I didn't have any tears because I couldn't believe what she was trying to say. She hadn't said it because he wasn't. He was fine. He was going to be fine. I could not make my brain conjure the word for what my mother seemed to have implied because he just couldn't be anything other than okay.

I threw on mismatched socks and no makeup, jeans and a t-shirt that I wasn't sure was clean. I brushed my teeth, but that's all I did in the way of personal hygiene. Maybe I thought if I got there in record time, none of this would be true.

I flew into the house, having barely put my old Honda Accord in park. "Mom!" I called to her as soon as I opened the door.

"Good. Let's go," she said, grabbing her purse and heading toward me. "They were on their way to University Hospital in Augusta with him when I called you."

"I thought..." My head swirled and a rush of relief came over me.

"I know, Baby." My mother never called me Baby except on rare occasions. "But, you need to prepare yourself. Granny said he wasn't responsive when they loaded him in the ambulance."

She put her arm around me as we rushed out the door to her car.

"He's not alone, is he?" I cried.

"They were working on him so there wasn't room in the ambulance for anyone to ride with him. Granny and Uncle Dwight are right behind the ambulance."

My mother drove at breakneck pace. The towns between Sandersville and Augusta went by in a flash. Mom rarely let off of the gas and the whole trip was a fuzzy spot in my mind. I cried all the way there.

Just outside of Augusta I said, "We have to get there in time, Mama. I have to tell him I love him."

"Cara, he knows you love him more than anything in the world."

"He's the best person I know."

"I know." Mom reached over and took my hand. She took her eyes off the road just long enough to give me a reassuring smile.

Never once did she tell me he was going to be okay and that spoke volumes.

We were still at the hospital, waiting on the funeral home to come and pick up the body when I started making calls. I called work first to let them know I would not be in that week. The club receptionist was off due to it being Monday, she never worked on Mondays and neither did any of the restaurant staff. Pam, the club accountant finally answered. I had the work number memorized, an eight hundred number ending with the numbers that spelled out "Port". I had not memorized Andy's number so I asked Pam to get it from the list of all of our numbers that Gabe kept in his office. I needed to let him know not to worry about picking me up for work. I also had a burning urge to talk to him.

Andy answered on the second ring.

"Hey," I held it together through that one little word.

"Hey," he replied, but I could barely hear him over the noise in the background.

I struggled not to break down at the sound of his voice. "I don't need you to pick me up for work on Wednesday."

"Why? What's up? Is it about how I ran off last night? I'm..."

I broke down then, "Pops died about an hour ago."

"What?" I could hear Andy sit up in his chair.

"He had a heart attack during the night and..."

"Do you need me to come be with you?" Andy asked.

"No..." I sniffled. "Yes. No, you have class and my family's here and I don't want you to... I'll be okay. It's okay. Everything's okay."

A nurse passing by and noticing me in the hall handed me tissues. I paused for a second to blow my nose.

"Tell me where you are and I will come to you," Andy insisted.

"No, seriously, I'll be fine. I'm with my mother and Granny and..." The thought of why I was in the corridor of the hospital came over me and the word that usually went after "Granny and" was "Pops" and the reality hit me again.

I held my head in my hand and cried to Andy, "He was the best man I ever knew."

I took ragged breaths in between words and coughed out, "He was the closest thing to a dad I had."

Andy insisted on coming to get me, but I convinced him it wasn't necessary and that he should go on to work.

"I need to be with my family. I don't know when I'll be back, but I'll call you later. Please don't worry about me." I hated when people worried about me.

"Okay. Tell everyone I'm really sorry about your grandfather." Andy paused. "And, Cara, we're friends, right?"

I sniffled again and was puzzled by his question. "Yeah?" It came out more like a question than it should have.

"So, friends worry about each other and that's a good thing, right?"

"Thanks, Andy, and I am going to hug you when I see you again."

Pops was buried on Wednesday afternoon in the graveyard at Pleasant Grove Baptist Church in Avera. The funeral preceded inside the church. The few times I'd been to church, Granny and Pops had taken me to Pleasant Grove with them. My favorite memory of going to church with them was wearing the blue dress with the ruffles and white lace that they bought me and the Animal Crackers Granny kept in her purse.

Inside the church, I sat on the front row between Mom and Granny. I glanced over my shoulder to the pew where we used to sit all those years ago. I wanted to see him sitting there even if he couldn't come sit with us. It was past time for making deals with God, but I would have bargained anything away to just have him sitting in that pew near the back.

Of course, I didn't see him back there, but I did see a church full of people who'd come to pay their respects. All of his friends from Mr. Gerald's store where all the old men gathered on stools in the hardware section to discuss politics, farming and the latest in Avera gossip. I also saw Millie, Jay and Andy among the crowd.

As I walked behind Mama and Granny on the way to the graveside service. Passing between those who had come from far and wide and who'd lined our path, a hand reached out and took mine. I glanced at the hand, a hand larger than mine, that of a man. For only a split second, a current ran through me. Quickly, my eyes traveled up the wrist, sleeve, shoulders and found the face that went with the touch as my hand slipped away. It was Andy.

After the funeral I lingered by the graveside while everyone else was invited to the fellowship hall for

74

refreshments that the church ladies had provided. I stood there admiring the casket and feeling sorry for myself. The person who loved me more than anyone else in the world was gone.

Millie joined me and put her arm around me. I think she meant for me to lay my head on her shoulder, but we were the same height so that didn't quite go as she'd planned. It took an even more awkward turn when my heel caught in the fake grass like carpet the funeral home had laid down under the tent and I stumbled toward the casket.

"Oh for Pete's sake!" I laughed and cried simultaneously.

Millie grabbed me tighter to keep us both from going down.

"That's all I damn need is for someone to go tell my mother I was flinging myself onto the casket!" I said, recovering my footing.

Once steady, Millie rubbed her forehead and said, "I'm still suffering from pregnancy brain." Millie was about two months post-partum.

I wiped my tear-stained cheeks and sniffled.

"Did you take a swig from Jay's flask too?" she asked. Millie had a way of making most any situation lighter.

"You didn't?" I asked accusingly.

Millie didn't drink, but she'd had some weird cravings with the pregnancy. "It's like I'm still pregnant," she'd told me and Stella earlier in the week. "I can't stand onions, yet when I was pregnant, I wanted one so bad that I sent Gabe to Macon to get me one of those blooming onions from Outback Steakhouse. I almost sent him to get another one the other night."

For all I knew, maybe she had taken a shine to something alcoholic.

A few minutes passed with us recovering from the near fall and Millie asked, "What's the deal with you and Andy?"

"Nothing," I replied in a casual tone just like I'd answered her other questions and keeping up my end of the conversation.

"Really, nothing?" she pressed as if she didn't believe me.

"Really. We're just friends."

Mille let it go and, although she didn't say anything else, there was a certain look on her face of holding back. There was no time for me to ask what the look was about as my mother called from the door of the fellowship hall.

"Cara, come on! They are about to say grace." My mother waived her hand, impatiently and motioning for me to come right then.

I hadn't realized Andy and Jay were milling around under the tent waiting on us. I felt what was left of my heart drop when I saw Andy standing there and a strange worry came over me that he might have heard what I said to Millie. The worry was a shock to me as I couldn't understand why it came over me. It was Andy and there wasn't anything going on with us yet I cared not to hurt his feelings. I cared not to hurt him and he cared to come here today to see if I was hurting and to see if he could help me. Maybe it wasn't anything, but I had no idea what it was.

Millie and I started toward Jay and Andy and I gestured to my mother that I would be there in a minute. I knew the look my mother gave me and it was one that shouted her displeasure.

"Are you all staying for dinner?" I asked. "There's plenty."

The church ladies had supplied a covered dish meal large enough to feed a small army.

"No," Jay answered for them. "We should be getting back before it gets too dark."

"Yeah, Gabe will send out a search party if I am out after dusk," Millie added.

76

"I don't want to intrude, but I can hang around and give you a ride if you want to go back to Milledgeville," Andy offered. "I drove separate just in case."

"I'm so sorry. You didn't need to do that." I laid a hand on his sleeve and gently shook my head while I smiled at him. "I've got my car so I'm not sure when I'm going to go back yet."

Millie stepped forward and my attention turned back to her. "I'm so sorry for your loss." She hugged me.

After Millie let me go, Jay took a turn hugging me and reiterating his condolences.

"Thank you for coming," I said as I looked over Jay's shoulder to Millie, thanking both of them.

"Of course," Millie smiled sweetly with understanding. "There's no place else would we be today, but here."

Jay gave me a little squeeze. "Millie's right, no place we'd rather be than with you today."

Andy waited a moment after Jay released me and a moment more as Jay and Millie said their final goodbyes and started toward Jay's car.

I figured Andy was going to hug me and a strange warmth came over me as I waited with anticipation.

I'd curled my hair and pulled it away from my face so the curls fell down my neck. My hair still wasn't long enough to flow much past the tops of my shoulders, but it was almost the same length all the way around. Some of the front had started to fall in tendrils around my face.

While Andy appeared to stall what I felt was a pending hug, he reached for one of the stray strands of my hair and gently tucked it behind my ear. Instinctively, my eyes locked with his and my face leaned into his hand. Slowly, Andy stepped closer to me and, with the hand that held my face, he guided me into his arms.

I thought he was going to say something sweet, some variation of "Sorry for your loss," but instead he whispered, "There's nothing going on between us, right?"

He'd heard what I said to Millie, but this wasn't the way he should have called me out. This was something that did not make my breath catch. It made me lose my breath.

Andy held me closer than a casual hug with the perfect combination of tightness and gentleness. My face rested on his chest and I could feel toned muscle beneath his shirt.

Breathless and melting into him, I answered, "No, nothing," but that was not true.

As I laid in bed that night in the room I'd grown up in, I kept myself from crying my way to sleep for the third night in a row by replaying the events with Andy. I knew it wasn't the right timing with my grandfather laying in his casket some ten yards away, but if ever I'd wanted to be kissed, it had been this afternoon. I wanted him to kiss me and I wanted to kiss him, but I didn't dare. I continued to remind myself who I was dealing with and I would not allow myself to be another notch on his bedpost.

We were friends and that was all. I reminded myself of that time and again combating the looming feelings for him. Nothing was going on.

Chapter 6

After I returned to Milledgeville, Andy and I went back to the way we were. Before Pops died, the nightmares had tapered off, but here they were again. They weren't as bad as they had been in the past, but Andy knew something was up and he continued to sleep in Jay's recliner a couple of nights a week. It was on odd setup we had, but I really appreciated it.

The bombing had caused the nightmares, but Pops' death brough on a new issue that ate at my mental health. I could not seem to shake the ache of Pops' death and I started slipping into a depression. I could barely drag myself to class and I called in sick to work more than once in the two weeks following the funeral. Each time I called in, Andy called to check on me and then made some excuse to show up and check on me in person. Most of the time, I had no ambition to get out of bed.

It was a sunny day in late April. I should have been studying or in class, but I was in bed with the covers pulled over my head at two in the afternoon. The phone rang and I didn't bother answering it. It rang and it rang and it rang until finally I snatched it up.

"What?" I snapped, expecting it to be a telemarketer.

"Hey! Get your ass dressed. I'm picking you up in ten minutes," Andy barked at me.

"I don't feel good," I whined.

"You'll be dressed when I get there or I will drag you out in whatever state you're in. Don't test me. Now get dressed!" Andy gave sharp orders and didn't take no for an answer. "And wear tennis shoes!"

Andy hung up before I could protest further or even say, "Okay."

"Get dressed now," I said to myself in a mimicking, mocking voice that sounded nothing like Andy. "Don't test me!" I stuck my tongue out at the phone.

In five minutes, Andy was at my door.

"Don't you have some studying to do? Don't you have class?" I smarted as I let him in. I knew he was enrolled in a master's program, but he never talked about it.

"Don't you?" he snapped back.

I walked to the bathroom and he followed me down the hall.

"I do, but someone called." I shut the door in his face.

Andy yelled through the door. "Someone's got a name. It's Andy and he said hurry up!"

We continued to snip at one another through the door until I was finished brushing my teeth, slipping on jeans and pulling my sweatshirt over my head.

Andy looked me up and down when I finally opened the door. "You look like shit."

"Thanks, asshole!" I slipped past him. "If you came over here just to be mean, I could have stayed in my pajamas."

"Nope. Come on, we're going out."

Once fully dressed and outside, Andy walked around and opened the car door for me. That was a new gesture and, any other day, I would have been impressed or touched.

Andy turned the car around and we headed back to Hancock Street, onto which Andy made a left. We crossed the Oconee River headed out of town as if we were going to Sandersville, but he made another left before the fork in the road that led toward Sandersville. A turn here and there, I stopped paying attention until Andy brought the car to a rest on a dirt patch in what appeared to be the middle of nowhere.

"Let's go." He opened his car door and got out.

"Where?" I was not amused.

"You'll see. Chop! Chop! Move it!"

I rolled my eyes in response and not without severe gripes in my head, I got out of the car. This seemed an awful lot like the old Andy, all bossy and I wasn't sure I liked him right then.

Andy took a path through the woods and I followed about ten paces behind, not entirely keen on keeping up, but afraid of losing him, too.

"Where are we going?" I yelled ahead to Andy.

"You'll see when we get there."

"Are we there yet?"

"How old are you?"

"Old enough!" I clipped off under my breath.

"You are in rare form today." Andy didn't even break his pace as he addressed me.

"Me?" I kept walking. "Hello, Pot, meet Kettle."

Tree branches encroached the path at various intervals and Andy held them back for me to pass. It wasn't my first walk in the woods, but most of the time folks in front of me just let the limbs fly. I had learned to keep a short distance between me and whomever was leading. No one ever stopped to hold back the branches for me before.

First the car door and now the branches, I noticed and the conflict within me started again. Was Andy the ass that I first thought he was? Maybe he was thoughtful and paid attention to little things like not letting the branches fly and hit me. I kept my eyes on his back as I walked and contemplated my reassessment.

Andy stopped as the woods opened up. I saw him stop, but my mind was drifting and my feet were on auto pilot. I barely missed running into him and stumbled to a stop.

"Look," he said, pointing to the right, "that's the dam to Lake Sinclair."

Andy didn't wait for me to fully take in the sight before he headed down the bank to the rocks below. These weren't like the rocks in the creek near my house, ones about as big as my foot that I'd strategically placed so I could jump from one to the next and cross the little creek.

81

No, these were giant boulders, big enough to have picnics on at the base of the dam.

"What are you waiting on?" Andy called.

I didn't dare give the real answer. I was waiting on my courage to arrive. All I could think was if that dam failed, I wasn't dog paddling my way out of it. I was not the best swimmer and this was giving me the creeps.

Andy stopped and waited on me. I took a deep breath and shimmied down the bank.

At the bottom, I jumped a stream of water that separated two of the rocks. To get to Andy I had to jump a bigger divide and he held out his hand to catch me.

Andy continued walking then jumping, crossing from one rock to another and I followed, my stomach knotting a little more and a little more until we were as close to the bottom of the dam as we could go.

"The dam was built in 1953," Andy explained.

"And its 1997 now," I mentioned, but he didn't pay much attention.

"My grandfather helped build it. That's how he ended up in Milledgeville. He was sent here by Georgia Power to help oversee the project."

"Have I ever mentioned, I'm not the greatest swimmer so if this thing breaks..."

"It's not going to break," Andy rolled his eyes.

The rock we were standing on was about ten feet by ten or twelve feet and mostly flat. I was in awe looking at the dam and, then, from the corner of my eye, I noticed Andy was not standing up anymore. At first, I thought he had slipped or something, but that would have made more noise. No, he'd sat down.

"What are you doing?" I looked at him curiously.

"Here," he patted the space next to him, motioning me to join him.

"Why?"

"Just do it."

I did as he commanded. As I sat down, Andy laid back, propping his head on an arm he'd folded behind him. The other arm, he stretched out to me. "Lay down, you can put your head here."

Again, I indulged him. For the next half-hour we watched the clouds and described what we saw. Andy saw a few of the Peanuts characters and I saw flowers. Trying to get comfortable lying on the rock, I'd squirmed until my head was resting on Andy's shoulder. He didn't seem to mind.

After a mild argument over whether it was Woodstock's head or a daisy, Andy got to the reason he brought me out here. He'd waited until my guard was down and I was relaxed.

"Cara, I know you're grieving, but it's time to get your shit together." Andy delivered the statement about as softly as one could while including the phrase, "get your shit together."

"Your grandfather wouldn't want to see you like this."

"I know," I said softly.

"There's a counselor on campus you can see. It's free. I got her number for you," he stroked my hair.

I laid there in silence and Andy continued.

"I don't mind staying over with you, sleeping in the chair every night if you need me, but..." he paused.

I sat up and Andy immediately sat up next to me. I looked at him and that tension I felt at Pop's funeral was back. That invisible rope that was pulling my heart toward him.

Andy's arm was still around me. My heart pounded in my chest and I'd never wanted to be kissed so badly in my entire life. I'd never want to kiss someone so badly as I'd wanted to kiss him in that moment.

I reached my hand up and touched his cheek and his arm flexed around me. It was happening. All apprehension fell away as the butterflies flapped their little wings in my stomach. Our faces inched together for a slow, drawn-out moment in which I assessed every inch of his face. Freckles, dimples, long dark eyelashes like every makeup company dreamed of creating for women, and his nose was long and straight and set dead center. It divided his face perfectly. His eyes, though, they were the best. They were pools of caramel that I would happily drown in and I couldn't believe I'd never notice before. I'd thought he was attractive, fun to look at, but he was more than that. He was beautiful and here with me.

A caress of his cheek urged him on and the soft tightening of his arm around me, brought me closer to him.

"You always smell good," I exhaled.

Other than the fact that my mind was completely slipping for him, I don't know why I said that other than the fact it was true. Even when we weren't outside, he smelled like fresh air and a trace of cut wood. After a long day at work, when there should have been a hint of his deodorant failing, Andy was a treat for the senses.

Andy gave a grin over what I'd said and I smiled, momentarily excited that this really was happening. I was past working up the courage. Worries of my fragile self-esteem had evaporated and, if he didn't kiss me, I was going to kiss him. Just maybe I was in the ballpark after all.

Just before my lips met his, a God-awful blaring noise flooded my senses and killed the butterflies. Andy snatched back and I covered my ears.

"What is that?" I shouted.

"We've got to get out of here!" Andy jumped to his feet, grabbed my hand and jerked me up. "Run!"

"What?" I stumbled.

"Just run! That's the alarm that they are opening the flood gates!"

"They're what? Shit!" I ran, jumping from one of the boulders to the next and never letting go of Andy's hand.

When we made it to the top of the riverbank, we were too out of breath from running and the moment had passed.

Silence filled the car as we drove back to town and it was about as thick as pea-soup, like fog. I was so frustrated as I sat wondering what he was thinking and where we were going. The second part of the question was quickly answered when Andy turned onto Jefferson Street. He was taking me home. The first part of the question was never answered. Andy pulled up in front of my door, said some gibberish about having to study for a test, gave me the name of the counselor and left as soon as I got out of the car. The afternoon had taken a turn and my self-esteem was right back where it was before.

Head down and dragging my feet, I schlepped back into my apartment and found Jay.

"Hey!" he hollered from the kitchen. "Are you ready for dinner?"

"No," I sulked and headed for my room.

"Well, too bad! I've made your favorite."

It was then that the smell of shrimp scampi overwhelmed my senses. Shrimp, garlic, butter, angel hair pasta, my favorite, but I was not in the mood to eat. For Jay's sake and the trouble he'd gone to, I forced myself. I didn't want to be rude and I was also curious as to what was up with Jay. I hadn't seen signs of him being home in weeks. He'd almost cleaned the place out of his belongings. He'd taken all of his clothes some time ago and only his furniture remained.

Over dinner I found out that Jay had gotten bored and decided that domestic life wasn't for him yet. While Chris was in class, Jay packed his car and moved back to our apartment.

"He was great at first, but..." Jay searched for the words.

"Things took a turn," I related.

"Every weekend we had to go visit his mother and she called incessantly."

I snorted.

"Yes, I know," Jay nodded, "And she made my mother's volume of calls look slim if you can imagine."

85

I continued to listen as I twirled noodles around my fork.

Jay made a flippant gesture with his hand, "I commend her for being so out and proud of him, but they were too much even for me. It was like watching peacocks fluff their feathers all the time, the two of them. He wasn't like that except when he was with her."

Jay also went on to add, "I want a man, not a mama's girl. She actually called him 'Gurrrl'." Jay said the last word in a mocking tone and added a gagging gesture with his finger aimed in his mouth.

When Jay finally wound down his story, he asked, "So what's been going on with you and why is my recliner in your room?"

I had some explaining to do, but before I even got started, Jay asked, "And what was the deal with you and Andy at your grandfather's funeral?"

I was relieved to hear that Jay had noticed. That gave my story a jumping off point. We were finished eating, but for the next half hour I recounted what I had going on or not going on with Andy. Jay listened intently with his chin propped in his hands, hovering over his dirty plate.

"So let me get this straight, he hasn't thrown it on you, he's been sleeping in the recliner, he hasn't even kissed you and you're together all the time?"

I nodded.

"What's wrong with him?" Jay squinched his face and shrugged his shoulders.

"What's wrong with me?" I was quick to counter.

"Nothing's wrong with you, but I assure you, if he was into you, he would make a move."

That was not helpful.

Chapter 7

Classes were over for the week and we had the first annual Delta Digital spring fling that night. The company's Christmas party had really been something to talk about and the spring fling set to be a spectacle as well.

The company hosted a Karaoke contest at Christmas and invited the staff of Port Honor to join in. They had a guy that sounded just like Elvis, but Millie gave him a run for his money each year. I could still picture her strutting her stuff to Joan Jett's "Do You Wanna Touch Me" and the look on Gabe's face. He was completely scandalized. It was priceless. Although I had to work the party, I had been looking forward to it all week. I'd also been looking forward to seeing Andy.

Hopes of things going back to normal and the anticipation of recapturing the moment by the Lake Sinclair Dam were dashed with a phone call around 2 p.m.

"Hey." I recognized Andy's voice just with one word.

"Hey." I bit my bottom lip and heard the breathlessness in my voice. That was not how I normally sounded, but my stomach did flips at the thought of him.

"I've got to go in early so you'll need to drive yourself today," he said with what I interpreted as no regret in his voice at all.

"Oh," I let out in defeat, but recovered quickly, trying to hide my disappointment. "That's fine."

"Yeah, so I guess I'll see you there."

"Right. See you there."

I hung up the phone and sat there on my bed wondering what was going on with him only to have Jay's words creep in. "He's not into you."

I arrived at work with fifteen minutes to spare. I entered through the side door of the clubhouse by the pool. As soon as I opened the door, I heard someone in the storage room where we kept extra tables and chairs.

Sometimes when we worked double shifts and, if the bathrooms were occupied, we changed clothes in there.

The door to the storage room was slightly open and I couldn't help but look. Andy was changing in there. Despite the fact that he'd slept at my apartment for the better part of few months, I'd never seen him in any state of undress beyond that of him just in his undershirt and slacks or shorts. Now, there he stood bare chested and the sight stopped me in my tracks.

"Hey!" Andy said, catching me looking.

I raked my eyes over him from the little V-pit in his neck to the V at his hips where his pants hung low enough to make smart girls go stupid. He was all pecks and abs and no tan line. I suspected he was fit, but I had no idea he was smuggling a Greek god under his shirt.

I was so dumbstruck I hadn't heard him until he said my name. "Cara?" Andy pulled an undershirt over his head and flexed, straightening the sleeves and back.

My heart pounded in my ears and I just stood there, looking and regretting having missed kissing him at the dam. If I had any thought at all, it was, "Damn, he was fine!"

"Cara?" he repeated and I realized I was caught.

Embarrassed, I turned around to give him the overdue privacy.

"It's ok," he laughed, "you can turn around."

"No, um, I've got to clock in," I said, briskly fleeing down the corridor that led to the kitchen.

Delta Digital was based out of Japan and as a treat for their local employees the management always had a sushi bar from Atlanta set up a station in addition to the food we served and, as a part of the entertainment, they hired a host for Karaoke. At this party the traditions continued and Millie even made an appearance to compete in the Karaoke contest. She won the first year we worked there, beating out a man who had a face for radio, but a voice that could easily be mistaken for the King himself. He'd beat her this Christmas, but I think if she hadn't been three weeks away from giving birth she'd have taken him again. The man sounded just like Elvis and he opened the night's performances with his annual serenade of his wife to "You Were Always On My Mind". He did not disappoint.

The night continued, but by the time the competition really got going those of us working were on the tail end of things. We had taken down the buffet and were pretty much done with the exception of resetting the dining room, which we couldn't do until they left. Most of us were milling around just watching and waiting for them to finish and go home. There was an open bar so, unlike those of us who were left that waited tables, Andy was still busy making drinks in the bar.

Daniel and I leaned against the hostess stand and watched. From the hostess stand I could take in all that was going on in the dining room and I could catch glimpses of Andy. I could not get the image of him shirtless out of my head and, each time I thought of it, I was afraid someone was going to notice me blushing. Thankfully no one did.

The singing continued and, this year, the Elvis impersonator added a lively rendition of Jailhouse Rock complete with leg wiggle and gyrations. Daniel and I howled along with the man's co-workers over the performance.

Millie only did one song and left off any dance number. She seemed to be holding back again. Her vocals were as competitive as ever with her performance of Bette Middler's "The Rose". It gave us all chills.

"Cara," Gabe called me, "could you get the trophy from behind the bar?"

"Sure," I replied and set about doing as I was asked.

For whatever reason the trophy for the Karaoke contest had been placed on the top shelf of the liquor cabinet behind the bar, sitting between the bottles of Patron and Dewar's.

I could have seen through the glass if I'd bothered to pay attention, but the surprise did not hit me until I opened the door. At the end of the bar, sat Miss Reese. That wasn't her name, I think it was Jessie or something, but she looked just like the volleyball star and there she was. Short skirt, legs and legs and legs, hair straight out of a shampoo commercial, and eyes that batted at Andy's every move. They were chatting it up, laughing as he dried highball glasses.

I glared at him and rolled my eyes. I marched around behind the bar, determined I wasn't going to speak to either of them. There was only one problem. Unlike his ex-girlfriend, I wasn't tall enough to reach the flippin' trophy without hopping up on the cooler at the base of the cabinet and stretching for it. I wasn't about to do that with them there so I had to ask him to hand it to me.

"Yeah, sure." Andy easily reached to trophy and handed it to me. "Here."

I should have said thanks or kiss my ass or anything, but I said nothing. I just snatched the trophy from him and gave an irritable grunt before storming off.

After giving the trophy to Gabe, I returned to Daniel's side at the hostess stand.

"I thought we were closed tonight," I said, directing Daniel's attention through the glass door to the bar. "Do you know her?"

"Oh, yeah, that's Andy's girl," he replied.

My head swam. He did not say ex-girlfriend. He said it in the present tense. I did my best to sound unconcerned when I asked, "Really?"

"Oh, yeah," he sighed, "she's been away studying in Spain the last semester."

In keeping with his envy, I added, "Must be nice," which had about as many translations as "Bless your heart," but in this case, it meant, "Bitch."

"Evidently she came in to surprise Andy."

"Looks like it's working out for her." I looked away to conceal Daniel from seeing me turn up my nose like I smelled road kill.

"Yeah, they are cute together."

"I heard she was dumb as a box of rocks."

Daniel took a long look at me. "Sweetie, I'm no expert on the straight male portion of the species, but I guarantee when you look like that, they aren't worried about whether you can do quantum physics."

That time I didn't bother turning my head. I gave a look like I smelled shit right to his face.

The judges of the contest were also the management of the company. At around 11:15 they announced the winner. It was Mr. Blue Suede Shoes and they took the trophy back with them when they finally left.

I could not help myself, I stole glances in the bar the rest of the night. Each time I saw her smile and fawning over him my blood boiled. I wasn't sure if she left or if she was waiting there for him to get off work. All I knew is that when it was time for me to drive myself home, my car wouldn't start. I had tried everything, even looked under the hood; jiggled some wires, disconnected the battery cables and reattached them and nothing worked. My Honda was dead.

Andy's car was the only one still in the parking lot. I would have rather died than walk back inside for his help. Just as I worked up the nerve and drag ass back in, Andy and one of the kids from the dish pit came walking out.

"Hey," Andy said, seeing me pacing around the trunk of my car. His voice and face lit up like he was happy to see me, but I was having none of it.

"My car won't start," I said, sounding as put out as I was at the whole night.

"Ah, okay." He headed toward the front of the car and Marcus trailed behind. "Pop the hood."

"Fine." I reached in the car and pulled the leaver. I then stood at the fender of the front passenger's tire and watched as Andy lifted the hood.

"You know anything about cars?" Andy asked Marcus.

Marcus shook his head. "Nope."

Andy gave a strained smile. "Try cranking it."

I got in and turned the key. It made a noise like, "Annh! Annh! Annh!" like a barking baby seal.

"Battery," Andy assessed. "I haven't got any jumper cables so I guess you're riding with me."

"Shit." I let fly under my breath.

"What?" said Marcus.

"Nothing!" I snipped back at him.

"Well, come on then. We'll figure this out tomorrow. It will be fine here tonight." Andy assured me, but his assurances didn't mean much to me right that moment.

I grabbed my keys and purse from my car as they headed to Andy's. Once at his car, I found Marcus had left me the front seat and he'd climbed in the back.

"Hope you don't mind the ride to Siloam. I've got to take him home, too."

I couldn't very well say anything but, "No, that's fine," although I'm sure I didn't sound like it was fine. I suppose my put out tone of voice warranted the side glance Andy gave me, but I just gave him one right back.

The ride to Marcus's house was silent with the exception of the blaring radio. Andy was a fan of Candle Box, Jesus Jones, Train and the like. I was doing fine until Interstate Love Song came on.

"Figures," I said just as the lead singer belted out, "You lied," and reached over and cut the radio off.

"Are you okay?" Andy asked.

Again, I said nothing, just grunted a little.

The silence continued until we dropped Marcus off.

92

"Some of the guys were going to Dockside, the bar over by the club. I told them I'd stop by. Do you mind?" He asked me, sounding the same considerate way he usually sounded lately. "I promise I won't have more than one beer and I'll buy you a Coke."

"Fine," I muttered, "but you don't have to buy me anything."

When we got there, the guys from the pro-shop were at the bar and a couple of the members from Port Honor were there, too. I'd halfway expected to see Miss Volleyball there in her little skirt. Praise Jesus she wasn't because I'd made up my mind that I'd wait in the car if she was. I'd seen enough of that show already.

Andy held to his word. He had one beer, bought me a coke, had some laughs with the guys and even included me and not as the butt of some sexist joke. For just a moment, I almost forgot about his girlfriend.

"Ready?" he asked, laying money on the bar for our drinks.

"Whenever you are." I forced myself to sound cordial.

Andy held the door for me and I went out.

The bar was in a building that seemed like it was constructed with the intention of being an office complex. It was all wood, almost cabin like, with a wraparound porch attaching it to other units in the complex.

Out on the porch, instinct took over and I waited for Andy to lead. He went down the two steps onto the walk way and turned back.

Meeting me at eye level, as I was still standing on the porch, he asked sincerely, "Why don't we go out sometime?"

The stewing I had been doing over seeing him with his girlfriend simmered to the top and bubbled over. I replied, incredulously, "Are you kidding me?"

Earlier today, I would have been all for it. I had let down my guard to him and I would have fallen all over him, but I had been reminded he was not for me.

93

A look of complete bewilderment overcame his face and he said, "You never take me seriously at all, do you?"

"No!" I brushed by him and went and got in the car.

Not another word was said all the way to Milledgeville. I had protected my heart and put an end to the foolishness I'd been feeling.

Little did I know that night, that was only the beginning of the foolishness of my feelings. For countless years, I regretted that night. I found out within days that Andy was not still attached to the volleyball goddess, but the damage was done.

Andy never spent the night in the recliner again. Another ride was never offered. There was a divide between us and a thickness in the air that told the moment had passed and he was not up for me fixing it.

Andy started dating another girl and, although I wanted him to be happy, I couldn't take seeing him so I transferred to a job at the Inn. The job transfer solved the problem of rarely coming in contact with him beyond passing him on the street in and out of Port Honor. I graduated college and left Milledgeville, but I heard about him from time to time from Millie and Jay. I heard soon after I left that he married that girl he'd started dating right after we stopped whatever it was we were doing. I heard when he had his first child, which wasn't long after the marriage. I heard when he finally left Port Honor. I had my own life events, but with each of his I wished him the best and I wished I was sharing them with him. Hearing about him never stopped breaking my heart.

The night I heard his grandmother died, I almost asked Millie for his number so I could call him. Instead, I cried myself to sleep, devastated on his behalf and remembering how it felt when I lost Pops, when I lost the person that loved me more than anyone else. That night, I didn't know if I'd ever tell him, but I knew he'd always have someone who loved him more than anyone else. That someone was me.

I had been so stupid and so blind and so cruel. I'd justified my actions and feelings, constantly questioning if whether Andy was an ass or not, whether I was in the ballpark or not. The truth was that I really wasn't in the ballpark with him and the ass had been me all along. I'd done it to protect my heart, but instead I broke the very thing I was trying to protect. I knew I did it, not him.

Chapter 8

I plucked the card from the standing spray of Star Gazer Lilies and white roses. "So pretty. This one would have been her favorite," I said, handing the card to Andy.

I moved to the next one. "She would have hated this one."

It was a simple bouquet of yellow long stem roses. It sat on a pedestal and in a glass vase between two standing sprays. Whomever placed the arrangement did their best to make the yellow roses blend with the others by placing them a little behind the sprays.

"Hold on a minute," Andy protested.

I cut a smile at him and handed him the card.

"I sent that one." He took the card and added it to the building stack in his other hand.

"I know." I blushed a little, having been teasing him. I didn't have to look at the card to know it was from him. "It's your signature thing." I moved to the next spray.

"You remember?" He asked, surprised.

"You sent the same thing to my grandfather's funeral. My grandmother told me she called to thank you for the flowers, she said you explained to her that you always send yellow roses because they were your grandmother's favorite."

Andy didn't look at me until I added, "I received yellow roses once too, but there wasn't a card."

I reached out and touched the sleeve of his sport coat. "You can never know how much they meant to me."

He lifted his eyes to meet mine. "Millie told me about the babies and I felt sick over it for you. I am so sorry that happened."

"Thank you," I smiled and blinked back the tears. Whenever I thought of the twins I lost, it still hurt.

"Millie said you had them buried in Avera with your grandparents."

I nodded. "They would have been six this year, but God had other plans."

We'd become distracted from our job, but I didn't care. I would have talked to Andy about anything, but I didn't like talking about my girls and I rarely did so. I never wanted to forget them, but the thought of them never failed to sting. Plus, people didn't tend to want to hear about how you carried twins full term, lost them at the bitter end when their umbilical cords became knotted and did not find out until you went through full blown labor.

Andy shifted the subject. "I hear you're living in Avera now."

I plucked a card from another of the standing sprays. "You seem to hear a lot."

Andy grinned and took the card. He still had noticeable dimples which I could see through the slight stubble he was sporting. I could not recall ever having seen him with the slightest bit of facial hair back in the day. Now, this mature look was working for him.

We were nearing the end of the line of arrangements. There was so much I wanted to say to Andy, but I didn't know where or how to start and there was no time to figure it out. Jolene started organizing everyone else to take the flowers away and called to Andy to help with an especially large potted plant.

"Daddy'll get such joy out of seeing these and thinking of Mama," she told him.

Jay threw up his hands and glared at Peter. Peter stood there with his hands full, awaiting dispatch to carry one of the standing sprays to Jolene's minivan. Jolene's husband doddled around, holding another of the sprays and waiting, too.

I grabbed the last two cards from the flowers and handed them to Andy who turned them over to Jolene. He then left with the plant, following her and the other two to her car. I felt the old pang of heartbreak as I wondered what to do with myself after fetching my purse. I didn't have to wonder long as Jay saw me and came over.

"Hey," he said, sidling up next to me. "I gave you some bad advice one time and I need to clear it up."

"What?" I asked, having no idea what he could be talking about.

"I told you a long time ago that he wasn't that in to you and I was wrong. I didn't know at the time and I'm sorry."

I remembered the conversation, but still didn't understand. "How do you know you were wrong?"

"I just know," Jay replied with an implication that he could not break a confidence placed in him. "I was wrong and I'm sorry."

"I'm sorry about a lot of things, too," I confided. "I feel I broke my own heart back then."

"Yours wasn't the only one you broke." Jay gave a pressed smile. He waited a moment and I could tell by the look on his face he was contemplating what to say next or whether he should say anything at all.

"What?" I asked again.

"Nothing." He still seemed torn. "I better go help before Jolene has my balls."

"Wait." I followed him. "What are you not saying?"

Jay stopped and gave me a pleading look. "I can't say anything. You know I would if I could."

"Why do you always have to be everyone's confidant?" I huffed, acting as if I was seriously put out, but I wasn't. He and Millie shared that role in our circle of friends.

Jay took the teasing as intended and smiled. "It's not all about you, Sweetheart."

I opened my arms and hugged him. "I'm so sorry about your mom. She was a wonderful lady. I'm going to miss her."

"Thanks." Jay gave me a squeeze.

I took that as my cue to say my goodbye. I had not gotten what I came for, an opportunity to apologize to

Andy, but it wasn't really the time or place so I couldn't be too disappointed.

"I'll call you in a couple of days to check on you," I said, as he released me.

"What do you mean? Aren't you coming to Seven Springs tonight?" While speaking Jay looked past me.

"You're not coming to dinner?" Andy's voice came from behind me.

I spun to see Andy had returned. "What are y'all talking about?"

"I thought you knew," Jay said with an implied apology.

"We're all staying there, the whole gang, Stella, Daniel and Jerry..." Andy started.

Jay added, "Anyway, you should definitely come."

I glanced at Andy, barely noticing Jolene's return as well. "Um, okay. What time should I be there?"

"Diner's at 7:00 p.m." Jay looked at his watch. "I guess we better get going. I still want to shower and change."

"I guess I'll go home and change and see y'all at 7:00," I shrugged.

"Get there at 6:30 so we can all have drinks," Jay insisted.

"Great idea," Andy added.

"Maybe they'll let you behind the bar and it can be like old times." I could not wipe the smile off of my face if I had tried.

Not taking his eyes off of me, Andy said, "I'd like for things to be like old times."

My heart melted and I felt all of the butterflies come back to life. My brain swirled, overanalyzing what he'd said. Was he implying something? I so hoped he was.

"Jay," Jolene called to her brother and, despite their ripe age, she still exerted her position as the older sibling, "if you could help that would be great."

Jay rolled his eyes, "Y'all excuse me. I'll see you there."

"I'll walk you out," Andy said to me as Jay left us.

On the porch of the church, I lingered and let Andy go down two steps ahead of me. Noticing me stall, Andy stopped at the bottom and turned to check on me. I seized the opportunity.

"The last time we were on a set of steps together, I said something I've regretted ever since." I watched Andy's eyes grow big as I spoke. I definitely had his attention.

I continued, "I was such a bitch to you and I am so sorry."

Andy didn't say anything and so I went on. "Not to excuse how I was, but I was terrified of you back then."

Andy's brows furrowed and he asked, "You," he emphasized, "were scared of me?" Andy ended with a laugh. "Really?"

I nodded. "Why is that funny?"

"Because I was so intimidated by you."

"No way." I could feel the heat in my cheeks rising.

"You were the first girl that didn't put up with my bullshit back then. You were the only real female friend I'd ever had and the closest thing to a best friend I'd had."

"You were friends with Millie and Stella." I shook off what he was saying.

"Not like with you. It was different with you."

I hesitated, but the question started forming on my face.

"What?" Andy asked.

I shook my head, shrugging off the temptation to ask.

"Seriously, we're grown adults," Andy reached out and took my hand. "You can ask me anything."

He thought we were grown adults, but I felt twenty years old all over again as I took in the wonders of his face. The slight twinkle in his eye begged the question so I took a deep breath and asked.

"Were we ever more than friends?" I narrowed my eyes and studied him.

Andy took a moment, choosing his words. "To me we were, but that night at Dockside."

"Right, when I was a..."

"Why?" he asked. "What happened? I've always wondered."

What better place than at the big white church in the center of Thomson, Georgia to make a confession?

Hearing the door grinding hinges on the front door of the church as it opened, Andy clammed up.

Jay and Jolene came out, followed by Peter and Jolene's husband. It was an interruption that ended the reunion Andy and I had been having. Everyone, but Jay was surprised to see Andy and I still there.

Jay hugged me, thanked me again for coming, as if there was anywhere else I'd be that day. While holding me, he whispered, "Don't breathe a word about meeting up at Millie's. Jolene doesn't know."

I wasn't sure how Andy and I left things. We all just disbanded with Jolene asking Andy if he could carry the last plant she was holding. Being the gentleman he was, he obliged. At that point all of the guys had an arrangement and were obligated to walk Jolene to her car.

Detached from actual driving with my Tahoe on autopilot, I hit the peaks and valleys on the road between Thomson and the cut off to Stapleton. The vision before me was not the road and landscape of where the Piedmont met the Coastal Plain near the Fall Line here in Georgia. Instead, I stared off in the distance watching as the movie before me skipped like an old record. It kept replaying the exchange between me and Andy, "Were we ever more than friends?" and his answer. I wasn't quite as timid as I once was, but I'd still shocked myself with the courage to ask the question, but his answer shocked me even more.

Like any movie, the one I was watching unfold above my dashboard had a dilemma and the dilemma was: What was I supposed to do with that information? Had we just been talking, rehashing old times? I'd come there to set things straight with Andy after all these years, just apologize, but I had not thought this far ahead. I hadn't thought out his response or reaction. I'd only hoped he would accept my apology.

With every repetition of his answer, "To me we were," the butterflies stirred in my belly. I couldn't unhear it. I couldn't unsee his face when he said the words. The boy I knew was still there, but the man before me was more than anything I'd dreamed. I wondered what more would have been said if Jay and his family hadn't come out of the church when they did. I wanted more time with Andy. I wanted to answer him. He deserved an answer.

I tried on half of my closet before I settled on my favorite jeans and sweater. I reminded myself I was going to a cookout and bonfire, not tea with the queen. I put on minimal makeup, way less than what I'd worn to the funeral. Glancing in the mirror, I could see the freckles across the bridge of my nose and the little lines starting to form at the edge of my eyes. I'd had my hair colored the day after Millie called about the funeral. I didn't have much gray, but now I had none.

"I'm not what I once was," I said to my reflection, "But this will have to do."

The hotel and restaurant that Millie and Gabe owned, Seven Springs, was about five minutes from my house. It was out in the country and, despite its locale, two dirt roads off of the grid, they did a surprisingly good business. They did such a good business, that I was amazed they were able to accommodate everyone coming to town on the three-day notice that the funeral gave. Millie was known for moving mountains for her friends and I guess this probably wasn't even a molehill for her.

I fretted over my clothes, my hair and whether to carry a purse or not, all in the name of killing time so I wouldn't seem so eager to get there. It was all I could do to wait and I made it as far as 6:30 before I headed out.

Upon arrival, I found the whole lot of them in the restaurant and, sure enough, Andy was behind the bar. I was relieved to find Millie and Stella dressed about as casually as I was. Caroline and Jack had conflicting schedules so they weren't able to come to the funeral. Caroline would have been the one who made us all look underdressed.

Anna-Cat, Stella, Jerry, Jay and Millie were seated at the bar with Alex, Daniel, Peter and Gabe mixed in but standing. Everyone turned to see me come in.

"It's about time you got here!" Jay yelled.

Gabe cleared a path so I could take a seat in the stool next to Millie.

"If Millie was a drink, what would she be?" Anna-Cat asked.

They were playing a drinking game that Andy used to play with the members at Port Honor. They would say the line with one of the member's names and Andy would make a drink to represent them. The subject was presented the drink and the rest of the onlookers chanted, "Drink! Drink! Drink!"

"What was that drink that you sent Gabe at the bar that night?" Jay snapped his fingers, trying to remember.

Gabe replied as the color rose in Millie's cheeks, "A Pink Panty Dropper."

Everyone broke out in laughter.

There was no guessing on Andy's part what drink was Millie as she would never live that story down.

"She definitely got my attention," Gabe pulled Millie in for a hug.

"A round of Pink Panty Droppers, please!" Jay shouted above the laughing.

Andy, having made himself acquainted with the stock of the bar, set to work making a shot for each of us. He slid the first of the finished product to Millie and everyone yelled, "Drink! Drink! Drink!" as Millie threw it back.

"Whew! Not bad," Jay praised Millie for her choice.

"Next!" Millie pointed to Stella.

103

Peter piped up, after tossing back his Pink Panty, "If Stella was a drink what would she be?"

Andy sized Stella up and then assessed the provisions behind the bar. He then pulled a bottle of Bailey's from the shelf behind him, searched the cooler and came up with heavy cream and a can of ready whip.

"Do you have any brown sugar?" he asked Gabe.

Gabe went to the kitchen and came back, sitting it down next to Andy who was mixing the liquids in a shaker. Andy took down as many martini glasses as there were and behind the bar he finished the creation.

"I give you the Stella," he said presenting her with one of the martini glasses.

A darker brown liquid spiraled down the inside of the glass with a lighter brown liquid filling it and a rim that was not salted, but sugared and salted. It was pretty.

Stella took it to her nose, inhaled and lifted her eyes to Andy with a huge smile.

"Drink! Drink! Drink!" we all chanted and Stella took a sip.

"Oh, this is good," she cooed over the concoction.

Andy slid five more martini glasses across the bar. Millie reached for one. She wasn't a drinker and we were all surprised.

"What is it?" she asked.

"It's really good, is what it is," Jay offered Peter some from the glass he had taken.

"A Salted Caramel Martini," Andy answered.

Stella raised her glass, "Salty and caramel, that's me!"

Andy took a pull off of the bottled beer he was holding and then shouted, "Next!" as if he was back in his days of working the bar at the club.

Stella pointed to me. "If Cara was a drink, what would she be?"

"Easy," Andy rolled his eyes. In thirty seconds, two bottles and an orange peel later, he was back.

Like Millie I wasn't much of a drinker either. Being a good sport, I stepped forward, but still shuttered to think what he'd made.

Andy slid the rocks glass toward me and everyone chanted again, "Drink! Drink! Drink!"

I took a sip and fought the urge gasp for my next breath. I didn't know what it was, but it burned like whiskey.

"Come on, throw it back," Jay demanded.

Everyone laughed at the sight of me struggling to finish it while Andy placed more glasses of it on the bar.

Gabe took one, turned it up and when he sat the glass down, he laughed the loudest. "An Old Fashioned?"

"Oh, ha ha!" I said to Andy and the whole place went into hysterics.

Carrying his glass, Gabe rounded the bar, headed in the direction of the kitchen door. "Dinner's almost ready if you all want to head down to the firepit," he said, continuing toward the kitchen door.

"Wait!" Millie called out to stop him and all eyes turned to her including Gabe's.

"If Andy was a drink, what would he be?" Millie raised her glass.

Jay slapped the bar top. "Yes!" and everyone chanted with him. "If Andy was a drink, what would he be?"

Before the chanting died down and above their collective voices, words jumped out of my mouth. "I know."

You could have heard a pin drop.

With both hands braced on the bar top, Andy gave me a stare. "Well?" With a flip of his hand, he invited me to join him behind the bar.

I eased off of my stool and made my way around. I slowed near Gabe and at the stock of wine bottles. "You probably don't have it."

"What are you looking for?" Gabe whispered.

"Port wine," I whispered in his direction.

"I've got some in the kitchen, but its table wine for cooking. It's not really for drinking," Gabe quietly explained.

The group started to chant again and, my cheeks heated with embarrassment, I really hadn't thought this through. I threw up a finger at them, gesturing for them to give me a minute.

"Just get it, please."

Gabe went through the kitchen door and it barely had time to swing back when he returned holding the bottle. He had the label covered and handed it to me.

I approached the bar, picked up a wine glass and poured. All the while I poured, I guarded the label. The red liquid swirled as I slid it to Andy. I did the same serving each of them.

They raised the glasses wondering whether it was Merlot, Cabernet or Pinot Noir. It was a ruby red color, but not deep purple enough to be Cabernet and not brick colored enough to be Merlot and way too sweet to be any of the three especially the peppery Pinot.

Letting it swish on their palates and not being able to distinguish the taste, I felt the need to tell them, but Andy spoke up before I could.

"Port?" His eyebrows raised and, although he recognized the taste, he was thoroughly confused.

All of the air left me and my cheeks really flamed then. I needed to explain myself and I knew that was coming, but this was going to be like walking on stage naked. I had not considered that.

I looked to the group before me and they were just as confused.

"When you think of Port Honor, who comes to mind?" I asked.

Jerry and Daniel nodded, smiling to each other, they were catching on.

I looked to Gabe. "Which one of us was there before you hired the rest of us? And he was there after I left."

Gabe dipped his head in acknowledgement.

"Whenever, I think of working at Port Honor, Andy comes to mind so, yeah, your drink is Port."

Jay added in a shamefully flirty tone, "And it's full bodied and sweet just like him."

We all howled with laughter at that point. Praise Jesus for Jay saving me any further embarrassment.

A little after seven, the party migrated down to the firepit area. The couples paired off for the walk down leaving me, Stella and Andy to walk down on our own. Being the gentleman that I remembered, Andy held the door for us and escorted the both of us down the steps. Stella and I took each step at the same time with Andy one step behind us. When we reached the bottom, he placed a hand on the small of my back and chills ran down my legs.

Gabe pulled a tinfoil packet out of the coals in the firepit as each of us took a seat in one of the dozen Adirondack chairs that circled the fire. Stella was about to take a seat next to me when Jay called her to sit between him and Peter.

"We are thinking about buying some rental property around the college," he said to her, guiding her to the seat between them.

Stella was a teacher at Baldwin County High School and sold real estate part time. She dabbled in property management and managed The Jefferson, which Millie still owned.

Jay then took the chair to my left and Andy took the chair to my right. Jay was very subtle, but I knew the favor he had done me.

Once we were all seated, Gabe gave us each a paper plate topped with one of the packets.

"Campfire Chicken," Gabe explained. "Be careful opening them so the steam doesn't get you."

Millie served us bottled cokes that she plucked from a wire basket in the creek. The amazing thing was that mine really was ice cold when she handed it to me.

107

Jay passed me the bottle opener after he'd popped the top to his. As he handed it to me, I gave a bit more eye contact in my, "Thank you," than was necessary for the small act. Jay nodded, knowing just what I was getting at.

I opened my Coke and turned to pass the opener to Andy, my eyes met his and the rest of the friends around us faded away for a moment. He didn't say, "Thank you," when I handed it to him and our hands touched.

"You still owe me an answer." A corner of his mouth turned up in that half smile, challenging me the way he used to, daring me to answer.

"What?" I asked, lowering my eyes, not being able to look at him for very long, fearing I'd humiliated myself blushing too much.

"Tell me what happened." Andy looked around, confirming everyone else was focused on opening their dinner packets. "Tell me what happened that night."

I focused on my plate, gently opening the foil as Gabe had cautioned. "Eat your dinner first."

Andy let out a jovial snort, "I've waited this long."

I cut my eyes at him, "You know you had my head spinning that day at the dam. Do you remember it?"

Andy nodded.

I wasn't used to this full disclosure thing we seem to have started so I returned my focus to the steaming contents of the pack, chicken, potatoes, asparagus and mini corn on the cobb in some sort of butter sauce. Changing the subject with Andy, I commented on the corn, "How does anyone successfully eat this in public?"

Again, Andy laughed.

The fire in front of us crackled and popped as Gabe threw another log on. Most everyone was quiet, eating their dinner, when Millie stood up and mentioned the game we used to play at the dinners she hosted for everyone at The Jefferson.

"So, whoever wins, gets..." she paused, thinking of a prize.

Daniel called out from the other side of Andy, "If we could pick our own prize, I'd like a free weekend here sometime."

"I second that," Stella chimed in.

Anna-Cat piped up, "We've never stayed here," she glanced at her husband, Alex, "We'll take one of those."

"Sure," Alex concurred, taking Anna-Cat's hand and kissing the back of it.

Before anyone else could make the same request, Millie made the offer. "Okay, okay. A free weekend at Seven Springs."

The object of the game was that we all had to tell a story and it had to be the most interesting or the funniest. Since Millie gave the prizes, she picked who went first, but there was no judge. Usually, the winner was obvious by the reaction of the group.

"There's one change to the rules," Millie held up her index finger. "Jay picks who goes first. And," she gestured again, "whoever makes him laugh the hardest, loudest and longest or entertains him the most, wins."

No one argued or balked, we all understood Jay had had a rough day and he deserved anything we could do to brighten his day.

Jay pointed Jerry to go first.

"Well, I was substitute teaching a class of Greene County's finest little minds last week. Their teacher is out on maternity leave so I've become the regular babysitter for prego's group of fourth graders. This one kid, who's more like us than he knows yet, said 'Mr. Clayborn, I got glasses too!' There ensued a discussion about going to the eye doctor and getting glasses."

"Holding up my end of the conversation, I said, 'You know what I hate about going to the eye doctor?'"

"On cue, he asked, 'What?' and I replied, 'When they put that little puff of air in your eye.'"

"'Yes,' and he added, exuberantly, and just as all of the other children went silent, 'That's how they test for Gonorrhea!'"

The whole lot of us started to snicker as Jerry continued.

"'Glaucoma! You mean, Glaucoma! That's how they test for Glaucoma!' I thought, 'Oh, great! The one gay guy they take a chance on and now I'm going to be fired because some little genius went home and told I was teaching about Gonorrhea.'"

At that point, we all busted into laughter including Jay.

When we started to taper off and Jay regained his composure, he added, "That's going to be hard to follow."

Jerry pointed to Anna-Cat to go next. She told a story about her son and baseball. He was about ten and it was the first time the kids had pitched to one another. The boy that was pitching threw a wild one and instead of Auggie, her son, turning away from it, he turned into it.

"It hit him square in the cup and rang out through the whole park. There was a collective gasp by all of the men."

"He waddled down to first base. Apparently, the cup can only do so much."

A shot to the balls always got some laughs, but it couldn't hold a candle to Jerry's Gonorrhea story.

"Nice try," Millie shrugged at Anna-Cat.

Anna-Cat then picked Stella to follow her. Stella's story was lack luster as well only getting a few laughs. Stella then picked Andy.

"I don't know if you all remember Chase. He was one of my friends who worked with us the summer of the Olympics."

Some of us remembered him and some of us didn't. Some were not around in college and had no idea who Andy was talking about, but it didn't really matter.

"Anyway," Andy continued, "He's my age and was having some stomach issues over the course of the last few months. His wife finally insisted he go to the doctor. One thing led to another and he was scheduled for a colonoscopy."

Strangely, everyone had put down their cutlery and Andy had their full attention at the word "colonoscopy."

"Chase still fancies himself a ladies' man even though he's been married about fifteen years and he could be a new member of the Hair Club for Men. Now, he said they were to put him in a bit of a twilight, but having the ability to drink any of us under the table, whatever they gave him had little to no effect. So, there he was laid up on this table in a paper gown with not only his bare ass hanging out, but also a tube that was God only knows how long running out of his butt and that's when he said the finest looking woman he'd ever seen walked in and introduced herself as the nurse or technician or whatever that would be performing the tests."

Alex was the first to snicker from his place across the other side of the fire.

"'Mr. Mason.' He said when she addressed him, he perked up to attention as best he could with what he equated to a tail hanging behind his legs.

"'I'm going to need you to turn over on your left side, please.' He said she sweetly gave the request and it sounded easy enough."

More snickers were coming from our circle as Andy went on. I also found myself anticipating what must be to come with a giggle already forming.

"Chase said he scrambled around and scrambled around, trying to remain suave, and follow her direction until he finally achieved the new position, all panting and out of breath."

"She thanked him and did whatever her job actually was and after a minute or two she said his name again and again he perked up, aiming to please. 'I mean, she was damn fine,' he told me."

"'Mr. Mason, I need you to roll over on your right side please,' again she said sweetly."

"'There was nothing sexy about the floppin' and rooting around that I did the first time and I knew I could do it better,' he told me. 'So, I thought for a moment, strategizing, about what to do. Finally, I threw myself into the air, kicked my legs out and flipped over. One swift move. What I hadn't accounted for was the fucking tail had gotten wrapped around one of my ankles and when I kicked my legs and flipped, I damn near snatched my intestines out my asshole.'"

Past Andy, I saw Jerry snort and spray the swig of his Coke that he'd just taken, not being able to hold back the guffaw he let out.

"If she'd never seen a grown man cry before she sure did that day," Andy started to laugh at his own story. "Chase said he laid there in the fetal position and squalled like a baby it hurt so bad."

My words came out in a laugh, "Not much of a ladies' man now."

Also spitting her words out through giggles, Stella said. "That's what he gets for trying to run around on his wife."

There wasn't a one of us in the group that didn't laugh until we cried over the mental picture Andy had painted including Jay.

"I think we have our winner," Jay said with a chuckle.

Peter peered around Stella to Jay, "But y'all haven't heard my story yet."

Millie asked through giggles, "You've got something that will beat that one?"

"I like to think so," Peter stood up and I put my cutlery down again, giving him my attention.

"There once was a boy who fell in love with another boy," Peter began as he stepped slowly in front of Stella's chair.

I could feel Andy scooch forward in his chair to see around me.

"Some family, some friends, and a whole bunch of people they didn't know said this was wrong, but it was right to them. They weren't hurting anyone else and all of their real friends just wanted them to be happy."

I had an idea of what was coming and I felt tears started to fill my eyes. I don't know what possessed me, but without looking, I reached back for Andy's hand and found it. I held on as Peter dropped to one knee in front of Jay.

"One of them," he smiled hopefully at Jay, "just wanted to live happily ever after with the other."

Jay covered his mouth with both hands, attempting to hide his surprise, but his eyes wide and bright gave away the joy and love he had for Peter in that moment.

Peter took Jay's hands down from his mouth and held them as he asked, "Will you marry me?"

Jay started to nod his head feverishly ever before Peter took his hands.

"Is that a 'Yes?'" Millie demanded.

Jay flung himself into Peter's arms and we all applauded and cheered.

"Get the champagne!"

Chapter 9

Champagne was served, toasts to Peter and Jay were made, hugs were exchanged and who knows what happened to our dinners. Stories were told about how they met, who said I love you first, how long they'd been together and how Peter was so intimidated the first time he met all of us.

"I never had a circle of friends. Not to sound self-centered, but my friends were mine and independent of one another. They weren't friends with one another like you are," Peter explained.

As the night wore on, stories were also told about the good old days when we were all in college and updates were given about who was doing what. Most everyone knew that I had built a house on the lot across from the playground in Avera where my grandparents' house had previously stood. I wrote cookbooks and had a cooking advice column that was syndicated in several newspapers including our local paper, The Jefferson Reporter, and several other small papers throughout Georgia, South Carolina and Alabama.

"Do you get fan mail," Stella inquired.

"Occasionally. Mostly I get letters asking how to recreate someone's grandmother's famous something or another. I usually have to fill in the blank of the missing spice or ingredient."

"Sounds interesting," she gushed.

It really wasn't that interesting. Millie said it left me with too much time on my hands.

Alex and Anna-Cat weren't original members of our group and, although Alex had been around for a few years, this was the first time he'd been with all of us at once. From across the fire pit, Alex asked Andy what he did. I had been wondering the same thing.

"I am actually back where all of this started," Andy replied.

All eyes and ears honed in on Andy.

114

"I just took a job as the General Manager at Port Honor. I've been there a couple of months."

"Congratulations!" I told him.

"So, General Manager." Gabe raised his glass, toasting Andy's success.

Years ago, Gabe had been offered the GM job at Port Honor, a promotion from Club House manager, but he left when Millie finished law school and they opened Seven Springs.

With questions flying around about what the place was like now, Andy started, "They are expanding and needed someone with real estate experience as well as that of overseeing the clubhouse and the grounds. There's some major renovations going on around the club and they are planning to expand."

"I think most of my college memories are tied to that place." I didn't hide the longing for what I considered the good old days in my voice.

Jay reached over to console me. "I doubt any of us will ever forget what all went on there and how that place brought us all together."

Jay didn't ever work there, but he was so involved with all of us and he came out from time to time and hung out while we were on shift.

Gabe corrected Jay, "You mean how it was the setting for Millie bringing everyone together."

At that statement, we all raised our Coke bottles to Millie.

The night carried on with more stories, more updates and more reminiscing. Finally, the fire started to die down and we passed yawns from one to another. Peter and Jay were the first to go up to their room. The rest of us milled around the campfire for a few minutes starting to say our goodbyes.

Anna-Cat and Alex had to drive back to town where they lived and Millie and Gabe had to get home to their girls. They were the next to go.

"Teenagers," Millie shrugged, "like herding cats and that's what we have to get home to." She hugged me goodnight.

Soon, Stella called it a night and walked up to the old hotel with Daniel and Jerry, leaving me and Andy standing by the fire.

Andy was standing back as I pulled my hands from where I'd been warming them. I turned to him and smiled. I didn't want the night to end, but it had to be getting on toward 11:00.

"I should probably be getting home," I said. "I don't live far, but the later it gets the more deer I have to dodge."

Moonlight shown through the trees and lit up streaks across his face and including one of his eyes. He was still the best-looking man I'd ever seen and the thought of leaving then caused a stirring ache within me, wondering if I'd ever see him again, wondering if he'd ever want to see me again.

Andy smiled and I added, "It's been great seeing you again."

I thought he was going to bid me goodnight, maybe even hug me, but he didn't.

Andy stood firm, blocking the path I would take to leave the circle of chairs by the fire. "You still didn't answer the question."

"What?" I blinked, not really having forgotten the question, but back in the headlights.

"I've always wanted to know why?"

"Because I was a stupid girl," I said flatly.

I didn't particularly want to elaborate, but Andy didn't budge.

"Come on," he widened his stance.

I found the courage I didn't have in my early twenties and told him, "You had my head spinning from the moment I first saw you." I shook my head remembering that day. "God, you were so good looking and then you spoke and you were such a chauvinist."

116

"But you knew I wasn't serious..."

"That's the thing. I didn't. No one ever talked to me the way you did and in front of the other men at the bar..."

"You always had a come-back. You were so witty and gave as good as you got. You were awesome."

"Well, I didn't see it that way and the come-backs were my way of fighting back. I didn't like you. At all. You kind of scared me. Then there was the bombing and everything scared me, time was passing and I was standing still." I shook my head, "Then there was you."

I paused, choosing my words. "You were *different.*"

Andy just listened.

"You didn't tease me anymore, but that impression of you was always lurking in my head. Pig. My mother warned me about boys being out for only one thing and the way you had talked to me, 'When ya comin' over? Don't wear no panties!' And I never thought I was in your ballpark."

"Ballpark? What?" Andy was genuinely confused. "You used that term before."

"The girl you had been dating was basically a supermodel. She was almost as tall as you and I'm sure she was...well versed in some things I was not at the time."

"I don't understand," Andy gestured for me to sit back down in my chair as he took his and turned it to face mine.

"I could tell you every detail of every night you stayed over and how things changed. We were friends and you helped me more than you will ever know and..." I fidgeted with my grandmother's ring that I wore on my right hand.

"And?" Andy probed.

I looked at him and bit my bottom lip. Regret of what might have been was filling me as I explained.

Andy reached over and stilled my hands, taking mine in his.

"Remember the day you took me to the dam?"

Andy grinned. "I almost kissed you that day."

"I almost kissed you that day," I said back. "And there was that siren and we had to run. Then you just dropped me at my house and took off. Why did you do that?"

"Yeah," he looked down at our hands, "I was trying to keep myself in check because I didn't want to ruin our friendship."

"Well, I thought about nothing but kissing you for three days. It was so frustrating."

Andy looked back up at me and his grin was huge. He still had dimples.

"I can't believe I'm telling you this." I bit my lip and shook my head, trying to rationalize that this was really happening. "I can't believe I've told you any of this at all."

Andy snickered. "Go on," he coaxed me. "And stop biting your lip. It's as unnerving as it ever was."

I looked away, unable not to bite my lip as that was another thing I did when I was nervous. I whipped my head back around to him. "Unnerving?"

A nod, an index finger placed gently on my bottom lip and the slide of his tongue across his own bottom lip and I fully understood unnerving without any verbal explanation.

"Go on," Andy said with a deeper, huskiness to his voice.

Yes, I knew unnerving. I didn't remind Andy that I saw him shirtless that one day and that I'd never forgotten the sight. The day I saw him I knew what unnerving was and I knew it every time I conjured the memory, even now.

"I was anticipating riding to work with you and then you called and said you had to go in early. I was disappointed and then, I can't remember her name, but the goddess you dated, showed up and Daniel said what he did about your girlfriend just getting home. I thought you had been toying with me until she got back from her semester in France or England or wherever it was."

"What? Oh, wait, that's why…" Andy trailed off, taking his hands and running them through his hair.

"Yeah. I was an idiot."

There was a turn in the creek and rocks that made a slight rapid. The gentle lapping at the rocks coupled with the crackling of the dying fire had been the soundtrack of the night. The moonlight came through the trees lighting a path to the edge of the water. I got up and followed the path. I stood there watching the water sparkle in the night.

Andy came up behind me. "I was the idiot."

"Maybe we were both idiots, but I'm really sorry," I said, turning to face him. "I've wanted to apologize to you for so long. I'm so sorry if I hurt you."

"I'm sorry I gave up on you." Andy met my eyes again.

"I mean it. I have felt bad about how things went with us for so long and I was happy for you when I heard you were getting married. I was equally sad when I heard you got divorced. I wanted you to be happy."

"Ha!" Andy let out in a huff. "I was pissed when I heard you were getting married and I was happy you divorced that bastard!"

Shocked, I covered my mouth to hide the giggle. "Huh?"

"Since we're having full disclosure." Andy got that cocky smirk that took me back to all those years ago. "That fucking asshole got my girl. I hated his ass so, yeah, I was pissed when you got married and delighted when you got divorced."

My knees went weak and I felt the need to fan myself. I didn't correct him regarding my marital status. Whomever he's gotten his news from was wrong. I wasn't divorced. I was widowed.

"I should have kissed you that day at the dam. I should have kissed you as soon as we got up the river bank, again in the car, at your apartment and I should have..." Andy trailed off and just looked at me.

I didn't know what to say and just stood there.

"The ballpark," Andy said as if he finally understood. "That's funny because I thought I wasn't good enough for you and you were thinking the same thing."

"And I wasn't a one-night stand kind of girl and I thought that's all you were after and you could never be seriously interested in me."

"Which is so ridiculous because you were the first girl I was ever genuinely serious about," Andy just kept shaking his head.

"Let me ask you," he said, "Why would I have kept sleeping over at your place and I was a complete gentleman, why would I do that if I only wanted in your pants?"

I hung my head, ashamed of myself. "I don't know and I wondered the same thing. It just didn't make any sense. You totally confused me and..."

I leaned in closer to Andy and laid bare the truth. "I broke my own heart over the way I felt about you and my stupid notions."

"Your heart was broken?" He sought clarification.

"It's been broken ever since."

Andy took a step closer to me. My eyes locked with his and all of the years faded away. The chill in the air was palpable, but the proximity to Andy lit a fire in me that could have warmed a small country all winter.

"You still give me butterflies." I bit my bottom lip and smiled.

Andy inched closer and took my face in his hands. He cupped my face and with gentle direction, drew my face toward his as he leaned down. I followed his lead and, went up on my toes, with my knees shaking and my heart pounding. Every single one of my senses came alive when my lips reached his.

Soft, but firm, his mouth sealed over mine. My hands in his hair at his nape. His arms around me. We tightened our hold on one another, each deepening the kiss. I could have forgotten my name, my address, the way home, the way anywhere, but to him right that moment. I could have become lost there forever.

Like teenagers we kissed with complete abandon until we were breathless and panting. Pulling away, there was no confession of undying love, but the whole night had been about confessions and there was yet another.

Andy held me close and I could feel his heart beat through to my own chest. He twisted a strand of my hair in his fingers, toying with it.

"I had been dreaming about that since..."

I drew myself up to my full height, standing on my toes once more, and nuzzled into his neck and whispered, intentionally letting my breath tickle over his skin, "Do it again," and he did.

Twenty, thirty, sixty seconds, two minutes or ten, I'm not sure how long we devoured one another, but it could have gone on forever as far as I was concerned. Andy wasn't the only one who'd burned with anticipation over our kissing and it was everything I'd thought it would be and more.

When we parted to catch our breath, Andy stepped back, ran his hands through his hair and simultaneously said, "God Bless America, that's what I've been missing all these years?"

I dropped my eyes to the ground. "Is it bad that I want to kiss you again?" I brought my eyes back up slowly to meet his again. "I know you should probably go inside before you get locked out."

"I hear three times is a charm," Andy brought my hand to his mouth, kissing it before urging me into his arms again.

This time, Andy buried his face in my neck, licking and sucking and whispered, "If I get locked out, I am definitely coming home with you!"

We weren't teenagers. We weren't twenty-somethings either. We were grown adults and we could have taken this up to his room at the inn, but Andy didn't make that move.

I reached out a hand and pulled Andy back to me. "It's all I can do not to ask you to come home with me now."

"Say the word and I'll go with you."

I smiled coyly, "You better go inside."

Hand in hand, Andy and I walked up the railroad ties that made the steps leading between the grounds by the creek and the hotel.

"I didn't expect this," Andy nudged up against me as we took the steps. "If I'd known Jay's poor mother's funeral would end like this, I would have killed her myself years ago."

I shrieked with shock, completely scandalized that Andy had said that. "You haven't changed a bit."

"And neither have you. Praise Jesus."

Chapter 10

I drove home high on kisses and thankful I didn't have far to go. I could barely see from the edge of one tree line and across the road to the other, scanning for deer, the vision of Andy's face stuck in my mind's eye. For a moment I considered pinching myself to check and see if I was dreaming as this was not at all how I expected the day to have gone. I must have been dreaming.

That night I did dream. I dreamed of Andy and relived our kisses. When I woke to my phone boring a hole in my bedside table, I was not happy. The vibrating of my phone had interrupted the progression of the kiss and, like last night, I wasn't ready for it to end.

The black-out curtains were doing their job and it was dark enough in my room that it took me a moment of swiping my hand around to find my phone. "Hello?"

"Where are you?" Jay sounded demanding.

"At home..." I sounded curt.

"I mean, why are you not here?"

"Because I'm asleep..."

"Oh for God's sake! I saw you and Andy last night. I expected to see you here for breakfast. I need details."

I rubbed my eyes and yawned. "Why don't you stop by here on your way home today? We'll talk then."

"Why don't you get your ass out here and hang out with all of us?"

I fumbled around and found the switch to the lamp on the side table. "Because I don't want to seem too eager."

Jay laughed manically. "The two of you have been in love with one another since 1996 and you don't want to seem too eager. I assure you, NO ONE would ever think of you as eager!"

"Thank you for your assurances, but I am going to stay right here." I yawned again.

"Ugg!" Jay let out a huff and then changed directions. He lowered his voice and asked, "Was it worth the wait?"

I sat bolt upright in my bed. "No! I mean, it yes, I can't believe..."

"That you all waited that long? I can't believe that either! ...But was it..."

"Oh my God, yes!" I clutched my covers to my chest. "Talk about finding out what I was missing all these years."

"Best ever?" Jay asked gently.

"Bar none, best ever!" Even then, I could feel Andy's lips on mine.

"I knew it!" I pictured Jay giving Peter a high five.

"Yeah, well, we'll see what happens..." I fell back into my pillows, knowing we hadn't exchanged numbers.

"Why do you say that?" Jay wasn't the eternal optimist that Millie was so he wasn't planning a double wedding for us, but he was definitely picturing my future with Andy.

"He didn't ask for my number," I sighed.

"What?" he gasped. "And you didn't ask for his?"

"No."

"Why not?"

"I wasn't going to..."

Jay interrupted me with exasperation, "Let me guess, you didn't want to seem eager?"

"Forward. I didn't want to seem forward." I slapped my forehead realizing that there was nothing forward about waiting on someone for as long as this.

"I'll give him your number." I could just picture Jay shaking his head. "Don't worry. I've got you."

I pulled the covers over my head and smiled all giddy-like. "Thanks!"

I had barely hung up the phone and snuggled back into my spot when the phone started buzzing again. I had intended to go back to sleep, but instead I found the phone again and cut the light back on.

"Hello?" I answered, thinking it was Jay calling back to tell me something he'd forgotten.

"Girl! You and Andy? Really? How long has this..."

I knew her voice, but sought confirmation, "Stella?"

"Are you the woman he was fooling around with?" Stella demanded.

Again, I sat straight up in bed in one swift move. "Excuse me?"

"I saw you two down by the creek after everyone else went up to bed."

I could not believe how accusatory Stella sounded. She'd never been like that to me before. I hadn't ever heard her speak to anyone in the tone she was using with me and before I could say another word she continued.

"Yeah, I work with his wife, she's a friend, and she thinks he was running around for the last half of their marriage."

"You work with his ex-wife," I gave a tone in my voice, making the point of the prefix "ex". I also added, "And, if he was running around, it sure wasn't with me! Stella, this is me you're talking to. We're friends too and you know me."

"I thought I knew you." Stella sounded so snide and accusatory.

I slammed down the phone as much as one could slam down a cell phone. I was not about to listen to one more word or defend myself to someone who clearly had their mind already made up.

I left it on the nightstand and headed out of the room. I needed coffee and, clearly, I wasn't going to be allowed to go back to sleep.

The phone buzzed again. I figured it was Stella and whatever she had to say, I didn't want to hear. I kept going down the hall toward the kitchen, but the phone didn't stop. She wasn't giving up.

I turned around and marched back to my bedroom and snatched up the phone. Believing it was Stella, I barked, "I don't care if he ran around on his wife!"

"Excuse me?"

Shit! It wasn't Stella and it wasn't Jay either. Jay had very quickly done what he said he would do. Jay hadn't wasted any time giving Andy my number and Andy hadn't wasted any time using it.

"Nothing. Hey."

"No, seriously, what was that about?" Andy inquired, full of concern.

"No, really, it's nothing..."

"It didn't sound like nothing. I remember how you sound when you are pissed and when you try to lie. So, you can tell me now or I'll be at your door in ten minutes and you can tell me then." If he thought he was threatening me, the only threat was that he would arrive before I could make myself fully presentable. All I had been able to think about since leaving him last night was when I would see him again, but I didn't want him to see me like this.

"Don't come..."

He cut me off. "Then tell me!"

I didn't want to tell him while he was there with Stella. I can't imagine he would take it well whether it was true or not. I didn't want him to say anything to her so, despite my caution of not wanting to seem too eager, I invited him to stop by on his way out of town.

"I'll tell you about it when you get here."

"Okay. I'll see you in about thirty minutes."

"You don't have to rush."

Andy laughed, kind of like Jay did, and he repeated the word, "Rush," like it was the best joke in town. He then repeated, "I'll see you in thirty minutes."

Shit, I thought as I ran back to my room. The debate over what to throw on was in full swing when I realized my hair and makeup needed attention as well. There just wasn't enough time for everything to get the attention it needed and brush my teeth and straighten up the house. There was no team to help me, but hot rollers worked their magic in five minutes to calm the bed head I had going on and mascara and lip gloss did the trick for makeup. I managed to brush my teeth while making my bed, not that I intended to let Andy in that room, but I hadn't intended him coming over this morning either. By the time Andy knocked on the front door, I was out of breath, but the house and I were presentable.

"Hey," I said opening the door.

My heart nearly stopped at the sight of him. His hair was still damp from his morning shower and the breeze caught a scent that was obviously him, like a hint of lavender in the woods. I still couldn't believe he was at my door and I couldn't believe anyone had the power to set me on fire the way he did.

"Mornin'." He smiled, nothing big, but it reached his eyes and put his dimples on display. He just stood there, smiling and looking at me.

"Wanna come in?" I held the door a little wider. I could feel I was biting my bottom lip, but I couldn't stop myself.

Two steps toward me, Andy took my face in his hands and gave me another helping of what I had last night. Butterflies in my stomach, weak knees and a vacancy between my ears that left me with only one hope, that this never stopped.

"So," Andy backed off from my lips, but nuzzled his nose around my right ear. "I made Stella tell me what she said to you."

I fisted the lapel of his white linen shirt and held on to steady myself before sliding my hands down his chest and backing up.

"I don't care about that." I shook my head.

"Oh, please, you haven't changed so much that something like that wouldn't make you wonder what I was capable of. That's what went on before." Andy twirled a strand of my hair between his fingers.

I reiterated, "It doesn't matter." I stepped farther back, my hair slipping from his fingers.

"It will eat at you until you have convinced yourself..."

I turned and retreated into the front hall. "Well then?"

Andy closed the front door and followed.

"Come on. I'll show you the house," I said, stopping at the door that led to my office.

"Is this the same house where we came for Easter that year?" Andy asked.

"No, I mean, kind of," I answered.

Andy raised a brow so I explained further.

"I inherited the old house from my grandparents, but the attic was full of bats by the time I decided to come live in it and termites were making a buffet out of other parts of it so I kept the bones and the foundation." I gave the pocket door a slide to the side, opening it. "This was the living room where my grandfather offered you a cigar and you told him you didn't smoke."

"I was telling the truth," Andy insisted. "You didn't notice, but I quit for you."

"You what?"

"You didn't like it and I didn't feel the need for it when I was with you, so I stopped."

I dipped my eyes and fidgeted, tucking a tendril of hair behind my ear. "I didn't know."

"There's a lot you didn't have any idea about. I think that's part of what..." Andy trailed off, looking around the room. "Now it's your office I see."

I would have loved for him to have finished his sentence, but I went with the change of subject.

"Yeah, I liked the idea of looking out over the street at the flowers in Mrs. Sally's yard like my grandparents used to do while I work."

I had a desk in the room that faced the double windows on the front of the house.

"Where did you put the living room?"

"I moved it to the back of the house. I tugged his hand and we walked back into the hall.

"What's over there?" He pointed to the door across from the office.

"In the original layout it is where my grandparents' room was. Now it's a guest room." I don't know what made me elaborate further, but I added, "I don't go in there much. I know it's weird, but I like to think they are in there and so I give them their privacy."

I led and we continued toward the back of the house. "There's bathroom there." I gestured.

Andy acknowledged the bathroom door, but kept with the previous line. "Wouldn't you just give anything to have one more day with them?"

With that question I was certain he was thinking about his grandmother.

"I heard your grandmother died a few years ago. I should have called you or something to let you know how sorry I was."

I had my own drama at the time that kept me, literally, on lockdown. I wasn't exactly free to call anyone, let along someone my husband had figured out was what he saw as a threat.

The hall opened up to the living room, dining room and kitchen.

Gesturing toward the couch, I offered Andy a seat, but he kept standing there in the entrance to the room. "You never met my grandmother, but she loved you."

"What? Why?" I asked, slightly embarrassed.

"Because you made me a better person."

"I think you did that all on your own. As I remember things, I was a real bitch to you."

Andy gave a smirk and a nod of his head. "At times, yes, but not all the time."

I could hardly tear my eyes away from him. I still couldn't believe Andy was standing in my house. I couldn't believe we had kissed last night. I'd dreamed of kissing him and it was so much better than any dream. As he glanced around the living room, to the dining area and to the kitchen, I just watched him. His eyes finally landed on the stair case.

"I don't remember an upstairs."

"I had it added." I elaborated. "The master suite and another bed and bath are up there and loft sitting area."

"So it's a three bedroom?"

I shook my head. "There's another bedroom and bathroom off of the kitchen and my grandparents' room adjoins the bathroom in the hall. Four bedroom, three full baths."

"Ah, okay," Andy nodded and watched our hands as he circled his thumbs around mine. "As much as I would like to hang out here with you all day, I have to go by the club and then make it back to Milledgeville for a recital."

"A recital?" I questioned.

He looked back up, meeting my eyes and smiling. "My niece plays the piano and my brother insisted I attend. He seems to think I have no life since the divorce."

Each time he smiled at me, my stomach performed like Mary-Lou Retton at the '84 Olympics.

"I think that's nice that he includes you."

"Yeah, well, I also have to pick up flowers for her."

"I can help you with that."

"How?"

"Come with me. I have just the thing."

Again, I led and Andy followed. As we passed through the kitchen, I picked up a pair of sheers and continued out the side door to the porch. Along the edge of the porch and all the way down the side of the house I had planted yellow rose bushes and they were in bloom.

"Will these do?" I asked.

"You know they will." Andy beamed.

"Everyone needs a signature flower," I shrugged and started down the steps.

I cut six buds. I could have cut more, but didn't want to go overboard.

"I have a vase inside."

"Perfect!"

I dug under my kitchen sink for a particular vase and, not finding it, I moved on to the pantry. Spotting what I was looking for on the top shelf, I stood on my toes to reach it. I was stretching for it when I heard Andy.

"I didn't run around. I checked out a long time before it was legally over, but I didn't run around. I want you to know that."

Coming down with the vase, I turned around. "I know you're not the guy I thought you were when we first met. You don't owe me anything and you don't have to prove anything to me."

"But, I want you to know that..."

I put a finger to Andy's lips. "I may not have seen you in what seems like forever, but I know what kind of man you are. I figured it out a little later than I should have, but I did figure it out. You understand you weren't the problem, right?" I paused for emphasis on my next statement. "I was."

"No," he shook off what I had said. "What were you supposed to think of me when I behaved the way I did at first? You pegged me right, I was a pig."

"I know now that was just an act, kind of like me and the bleached blond hair and the super blue contacts. My God I look at photos of myself from back then and cringe."

"You were cute, in a Pamela Anderson wanna-be kind of way."

I laughed, knowing I didn't have the boobs to complete that look.

"We need to get these in water," I said, still laughing and referring to the roses I'd laid by the sink. Turning on the faucet and filling the vase, I also added, "Maybe that's something good that came out of the flippin' bombing, that I gave up on my looks and let go of the bleached hair and stupid contacts."

Andy closed the space between us as I finished putting the roses in the vase. He slid an arm around my waist and, with the other, he moved my hair and exposed one side of my neck. Andy lowered his lips to my neck and breathed the words. "I wouldn't say you let go of your looks and it wasn't the only good thing that came out of the bombing."

Chills went down both my legs and one of those gymnastic ribbon dances started in my stomach and swirled all the way to my toes. I left the unarranged flowers just sitting in the vase and grabbed hold of the edge of the sink with both hands to steady myself. Within a moment, I found myself, not only steady enough to let go of the sink with one hand, but to mindlessly take hold of a fist full of Andy's trousers with one hand and pull him closer to me.

Andy, likely feeling the encouragement I gave with the tug of his pants, leaned closer into me and drew his arm around me tighter. His other hand rested on my side, splayed.

Completely safe in his arms, I let go of the sink altogether. I leaned into him, arched my neck and back, lifted my free hand to run my fingers through the hair on the back of his head. My chest rose and fell with each breath more dramatically than any other I'd ever taken.

"You are very good at this," I exhaled.

Andy turned me in his arms. "I really should be going," he said, biting his lip.

"That's too bad." I stood on my toes, took his face gently in my hands and led his lips to mine.

When Andy eased away, he sighed, "I don't know when the last time was that I've been kissed like this."

I wasn't sure if I'd ever kissed anyone with this much enthusiasm, but left it at, "I'm okay with that."

Andy grinned, bashfully. "Well, I can definitely say I've been thoroughly kissed now."

"I'm not sure," I stretched up to him again, "I think I may have missed a spot."

I placed a chaste kiss on his lips as I thought of how I could die happy now.

Chapter 11

By 10:00 p.m. I settled into bed, snuggled up with one of the classics. I couldn't make it through Jane Austin when I was in college, but I loved the movie adaptations on Masterpiece. Being a grown adult now, I decided a few days ago that I was capable of reading Pride and Prejudice. For the past three nights, I struggled through the first few pages. Tonight, I started again, determined I would persevere.

By 10:15, I slammed down the book. I was wrong. Perseverance did not go with Pride and Prejudice.

In my previous attempts to get through it, I had no distractions. The other three nights it was the writing style that was the cause of the struggle, but not tonight. Tonight, I could not focus on the words on the page. Tonight, I dwelled on the fact that Andy had not called. I hadn't really expected him to call on Sunday night, but I'd hoped he would. I knew Monday night was a little soon, but I prayed he'd call. By Tuesday, not even Tuesday night, I was having something like boy withdrawals, like him calling me would give me some sort of fix. I needed that fix bad.

I picked up the book only to put it back down. I cut the TV on only to cut it back off. I found myself in the pantry one time with no clue as to why I'd gone in there. I found myself outside staring at the roses with no idea why I was out there either. From Sunday to Wednesday, this is how I was with everything. Nothing held my attention. I really was behaving like a teenager.

Would the boy call me? When would he call? Why hadn't he called already? Where did I go wrong? I spent enough energy obsessing over the answers to these questions to power the entire Plant Vogtle grid.

A flood of emotions ran over me every time the phone rang. Sweaty palms picking up the receiver, hopeful "Hello," bitter realization when it wasn't him and that was just a small sample of what I was experiencing. I'd just about driven myself crazy and given up by Wednesday night when the phone rang. Almost given up, but not quite. I snatched up the phone from my bedside table.

In response to my impatient, "Hello," I heard the voice I'd been longing for all week.

"Hey! I didn't wake you, did I?" Andy asked.

"No." I tried to hide a yawn. I was in bed, but not asleep yet.

"I'm sorry for calling so late," he apologized.

"Its fine. Don't apologize." I didn't care when he called, just that he called. That was a lie. I'd cared all week that he hadn't called.

"How's your week been?" he asked.

"Fine. Nothing to write home about." I shifted in bed, apparently rustling the covers loud enough for Andy to hear on his end of the line.

"You're in bed? Seriously, did I wake you? I'm so sorry. I can call back tomorrow."

"No. No. I wasn't asleep," I protested. "I was just in bed, reading."

"I'll let you go and you can get back to reading." Andy all but apologized again.

"I swear, if you hang up, I am going to hit redial and call you right back."

Andy chuckled. "It's been a rough week."

"Really?"

"I would have called sooner, but, yeah. No picnics around here."

"I never really took you for a picnic guy anyway."

"Rustle the covers again and let me picture you in bed." The way he said it came hot and clear through the phone.

I giggled on instinct, but gave my duvet a tug and flapped it hard so Andy would hear it.

"Good." He let out a long exhale. "I still remember staying over with you and watching you sleep."

"You watched me sleep?"

"Between your thrashing about and that corner chair, yeah, I certainly wasn't sleeping," he recalled.

"But once we moved the recliner in there..."

"I slept some, but I watched you some then, too. Plus, that was the smallest recliner ever made. It was better than the chair you had in there to begin with, but you had to notice."

"I was just so thankful for whatever magic allowed me to sleep when you were there that I'm sorry to say, I really didn't notice. Sorry."

That first night on the phone Andy and I took an hour-long trip down memory lane.

"We established I'm in bed and it's close to 11:00, but where are you?" I asked him, wondering if he was sitting in his bed, too. He'd seen me in my bed so many times that winter and spring after the bombing, but the most titillating view of him that I ever got was the time I caught him changing shirts.

"I'm sitting on the back deck, having a beer, talking to you and I just lit a cigar." He took a drag off the cigar that was just barely audible through the phone.

"Cigars, that's your thing now?" I still didn't like any form of smoking.

"I don't have a thing."

I laughed out loud as soon as he said it and Andy immediately realized how he'd misspoke.

"Oh, for God's sake, you know what I mean!"

I couldn't stop laughing, but I wasn't the only one laughing.

"Get your mind out of the gutter."

"Why, so yours can float by?"

"What?" Andy continued to laugh right along with me.

I didn't answer right away. I tried to get myself under control and let the lingering chuckles die down. "I missed laughing with you."

"I miss everything about you."

136

Andy's words hung in the air as I was speechless. I felt the same way about him and I wanted so badly to tell him, but felt the need to hold back. I didn't want things to go so fast that they fizzled out before they even got started.

"I'm not the same needy-neurotic girl you knew in college." I paused, before adding. "I've got a whole new brand of neurotic."

"I'm looking forward to it."

We continued to talk about what felt like everything and nothing all at the same time. Although I would have been perfectly fine to stay up all night talking to him, it was approaching midnight so Andy got the point to his call.

"So, I wanted to ask you something," he said.

"Okay."

"Why don't we go out sometime?"

Those were the exact words he'd used before I turned everything to shit.

"I think that's long overdue. When do you have in mind?"

"Saturday." I could hear the smile in his voice. "I'll pick you up."

"Don't pull up and honk because I won't come out," I teased him, knowing it would be all I could do not to be sitting in my front porch swing and watching for him to drive up the street.

"Woman!" Andy said with an air of authority in his voice, which made me bite my lower lip. "I'll kick the door down and drag you out this time."

"Or maybe I'll just invite you in."

"You keep teasing me and rustling those blankets and I'm liable to drive over now."

I squealed and drew up the covers as if I was shielding myself, like he could see what he was doing to me.

"So, Saturday?" I redirected, barely able to hide the excitement in my voice.

"How's 6:00 p.m.?" Andy asked.

"Long overdue," I teased him again.

"And who's fault is that?" He said with a helping of jest.

"Mine." I said flatly, letting him hear my exaggerated frown.

"Nah," he corrected me. "It wasn't all your fault."

We continued to talk for another thirty minutes or so until a point where we were exchanging more yawns than words.

"I'll call you tomorrow night, okay?" Andy asked.

"I'll be here." Even though he couldn't see me, I still shrugged and smiled from ear to ear.

By 10:00 p.m. on Thursday night, I'd settled into bed and had just opened Pride and Prejudice. I was both equally determined I was going to make it through chapter one and frustrated that the struggle was real. I'd navigated a few pages when the phone rang and to my surprise it was Andy.

"Still trying to read your book?" he asked and I immediately recognized his voice.

"Yes."

"So, I didn't wake you?"

"No." The smile was still in my voice, still excited to hear from him.

For the next hour we talked and talked and talked about any and everything, Jane Austin books to James Bond movies.

Leaning back on the pillows I'd stacked against my headboard, I said, "Tell me something you like."

"Like what?" he asked.

"Anything."

I closed my eyes and listened as Andy explained, "I like listening to my daughter play the piano. She thinks she's just practicing and no one's listening, but I listen every chance I get. Her mother likes for her to play church hymns, but I bought her a book of sheet music with songs like 'The Rose,' 'Endless Love,' and 'Great Balls of Fire.' You should have seen her mother's face, the day she

138

cranked out 'Bohemian Rapsody.' It took her a minute to figure out what she was playing, but once she did, she was pissed. The veins were all popping out in her head. I, on the other hand, was proud. My girl had just nailed that song at ten years old. I figured I'd gotten my money's worth on all of the lessons. I love hearing her play."

"She sounds very talented and it sounds like you like putting a bee in your ex-wife's bonnet," I observed.

Andy chuckled and confessed, "Sometimes."

"What was her name?" I asked.

"Who?"

"Your ex-wife."

"Ah," he sighed. "Right. Stacey. Her name is Stacey."

The phone fell silent and, for a moment, I thought I finally knew the name of the girl who'd beaten me for Andy's affections back then. As quick as I'd repeated her name in my head, I remembered, she hadn't beaten me at all. I'd beaten myself. Andy didn't even know her when I let him get away.

"Tell me something you like."

Snapping back to reality, I heard he had spoken, but I had no idea what he said.

"Excuse me?"

"Tell me something you like," he said again.

"I like listening to you talk about your daughter." I did, it was the sexiest thing I think I'd ever heard.

"No, seriously," he chided.

"I am serious."

"Okay, well, tell me something you don't like," Andy probed.

"I don't like closets."

"What?"

"Closets."

"Why?"

I answered flatly, with no emotion, "Because my husband used to lock me in them when I 'misbehaved.' The first time was when I tipped over a glass of wine at a fancy restaurant and embarrassed him. I was in there all night. One night, I looked at him in some unsatisfactory way and I was locked in the coat closet all weekend."

I repeated, "All weekend," for emphasis. I didn't describe it further, but figured Andy could just infer and he did.

The line went silent for a while. I'd clearly shocked him. I hadn't wanted the conversation to get so deep, but there would never be a good time to tell someone what the new brand of neurotic really was. Before I realized what I'd said, I took the conversation to the deepest aspects of my ocean. I'd just told him things that no one other than Millie knew about me, not even my mother.

"So, I'm not a fan of closets." I glanced toward the one in my bedroom. "I had them leave off the doors when they built the house. I told the contractor I liked curtains and those beads like they used to have in Wendy's restaurants when we were children. Kind of hippie and seventies, I told him. You should have seen the look he gave me. It was quite grave, but he did as I asked."

"Forgive me. I just don't know what to say. I mean, how did you... You sound so..." Andy searched for words to describe how I'd presented the situation and came up with, "well adjusted."

"He didn't beat me because that would have left marks that others could see and he was too smart for that. He didn't rape me. The worst he did was lock me up like putting a dog in a kennel." I delivered the story like one would just delivering the facts.

"Cara, I'm so sorry. I can't imagine how you got through..."

"How I got through it?" I gave off a slight breathy, "Haa" snort of a noise. "I thought of you a lot."

"You thought of me?" No doubt he was puzzled.

"Sometimes," I hesitated. "I imagined you were..." I treaded cautiously as one would when airing all of their inner most frights and secrets. "I imagined that I hadn't turned you down that night on the porch. I imagined life with you. I imagined we were happy and everything was normal and..." I stopped before the flatness in my voice gave way to anything else.

I took a deep breath and began again, "I wouldn't have endured punishment on top of punishment for giving birth to girls and then letting them die. Like I had any control over that and like he was the freaking King of England, I couldn't even give him an heir. I guess I should be lucky I still have my head."

I paused again. "I was such a stupid girl. I was so afraid of you and how you were going to break my heart that I pushed you away and ended up with a man that was Hell bent on breaking my spirit, breaking all of me."

"Oh, Cara, I'll kill him if I ever see him."

"Thanks for the offer, but there's no need. I shouldn't have told you all of that. I warned you I had a brand-new version of neurotic." I laughed again. "I haven't thought about all of that in a while. Millie knows about it, but no one else. It's not something I usually talk about."

"It's okay. I didn't have the best marriage either, but it was nothing like that. I think emotionally vacant is about the worst I can say about it."

"If you count hate, anger, fear and the many forms of abuse, there was plenty of emotion in mine."

"How did you get away from him?"

I gave a slight grunt of amusement. "Two years ago, he dropped dead of a heart attack while on top of his mistress."

"Seriously?" Andy voice reached a new level of intrigue. "I thought you were divorced."

"No, widowed," I corrected him. "He's definitely dead and get this..."

"There's more?" I could picture Andy leaning in.

"Oh yeah, his mistress was pregnant when he died and she's suing me for his estate on behalf of the child, which happens to be a boy. He got his son after all. I mean, he died to do it, literally, but he got his heir...Illegitimate, so, kind of."

"Well, that's some karma!"

"Did you know there are laws still on the books in Georgia that say a spouse has rights to any child produced by the other while married? No? I didn't either, but according to Millie if you were still married and your wife got pregnant by someone else, the child would be, by law, yours since she was married to you at the time of conception. So, Millie filed a counter suit for me demanding custody of the child and added in the suit a claim of wrongful death of my husband since she screwed him to death."

"Wait, hold on. You sued his mistress for custody of his child by another woman?"

"It's more of a tactic to keep her tied up in court. Wrongful death, ha, whatever! Do you know how I prayed for him to drop dead? Seems kind of hypocritical, but Millie and I figure I earned every penny in his estate."

I paused realizing how I must sound. "Oh God, you must think I'm awful."

"Noooo," he drew out the word. "I don't think you're awful, but what would you do if you won?"

"I hadn't really thought about that. We are a year and a half in at this point. I've just been hoping the legal fees would eat her alive and she'd lose interest and go away. We have another hearing in a few weeks. We lived in Atlanta at the time of his death so she filed suit in Fulton County. Millie tried to get the case transferred here since I live here, but that motion got denied. Each time we file a motion, it runs up legal fees for her. Millie filed a motion for summary judgement recently for the custody issue to push it along. That's what the hearing's about in a few weeks."

"Your husband was a doctor, right? I would guess all of the dollar signs in her eyes probably won't let her see her way out of this. And, what kind of mother would risk giving up her child?"

"You're probably right. Plus, her attorney is arguing that the custody law that Millie has cited is antiquated and frivolous."

"I don't think you're neurotic," Andy left that hanging in the air and I waited, feeling there was something else he was going to add.

"What?" I asked.

"I just can't see you taking someone else's child and, no doubt Millie is a good attorney, but involving the child like that seems a bit low down. Tactic or not, Cara, it's not right."

"I know and I promise you, it won't get that far. Seriously, Andy."

"Money's not everything, you know."

Never in a million years when I first met Andy, would I have ever thought he would be the voice of moral reason for me.

Silence strung through the line for a moment until I broke it.

"I wish you were here," I sighed.

Chapter 12

Friday, I met Millie and Anna-Cat for lunch at Peggy's restaurant in Wrens, about fifteen minutes from Avera and where Millie and Anna-Cat both had offices. Millie was one of the few attorneys in town and Anna-Cat was one of only two doctors. Then there was me, a former doctor's wife turned cookbook author.

I went through the cafeteria line at the restaurant, but Millie and Anna-Cat ordered salads off of the menu. What Andy said about me taking someone else's child if I won the case had been eating at me. I wasn't up for watching what I ate. I needed to eat my feelings and I had been thinking about my selections all morning.

Andy sounded judgy last night and I didn't blame him. I knew it was awful from the first time Millie mentioned filing the counter suit for the child, but I went along with it just being a strategy. I'd never really given it a second thought until the conversation with Andy last night.

Returning to the table with my plate of meatloaf, mashed potatoes and creamed corn, I brought up the subject of my case with Millie. "What happens if I win?"

"You get to keep all of your money," Millie replied as if it was a ridiculous question.

Anna-Cat looked on wondering what we were talking about. I gave her a brief summary and brought her up to speed and told them both about Andy's opinion. Anna-Cat knew the detail of David, my husband's death, and that I was being sued, but she didn't know all of the details until just now.

Anna-Cat was stunned. "Oh, yeah, that's not cool and it's not cool that you're letting some guy you haven't seen since college make you feel like this."

"Well, clearly he has a point," I said to Anna-Cat before turning to Millie.

"See," I told Millie. "That's the sound of the Hell train pulling up for me."

"Look," Millie insisted, "it's not going to come to that."

"Millie, we're a year and a half into this and she hasn't backed down yet and you keep swearing we have a good case."

"I can't believe you're still dealing with that," Anna-Cat stated with amazement.

"Yes," Millie kind of snipped. "Just because we haven't talked about it lately doesn't mean it's gone away."

Anna-Cat cut her eyes at me, with the question of what was Millie's problem.

"You've got a good case. You just need to hang in there and trust me. You're not going to take that woman's child," Millie said in a bit calmer tone.

"I'm just saying," Anna-Cat interjected, "if you had come at me for Auggie," Auggie was her son, "I would have killed you. At the very least you would have woken up with a horse head in the bed with you. You don't mess with a mother about her child."

"She's just after the money," Millie said, waving a hand and motioning for Anna-Cat to simmer down. "In all of the back and forth, it's only been about the estate. In the beginning, her attorney filed a motion to exclude our demand for custody, but I argued and got his motion dismissed. There's not been one other word mentioned on the subject. She's supposed to be producing a copy of his DNA and that's overdue so in a way we've won by default. Just let me do my job and stop fretting."

The waitress brought their salads and Millie raced through the blessing before Anna-Cat and I had time to bow our heads. I wasn't sure what the deal was with Millie, but she was in rare form that day. She usually had the sunniest of dispositions, but today she was testy to say the least.

"Wait? If we've won, then that mean's I am taking him. No. No, Millie!" I suddenly felt a little sick. I'd been dreaming of the meatloaf and corn well before this morning and now I could hardly look at it.

145

"It's not like that. There are steps I'll have to take to have the court enforce it so she's still got time to negotiate. It just means things are currently in our favor."

Even Anna-Cat needed clarification, "So, it's complicated and we should just trust you?"

"As always," said Millie while she chewed. She swallowed and emphasized, "You know me."

I did know her. I knew she'd do anything to protect her friends and I also knew she was raising a child that wasn't hers, too. She and Gabe had adopted their daughter, Gabby, when she was an infant. Gabby's mother had been a real piece of work and dumped the baby on Gabe, a former boyfriend and accused him of being the father. This was not the same.

My husband's mistress was a stripper named Darla Hopewell and she was what I imagined when Granny used the term "from the other side of the tracks."

"I do know you, but I also know I'm tired of this dragging on. I'm ready for it to be done. I'm ready to move on."

Millie just shook her head. "I'll get it done and," looking perturbed, she added, "And, tell Andy to stay in his lane."

"So, tell us about Andy," Anna-Cat turned the conversation. "What's he like? I mean, you've had several offers in the last two years but you couldn't give two hoots."

Millie laughed. "Wait until you see him."

"What does that mean?" I asked, indignant.

Millie was glad to elaborate. "He's still as hot as ever!"

"Hot?" Anna-Cat cocked her head back and looked me over. "Really? Do tell."

Anna-Cat added another bite of salad to her mouth as I gave a playful shake of my fork in her direction. "Oh stop!"

"He's taller than Gabe," Millie described. "You saw him the other night at the inn."

"Right..." Anna-Cat recalled, "Dark hair, the bartender. Wow! Yeah, he was hot. Cara, good for you!" Anna-Cat touched her glass of ice water to mine filled with sweet tea, clinking them together.

We all chewed quietly for a moment before Anna-Cat asked, "So y'all know him from college?"

Millie shifted her food to one side of her mouth to answer. "Yeah, he worked with us at Port Honor. It's funny. I didn't think you liked him."

"I didn't at first, but after the bombing..." I went on to tell them how Andy stayed over and took care of me while I recovered from that experience.

"He slept over? I still can't believe I didn't know about this last weekend," Millie shook her head.

"I can't believe he slept over and didn't try anything," Anna-Cat shook her head too. "You know that's weird, right?"

"It's not weird," I argued. "It was gentlemanly. He was being kind to me."

"No, it's weird," Anna-Cat argued back, adamantly.

Finally, Millie announced she had to go. "I've got to be in court in Louisville at 1:30."

Anna-Cat and I took care of our bills and followed Millie out.

"I expect to hear all about your date so call me Sunday morning." Millie hugged me.

"Yeah, I'm looking forward to hearing about this one, too. Hopefully he'll do more than just watch you sleep this time."

"Anna-Cat, I swear I never knew you were such a perv," I teased her.

"I'm just saying, we aren't getting any younger, and medically speaking, he needs to use it before he loses it."

Again, Millie told us she had to go and our little lunch date came to an end. Millie made off to her office with Anna-Cat walking back with her. I waved at them as I drove by. Short of Jay, they were probably my best friends and I loved our Friday lunch dates.

The rest of the day drug on. I hoped Andy would call that night, but mostly, I passed the time counting down the hours until I saw him again. I could hardly wait for Saturday evening to arrive.

The phone rang shortly before 8:00 and his voice caught me off guard. My heart dropped at the recognition and my face flushed.

"So, we've got a golf tournament at the club tomorrow and I have to make an appearance. It'll be done in plenty of time to pick you up," Andy explained.

The anticipation of seeing him again was consuming me.

"Where are you taking me?" I asked. "I need to know what to wear."

"Wear whatever you like," he replied.

"Could you be more specific?"

"You know the area. Why don't you decide and tell me so I'll know what to wear?"

"Okay. How do you feel about going to Augusta?" I immediately back tracked. "No, we'll go somewhere around here."

Augusta was the second largest city in Georgia. I knew the perfect place to go for dinner and dessert, but I felt it was too much to ask if he was going to drive from Greensboro to Avera and then have to drive home that night. Each segment of that trip was an hour to an hour and a half then add another hour for going to Augusta and back. It was too much.

It was as if Andy read my mind. "I got a room at Seven Springs for the night so I don't have to drive home. We can go to Augusta if you want."

"Are you sure?" I asked.

"I'd drive to the ends of the Earth for you."

It was lines like that that made me melt. With just a few words he fired off all of my senses, brought back the feel of his lips on mine, the sight of his chest in that white

148

linen shirt and the smell like a forest, damp, sweet and woodsy.

"You can't say things like that to me." I touched my forehead, shielding my face as if Andy could see my embarrassment before running my fingers past my temple to tuck my hair behind me year.

"Why?" He drew out the word in a way that made me blush even more. That one word had the same effect as if he'd just ran his tongue over an erogenous zone, over my shoulder or from my ear to my collarbone or the back of my knee.

"Because." I replied in just the same drawn-out manner and lowering my voice to barely above a whisper.

I wondered if a word from me had the same effect on him, but I didn't have to wonder long.

A long, jagged exhale was audible.

Andy and I talked until well into the night again.

"What are we going to talk about tomorrow night?" I asked him just before we hung up. "I think we've touched on every single subject and then some."

"I don't know, but I can hardly wait to find out," Andy answered. "I'll see you at 6:00."

Saturday went by even slower than Friday. I didn't have a lunch date to break up the day. The only thing that made it pass at any rate was the phone calls from Millie and a visit from Jay. He stopped by on his way out of town. Were it not for him, the whole day would have drug on to the point of boring me to tears.

"Well, they finally got Mama in the ground," Jay started, taking a seat on the porch swing and sounding quite over it all.

"Surely it didn't take them until today to get that done?" I inquired.

"Not quite. They finished up yesterday around lunchtime," he explained.

I rocked in one of the chairs on the front porch, listening with disbelief as Jay floated back and forth in the swing, giving me an account of how things had gone.

149

"It took 'til Wednesday for the ground to dry out enough to keep the walls of the grave from falling in on itself. On Tuesday, Daddy insisted on riding out there to check the progress."

"I'm so sorry for you and your family." I didn't know what else to say. Jay and his family seemed to be going through something like the funeral that wouldn't end.

Jay went on, "They had two other funerals on Wednesday and Thursday and, since Mama was already on ice, they thought it best to move forward with the others and let her keep."

"I imagine all of this has just been insult to injury for y'all."

I knew Jay's father was always on the tender-hearted side and Mrs. McDonald was his whole world, her and their children.

"Oh, Daddy is absolutely beside himself. You know Mama hated being cold and they had to keep her on ice for days and days. He's been fretting and worrying about her being cold all this time. He's clearly out of his head with grief so there's no need trying to explain to him that she couldn't feel anything anymore."

I held my hand over my mouth as tears began to build, feeling so sorry for Mr. McDonald.

"I finally told him I was going to take her a blanket." Tears were starting to build in Jay's eyes as well, but he looked away, past the street and at the azalea bushes across on the other side. The age and size of those bushes were one of the seven wonders of the world according to the citizens around Avera, Georgia.

Jay continued, "I got the old comforter off of their bed..."

"You what?"

"Oh, don't worry. I didn't actually carry it up to the funeral home. I drove it out Pylant Crossing Road, turned down the first field road I saw and threw the thing out in the woods."

"You threw it out in someone's woods?" I couldn't believe he would do that.

"Yep. Then, I smoked and entire pack of cigarettes before driving back home. I haven't had a cigarette in fifteen years and, my God, they were just as good as I ever remember they were."

Jay hadn't lived at his parents' house since the day he left for college when he was eighteen, but I guess like most of us, the house he grew up in would always be home. Peter had gone back to Atlanta the day following the funeral, but Jay had stayed, keeping the room at Millie's Inn. He'd intended to stay at the inn and go back and forth to help his dad get things finalized after the funeral and clean up the house, but once at the house he couldn't bring himself to leave his dad.

"See, you think I should feel ashamed throwing the bed spread out in the woods? Nah, that thing was so old and thread bare that left to the elements it will disintegrate in a month, tops. The part that made me feel bad was when my dad thanked me for taking it up there." Jay choked up a little. "Then he hugged me and told me what a good son I was."

I leaned over and took Jay's hand. "You are the best son they could have ever hoped for."

Jay really broke down then and it was worse than I'd seen him cry at the funeral.

"I hated leaving him," Jay sobbed.

"I'm sure you did."

Jay did stay at the inn last night.

"I needed a night alone to cry it out and process everything alone before going home," he described and dabbed at his eyes. "I can't seem to stop," he said, showing me the tears, damp on his fingers.

I moved to the seat next to him in the swing, stopping the back-and-forth motion. I put my arms around him and we just sat there.

Jay straightened up, wiped his face and, in true Jay fashion, tried to think of a way to make the best of things. "I don't know how much longer he's going to be able to live by himself and Peter will never agree to move here. I guess we'll just have to get a bigger house and he'll come live with us."

"That's an idea," I stroked my hand up and down his back, still trying to comfort him. "I'll be glad to check on him for you until you get him settled. I'll take him dinner once a week and, well, I'll just do whatever you need me to do. And, Millie will help too and we'll put together a meal train for him."

Jay looked at me, "You are the best. You really are."

"Thanks, but I think you are the one that is the best. I mean, you're the best friend I've ever had. You don't have to take all of this on by yourself. Also, your dad could go live with Jolene too," I suggested.

"Lord, no!" he almost laughed. "He'd be in the grave alongside Mama in a month. He's allergic to cats and she's got a dozen of them and a ferret."

"A ferret?"

"Yeah, I was passing through on business about a month ago and stopped by for a visit. I still had a two-hour drive home and decided to spend the night. Not one of my best decisions, but I had a sinus infection and just didn't feel good. Anyway, I woke up at two in the morning to the sensation of something licking my nuts. In my delirium, I felt around the bed for Peter, and came to pretty quick when I remembered I wasn't at home. That little bastard had crawled in the bed with me and run up the leg of my boxers. I woke the whole place up then when I kicked him upside the wall and he started crying. You ever heard one of those things cry? It's more like whining. Anyway, I'm not sure Daddy could handle a night with the ferret at his age."

Since Jay mentioned the ferret I had the urge to laugh, but when he mentioned waking to it licking his balls, I doubled over and almost fell out of the swing.

"Yes, probably best that he avoids your sister's house," I laughed, "and her ferret."

"I didn't even tell you what its name is," Jay gave a challenging smile as if he dared me to ask its name so I did. "Frisky, his name is Frisky."

I busted out laughing again, "And he tried to get frisky with you!"

Jay and I laughed until our faces and sides hurt.

"I needed this," he said and we floated back and forth some more, just letting the sounds around us take over.

I laid my head on Jay's shoulder and held my arms around him. Eventually he sighed. "So you forgive me about the whole thing with Andy?"

"What's there to forgive? You didn't do anything." I shrugged my shoulders even with my arms still wrapped around Jay.

He laid his head against the top of mine. "If I hadn't told you he wasn't that into you all those years ago..."

"Well, you were right. If he had been that into me, he would have made a move."

Jay lifted his head. "I was so intimidated by Peter when we first met that I would have died before I spoke to him."

"What?" I threw down my feet and stopped us.

I had no idea Jay was even capable of being intimidated by anyone. I didn't even think he knew the meaning of the word.

"He was so Neiman Marcus and I was so..." he paused looking for the right description. "I was so Wal-Mart."

"Oh, please. You might be Target, but you're no Wal-Mart. Give yourself some credit," I teased Jay.

I let my feet up with a push off the porch floor and we started to swing again. To and fro we went and, gradually, I took my arms from around Jay. We sat there, just swinging and feeling the breeze and holding one another's hand for God only knows how long.

"If you want to wait and drive back tomorrow, you can stay here," I offered.

"Oh, God no, and ruin your date? I would die first," Jay protested.

"You wouldn't be ruining anything," I lied. I loved Jay and I would do anything for him, but if I had to cancel with Andy, it would be the ultimate in having my balloon popped. I had been dreaming about this night all week. Really, I'd been dreaming about it for much, much longer than that.

Jay stayed until about thirty minutes before Andy was due to pick me up. He threw back the curtain that acted as the door to my closet and rummaged through. It took him a few minutes, but he finally emerged with what I was going to wear. He would have picked out everything right down to my underwear, I suppose if I had let him.

"And these shoes," he said twirling a pair of three-inch heeled sandals by their straps.

"Just like old times," I said, looking past myself in the mirror and back at Jay.

"Sometimes I miss the college years," he shrugged.

"Me too."

Chapter 13

At precisely 6:00 p.m. my doorbell rang. I opened the door to find Andy, right on time. The sight of him took my breath away. He didn't just look good. He looked clean, showered and freshly shaven. And, he smelled good. Yes, a scent to behold, a scent that my brain had in my nostrils all week. It smelled like what all of the flowers and trees that grew in my version of Heaven would smell like.

"You don't look like someone who's worked all day," I said, sizing him up.

Andy was wearing a baby blue linen shirt, identical to the white on he had on at the after party for Mrs. McDonald's funeral, and dark blue jeans. He looked great in the white shirt, but the blue made him look like model straight out of a Polo catalogue.

Andy gave an amused grunt. "I grabbed a shower before heading over."

I reached and touched his cheek, "And a shave." I smiled, liking the feel of his smooth skin.

"You clean up nice yourself," Andy looked me up and down.

"Thanks," I blushed. "Just let me grab my keys and we'll go."

Out the front door and around the house, Andy held my hand on the way to the car which he'd parked in the driveway. I hadn't seen him drive up so I was stunned to find the old yellow Mercedes parked there. My eyes went wide and, instinctively, I put a hand over my mouth.

"Oh my God! I can't believe you still have it."

Andy stepped forward and opened the passenger's side door for me. "I could never get rid of this car. It's one of the few things I have from my grandmother. Plus," he said, gesturing for me to get in, "some of my best college memories are from inside this car." He gave me a wink.

Andy shut the door and headed around to the driver's side. My eyes were glued to him as he rounded the front fender.

"You know," I said, "I'd never ridden in a Mercedes before the day you picked me up in it. Every time you showed up to get me in this thing, I felt like I'd really arrived. You must have thought I was such a simpleton back then."

Andy gave that amused grunt again and turned the key, cranking the car with more ease than most twenty-year-old vehicles would give. "My truck was in the shop the first time I picked you up in it."

"I remember that," I nodded.

"Well, I don't think you noticed the color of the car that day at all. And, let me tell you, a canary yellow car of any kind doesn't exactly scream college man on the prowl, but it seemed to impress you so I borrowed the car every chance I got."

"I had no idea, you did that." My cheeks reddened again.

"You were pretty oblivious to a lot of things."

Andy turned the wheel and we headed down Main Street, back toward the stop light in the center of town. I gave Andy directions toward Wrens and then toward Augusta in the midst of our conversation which worked its way back around to our marriages.

"We rarely fought, but one day, we had one Hell of a knock down drag out and she told me she set her sights on me and did what she had to do," Andy said.

"What did that mean?" I asked.

"As soon as things went to shit with you and you transferred to the Inn, Gabe hired Stacey and we started...dating." He seemed to use the word "dating" loosely and went on cautiously. "I wasn't exactly thinking with my brain and I hadn't noticed that she was basically living at my place."

"Hey, no judgement here," I threw up my hands up in a sign of assurance, but my mind swirled at how this Stacey girl had gotten my job at the club and gotten Andy. I hadn't even known how it went down until then. I was kind of pissed, but I kept it to myself.

"Anyway, it wasn't long before I was presented with the pregnancy test one afternoon."

Andy was really blunt with his next statement. "I stopped thinking with my dick fast enough then."

I gasped, just a touch shocked.

"I thought of what my grandmother would think of me. I felt I was doing the right thing at the time and a month later we were married, tux with tails, white dress with puffy sleeves. Yeah, she's dreamed of a dress like Princess Diana since she was a child."

"What about you?" he asked.

"Well, I never started thinking with my dick so..."

Andy snorted, equally shocked by my use of the word "dick."

"I meant, how did you come to find yourself married to a big time Atlanta doctor?" he clarified.

After instructing him on the lane he should be in for the upcoming turn on to Gordon Highway, I began to explain how I met David.

"He was tall like you. Dark hair and good looking too. He was younger than Mr. McConnel, but they were friends."

At that I point I noticed what was left of Regency Mall on our left. For a brief moment, I pointed to the building. "It's nothing but a shell now, but my grandparents used to take me shopping there and they would treat me to lunch at Piccadilly. I thought I was something special when my Easter dresses came from J.B. Whites. You can't see that store from here. It was on the far side of the mall."

"My grandmother had a cousin that lived down here. She brought me with her to visit one time. I had mowed grass all summer and saved up money for a particular pair of cleats for my freshman year of baseball. I spent fifty bucks on a pair of Nike Sharks. We parked there," Andy pointed, "right outside of Montgomery Ward. I still have those shoes. They're probably dry rotted, but I still have them."

"It's funny. For all we know we could have been there at the same time." Remembering we needed to turn soon, I twisted in my seat and checked for traffic coming up in the lane next to us.

While changing lanes, Andy diverted the conversation back to how I met David. "Mr. McConnel from Port Honor way back then, he introduced you to your husband?"

"Yeah, the nice old man that used to work for UPS and gave us all their swag from the Olympics. Anyway, Mr. McConnel put him up at the inn one weekend while I was working there. Mr. McConnel, his son, David and some other guy played golf all weekend. One night David couldn't sleep and since I was up all night as the night auditor, he kept me company. I told him I was moving to Alpharetta after college and he gave me his card, told me he lived in Alpharetta and to call him if I ever needed anything. I didn't think anything of it and never had any intention of calling him. Of course, I didn't call him, but a couple of months after I moved up there, I ran into him at Publix. I ended up helping him pick out a fresh watermelon. I still don't know how he got my number, but he called me the next day."

"That's all it took? I'll have to remember to take you to a grocery store and act helpless with fruit." Andy was making a joke, but he didn't sound amused.

"He was obvious about what he wanted and I was young and stupid. He was a doctor and interested in me, this wet behind the ears girl from Sandersville." There was no amusement in my voice with that statement either. "I was enamored with him the way I was this car, but looks, titles and name brands, don't mean squat. My grandaddy used to say, 'The more expensive it is the more it takes to fix it.' There wasn't enough money in the world to fix David."

As we continued around Gordon Highway toward downtown Augusta, the conversation transitioned to me pointing out various points of interest from what used to be a decent area of town. I gestured across the opposite lanes of traffic to a shopping center whose hay day had come and gone.

"Duff's used to be located in the back corner over there. It was my grandfather's favorite restaurant. It was a buffet, kind of like Golden Corral, but the actual buffet table rotated around so you had to walk up to it and wait for the item you wanted to pass by. As a child, I thought it was amazing. Mashed potatoes would come around, then whole kernel corn, fried chicken, fish, green beans, you know, all the soul food standards. Three fourths of the buffet was exposed for guests to serve themselves and the other forth rotated through the kitchen for the staff to replenish as it went around. It was a neat concept."

"What happened to it?" Andy asked.

"I don't know. This side of town just started dying off. Jay and I joke that it looks like a swarm of locusts came through."

"So you think God smited south Augusta?" Andy smirked.

"Look around, don't you think so?"

"I grew up going to Macon and have the same kind of stories from there. There's parts of Macon that look like a swarm of locusts went through there too."

We made it to the parking lot, a dirt patch next to Beamie's and as Andy came around the car to open my door something occurred to me. Andy offered his hand to help me out and I took it. I locked eyes with him as I stood.

"There's something I need to tell you."

His eyes narrowed and he said, "Okay?" Clearly, concerned by my serious tone and not knowing what I was going to say.

"I don't want you to think I picked David over you or instead of you. It was two equally bad but separate decisions and one didn't have a thing to do with the other. I was all kinds of screwed up back then and I was so naive about so many things. I had a shit ton of low self-esteem

159

and... Well, I just made some bad decisions that hurt me and..."

Andy smiled warmly and nodded. "Its water under the bridge now." He stepped back allowing me room to move from between the car and my door, but never let go of my hand. "Let's go get some dinner. I'm starving."

Waiting for our order to arrive, Andy told me more about his marriage.

"I married Stacey because I wanted my child to have a better start to life than I had," he explained.

"Did you love her?" I asked.

Andy pondered the question a moment before formulating an answer. "You were the first girl that ever needed me and I wanted to help and take care of. Other than my grandmother, I'd never wanted to help anyone before, but you had me pegged right. I got with girls left and right just because I wanted to. They wanted to and I wanted to and it was on. That was me and then you came along. When things went south with you, I went back to what I was used to. Stacey was the kind of girl I was used to, fun, wild, and in the sack... I won't spell it out for you. The thing was, I was different. Unfortunately, I didn't figure that out fast enough or with my pants up."

He didn't answer the question directly, but I got the picture.

Again, Andy's face shifted to that of pondering. I looked on attentively as I took a sip of my tea and waited for him to proceed.

"I like this openness." He motioned between us. "I feel like I could tell you anything, but I don't want to say too much and scare you off either."

"We're adults, right? So, you *can* tell me anything. No judgement. No fear. We're not kids anymore and there's no need to play those stupid games that try to keep from giving away too much or letting someone else have the upper emotional hand or any of that nonsense. Just be yourself."

160

Andy held up his beer to toast, "Cheers to no bullshit and to being adults."

I touched my glass to the side of his. "Cheers."

The waitress arrived an sat down my plate of fried shrimp first followed by Andy's oysters.

"Can I get y'all anything else?" She looked at Andy and batted her eyes.

Andy raised his brows to me and I replied to the server. "I'm good. Thanks!"

"Maybe some tartar sauce?" Andy asked politely.

The young girl waiting on us motioned to the end of the table to the bottles of condiments. The bottle clearly marked was full, but she offered, "If that's not enough I can get you some more."

"No. That should do it," he replied, slightly embarrassed.

We dug in to our dinners, but that didn't stop the conversation.

"Why did you get divorced?" I asked before offering Andy one of the shrimp I had just forked off of my plate. "Here, try this. They are the best in the CSRA."

"What's the CSRA?" He bit the shrimp from my fork with no hesitation.

"That's what they call the area in and around Augusta. The Central Savannah River Area."

"Oh, okay." He picked up one of the oysters with his fork. "Try this."

Showing the same lack of inhibition for eating after him, I leaned forward and took the oyster.

As I chewed the rubbery little mouthful of nastiness and tried to hide my distain, Andy explained what happened or more like what didn't happen that led to his divorce.

"I settled into fatherhood. I finished my master's degree and got a job in my field, but tended bar every now and then to make extra money while times were tough. I coached little girls' softball every season. I ran for PTA president and won. I did everything my father didn't. I worked fifty and sixty hours a week. I stayed busy." He shrugged, as he paused to take a bite. "I got my real estate license because that would make more side money than tending bar, plus who wants a forty-year-old bartender?"

Andy pushed his food to one side of his mouth and added, "I became boring."

I choked down the mushy mouthful with a tea chaser and asked, "You became boring?"

"That's what she called me. Irreconcilable differences. That's what she put on the divorce complaint she served on me completely out of the blue." He continued to chew.

"But Stella said your wife thought you were having an affair," I reminded him.

"Again, probably TMI, but we hadn't had sex in something like two years and she was of the mindset that if I wasn't getting it from her, I was getting it somewhere."

"But you weren't?" I believed him when he told me the first time, but sought reassurance only for the sake of me keeping up my end of the conversation.

"To be perfectly honest, working sixty hours a week, keeping up with all of Stephanie's extracurricular activities, being exhausted and coming home to someone who looked perpetually put out, didn't exactly inspire one to feel in the mood."

I shook my head. "You don't sound boring to me. You sound like a good family man and every marriage hits snags sometimes, right?"

"As it turned out, I was the snag in her life, but it's okay. You can't imagine the relief I felt the day she served me the papers."

I challenged his statement with the raise of one eyebrow. I would never really wish anyone dead, but the relief I felt the day the police arrived on my doorstep and told me what had happened to David was like God himself had smiled on me. I didn't give that full disclosure, but simply commented, "Oh, I can totally imagine."

"Don't get me wrong. It went from relief to complete panic when I saw that she was seeking full custody. It's been rough learning to live without seeing Steffi every day. I still feel I was her primary care giver, but my attorney said no judge would give me primary custody since there was no proof that her mother was unfit."

I did the math in my head with ease. "Shouldn't your daughter be old enough to choose which of you she lived with?"

"Oh, not quite, but I would never ask her to choose. Now if she came to me and told me she wanted to live with me, 'Of course,' would be my response. She knows she can come to me whenever she wants, but I drew the line there."

I was getting the picture that Andy was completely selfless when it came to his daughter and that just served to draw me closer to him.

"I agreed for Stacey to keep the family house until Stephanie graduated from high school so everything stayed stable for her. We've got about four more years before then so Stacey can buy me out of my part or we can sell it and split the equity. I don't care either way."

I sat listening, finishing as many of my shrimp as I could hold and a few of the fries, I waited for Andy to go on. Perhaps sensing the depths to which our conversation had gone, he changed the subject.

"You don't like oysters, do you?" he asked.

As Andy took a sip of his beer, I hung my head. "No."

"Then why didn't you say so?" His face conveyed the combination of amusement and confusion.

"I was being polite," I said shyly. "I didn't want to offend you."

"Oh, for God's sake! Don't be polite. Just tell me straight out. If you don't like something I like, it's fine. What did you say earlier about being adult and no judgement? It goes both ways." Andy reached over with his fork and took another of my shrimp. "And, I like shrimp so I'm taking this one."

I cracked up. "Okay."

"No games and no guessing either," he added.

"Fine."

"Are you done with those?" He forked another of my shrimp.

"Yes."

"Good."

The waitress came and dropped the check. I saw the total and the bills Andy handed her. He tipped generously and told her, "Someone said you all had best shrimp in Augusta and they were right." He winked at me. "They were great."

"Thanks," she replied, taking a page out of my book and blushing at Andy. "Y'all come back anytime."

I smiled as she picked up our plates and excused herself, but not before I gave her a bit of a glare, thinking, he's old enough to be your father. She was probably just being nice, working it for a good tip, but I suddenly felt territorial over him.

"Wouldn't you give just about anything to be that age again?" I asked Andy.

"Only if I could know then what I know now."

He got up and offered me his hand and, as was my new norm, I took it gladly, loving the feel of my hand in his.

We walked hand in hand as we left the restaurant and we walked along Riverwalk, the bricked walkway along the levee that separated the downtown area from the Savannah River.

"Briefly, during my senior year of high school I dated a boy from Augusta and he brought me down here one night, intent on impressing me with a view of the moonlight across the river. It was pretty and supposed to be all romantic and all," I explained while trying not to laugh at my own story, "but the moment was totally ruined when two river rats the size of small dogs came swimming past."

I could feel Andy cringe through the vibration from his hand to mine.

"They were so disgusting."

"I'm guessing there was no moonlight make-out session that night?"

"No," I snickered, "As it turns out, river rats are total cockblockers. Not that I was going to give it up anyway. I wasn't like that."

Andy laughed. "I'm well aware."

The farther we walked the closer he drew me with not only our fingers interlocked, but our arms intwined.

I noticed the Radisson Hotel in front of us and asked, "Do you mind if I step in there and use the restroom?"

"No, that's fine," Andy replied and we headed to one of the side-door entrances of the hotel.

As it happened, we entered into the convention center portion of the hotel with meeting and ballrooms on each side of a grand aisle. It only took a moment, but we found a set of restrooms. I excused myself and said I would be right back.

In less than three minutes, I was back in the hallway, but there was no sign of Andy. I waited for a moment, thinking he must have gone into the men's room. While waiting I started to hear a familiar tune from a lone piano, Desperado by the Eagles. I didn't know he played the piano, but a feeling drew me toward the sound of the music.

A crystal chandelier the size of a six-man dome tent hung directly above a grand piano. The bulbs shaped like candle flames were dim and the majority of the light came from the refraction through the crystals. It gave the area, not a room or a hall, a warm feel unlike the cold walkway where we'd first entered.

The piano was black, but it was polished to such a shine that I could see Andy's reflection in it as I approached. For a moment, I hesitated not knowing whether to join him on the piano bench or not interrupt him. It was moving just to watch him play.

When he started to sing, my feet made the decision to move all on their own. Perhaps, my heart was directing them, there was no telling, but I walked toward him.

As soon as I was within arm's reach, I slid my hands over each of his shoulders, down over his pecks and crossed them over his chest as he played. Andy never missed a key or note as I rested my chin on his right shoulder. It was as if I wasn't there at all, but I was.

I closed my eyes and let the sound of his voice and the softness in the melody of the piano ring through me. Beneath my arms, I could feel the rise and fall of his chest with every breath and every word.

"You're losing all your highs and lows ain't funny how the feeling goes away..."

I was lost and found in that moment all at the same time.

"Come down from your fences..." I could hear Don Henley in my head as clear as I could hear Andy right next to me.

"I love to hear you sing," I whispered in his ear.

Andy struck the final keys and held them with the pedal before he turned on the bench. He pulled me into his lap, and weak kneed, it took no effort to sweep me off of my feet. My breath hitched in my throat as I was caught off guard by the move.

A firm arm around my back, directed me, twisted me until my body was pressed against his.

His eyelashes floated across my cheek, giving the sweetest, slightest tickle and Andy whispered in a husky, needing voice, "I've thought about you all week."

His touch and his words sent a passionate need for him throughout every inch of me. I felt I would melt right into him.

Gently grazing his lips over mine, he added, "I've thought about this for years."

Andy pressed his lips to mine and once again I yielded to him.

A sigh of "Oh God," escaped my lips as Andy grasped me tighter, which I didn't even think was possible. Somehow his arm wound up my back and he gripped my hair, urging my head back and arching me as he buried his face in my neck. Goosebumps shot down my legs and I could feel the heave of my breast with every breath as Andy headed south, down my neck, down my sternum and toward my cleavage, hindered only by the top button of the collared shirt I was wearing. He seemed to kiss me with complete abandon leaving me keenly aware of how badly I wished we were at my house and not in the halls of a hotel, a hotel where we didn't have a room.

"Hey, you there!" a man's voice came sternly from the other end of the hall.

Both snatching our heads, Andy and I spotted the security officer at the same time.

"Oh shit!" I said, jumping out of Andy's lap.

Andy laughed, and grabbing my hand, he said, "Run!"

Hand in hand we ran around the piano in the opposite direction of the oncoming security officer, found a grand staircase and down it we went into the main lobby of the hotel.

Spotting the bank of doors at the front entry, Andy pointed, "There. Let's go."

"Stop them," the security guard yelled from behind up. People looked at us to see what the commotion was, but no one made a move.

Out onto tenth street we went. Still clutching hands, we slowed to a brisk walk filled with laughter and maintained that pace all the way to the corner at Reynolds Street. We turned the corner and Andy let go of my hand. He doubled over with laugher as I stood tall trying to catch my breath.

"I'm damn near forty years old and I just ran from the equivalent of a mall cop," he laughed almost hysterically.

"I think I forgot I was an adult for a moment..." I trailed off unable to speak coherently due to the giggles.

With his head between his knees, Andy noticed my shoes, the strappy heels Jay had picked out. "You just kept pace with me running in those shoes?"

"Impressed?" I wiggled my toes.

"Hell, yeah!" Andy continued to laugh.

Once we could compose ourselves, Andy took my hand again and we headed back toward Beamie's.

"Why don't we get dessert and take back to my place? My treat," I offered.

"Sure, but you don't have to treat," Andy pulled me close again, entangling our arms so that we were connected from my fingertips to my shoulder.

We picked up a slice of a Perfect Chocolate cake to share from the Bole Weevil. We made it back to the car just as the sun was setting.

I gave Andy directions from downtown Augusta back to Gordon Highway and around to Highway 1. All the while we held hands and chatted. This time the conversation wasn't about our marriages or anything deep. As we rode along toward Wrens, I eased in as close to Andy as I could get, propping myself on the arm rest.

Just after we passed the exit for Fort Gordon, I mentioned, "I don't know if you know, but I saw you once without your shirt."

"Really?" He flicked his eyes from the road to me.

"Um hum," I confirmed, instinctively running my tongue over my lip at the memory. "It was the night of the epic misunderstanding. You were changing shirts in that closet by the door that we all came in next to the pool."

"Yeah?" Andy cut his eyes to me again. "What did you think?"

"I thought I had never seen anything like you."

168

"You know in all the time I slept over in the recliner I never caught a look at you?" He flashed a grin. "It was so disappointing."

I scootched back and raised up the arm rest, securing it between the seats. I unbuckled my seatbelt and turned around facing the passenger side window. I glanced over my shoulder and said, "Promise me you won't wreck."

"What? Why?" Andy stuttered trying to see what I was doing and watch for the car that was passing us. "What?"

"Promise." I demanded.

"Of course, but what are you doing?"

I lowered myself until my head was resting on his thigh between his hip and the steering wheel and my legs drawn up by my door.

"Behaving like a teenager again," I said unbuttoning the first button of my shirt.

Andy struggled to keep his eyes on the road. "That's not really fair. You saw me yet I can only steal a glance while driving."

"Pretend your blind and feel your way to second base," I said, pulling his right hand down to the next button on my shirt.

"Oh, sweet Jesus," Andy inhaled deeply and unbuttoned the button.

Taking his time, Andy traced a line with his index finger from the pit of my neck down to the third button. Goosebumps sprang up down my legs again. Without looking he unfastened the third button. I closed my eyes, reveling in the feel of his touch and the anticipation of where his fingers would travel next.

Andy unbuttoned all of the buttons and with the slide of his hand across my belly, he spread my shirt wide. I was exposed completely save for my bra.

"I swear to God your nipples have been staring at me through this thing all evening," Andy said, glancing down for a split second as the headlights of an oncoming car lit the cab giving him full view of the thin black lace contraption with wire support, but no padding at all. "I could hardly keep my eyes off of them."

"Look all you want, but remember fair is fair."

Andy continued to trace the outline of the bra, back and forth across the top and I moaned just enough to encourage him onward. I wanted his hands on every inch of me and unlike a horny teenager, I didn't have to hold back, push him off or save anything for later. I was his for the touching and taking right then if I wanted and if he wanted and I definitely wanted.

I felt the bumps in the road as we crossed the bridge for Briar Creek and entered Jefferson County. We had ten minutes until we made it to Wrens and another ten until we made it to Avera.

Just past the bridge, Andy stopped teasing me. He slid down the strap on the right side of my bra and, using a finger and his thumb, he peeled back the lace cup that had been camouflaging my right breast and it was free. He palmed the entire breast at first, giving it a gentle squeeze and then traced his thumb around my nipple. It stiffened and rose to a peak, but he didn't stop. He did it time and again, softly rolling it around, and it sent the sweetest tickles through my groin and down to my toes.

"God almighty, Cara," he said after freeing my left side the same as he'd done my right. "I just want to look at you, but you are going to make me wreck."

His words made me laugh and arch more. I wanted him to look at me, look all he wanted.

Andy circled my left nipple with his thumb in the same manner as he'd done with my right. I knew I was wet and things twitched inside of me.

"Holy shit, can someone actually orgasm from this?" I asked as I bucked my hips and clutched a fistful of his shirt near his right peck and a fistful of his pantleg with my other hand.

Andy moved his hand lower, flipped open the button to my shorts and slid his hand into my panties. Keeping a hand on the wheel and eyes forward, he leaned a bit to reach. I opened my legs and he slid a finger over my clit and inside of me.

"Oh, God, you're so wet," Andy growled.

I dug in my heels into the leather seat and tilted my pelvis, drawing him in deeper.

I panted and felt the tide rising.

He slid out and in again and that was all it took. Contorting and grasping his shirt and pants tighter, I came undone. "Andy, oh God, Andy!" I called his name as I shuttered and pulsing waves of ecstasy crashed all through me.

Streetlights started to illuminate the car one after another as we came into Wrens. I just laid there recovering, coming down off of the high.

"Sorry that was so quick. It's been a few years," I said bashfully.

"Years?" he asked.

"Four," I said breathless.

To be honest, it was four since I'd had sex and God only knows how long since I'd had an orgasm. I'm not sure if David's mistress found him as fumbling in the bedroom as I did. Sex with him had been like an extended gyno exam, all poking and probing, but never really finding the object of the search. I faked it for years just to get him to give up the hunt and get it over with. Perhaps it was just the idea of being touched by Andy, but he seemed to know where to go and what do when he got there even if it was just a hand job.

Chapter 14

It seemed strange to take things slow after that ride home. It seemed strange to take things slow seeing as I'd been in love with Andy since college. It seemed strange to take things slow since we were both consenting adults. Unfortunately, taking it slow is just what happened.

I was up and covered by the time we reached my driveway, but I would have been perfectly content to continue reliving my youth by taking the action to the backseat. I'd never gotten it on in the backseat of a car before, but I'd sure thought about it. In the few times that I'd allowed myself to fantasize about Andy back in college, I'd fantasized about what he would do to me in the backseat of that yellow Mercedes if I let him. My mother said girls who got it on in the back seat of cars were cheap, but now I was old enough to know that my mother wasn't always right. I was also too old to care.

"So," he said, putting the car in park, "I'm going to walk you to the door, borrow your restroom if that's okay, and then I'm going to kiss you goodnight."

That sounded kind of final and concerned me, but I agreed. I hadn't expected, nor wanted, the night to end yet.

Andy got out and while he headed around to open my door, I finished buttoning my shirt. He offered his hand as soon as he opened my door.

Looking up at him I noticed how I'd wrinkled his shirt, wadding it in my hand and holding on during my orgasm. I grinned somewhat embarrassed. "I'm sorry about your shirt."

Andy glanced down to the spot where my eyes had landed and grinned. "I'd actually prefer all of my clothes to get wrinkled like this."

Andy did just what he said he was going to do. He walked me to the door, used the restroom and then gave me a somewhat G-rated goodnight kiss. He said his goodbyes and he was gone. It all left me analyzing whether

I'd done something wrong. I tried to put that out of my head and reminded myself that I might have behaved like a horny teenager tonight, but I was not alone. I was a grown ass woman and I wasn't doing this.

I was showered, changed and in bed with Miss Austin's finest when my phone rang.

"Hello?" I answered, wondering who was calling at nearly 11:00 and thinking someone was either dead or on the way to the hospital.

"Hey."

A smile stretched across the entire width of my face when I heard Andy's voice.

"Hey," I reciprocated.

"I was thinking about how things went tonight and I just... I..." Andy paused as if he was trying to say something, but didn't know how to get it out.

I laid my book to the side and waited. He stopped and started a couple of times, but just couldn't get it out. When he didn't come up with his words after a minute or so, I said, "I had a great time tonight."

That seemed to be the prompt he needed.

"So did I and I wanted to apologize for running out. I know this is just going to sound like an excuse, but I've got to be up early in the morning and I didn't bring clothes for staying over and...Well, I was going to stay at the inn, but maybe next time."

"It's okay. And it's not like we could run down to the Avera corner store and buy you a toothbrush or anything." I tried to lighten the moment with a little joke. We both knew there was no store in Avera anymore.

"I just didn't want you to be disappointed," Andy said solemnly.

"Are you kidding me? Could you not tell how far from disappointed I was?"

That perked him up. "Yeah, about that. I'm sorry. I probably shouldn't have taken things that far."

"Again, are you kidding me? Did you feel me try to stop you? No. Did you hear me ask you to stop? No."

I looked at the book lying next to me. "I may be reading Jane Austin, but I'm no eighteenth-century waif."

Andy laughed.

"You know what I thought about when I first saw your car tonight?" I asked.

"No. What?"

"I thought about how I used to fantasize about you and me *in* that car when we were in college."

"Fantasize how?"

"You know."

"Really? How did I not know this?"

"Yep, had things not taken the turn they did, I am pretty sure I might have lost my virginity in that backseat."

"Your virginity?"

"Um-hum."

"We've got to change the subject or I'm going to have to make a U-turn."

"Just go home and take a cold shower. I did."

Andy laughed again at the mention of me taking a cold shower.

We continued to banter and verbally toy with one another until Andy reached Milledgeville.

"I thought you had place at the club," I said in reaction to his mention of the city limits sign.

"I do, but I also have my grandmother's house in Milledgeville. I only stay at the club when I'm going to be there a few days in a row and I'm not on dad duty."

"Ah, okay."

"I want to see you again tomorrow, but I've got plans with Steffi. It's been on the books for a while. I'm taking her to the Braves game. It's a daddy/daughter thing. Sorry."

"No worries. It's okay."

"I don't suppose you'd be interested in having dinner with me at the club on Friday night?"

"I think I could be persuaded."

Andy and I continued to talk until he reached his driveway.

All the next day I tried to keep busy, but it was no use. Every time I sat down I drifted back to the ride home last night. The few times my mind ventured to another topic, it was only to wonder when he was going to call.

As promised, Andy called after he got home from the Braves game and after Stephanie went to her room for the night.

"My Lord, she's thirteen going on twenty-four." I could imagine Andy throwing up his hands as he described his daughter and the whole picture amused me.

"Did I mention she's about five foot eight and has the curves of a grown woman. Yeah, at thirteen years old, curves! Sometimes I wonder what I did to deserve this." Andy laughed, but went on. "You should see the way men check her out. At first it unnerved me. Oh, the restraint it took at first to keep from punching them in the face, but here's the thing, she's completely oblivious to how she looks and she's still kind of child-like."

"Child-like?" I asked.

Andy then gave an example of what he was talking about. "So, we're walking to our seats in the club level of Turner Field today and these college guys were checking her out. Long brown hair, dimples, big hazel eyes, long legs, and, like I said, the curves. She's gorgeous. And, yes, I feel a little weird describing her like this, but it is what it is."

"Well," he continued, "we're walking along and these guys are totally perving on her and I'm seeing all of this, but I've learned something and I just wait for it. Like I knew she would do, she grabs my hand and starts skipping. You should have seen their faces. Each and every one of them released an 'Awe, she's special,' in their heads and their stomachs churned a little for what they'd been thinking. It's just priceless and she has no idea."

I loved listening to Andy talk about his daughter.

"Does she look like you?" I asked, crawling into bed and snuggling in for the night.

"Yeah, but better," he replied.

"I find that hard to believe," I sighed, thinking about him.

I stole glances at Andy every chance I'd had since meeting him again at Mrs. McDonald's funeral. His eyes hadn't lost the boyish sparkle and his cheeks still had the dimples that made him absolutely adorable. Although, I had not felt it, his ass appeared to be as firm as ever. Just looking at him, and even the thought of him, brought the butterflies that had died in my early twenties back to life.

Andy called again each night after that. He didn't always wait until 10:00 p.m. Sometimes he called earlier, but each night we talked until midnight.

Throughout the week, I thought about the events on the piano bench in the hotel and those in the car on the ride home. I thought about the orgasm and how easy it was with Andy. I recalled reading some article once that made the argument that female orgasms were mostly mental and if a man couldn't stimulate a woman's mind, in part, if she wasn't attracted to him, it didn't matter what he had in his bag of tricks. Thinking more about the subject and comparing my time with David to my mere minutes with Andy, I found this to be true.

It wasn't long after we were married that the gig was up. The person I'd fell in love with, Dr. Jekyll, didn't really exist. It had just been one big trick by Mr. Hyde all along. At first, I thought if I could just learn to please him, to make him happy, he'd be like he was before, but it was impossible to please him. Quickly, the love turned to fear and then to hate. It didn't take long for me figure out this version of the man I married couldn't give me an orgasm if his life depended on it.

Thursday night during our conversations, we reverted back to the subject of David. After describing some of the things he did to me, Andy asked in a timid voice, unsure whether it was okay to ask and probably unsure if he really wanted to know the answer, "Did he rape you?"

"He did not hold me down and force himself on me, if that's what you're asking," I replied.

There was an audible sigh of relief that came from Andy's end of the line.

"But," I continued, "he had a way of badgering me with verbal and mental abuse when he didn't get it, that I often just gave in and let him use me so he'd leave me alone."

"I'm so sorry," Andy said.

"He seemed to think foreplay was bitching about how he hadn't gotten any in a certain amount of time," I said flatly. "I could tell you almost to the day when he started seeing Darla Hopewell. That's her name. Darla Hopewell, the finest East Dublin, Georgia had to offer in the way of trailer trash, but I prayed and thanked God for her even before she screwed him to death." I kind of laughed at the end of my statement, signifying one of those funny, not funny, but true moments.

"You thanked God for her?" Andy asked in disbelief.

"Yeah. Remember what you said about your wife's theory about if you weren't getting it from her, you were getting it somewhere?" I asked back.

Andy snickered, getting my meaning.

"It's a pretty common theory. In my case, it happened to be right. So, yes, praise God for Darla Hopewell because when he stopped bullying me into it, is when he started getting it from her."

Friday, I had lunch with Millie and Anna-Cat again. The three of us met at Peggy's. Millie had been to court that morning so she drove straight in from Louisville. Anna-Cat walked down from her office and I took a break from counting down the hours until I needed to leave for my drive to Port Honor.

"I need a job," I said as we took seats at our usual table.

"I thought you had a job," Anna-Cat said, curious as if she'd missed something. "You write cookbooks."

177

"Oh, please," I snorted. "I complied a group of old family recipes. That was a year ago."

I'm not sure Millie knew what to say since she was sitting so quietly and perusing the menu. Everyone who lived in the general vicinity of Wrens knew what was on the menu at Peggy's. It hadn't changed in twenty-something years and it didn't take a rocket scientist to have it memorized cover to cover after less than a handful of visits.

After Anna-Cat and I gave our orders to Dolly, one of the usual waitresses, Millie asked for a few more minutes since she couldn't decide. After Dolly rolled her eyes and excused herself with a huff of, "I'll check back with you girls in a few minutes."

"Thanks," Millie said, having never taken her eyes off the menu.

"Are you okay?" I asked her.

"Yeah, what's up?" Anna-Cat added.

Millie replied with an obvious lie, "Oh, nothing."

"Seriously?" I reached over and, with a gentle finger, I pushed the menu down so we could see her face.

"Yeah," Anna-Cat leaned in closer so the whole dining room wouldn't hear us. "There's something going on with you. Now spill it."

Millie sat the menu down and locked eyes with me. She filled her cheeks with air and let the breath out in a huff that rolled her bottom lip. "The opposing counsel in our case called. He can't find his client."

"Is that bad?" I asked, not seeing why Millie seemed unnerved by the news.

"I expected her to fade away, but..." Millie trailed off.

"But what?" I asked, a bit more-testy than before.

"Didn't you say if she drops the suit, then Cara gets to keep all of the estate? So this is a good thing, right?" Anna-Cat asked, thinking this was good news. She didn't understand any better than I did why this was not good.

178

"Remember what I told you about a default judgement?" Millie straightened her face.

The legalese, didn't register with me and I am sure it showed.

"If she files a motion to withdraw her Complaint or if she files a dismissal," Millie began to explain, "then the case goes away and you get to keep the estate. Both of those options make the case go away, but if she's just in the wind then the case goes on."

Millie continued to describe. "With her having filed the Complaint, the suit," she clarified, "against you she is the offense and you were primarily the defense, but because we filed a countersuit, we are also on offense."

Anna-Cat and I leaned in closer as Millie made a comparison to the sport of soccer. "Now, we can score on her goal without the goalie there to block."

"But what does that mean?" I still didn't fully understand.

"It means you're going to win," Millie said flatly.

A smile came over my face and a wave of relief swept over me.

"Congratulations!" Anna-Cat held up her hand to give me a high five.

"Because we counter sued, the little boy is now yours."

My head whipped from Anna-Cat to Millie. "Wait, what?"

"She left him with her mother who's seventy years old and already has custody of two of the child's siblings. She can't keep him so he's yours."

"But this was only supposed to be a tactic."

"I know," said Millie. "But..."

"What am I supposed to do..." I was going to finish with the words, "a little boy?" but Millie cut me off.

"Take the weekend to think about it. If you don't want him, he will be turned over to DFCS in Fulton County in about a week. Here's a picture of him." Millie pushed the photo across the table to me.

"I don't want to see that!" I snatched the photo from beneath Millie's fingers and flipped it over with a slap on the table. "I don't want anything to do with him! I only went along with your scheme so I could keep what was rightfully mine! This is not how this was supposed to go! I'm not raising someone else's bastard."

I'm sure every head in Peggy's turned toward me, but I couldn't say that I noticed or cared. I grabbed my purse and stormed out of the side door of the restaurant into the parking lot. Millie threw back her chair as she stood and followed me out.

"Now wait just a damn minute!" Mille said, raising her voice in a manner I'd never heard from her before. "I think you forget who you're talking to when it comes to bastards!"

I had forgotten. I'd completely forgotten that Millie was raising someone else's child and Millie herself had been raised by her aunt. I also spotted Anna-Cat who'd gotten pregnant out of wedlock and had raised her son by herself for the first twelve years of his life. I regretted my use of the term, but I stood by the meat of my argument. I was not the child's family and I shouldn't be made responsible for him.

"I'm not you, Millie!" I shouted back.

"That's for damn sure!" She came back at me.

"Hold on ladies," Anna-Cat said softly, trying to intervene.

Millie didn't hold on. "You were just whining about needing a job. Seriously, you live in that big house all by yourself doing nothing. Oh, wait, now you count down the hours until Andy calls you. Big damn deal! That's some real meaning to your life right there!"

Millie hardly took a breath and went on, "It's past time for you to get over what that asshole husband did to you and start being productive and we all know about your twins and how devastated you were. You wanted to be a mother more than anything. You thought it would bring meaning to your life, well this is it. This may be the Lord's way of giving you a second chance and it's definitely this little boy's shot at a second chance."

"And furthermore," she added, "children don't ask to be brought into this world. He's more than a bastard, he's an orphan. You should know what that feels like since your dad ran off when you weren't much older than this little fella is. Yeah, I admit it was just a tactic, but he's a real person and he needs you and you just might figure out what the rest of us already know, you need him too!"

Before I could reply, Millie turned on her heels and started away. I stood there just watching her, completely floored. About fifteen feet from where she started, she whipped back around and said, "Take the weekend to think about it!"

"Anna-Cat," Millie said, a little bit calmer than how she'd just spoken to me, "I know you picked up the photo. Give it to her! I'm sure you'd appreciate it if Auggie ever became an orphan, someone would look past his parents' not being married and do what's best for Auggie even if it was a stranger who owed him nothing." Millie shot daggers at me with a glance. "But not to worry, I'd take him and love him as my own because that's the kind of person I am."

I stewed all the way home. The thought of how Millie spoke to me like that would not leave my head. She'd basically called me a piece of shit to my face and in front of Anna-Cat. I waited until I cut the car off and went inside before I dialed Jay from the house phone.

"I know why you're calling," Jay said before I got anything more than "Get this!" out of my mouth.

"I just hung up with Millie," he added.

That just pissed me off even more. Whenever I couldn't reach her to pour out my problems, I called Jay. Being put out with her, I couldn't very well call her and now she'd cut me off at the knees with my backup.

"Ugh!" I huffed.

"Oh, calm down! I told her if you didn't want him, Peter and I would take him." Jay was so calm about everything.

That did not help. "How dare she! That's a violation of attorney/client privilege!"

"Seriously? I think that went out the window when you screamed all of your business in the middle of Peggy's restaurant."

I hated when he was right!

Chapter 15

I was just about out the door to the point of turning the lock and pulling it shut behind me when I heard the phone ring. It was the house phone and, out of some compulsion, I ran back to answer it.

"Hey, I don't know why I didn't call you on your cell and only thought to catch you before you left," Andy went right into it.

I could hardly wait to see him and smiled at the sound of his voice. "What's up?"

"I know I told you to meet me at the clubhouse for dinner, but," Andy paused, "but," he started again and stopped.

"Do you need to cancel?" I asked, feeling dread, but not dare letting it show in my voice and trying to help Andy with what he was trying to say.

"No! Oh, God, no. It's not that," he replied, finding his words quick enough.

"Okay..."

"It's just... Forget I called. I'll leave word at the guard shack for you and I'll see you when you get here."

"Okay," I repeated myself, not knowing what else to say or what to make of the phone call.

An hour later I saw the sign along I-20 indicating the next exit was the one for Greensboro-Eatonton. Up the ramp and to the right was the town of Greensboro and to the left toward Eatonton was the lake and all of the country clubs like Port Honor. I'd never come to Port Honor in this direction before and I'd only gone to Avera after work a couple of times via this route. As far as I could tell, it seemed like more businesses had popped up between the lake and the interstate.

I paid more attention to my surroundings along this stretch of the drive, taking in every sight, trying to stave off the butterflies in my stomach. There was no distraction, I couldn't take my mind off the anticipation of seeing Andy again and seeing the clubhouse. I wondered what all had changed since I was last there. Was the carpet still blue? Was the giant deer antler chandelier still hanging upstairs in the lobby area and was the piano still here, too?

My mind stuck on the piano for a moment. I recalled having heard Millie play it several times while we worked there and I heard her sing, but looking back, I'd never heard Andy play it and I'd never heard him sing. My mind flicked back to the piano bench in the Radisson from last Saturday night. I wondered if he might sing to me again and recreate that moment on the piano bench there at Port Honor, if it was still there.

I turned in at the guard shack and halfway expected to see friendly faces wave me through like old times. It was a silly notion as most of those men, already retied sheriff's deputies, had been in their late sixties and early seventies back then.

I pulled to a stop in front of the gate and a new face greeted me. He was much younger than the old guards. He could have even been younger than me.

"You must be Miss McConnell," the guard said.

After David died and I left Atlanta, I'd gone back to using my maiden name. I didn't want any part of him tainting the rest of my life. Now, going on three years later, hearing my own name was still refreshing.

"That would be me," I replied, cheerfully.

"Yeah, Mr. Sheppard said you would be driving the white Tahoe," he tipped his hat.

"Do you not get very many white Tahoes?" I asked, knowing that my vehicle wasn't exactly a rarity.

"Actually, you're the fifth one this evening," he replied.

"Then how'd you know it was me?" I'm not sure why it mattered.

"The others have a Port Honor tag on the front and they're residents. You're the first without the tag."

"Ah, right." I replied, having forgotten about the plate on the front of the cars. Gabe had given each of us a

Port Honor tag for the front of our vehicles when we worked here. The tag kept us from having to stop and have these discussions with the guards each time we came to work.

Concluding that subject, the guard moved on. "Mr. Sheppard told me to tell you to meet him at the clubhouse." The man took his cap off and scratched his head. "I can't tell you what he meant, but he said to tell you not to follow the signs. Just go the way you know."

I wasn't sure what that meant so I replied simply, "Okay," thanked him, gave a wave and went on my way.

The road appeared to be under construction with cones and barrels all over the place, outlining a path which I did my best to follow. I wasn't sure whether I was on an endless driver's ed course or trying to thread a needle with a tank, but I managed to squeeze through. There were signs along the way providing directions starting with all arrows pointing forward just beyond the guard gate for the marina, the real estate office, the clubhouse, but not the inn. The next sign had an arrow indicating the turn for the marina, but more straight-ahead arrows for the clubhouse and finally I came to an arrow indicating a turn. From what I recalled, that road was not there and the turn was too soon. I wasn't sure about it, but I inched by more orange cones and kept going.

When I came to the area where the road used to fork off to the right and continue into the residential portion of the property and the fork to the left headed toward the inn and the clubhouse, there was no fork. There was a round-about where the fork used to be. I headed into it, noticing two additional roads had been added, but the road for the clubhouse was still there. Continuing around, I saw the curb did not break for the opening to the old road and a gate had been put up. The gate was open so I slowed down and hopped the curb one wheel at a time.

I continued on, following Andy's instruction about going the way I knew and studying the changes. The view

185

to the circular driveway in front of the inn was now blocked by thicket of Leyland Cypress trees. The row of trees kept going and by the look of their size, they were probably planted shortly after I quit working there. I marveled that I couldn't see any more of the inn than the roof, but it was still there and I took comfort in that.

The cypress trees curved and lined the cart path which was new. The croquet courts that were once world famous were gone, cut in two by the trees and the path. I couldn't see what was on the other side of the trees, but on the other side of the cart path, it appeared one of the greens for the course had been repositioned and now encompassed the lower court.

Getting the feeling that nothing was the same, I rolled down the hill and finally looked toward the clubhouse. A little worse for wear, but it was still there. Despite the arrows indicating the premature turn, despite the gate that had been put up to block this road, the reality that lay before me had only started to register. I didn't know why the new roads had been built. I didn't know why this one was deserted. I didn't know why there were no young boys collecting the remainder of the carts at the end of the day and no one hitting range balls into the twilight. I didn't know why it was 7:00 p.m. on a Friday night and the only car in the cracking and weed infested parking lot was Andy's, but I was starting to catch on. Our clubhouse was no longer the clubhouse.

As I came closer, I saw Andy standing beside the Mercedes, jeans, a white Port Honor logo shirt, flip flops and shades. He was a sight that made my heart stop.

Although the lines had long since faded, I pulled into a space next to Andy. Before I was even stopped, he rounded my SUV and headed for my door. Opening it, he offered his hand.

"I like this," he said, like it was the first time he'd seen it.

"I like yours better." I raised an eye.

"This has more room." He matched my look and I could not help but laugh.

With my hand in his, he pulled me close, "Come here."

My chest went into his and I went up on my toes as he leaned down. His free hand went around my neck with a firm, possessive grip as his face went into my hair. His lips were so close to my ear I could feel his breath as he said, "I can't stop thinking about the other night in the car."

My breath hitched and all I could do was exhale. I could almost hear the blood as I felt it carry the heat all through me because it's all I had thought about too.

"I want to kiss you, but I'm not going to yet," he whispered in a way that made my toes want to curl.

Again, all I could manage was to breathe. I was putty in his hands whether he knew it or not.

"Later, okay?"

I nodded in response. I was weak kneed and unable to articulate much with him pressed against me like that. I was certain I could feel an erection through his jeans.

"Okay," he inched back, dipping his stance a little and discretely adjusting himself.

Yes, he had an erection and, for a moment, I imagined what that was like. Before I could get the full picture in my mind's eye, Andy led me by the hand toward the clubhouse.

"Through the front door or through the kitchen like old times?" he asked.

"I don't know. You choose."

"Front door it is."

At the door, Andy took out a set of keys. I peered through the glass as he tried three keys before the lock gave. The glass was so dirty I could hardly see anything. Andy held the door and I walked in.

Just as I noticed along the road to the clubhouse, so many things were different. In this instance, not only were they different, they were missing altogether. The desk next to the front door was gone. The plush couches, the big antler chandelier, the silk floral display above the mantle and, most disappointing of all, the piano; they were all gone. The entire loft area that overlooked the dining room was empty.

As I broached the top of the stairs leading to the dining room below, I braced myself for what I'd find, or more likely, what I wouldn't find. I'd spent so many hours there that I could still picture it exactly as it was. I remembered the placement of the tables for day-to-day service of guests. I remembered where the dance floor went when we hosted wedding receptions. I remembered where the buffet tables went, in the Florida room off of the left side of the dining room that had a view of the pool, and I remembered all of the food that used to cover the tables.

Picturing how everything should be, I opened my eyes, looking down to the floor below and I found nothing was left but my memories. The blue carpet with the pretty gold woven in it was all ripped up and gone. The six top table in the far corner where Mr. and Mrs. Bay dined with Mrs. Macy and her husband along with State Senator Channell and his wife on Friday nights was gone. The table where I'd waited on Wild Hands and Roaming Fingers Howie Wollows, also gone. Rumors about him holding a girl hostage at the inn turned from rumors to charges spelled out on the front page of the local newspapers one summer. The Olympics was the summer of 1996 and the next was the summer of the Howie Wollows' trial. He was still sitting right where he was at the end of 1997, in some south Georgia correctional facility, but everything that had been there was gone.

Andy's voice interrupted my recollections. "I guess I should have warned you."

I looked to him curiously and followed as he started down the stairs.

"They remodeled the inn and that building now holds the clubhouse. They're only weeks away from demolishing this place. I just thought you might like to see it one last time."

We reached the bottom of the stairs and I surveyed the room once more. I looked to the corridor that led behind the fireplace, to the bathroom and to the storage closet where once I'd caught Andy changing clothes. I blushed at the thought of where that opening in the wall led and what I'd seen.

"Penny for your thoughts." Andy nudged me.

"My thoughts are not that cheap, sir."

Andy gave a snort of a noise. He turned and opened the door to the bar. Unlike much of the rest of the room, that door was still right where it had always been, at the bottom of the stairs and to the right.

I stepped through and found two bar stools sitting at the counter. On the bar was a bottle of wine, two glasses and two dome covered plates.

"Dinner at the club," Andy motioned toward the bar and moved ahead to pull out the stool for me.

"In all the years I worked here, I don't think I ever ate in here."

Over a dinner of New York Strip, roasted potatoes, and whole green beans, Andy recounted a few of his own memories of the place.

"Over there is where I first noticed you." He pointed toward the end of the bar near the kitchen door.

"But, we first met in the parking lot out back," I corrected him.

"Right, but I didn't really take notice of you until the day I asked you if you were coming over and told you not to wear any panties."

I laughed and nearly choked on my bite of steak. "What?"

"Yep, you snapped back and asked me, 'Why, are you going to be wearing them?' All of the men at the bar laughed at me. You got me good and it wasn't the last time. That was the first thing I liked about you. You gave as good as you got."

For a second, I thought about that and wondered why I hadn't been fisty like that to David. Maybe if I'd fought back more and not just been paralyzed by shock, I wouldn't have an aversion to closets now. I brushed those thoughts away as soon as they entered my head.

"You liked that I zinged you and got the other guys to laugh at you?" I asked.

Andy nodded as he shoved another cut of steak in his mouth. He chewed and washed the swallow down with a sip from his wine glass.

"Seriously, though," he started again, "I noticed you, I mean, really noticed you for the first time after you came back to work following the bombing. You looked so completely different. I know you thought you'd let yourself go, but you looked like a different person."

He reached over and twirled a lock of my hair between his fingers. "Everything about you was natural and it suited you."

"I was a mess after the bombing," I said.

"You had every right to be a mess after that, but it brought back the real you. I think it took that incident for you to stop trying to be something you weren't."

"I guess you're right, but I still don't know that I'd want to relive that night again." I took a drink of my wine.

"I wouldn't want you to go through that and I wouldn't want Millie or all of those other people to get hurt again, but it did set me on the path to you." Andy touched his glass to mine and smiled warmly.

Throughout the rest of dinner we continued to share memories of the club. Andy told me about the time he and Matt got so high they couldn't drive home after work and had to sleep it off on the couches upstairs.

"It wasn't one of my proudest moments," he said in an apologetic way.

"What would you do if you ever caught Steffi with pot?" I asked him.

"I'd beat her ass!" He answered without hesitation.

"Well, that's kind of hypocritical, don't you think?"

"Hell, yeah, but I'd beat her ass anyway!"

I could not help, but laugh.

Once I could talk again without fear of snorting, I ask Andy, "So, you don't do that anymore?"

"I couldn't tell you the last time I touched anything stronger than beer." No sooner had he said that than did Andy correct himself. "That's not true. I had whiskey for a cough this past winter and," he started with hesitation, "I got shit faced after my grandmother's funeral. I hadn't been drunk like that in years. I probably would've smoked myself into an oblivion if I'd known where to score the stuff but the PTA circles aren't exactly real open about whether they keep bags of weed in their gloveboxes."

"Speaking of Matt, did you have any idea?" I asked.

"None at all." A puzzled look flashed across Andy's face. "You two never..."

He didn't finish his question, but I knew what he was asking and I didn't mind. "Nope. He didn't even get to second base. I don't even recall that he tried."

Andy laughed. "It took me fourteen years, but I've gotten farther than that."

I smirked.

"Seriously, we were roommates and he told me he was sleeping over at your house all the time." Andy stood up and reached over the bar and pulled up a mini cooler.

"He never," I emphasized, "as in, not ever, spent the night at my place."

From the little cooler, Andy pulled out a small plate and placed it between us. "Strawberry cheesecake?"

"My favorite!" I readied my fork and then put it down, thinking again of Matt. "If he wasn't at your house and he wasn't at mine..."

"If we use Stacey's logic, if he wasn't getting it from you, he was getting it somewhere." Using his own fork, Andy cut the end off of the slice and offered it to me.

"I was such a simpleton back then."

Andy and I polished off the cheesecake and when we were finished, Andy pushed back from the table.

"So, not quite what you expected when I asked you to have dinner at the club?" he asked.

"Not quite, but I wouldn't change a thing. Well, except I hate to think about this place being torn down. This was the best," I looked around, "Really, it was the best part of my college experience. I met all of my friends here or because of here."

"Glad you got a chance to see one last time?"

"Of course. For years I've thought about coming back here, seeing if it was all that I thought it was, seeing if it was really here or if it had all been a dream, seeing if I would find myself and could start over."

"Come on." Andy hopped down from his bar stool and took my hand.

Out through the doors, across the deck, down the steps and to the far side of the cart path we went.

"Take off your shoes." Andy stepped out of his flip flops.

"Okay?" I said curiously and bent over and unhooked my sandals.

"When Millie finished her first shift at Port Honor, she ran right out here, kicked off her shoes and just walked around barefoot, feeling the grass and taking it all in." Andy stepped onto the grass and again offered his hand for me to join him.

Placing my hand in his, I took a step. It felt so cool between my toes, but like carpet, too. Cool, fluffy carpet.

I looked back at the clubhouse and could not believe it would all be gone soon. Everything changing.

Chapter 16

With our shoes in tow, Andy and I walked barefoot across the eighteenth green, and down the rolling hill that led to the head of the cove. The dock was still there where members like Mr. and Mrs. Boudreaux parked their boats and pontoons before coming up to the clubhouse for dinner. From the far, right side of the dock you could see the Highway 44 bridge that connected the Greensboro side of the lake to the Eatonton side.

All night the argument with Millie kept eating at me. I wanted to tell Andy about it, get his opinion on the situation, but I already knew his opinion so I tried push it toward the back of my mind. Very much like Scarlett O'Hara, I kept telling myself I'd think about it tomorrow.

We spent the remainder of the evening sitting on the dock. Our feet were already bare so it only took Andy rolling up his pants leg for us to be able to sit there, dangling our feet in the water. At first, we sat there talking and looking out over the cove, just watching the ripples made by passing boats roll in from the deep water to the shore.

"I was wondering..." Andy paused and I felt like what would be a big question was coming. He stroked his foot against mine and asked, "I know it's probably my turn to drive to you, but I was wondering if you would mind coming back out here tomorrow night?"

"I think I could be persuaded," I said, giving Andy all the encouragement I could with my eyes. I'd been dying for him to kiss me again.

"And just how," he leaned closer, "might I," taking a breath, "persuade you?" He inched even closer until his nose stroked mine.

"I'm sure you can think of something."

Slow, deep and possessive is how Andy kissed, lighting a fire all the way to my toes. They could have boiled the water in the lake.

"Meet me at the marina tomorrow at 6:00 p.m." Andy told me before he put me in my car for my drive home. "I'll tell the guard gate to expect you. Just follow the signs and come to boat slip number 15A. I'll be waiting."

I thought we were done. I waved goodbye to him once more and started to back up. Andy stood there watching me leave. When I put the car in drive, I noticed him motioning something. I stopped and he walked over and motioned again, indicating for me to roll my window down and I complied.

"Bring a bathing suit even if you don't bring anything to stay over," Andy instructed.

"Okay."

Andy leaned in my window and kissed me again.

Thinking about his kisses was what kept me awake on the drive home and how he'd asked me to feel free to bring an overnight bag if I liked. We'd only been dating for two weeks so what I thought was on the horizon seemed fast, yet due to our history, it seemed long overdue.

I'd never wanted anyone the way I wanted Andy, not even David in the early days of our courtship or during our engagement. David was so restrained and only displayed a passion for punishing me. In the time I'd been with Andy I'd already experience more tenderness and burning passion than all of the days of my marriage combined.

I arrived at the marina ten minutes early. I grabbed my travel bag and purse from the backseat. I stood looking down the hill from the parking lot toward the marina. I'd never been to the Port Honor Marina before. It was only in its infancy when I worked there in college. It wasn't nearly as big as where David's doctor friends kept their boats at Holiday Marina on Lake Lanier, but it wasn't super small either.

I walked down the hill taking it all in. From what I could see on my approach, mostly pontoons and ski boats were docked there with only a couple of small house boats.

Again, I compared it to what I'd seen at Lake Lanier, no yachts and no cigar boats, nothing intimidating.

I wandered along following the numbers of the boat slips until I found 15A. Docked in that spot was one of the small houseboats. It was older, but looked to have been freshly painted and well maintained. It was white like the others, but the trim was navy blue. It had a deck area with a bench along the wall of the cabin and a couple of folding lawn chairs near the rail. I could picture Andy sitting out there drinking his beer and smoking his stogies while we talked on the phone.

I was about to step on to the deck when the sliding door to the cabin opened and Andy stepped out.

"Hey there!" he said, taking my bag and offering his hand to help me aboard.

"Hey!"

Stepping from the steady planks of the dock to the deck of the boat, I looked Andy over. I felt underdressed in my bikini and cover-up compared to his jeans, t-shirt and boat shoes.

Andy looked me up and down and licked his lips. "I see you came prepared."

I smiled. I'd worn the tiniest red bikini I could find at the Augusta Mall that morning and a white, almost sheer cover up, with some cut off jean shorts and flip flops. I'd never dressed so brazen in all my life, not even when I went through the look at me bleached blond hair and crazy contacts phase.

"This?" I asked, as if "this" was completely innocent. "You said bring a swimsuit and meet you at the marina."

I'd also had a spa visit this morning which I hadn't had in years. A full visit complete with Brazilian wax. Things weren't out of sorts when he had a blind man's visit the other night, but now there was no litter on the playground at all. I'd also taken the time get a pedicure and to use a mild tanning lotion so there was no sign what-so-ever of my farmer's tan. Unlike some bottled tans,

195

this one didn't leave me orange. I was a light copper from head to toe and absolutely everywhere in between. Thanks to my dead husband, everything had been put back in place, tightened trimmed and tucked not long after I lost the twins and I'd worked out religiously to keep my thirty-five-year-old body in better shape than it was at age twenty. I was rocking that bikini.

Andy escorted me down the walkway along the edge of the cabin. He slid open the glass door to the cabin as he explained, "I told you I have a room at the club. What I didn't tell you is that the room is actually one of the member's houseboats that I rented."

Andy sat my bag on the built-in sectional. "This converts into a queen size bed and there's a bedroom in the back with another queen." He nodded toward the front of the boat. "It's a 1981 Gibson 50 and it has been completely remodeled with a full kitchen, small, but full." Looking toward the other end of the boat, "There's a bathroom, three-fourth's bath, a shower, but no tub, toilet and sink. Everything works."

I stepped toward the back and peeked through the door to the bedroom. "No curtains?"

"Nope. Wake up on full display with the sun each morning," Andy grinned.

"Can you drive it around or do you have to leave it docked here all the time?" I asked looking at the station containing the instrument panel, gear shift and steering wheel on the front wall of the cabin.

"Oh yeah. It actually runs great for its age. There's another captain's chair and steering wheel up top too. I'll show you."

We went back out on the walkway along the side of the cabin and to the back of the boat. We climbed up a small ladder to the upper deck, the roof of the bedroom area, and then up another small ladder to the roof deck over the living room and kitchen where, like Andy said there was, another driver's seat.

"Shall we take her out?" Andy asked.

"Sure," I replied. I'd never been out on a houseboat before.

"Wait here. I'm going to go down and untie us." Andy climbed down onto the cabin level, secured the folding chairs that were on the deck, then jumped onto the dock and untied three ropes that held the boat in place. When he untied the last rope, he jumped on, giving us a shove away from the dock with his back foot. I watched him over the edge of the top deck.

Andy quickly ran up both ladders as the boat floated away from the dock. "Let me teach you how to start her so next time you can pull us away once I get us untied."

Andy quickly showed me how to crank the boat and steer it away, he explained that it was really a two-man job and I was better suited for driving than shoving the boat away from the slip. I heard most of what he was saying, but standing there with him pressed against me and his arms around me, I couldn't say his words had my full attention.

We putted along no more than about ten miles an hour. We made a left out of the cove and headed under the Highway 44 bridge toward the Reynolds Plantation and Great Water's side of the lake. Once we were on the other side of the bridge Andy backed off. He took a seat in the chair across the aisle.

"I was thinking we find a private cove and anchor. We can have some dinner, go swimming, hang out...Or swimming and then dinner."

I cut my eyes at him, from my place at the wheel.

"Or we can go back to the marina if you like."

I smiled. "No, we can do whatever you want to do."

"Okay. Watch for the channel markers." Andy glanced ahead. "I can't have you hit one and sink us."

I snapped my head back toward the water beyond us. "Oh! Shit!" I jerked the wheel, but the boat, at the

197

putting along speed we were going, barely drifted off course enough to miss the marker.

Andy leaned back and laughed heartily. I loved hearing him laugh. I loved being here and for a moment I laughed with him, but the moment stopped as memories of the conversation with Millie crept in. I couldn't do this, be free with Andy, if I was suddenly saddled with a toddler. My face fell at the thought and I looked away.

"What is it?" Andy seemed to notice everything.

"Nothing." I wiped my eyes and shrugged it off.

Andy stood and approached me. I shrank away, trying to compose myself. I'd determined I wasn't going to tell him, not yet. If I told him, I would lose him and I didn't want that. I wasn't ready to lose him.

I shook him off again. "It's nothing. Really."

He just stood there as I continued to man the wheel. We were in open water and the lake was wide and there were no other boats out. Other than the occasional marker, driving the boat didn't take my full focus.

"Liar," Andy said, half joking, half serious. "You might as well spill it."

I remembered one of my offences which landed me a weekend in the closet was lying. To this day, I maintain I didn't lie, I just didn't tell David all that he thought he was entitled to know. David said I would learn and I did.

I let out a long breath, an exhale I hoped would carry out my fear and insecurities and usher in air of relief as I drew in the next. Still, I hesitated, beginning cautiously. "There's been a development in my case."

"Okay?" He pronounced it as if the word had three syllables and fluctuated his pitch higher at the end, volleying a question and urging me on.

"The timing just stinks!"

"Why?"

"The thing you cautioned me about..." I let it hang in the air hoping Andy wouldn't make me spell it out.

Andy narrowed his eyes and a hint of confusion rose in his face.

"As it turns out, I'm not stealing anyone's child."

Andy really looked puzzled then.

"The opposing counsel in the case called Millie. David's mistress has disappeared and abandoned the child with her seventy-year-old mother. Her mother has no interest in raising the child and with the attorney not being able to contact his client..." I rung my hands, fearing this was the point where things came apart for me and Andy.

"You said something about the laws in Georgia being that you have claim to the child since he was still married to you, right?" Andy asked.

I nodded.

"So are you telling me that..."

I didn't let him finish asking the question. "Millie wants me to take the boy."

"Well of course," Andy said.

My head nearly snapped back as I looked at Andy for clarification. This was not the reaction I'd expected.

"But, you said I shouldn't..."

"I said you shouldn't just take him. The way it sounded was as if you were stealing him from his mother just to keep your inheritance, but if he has no one else...I'm not telling you what to do, but..."

"Did you talk to Millie? You sound almost just like her right now."

Andy grinned. "No, I haven't talked to Millie."

"Then why are you grinning?"

"Because Millie is the poster-girl for righteousness and I'm certain that's not how you would have ever described me in the past."

"Oh, ha-ha." I said, mockingly and flipped my hand dismissively. "I'm being serious."

"So am I." Andy grabbed my hand and pulled it flat to his chest, making a more permanent connection than I'd anticipated.

For a moment the boat drove it self.

I dropped my eyes to my feet. "Millie's pissed with me right now."

"Why?"

"Because I refused to take him and I used the word 'bastard'."

At this juncture of the conversation, Andy managed to put two and two together. "You refused because of what I said?"

Still hanging my head, I nodded.

Andy lifted my chin with a finger. "This is different and you don't need my approval or permission or anything. Who cares what I think anyway?"

"So, you think I should take him?" I asked cautiously.

Andy shook his head. "Oh, no, I'm not telling you what you should do. This is your decision."

"You are no help!" I huffed.

"What do you want to do?" Andy asked me.

"I don't know." I then tried putting it into a different perspective. "What would you do?"

"Again, I'm not telling you what to do." Andy held firm. "Just do what you feel is the right thing to do."

I let out an exasperated sigh.

"Have you ever even seen him?" Andy asked.

"No." I rolled my eyes. "Millie tried to give me a picture of him, but I refused to look at it."

"Then perhaps you should schedule a time to meet him first."

"I'm telling you right now, if he looks like David. I can't do it. It's taken me years of therapy to get anywhere close to over what he did to me. What kind of mother would I be to this little boy if I can't look at him without cringing? How could I ever tell him I loved him? What kind of life would that be for him?"

"Okay, start with looking at the picture then."

"It's all so overwhelming." I wiped my face with both hands.

"Overwhelming," Andy scoffed. "That's every day of parenthood, but you have me and Millie and Jay and everyone else to help you. No matter what you decide, it will be fine, but I get it. If Steffi had come out looking like my former mother-in-law, I can't say I wouldn't have struggled. That woman was a piece of work and she never physically or mentally abused me the way you've described."

I could feel my cheeks swell and the smile spread across my face. I cared what he thought because I'd been in love with him for fourteen years.

I ran a hand through my hair, flipping it out of my face and letting my smile fade a bit. "We're so new." I eased my hand that had been resting on his chest up and over his shoulder. "I don't want to mess..."

"You think I'd run off because..."

I finished his question with another nod.

"No." Andy let out a breath in a manner that said I was a fool without actually saying the words. "Come on. We've been over this. We're not stupid college kids anymore. We're grown adults with grown adult issues and obligations and we're capable of multi-tasking, right? I mean, I have a kid and you're not going to ditch me because I just said that out loud, are you? Seriously, she could call at any moment and I might have to run out on you. It's going to happen at some point, I promise, I'm going to come back, but does that mean you won't want to see me anymore?"

My smile returned as I shook my head.

"Okay then, so you're going to be a mom?"

A flush came over me and I threw both hands over my mouth and through my fingers came, "Oh my God. I'm going to be someone's mom!"

"And without the stretch marks!" Andy joked.

"No, seriously," I remained, eyes wide and hands clasped over my mouth. "Am I really doing this?"

Andy searched around, looking until he found where he'd put his cell phone. "Here." He handed it to me. "Call Millie and tell her you want to see that picture."

I dialed Millie's number as Andy added. "And you might want to tell her to start planning a shower. You're going to need baby stuff."

"Toddler stuff," I corrected him. Then something hit me and I stopped and hung up the phone.

"What?" Andy asked.

"I guess tonight's the night for full disclosure so I'm on three different anxiety medications..."

"Three?"

That was exactly the reaction I was expecting earlier about me getting a kid and pretty much what I should have expected on that bit of information as well.

"The bombing and the closet phobia." I paused a split second before adding, "Really, it's two anxiety meds, nothing as strong as something like Lithium or any anti-psychotic like that, and prescription for insomnia. I am not exactly the spokesperson for picture perfect mental health and I still see a psychiatrist once a month."

Andy chose his words carefully. "You seem fine?" came out like a question as opposed to a statement and I couldn't blame him.

"I am. You've actually seen the worst. The trauma's manifest in nightmares. The two medications and, just not being so near the events anymore, keep them at bay for the most part. Depending on how you look at it, the two meds have the fortunate or unfortunate side-effect of insomnia. One might think that's good because if I'm not asleep, I can't have nightmares, but who wants to never sleep? No one."

"I really don't see the problem." Andy didn't respond in a question that time and it was comforting. "If you have things under control then what more could anyone ask, plus you've been through a lot and yet you look fine to me." He looked me up and down in an attempt to lighten the mood.

"Oh funny."

I hadn't noticed, but we'd floated along a fair distance from the highway 44 bridge and well past the lake houses of Reynolds Plantation and Great Waters. At some point during the conversation, Andy had taken over steering which I'd almost forgotten about.

Scanning the shoreline, Andy pointed to a cove over to the left. "I used to fish up in there with my grandfather. It goes back a ways."

Andy turned the wheel and the houseboat chugged along into the cove.

After Andy found a spot to anchor the boat way back in the cove, he handed me his cell phone. My phone was in my bag on the couch in the cabin below. "Call Millie while I get dinner together."

I took the phone with one hand and pulled Andy close to me with a gently tug of his collar with my other. My eyes fluttered as I brushed my cheek to his. I gave a relieved smile, "I thought surely I was going to lose you over this."

"Not a chance." His lips barely grazed mine.

"I've been thinking about kissing you all day," I sighed and eased on to my toes to better accommodate the height difference between us.

Chapter 17

I'd followed Andy down into the house portion of the boat as I waited for Millie to answer and wandered out onto the front deck watching him anchor us. While I smoothed things over with Millie and set her on the path to arrange for me to meet the little boy, Andy disappeared inside. He heated up dinner and changed into swim trunks. Just as I hung up with Millie, he returned with wings and salad he'd picked up from The Brick, a place where we all used to eat in college. The food wasn't the main thing I noticed when he returned. I looked right past what he was carrying, completely distracted by his shirtless form.

"You hungry?" Andy asked.

He handed me a plate and I stuttered through the two simple words, "Thank you."

We ate dinner on the front deck of the boat with our feet dangling off the front edge into the water.

"His name is Gavin, Gavin Hopewell," I said, before taking a bite of one of the drumettes.

"I suppose if you adopt him, I guess you'll have to do that, you can change his name if you want?"

"I really don't mind the name Gavin. One of my grandfather's best friends was named Gavin and he was such a nice man. Always wore overalls and a striped cap, like a train conductor." I smiled at the memory from my childhood.

"But you'll change his last name to yours?"

"I hadn't given that any thought, but I guess. That would just make David spin in his grave."

Andy shook his head.

"Yes, I'm still bitter. I will be bitter for the remainder of my life," I assured him.

"That's fine with me. I didn't know the asshole and I hated him when he married you so hate him if you want or let him go of what you can't change if it makes you feel better."

I grinned and gave a fake disapproving shake of my head. "If I could forget what he did to me, I might be able to let go and not hate him."

We finished eating and Andy took our plates away and I waited there on the edge of the boat. He's positioned the boat facing out into the opening of the cove, but due to the curve of the lake, I couldn't see anything in front of us but woods. It was definitely secluded back in there and the water looked clean and still. I could almost see fish swimming below my feet.

Andy didn't say anything when he returned, he just dove over me and into the water he went. He made a small splash, some of it flying back at me. Instinctively, I drew up my knees and squealed.

Andy popped up, slung the water from his hair and wiped his face. "You coming in?" he asked.

I pretended to contemplate for a moment before standing up, flinging one of the life jackets he'd put out on the deck out in his direction and then jumping in. I popped up and within a few strokes, grabbed the life jacket. I could swim, but having the life jacket to float on would save my energy.

"According to the depth finder, it's about eight feet here."

"Ah, okay." That was two and a half feet deeper than I was tall. I didn't put the lifejacket on, I just leaned over it and kicked my feet underwater like a duck, moving closer to him.

I looked back and the anchor was holding and we weren't that far from the boat.

"Is there something wrong?"

"Nope, just making sure it was still there and not floating away."

We gently bobbed around in the water, drifting with the ripples that rolled into the cover from the rest of the lake, no more than an arm's length from one another. Each set of little waves brought me closer to Andy.

205

"You don't need that thing, you know." He gestured to the jacket.

"I wanted something to hold on to."

"You can hold on to me."

A moment or so later, Andy took the life jacket and flung it back up onto the boat. Everything he did seemed to draw a smile on my face that I could not hide.

Andy's chest was firm and I rested my chin on his shoulder as we drifted in the water with the little ripples that came along and with Andy moving just enough to keep us afloat. I held on to him with my arms around his neck. We seemed to turn in gentle circles, coming around and allowing me to make sure we hadn't moved too far away from the boat. Minutes passed and we just lingered there in the silence.

There was a breeze in the air, nothing chilly, but it moved just enough to carry the scent of honeysuckle from the woods all around us and breaking the heat of a June evening in Georgia. I was surprised there weren't more people on the lake, but thankful we had this cove all to ourselves.

It was enough just being there with him, but I finally broke the silence. "Have you ever been skinny dipping?"

"No."

"Really?" I was stunned by his answer. I'd just always assumed he'd done *everything*.

"Really. And you?" He inched back to study my face.

"No." As I said the word, I felt the tug of the string and the knot slip, untying the strings across my back.

Andy grinned.

"So, we're doing this?"

"Why not?"

"I can't believe you haven't done it before."

"Nope." Waves stroked over my shoulder blades as Andy brought his hand up, broke the surface of the water and slipped the knot holding the strings around my neck.

With my top twirled around his first to fingers, he saluted, "Scout's honor," and tossed my bikini top onto the deck of the boat the same as he'd done with the life jacket.

The water barely covered my cleavage. My nipples were already hard, the chill of the water, the proximity to Andy, but this took them to heightened forms of arousal.

"And..." I said to Andy.

"And, what?" he cocked an eyebrow.

"Your suit. Throw it up on the boat."

"Ah, right."

I floated on my own while Andy shimmied out of his suit and flung it to the boat.

Each time he tossed anything to the boat, I got a glimpse of the muscles in is arms at work and they were still quite impressive. I assumed he must have made time to work out.

"And..." Andy said to me the same as I'd just done to him. Challenging me to ditch my bottoms.

I rose to the challenge and untied mine and flung it toward the boat. I over-estimated the strength it would take, missed the pile of other items and hit the window of the cabin. Even worse was it made this splat sound and the red bottoms just stuck there all splayed out.

I looked from the window to Andy and back again. "Well, that's not how that was supposed to go."

"It looks like bug guts on a windshield," Andy chuckled and I just shook my head, embarrassed.

"I guess I should go get that down..."

Andy grabbed me before I could finish my sentence and pulled me back toward him. "Fuck that!"

"Oh, um, okay," I stumbled through my response, still giggling over the bug splatter and Andy's exclamation.

Our fingers were intertwined and we floated with a little distance between us initially, each of us feeling for the first time the freedom of being naked in the water. Within mere moments my arms were around Andy's neck again and we were chest to chest.

207

"I'll never be able to swim in public again," Andy said, moving my hair and leaving my shoulders bare.

I could hardly breathe let alone speak as he kissed the top of my shoulder and his dick grazed my pelvic bone, but I managed to squeak out, "Why's that?"

"You can't expect me to go back to using trunks after this?"

He had a point. I never knew swimming could be like this. I admitted, "I've never really been a swim in the lake person before. I'm more of a pools and rivers and streams kind of girl. If I can't see the bottom, it's not really for me, but I think I could stand to do this again."

Andy picked up on my sarcasm. "You think you could?"

"I think I could."

I closed my eyes and let my head rest on Andy's shoulder, moving with him and the water as he kept us afloat. We just lingered there. Crickets and tree frogs started to sing in the woods and the few waves lapped against the shore. As we turned, I opened my eyes just to confirm the boat was still holding as time drug on and the sun started to set.

"Did you ever think things could be like this for us?" Andy shifted, moving me from his left side to his right.

It was really something feeling his body completely against me with nothing between us but a few molecules of H_2O. Exhilarating was that something. Titillating was that something else.

"Not in the slightest," I replied. "But, I imagined. And you?"

"I wanted to call you so many times. I asked Jay for your number once."

I stretched back, looking Andy in the face. "That explains it."

Just as Andy asked, "Explains what?" but before I could answer, his phone started to ring. "Sorry. Hold that thought."

Andy let go of me and swam for the boat. We had jumped off the front of the boat and the ladder was on the back. There was no way he was going to make it to the phone before it quit ringing if he had to swim all the way around the fifty-foot length of the boat, get up the ladder and then run from one end to the other, but he tried. The caller rang again and again, likely having hung up and called again. Andy didn't even make there on the second round either, but he didn't give up. About five minutes after the phone first started ringing, Andy made it to where he'd laid it on the built-in seat on the front deck. I watched him, slightly disappointed that he'd grabbed a towel and thrown it around himself on the way to check to see who was calling.

Seeing that it would be dark soon, I started to make my way to the back of the boat. All of the sudden, being in the lake alone reminded me I was a rivers and streams girl, not a lake girl even if I was naked. It wasn't fun without Andy. Plus, I decided it would be the perfect time for me to climb the ladder. I couldn't imagine anything sexy or graceful about having to climb up the ladder out of the water while naked so I seized my chance to do it while Andy was distracted.

As I made my way around the side of the boat, Andy called down to me, "Are you okay?"

"Yeah, I'm fine." I yelled back. I then started to use the life jacket like a kick board.

"I'm so sorry about this. It's Steffi. I need to call her back."

"Go ahead," I waved back to him.

Getting up the ladder was certainly not graceful and there was no way that could have ever been considered sexy. I had to get my knee up nearly to my ears before my foot found the bottom rung. Then, I had to pull with all of my upper body strength to get my ass out of the water. I know the veins in my head bulged a little at the straining I had to do. No, this could not have been pretty.

Once on the boat, I grabbed my overnight bag and headed for the shower. I didn't stick around to overhear Andy's conversation. I opted to give him some privacy.

Fifteen minutes later, I returned to the front deck, free of the smell of lake water. I'd towel dried my hair and put on a robe with matching bra and panty set underneath. The sun had set and it was dark out save for the string of lights woven around the railing of the deck and gang way. Through the front window of the cabin, I could see Andy was still on the phone.

Andy had heard the sliding of the glass door and was looking my direction when I rounded the corner to the front of the boat. His face perked up at the sight of me and he immediately wound down the conversation with his daughter.

"Alright, I'll call you tomorrow. Don't worry about Jesse Baxter."

After mentioning the boy's name, Andy proceeded to give her the speech about there being more fish in the sea. I almost laughed, but did my best to act as if I hadn't heard a thing. I was going to pick up our wet bathing suits and hang them on the rail, but seeing as Andy had already done that, I went back inside and searched the refrigerator for drinks. I returned with a bottled beer for Andy and a bottled water for me.

Andy took the beer and mouthed both, "Thank you," and "Sorry."

I mouthed back, "It's okay."

I turned to leave, but Andy caught hold of my hand. "Seriously, Steffi, I've got to go. I'll call you tomorrow."

"But, Daaaaaad," I could hear her exaggeration of the word from where I was standing.

Andy glanced at me, gritted his teeth and shook his head. "Look," he said with a stern voice that I hadn't heard before, but found damn hot. "You're not old enough to date and that's final. We'll talk tomorrow, but this subject is done."

"Fine!" she said and I could hear that as well. "Goodnight!"

"Goodnight," Andy said in a more subdued tone. "I love you."

I assume she said it back to him, but I couldn't hear her.

Andy turned his full attention back to me. "Sorry about that."

"That's alright. You said earlier that she might call and you would have to run..."

"Indeed," he nodded. "You got a shower," Andy observed.

"Yeah," I shrugged. "I thought you might join me."

"No, I can barely fit in there by myself."

For a few minutes, Andy informed me of Steffi's boy troubles, his difficulty wrapping his mind around how little time he had before he wouldn't be able to stop her from dating. He also explained how he wished Stacey would take a firmer stance with Steffi and stop making him be the disciplinarian from a far.

Still donning his towel and not wanting to continue going on about his daughter, which he thought was a dating downer and I thought was endearing, Andy excused himself to take a quick shower. "I'll be back in a minute."

When Andy was finish, he found me lying on the top deck of the houseboat.

"What are you doing?" Andy asked, quizzically, as he topped the ladder.

The night was cool and the breeze from earlier had died down and the night was still, but the smell in the air was still the same until Andy arrived. He was shirtless, barefoot and only wearing a pair of black Adidas basketball shorts and the hint of the Dial soap I'd seen in the dish in the shower lingered on his skin.

"Watching the stars." I patted the spot next to me. "Come here."

Andy obliged. As soon as he was on his back next to me, I inched over and laid my head on his chest.

"I took astronomy as one of my science classes in college." I pointed above our heads to one of the obvious constellations that most anyone would know. "That's the big dipper."

Andy's chest quaked beneath my head. "I thought you were about to impart some real knowledge there."

I rolled over and propped my chin up on my arm, laying over Andy's left peck. "I can't remember shit from that class." I gave a little giggle.

Andy shifted, wrapping his arm around me and laying a hand on my ass. "I can't let you go tonight, but if you don't want to..."

I smiled and, borrowing a line from one of my favorite books, and asked, "Are we going to bed or to sleep?"

Andy cocked one side of his mouth, slyly he said, "Neither."

In a gentle, but swift move, Andy had me on my back. The skirts portion of my robe became tangled and my legs were bound and prevented Andy from the natural position of things. I jerked slightly to free myself, but to no avail. His knee was on some portion of the fabric and I was trapped. There was nothing graceful about this, but I wasn't about to lose the momentum.

"That's not how this was supposed to go." Andy snorted. "And, what are you wearing?"

I tugged again, but still nothing. "A robe and..."

Andy sat up and straightened the material, but there was no need.

I got to my knees. With the robe flowing behind me, I stepped over his lap with one leg and then the other and straddled him. "Tell me how it was supposed to go."

Gripping my ass with a hand and the other in my hair, Andy began. "I'd planned to have you on your back and settle my cock between your thighs in front of the moon and stars and God himself."

Andy planted soft kisses from my ear to the top of my shoulder. I untied my robe and, with the nudge of his nose, the satin slid down one shoulder, exposing the strap of the black lace bra I had on and the one cup.

"And what's plan B?" I panted, feeling his growing erection as if there were no shorts or panties between us.

The hand left my ass and moved to the exposed strap of my bra. He eased it over my shoulder with a finger, but seemed to think better of taking the whole bra down on that side. "I'm gonna suckle you through this lace and rake my teeth over your nipple until you beg me to do it to the other." And he did just that.

When Andy came up for air, I lifted his chin, giving me access to his mouth. I kissed him deep and hard and possessive and simulated riding him as I devoured him.

I didn't just want him. I wanted all of him and I didn't care if all of the satellites in the sky were tuned in.

I drew back to catch my breath only to bury my face in his neck near his ear. "What else?" I whispered, deliberately letting my lips graze over his ear before catching the lobe between my teeth and giving a gentle bite.

He unhooked my bra. "I'll have ya wet and wanting."

I shimmied and let the robe fall down my arms, sliding off and landing in a bunch around us. I was bare, save for the black panties.

With his arms bound around me, and my torso pressed firmly to his, Andy lifted me and again flipped me to my back. This time, my legs went wide around him as he came down over me.

"What are you going to do to me?" I said, wide eyed and eager as he hovered over me.

Andy locked his eyes with mine. "Everything you never knew you wanted."

My breath caught and I almost came over a phrase. I pulled him down to me. "And what can I do for you?"

"Try not to scream my name too loudly."

"Holy shit," I giggled, totally surprised by his candor. I'd never talked like this during sex before, but responded, "I'll do my best."

Andy took his time, traveled from mouth to ear to breast, flicking with his tongue, softly biting and sucking, he knew exactly what he was doing and seemed to enjoy it.

"Lay back," he said and he started southward.

He planted kisses down and down, crossing my belly and circling my navel before he drew up on his knees. He slid his hands down and rested one over the top of my panties, sliding his thumb down and fingering me through the lace. I arched my hips, enjoying the feel and the hint of what was to come. When I couldn't take anymore, Andy peeled down my panties and tossed them to the side.

Andy took my left foot in his hands and left a trail with his tongue from my instep to my knee and to my inner thigh. I realized where he was going and reached for him. I gently took him by the side of his face and urged him up.

"You don't have to do that," I said.

"Oh, but I want to."

Andy was right, I had to try not to scream his name so loudly, but I failed.

Two fingers in my vagina and a tongue on my clit working in unison, he knew just what he was doing when he asked me not to scream his name too loudly. He knew exactly what I was going to do. The way he used his tongue, the circles, the long licks, well I'd never experienced that before or anything like it. I knew oral sex was common place now, but I'd just never had it performed on me.

My back arched and my legs widened all on instinct, and I was compelled to try to turn myself inside out for him, letting him have every bit of me there was to have. Heat rose in my face and tears swelled in my eyes before escaping down my cheeks, but I wasn't crying. I was losing control, all control. My voice and my body begged for it as I screamed. I'd never screamed or made much noise at all in the past, but I hadn't even seen his dick and he had me screaming his name.

"Andy! Oh God, Andy! Jesus... Christ...ANDY!!!"

I was on the tail end of my orgasm when Andy took down his shorts and drove into me. I wrapped all of myself, all that was me, around him and moved when he moved. It wasn't like I was unprepared. I was still slick and ready and, surprisingly, still wanting more and Andy gave and gave.

There's no description for the amount of time that passed. There's no way of saying how long Andy went because what he did, he did so well it left me mindless. The way he moved not just in me, but all over me, connecting us inside and out. The feel of his chest, slippery with sweat, slid over mine reiterating the fact that he knew how to use his entire body.

"I'm going to come. My God, Cara, I'm going to come!" he said, all husky and breathless. He buried deep in me, shuddered and fell limp with a little more of his weight resting on me than I'd experienced before.

I hadn't expected so many firsts in one night or seconds and thirds. For the first time in my life, I'd thoroughly enjoyed sex and learned that multiple orgasms really were a thing.

Chapter 18

At some point, Andy and I migrated to bed and to sleep. The next morning, I awoke to the smell of bacon and having forgotten that there were no curtains. I sat up and stretched. Extending my arms, yawning and opening my eyes to the realization that I was on full display for the viewing pleasure of two elderly fisherman trolling past.

Taking in the show, the two men put down rod and reels down and gave me two thumbs up.

"Go away!" I screamed, and jerked the sheet all the way up to my chin.

Andy came running, holding his phone to his ear. He mouthed, "Good morning," and gave a shooing motion using his whole arm, telling the fisherman to move it along. Then, he leaned in and kissed me. It was little more than a quick peck and nothing to write home about. Andy barely broke stride with his conversation and was out of the room as quickly as he'd come in.

I rolled out of bed, wrapped in the sheet and followed him.

"You need me there to repair the green?" Andy asked whomever was on the other end of the line. "You have a grounds crew so I'm not sure what you think I can add."

I followed Andy all the way to the front deck where he started pulling up the anchor. Shirtless, I could see the marks I'd left on his back and the memory of the night before jumped back to the front of my mind.

"Fine," he huffed. "I'll be there in thirty minutes."

I'm not sure what the voice on the other end of the line said, but I anticipate they were as disappointed with his answer as I was.

"Yes, it's going to take me at least thirty minutes to get there." Noticing me in the sheet standing behind him, Andy corrected himself. "It may be closer to an hour."

Andy hung up the phone and let the slack out in the anchor again. I smiled wide.

"Care to remind me again of what I missed out on in my early twenties?" I asked him and, not seeing any more fisherman, I let the sheet drop.

With only fifteen minutes to spare, Andy drew up the anchors and met me on top deck where he cranked the boat.

"Just keep it in the middle of the lake and," demonstrating the controls for the speed, "After you get out of the cove, shift this upward to speed up and to slow down and stop when you get near the bridge. I'll be back by   then   and   take   it   from   there."
"Got it." I rested a hand on the lever and another on the steering wheel.

No sooner had he turned away, did Andy turn back. He wrapped his hand around my neck and pulled me in and kissed me. "Do not try to go under the bridge," he said with sternness.

"Okay," I nodded.

Andy kissed me once more before he ran below to shower and change. He was back in ten minutes and dressed, Polo shirt and khaki slacks. He looked ready for a game of golf, not work. I was still wearing one of his undershirts and a pair of panties. He'd refused to let me change, insisting he didn't have time.

"Anyone that notices will just think you have a shirt on over your bathing suit," Andy had assured me. "Plus, skinny dipping, making love under the stars last night, flashing the elders this morning," he looked me up and down, "you know you're an exhibitionist."

"I am not!" I protested.

"You are," he teased me. "And, I'm okay with that. Whatever floats your boat. To each their own. Who am I to judge?"

I drove the boat until we were in sight of the no wake sign before the bridge. Andy didn't ask me to move, he just came up behind me and took over driving the boat around me. He slowed us and lined us up to pass between the pillars while pressed firmly against me.

217

"I like you just like this."

I glanced over my shoulder, "Like what?"

"Wearing my t-shirt, smelling like me, barefoot, in my arms."

We floated under the bridge and I melted into him. I leaned my head back, resting it on his chest and feeling boneless over his words.

"Someone cut doughnuts on the third green last night and apparently my presence is needed for the repairs." I could feel him shake his head and the air of disgust he gave off for having been called in. Leaving a hand on the steering wheel, he lifted the hem of the t-shirt and ran his hand over the leg of my panties, tracing the elastic band where my leg met my torso with his thumb, sending goose bumps all over me. "Wait here and I'll be back as soon as I can."

I nodded. How could I refuse when he touched me like that?

The slip Andy's boat held at the marina was the last one at the very end of the dock. In fact, it wasn't so much of a slip like the other boats had, but a spot to tie up along the side of the dock. Had he held one of the other spots, he would have had to back the boat in and, therefore, anyone could walk by and see into his bedroom. Had that been the case, I would have disobeyed Andy and driven to Greensboro in search of curtains and a curtain rod. Instead, I ate the breakfast Andy had prepared, showered and then headed back to bed. Looking across the dock to an unobstructed view of the woods, I thanked God for this view and the spot at the end of the dock.

Feeling an exhaustion that compared with the handful of hangovers I'd had in my life, I allowed myself to nap while I waited for Andy to return. I also figured what would it hurt for him to return to find me naked in his bed. From 10:00 a.m. until noon, I slept like the dead. Initially, I was all snuggled in, but I only woke up around noon to the sound of voices.

"I haven't seen tits like that in twenty years."

I opened my eyes, spotted the same two old geezers from this morning. I snatched up the sheet again, thinking, "What are the odds?"

Earlier they didn't speak, just gave hand gestures, but now they were actually commenting.

"Well, that's twice in one day. With this kind of luck, I'm going to play the lottery on the way home," the other one replied.

Then I heard a familiar voice and the boat barely rocked.

"Hey! I know you two dirty perverts! Now, fuckin' beat it or I'll tell your wives your pervin' on my girl." Andy was back. His voice was jovial, and I liked to think that he would have followed through on his threat. More importantly, I wanted to believe he meant it when he called me his girl.

The two old men laughed and one yelled back, "Bravo, Andy!"

The other one asked, "Does she have a sister?"

Andy and I did not spend the afternoon in bed. We spent it having lunch at The Yesterday Café in Greensboro followed by purchasing and hanging curtains in the bedroom of the houseboat.

On Sunday Andy and I said our goodbyes for the week. He tucked me into my car and added, "If Millie arranges a time for you to meet Gavin, let me know and I'll be glad to go with you."

"You don't have to do that," I assured him. "I'll be fine on my own."

"But, you aren't on your own anymore. You've got me," Andy added firmly.

I smiled, "Thanks, but..."

Andy cut me off. "The only but, is whether or not you are going to take him and I'm going to tell you again, it is your decision. I won't think any less of you and I don't want you to think this is something you don't have a choice in."

This was a subject we had touched on all weekend. Each time Andy reiterated that it was my decision. He also reiterated that I would have his support no matter what decision I made.

There was no perfect ending to this weekend. The fact that it had to come to an end meant there was no way to achieve perfection, but it had been an absolutely perfect.

On the drive home, I called Jay. I hadn't talked to him all weekend and I wondered how he was doing.

"I'm fine. Adjusting, is more like it," he described.

"And, Peter? How's he doing?" I asked.

"He beats the Hell out of that ferret," Jay joked. He always had a way of turning a serious conversation on his head.

"You are nuts!"

I told Jay all about the weekend right down to the last detail. Jay was a junkie for details.

I summed up by saying, "It was better than I could have ever imagined."

"He was that good?" Jay inquired.

"Let's just say, even if I was a smoker, I wouldn't have needed a cigarette afterward."

"Lord, I'm gonna need a moment to fan," Jay sighed. "Who would have ever thought I would live vicariously through you?"

I laughed. "I doubt you need to live vicariously through anyone. Peter is everything you ever wanted."

"You're right, but like I've always said, 'I'll look at anything naked once.' I'll also listen to any sex story, too," Jay snickered, "Plus, not that I call them anymore, but hearing you describe Andy is almost as good as calling a phone sex hotline."

"Oh my God!" I felt myself blushing. "Did you have a crush one him too?"

Jay just giggled before giving the most unconvincing "No," never.

Jay kept me company the rest of the ride home and mostly we talked about his and Peter's wedding plans.

"I don't know why you bother," I said.

"Why bother what?" he asked.

"Getting married."

"Oh." He started to give me the speech about how they had every right.

"Yes, I get it about your rights, but let me tell you, it's not all that everyone makes it out to be."

"We're practically married now so we're just making it official."

"Everyone you know and love already knows your official. Sounds like you're the only one that doesn't."

Jay huffed. "We're doing this and you are a, well, not a bridesmaid or a groomsman, but you're standing there in some taffeta contraption looking like Scarlett O'Hara and that's that."

"Taffeta contraption? Scarlet O'Hara?" I rolled my eyes. "Really?"

"Really. And, you'll like it."

"I'll pretend to for your sake."

"You do that."

The snipping, bantering back and forth, continued all the way to my driveway. We parted with an exchange of "I love you" like a brother and sister.

It wasn't long after I arrived home that Andy called to make sure I got home okay. Then he called again as I settled into bed around 10:00 pm. He called each night thereafter and we spoke until midnight and sometimes beyond. I loved talking to him until the wee hours.

On Wednesday night, I was walking home from the weekly visit to lay roses on the graves of the twins and my grandparents and I was just about home when a truck rolled up beside me. Instead of passing on down the street and stopping at the four-way, it stopped just beyond me, making sure whomever was driving got my attention. It was a Silver Ford F-150 extended cab truck.

I stopped in my tracks, not having recognized the truck.

The front passenger's side door flung open and the voice of the driver billowed out. "Come on, get in! I'm taking you to dinner tonight."

It was Andy and I'd never been more surprised or glad to see someone.

I was barely in the cab before Andy started, "Well don't keep me waiting." He leaned over and kissed me. "How did it go?"

As we sat there in the middle of Main Street, in this whopper of a truck that no one could get around if they wanted to, I replied, barely holding my excitement, "It went just as you and Millie knew it would."

Andy feigned ignorance, "I have no idea what you're talking about."

Sitting as close to the console as I could get in an effort to reach Andy, I placed both hands on his face. "You know exactly what I'm talking about." I smiled and drew him to me for a thankful kiss.

"You both knew I would not be able to resist him."

Millie had arranged for me to meet Gavin and his grandmother that afternoon.

"I hate that I couldn't be there with you, but I had a meeting with the contractors about tearing down the old club house. I couldn't get out of it on such short notice. I'm so sorry."

"No, it's okay. Millie and I didn't have much notice either. She got the call from the other attorney yesterday afternoon and that was the first she knew of it, too."

Most restaurants in the area were only open Thursday, Friday and Saturday nights with the exception of Peggy's. On the drive to Wrens, I further described how the meeting came about.

"As it turns out, Darla Hopewell, is straight out of a trailer park in East Dublin, Georgia which, strangely enough, isn't all that far from here. According to what her mother told us this afternoon, Darla got her ticket out by following some boy to the big city. At nineteen he'd left her with two kids and a meth habit. She'd dumped the two other children, now ages eight and nine, on her mother back in East Dublin. She got clean and got a medical assistant certificate from one of those tech schools. She even clarified that it wasn't Georgia Tech. You should have seen Millie give me the side eye over that. As if either of us would confuse Georgia Tech with handing out medical assistant certificates."

"You two are such snobs," Andy teased me, "with your Harvard degrees."

"Oh you know what I mean."

"Go on."

Pulling into Peggy's we got a parking spot in the back. The conversation was leaning more toward me giving him the low down on Darla.

Andy held the door to the restaurant for me. "So, are you going to tell me how meeting the child went?"

"I did tell you."

"No, you didn't." He followed me inside to a table and pulled out my chair.

Taking a seat, "I did. I said, 'It went exactly as you and Millie knew it would.'"

Andy stared down at me. "I'm going to need you to elaborate."

"Fine," I said and the giddiness returned. I'd been trying to play it cool, knowing I was due for an exclamation of "I knew it!" from Andy.

"Okay, so Darla's attorney arranged for Mrs. Hopewell to drive over with him from East Dublin where she still lives. We met at 2:00 pm in Millie's office."

"Yes, you told me that was the plan," Andy recounted.

Just as I was about to get going again the waitress approached. Not meaning to be sharp, Andy said, "Two sweet teas with lemon," before she could even ask and immediately directed his attention back to me. "And?"

The waitress turned on her heels and went away.

"And, he's got a head full of brown curls, the biggest hazel eyes and he seems to take in everything around him. And dimples, oh just the cutest dimples, and chubby little legs too."

"You know you just described me as a baby," Andy kind of laughed.

I looked him over. For just a split second I allowed myself to picture the child's real father. "I guess you're right. He looks nothing like my husband."

"I suppose that's a relief."

"To tell the truth, I hadn't even thought of it until now."

I quickly moved on and went back to telling Andy all about Gavin.

"Mrs. Hopewell said he's shy to talk around strangers, but he has about thirty words as far as she can think and he's learning more all the time. He calls her Mama because it's easy for him to say and there's no one else to call Mama so she figured why correct him. I thought that was so sad."

"Did you hold him?"

"He came right to me. He weighs about twenty-four pounds and he's walking, but still likes to be held. Oh, and he sucks his thumb. It's so cute!"

"You'll need to break him of that. Stephanie did that and it just about ruined the shape of her mouth. Thank God for braces. Trust me, there's nothing cute about beaver teeth and a three-thousand-dollar orthodontist bill."

From the way Andy worded his warning, it was a foregone conclusion that I would be taking Gavin, but I didn't get to correct him.

I snickered. "I will take your word for that."

Our drinks arrived, we ordered and we continued to talk over everything.

"So how did you leave things?" Andy asked between French Fries.

"Millie is going to arrange everything."

"You're taking him?"

I gave Andy a look. "You knew all along that I would."

Andy smiled and shoved another fry in his mouth.

When we arrived back at my house, I just assumed Andy was going to drop me off and head home, but instead he grabbed a duffle bag from the back seat and followed me inside.

"Staying over?" I asked coy-like.

"You bet your ass I am." Andy gave the front door a shove with the bottom of his shoe and dropped the duffle bag. "Where'd you say that bedroom of yours is?"

We didn't make it to the bedroom. We christened the floor in the main hall outside of the living room door. Praise Jesus I'd had the good sense to put little blinds over the transom windows around the front door or those slowing down at the four-way stop might have gotten a show. I would have been more of the talk of Avera than I usually was with my weekly walk to the graveyard.

I loved everything about the way he touched me. Straddled atop him, one would have thought I was in control, but that wasn't the case. With an arm wrapped firmly around my back and a grip on my left butt cheek, Andy guided me and set the pace. He also wound a hand in my hair and arched me allowing him to bury his face in my chest.

David treated me as a possession, something to be kept and controlled. With Andy, it was as if I was possessed. David took control, but to Andy I gave control. Although I could hear my mind describe both and make the comparisons, there was nothing alike in these experiences as they were so vastly different, so completely opposite.

Feeling spent, we laid intertwined on the floor, but not for long.

"I've got to get something out of the truck," Andy said, and he reached for his jeans.

"Okay?" I was confused because I could still see his bag sitting by the door.

"Stay here. I'll be right back."

Andy slipped his pants on and flipped me his undershirt. "Put this on."

He walked outside, shirtless and barefooted and I wondered if the neighbors would notice. Soon he retuned carrying a huge box that he could hardly manage. It was wrapped in baby shower paper with a huge blue bow.

"What have you done?" I asked as I got up to help him get it through the door.

"I picked up a little something for you. The lady at the store insisted on wrapping it." Andy said over the top of the box as we wedged it in the front door.

"Which room are you going to make the nursery?" Andy asked, sitting the box down.

The look on my face gave it away. I hadn't thought about that yet.

"Alright. Didn't you say there was another room upstairs near yours?"

"Yes."

"Okay, then. That's it." He picked the box up and started down the hall.

I wasn't sure what was in that box, but it was heavy and all of the muscles in Andy's arms and back were on display as he walked past me.

I shimmied between the box and the wall around to help. "Wait!"

"Right, I got ahead of myself." Andy put it down again. "Go ahead and open it."

"But...I just meant I was going to help you carry it."

He gave the box a little push in my direction. "Open it."

"Alright," I hesitated and he gave it another shove toward me.

226

Ripping off the wrapping paper, I found the writing and picture on the outside of the box. "You bought a crib?"

"Not just any crib. It converts!" From the sound of his voice, he was very pleased with his purchase.

"Converts?"

"When he outgrows the crib, we can turn it into a toddler bed and then when he outgrows that, we can turn it into a full-size bed that he can use forever if he likes."

I was really stuck on the word "we" and that Andy had gone ahead and bought a crib.

"We?" I asked.

"Yes, we," Andy emphasized. "You're not alone in this."

Memories of David jumped to the front of my mind again. I'd done everything for the twins myself, all of the purchasing, putting together of furniture, painting the room and, at his insistence, three weeks after I lost them, I dismantled the nursery and repainted the room.

I jumped into Andy's arms, hem of the t-shirt flying and my bare ass surely showing. "I love it!"

Chapter 19

Andy in jeans and me still in his t-shirt, we cleared the upstairs guest room, took down the bed, packed the bedding into the linen closet and set about putting the crib together.

I broke from reading the directions. "She seemed nice," I said pensive and handing Andy the Phillips head screwdriver.

"Who?" He asked, taking the tool and barely loosing focus on his task.

"Mrs. Hopewell." I flipped the page. "That's the wrong screw." I picked through the pile before handing him the right one and added, "how could the lady I met raise someone like Darla. Someone who only cares about herself?"

Andy didn't miss a beat with his answer. "Nice people raise piece of shit kids. That's what my aunt said and it's why she said she was a real bitch to my cousins and me."

"I guess that's one explanation."

"It's how I turned out to be the upstanding guy you have before you."

My husband's parents must have been damn near saints as evidenced by the way he turned out, I thought to myself.

"I did the math based on when she said Darla left home and the age of the two other children. I guess Darla's about twenty-seven now. From the looks of Mrs. Hopewell, she must have been forty when she had Darla or she's done some real hard livin'."

"Did she have any idea where Darla is now?" Andy tightened the screws and had the back and the sides on.

"If she did, she didn't say. She said she dropped Gavin off with her about six months ago and she hasn't seen her since. She calls just often enough to get the others' hopes up that she's coming back to get them. Mrs. Hopewell said that in all honesty she's more like the good witch in The Wizard of Oz to them than a mother, popping in wearing a fancy dress and a present for them every now and then."

"So, does she intend to keep them, but she's letting you have Gavin?"

"I think she loves all three of them, but one more was just too much for her and, well," I scrambled to hand him the next item in the list for attaching the front piece of the crib, "I think she sees me as an opportunity for Gavin to have a better life than the rest of them, kind of a way out for him."

I got to my knees and held the front piece in place while Andy drove in the screws, bolting it to the side. A moment more and we had it together and standing up right.

"I love it!" I announced again.

Andy gestured to the two pieces still laying on the floor and to the sides of the crib. "Do you have an attic? I'll put these up there until we need them." He also mentioned they were the rails that weren't needed until we converted the crib into the full-size bed.

"Thank you so much for doing this, but what would you have done if I told you I wasn't going to take him?" I asked.

"I would have taken it back to the store I guess."

We worked together again and got the bedrails up the drop-down stairs and into the attic.

It was nearly midnight when we stood admiring our work before going to bed.

"I know you said Millie was going to arrange everything, but do you have any idea when you might take custody?" Andy asked.

"I have a feeling it will be soon." I felt both nervous and excited about the idea. "What am I doing? You know, this is the only thing I have in preparation for a baby? Oh my God, seriously." I turned and faced Andy. "I am so unprepared."

He laughed. "You're going to be fine. You'll see."

My schedule was nearly non-existent and I could work from most anywhere so I'd stayed over at the boat house with Andy on the nights we stayed together. This was the first time Andy had slept over at my house. In fact, this was the first time he'd been upstairs.

"It's so white," he said of my bedding. "And so fluffy. Do you actually sleep in here?"

"Yes," I replied tersely, shaking my head and tossing one decorative pillow after another to the chair in the corner.

"Even the chair is white," he observed.

"I like white. It's so clean looking," I said.

Andy laughed. "Let me know if you still like white in a month or two."

He flipped back the covers on the side of the bed I'd offered him, right side as I slept on the left.

"Why wouldn't I?" I asked as I pulled them back from my side.

"Kids and white don't exactly mix well." He climbed into bed still fresh from the shower and wearing nothing more than boxers. I climbed in wearing his t-shirt which he'd handed back to me after I exited the shower.

Andy opened his arm for me to lay my head on his chest and I snuggled in. Andy settled into my bed and aired his observation. "This is what I imagine sleeping in a cloud might be like, but the bottom is firm."

"I like a firm bottom," I snickered, rolling over to cut the bedside lamp off.

He threw a hand over and grabbed my ass. "So do I."

Twice in one evening. Earlier we'd been overtaken with passion on the hallway floor, all ravaging and needy. Settled into bed, it was loving and tender and toe curling all the same. I looked back on the first night at the boat house and how many times that night as well. Each night I fell asleep wondering what we would have been like in our prime and so mad at myself for something I'd never be able to change and never stop wanting to fix.

230

That Saturday Millie threw an impromptu baby shower. It had been over a month since Mrs. McDonald's funeral and we all converged on Seven Springs. Now we were back again, as well as many of the ladies from around the county who I'd made friends with since moving back. Millie had been specific with her invitation and suggested gifts suitable for sustaining a toddler. By the end of the party, I'd opened over a hundred presents and received, not only enough to outfit a nursery, but to outfit the child himself. Jay and Peter gave me a glider for rocking him to sleep. Anna-Cat gave me a stroller. Millie gave me a high chair that she'd saved from when her girls were small.

"I saved it thinking we were going to have another one," she said. "It was mine when I was little so just ignore the bite marks on it. I'm not sure if those were from me, George-Anne or Gabby."

"I'll make sure you get it back when he out grows it," I hugged her in an additional thanks.

Two weeks later, I signed off on the equivalent of a copy of War and Peace accepting custody of Gavin.

"How long does it take before Gavin's officially mine?" I asked as I signed my name to the ump-teenth page

Not only was I taking over custody through default judgement in the case with Darla Hopewell, but Millie said she could come out of the woodwork in the next sixty days and appeal the case.

"I don't think there's anything to appeal, but there are judges out there who will entertain the appeal because it involves the removal of a child from their biological mother," Millie explained.

I flipped the page and Millie pointed to the next signature line. "Even though she abandoned him?"

"She left him in the custody of her mother. It's tricky. She could say she did it while getting clean so she could take better care of him or something. I've seen it a million times." Millie straightened the stack of pages that I'd already signed.

"I'm going ahead and filing a petition for adoption so we'll come at it from that angle as well. We discussed that before, remember? And that's what most of the documents are about." Millie continued explaining each of the documents.

"And this one," she pointed, "Is a petition to change his name. Just sign here and write the name you want to give him on the sticky note and I'll have my secretary type it in."

I had been thinking about it for days. When Millie first mentioned the option to change his name, I dismissed changing his first name, but the more I thought about it, the more I thought I would change it. Back and forth I went, change it, don't change it. As it turned out, his middle name was his father's middle name. Learning that, brought me to a compromise. Wherever his mother got the name Gavin from was more important to her than his father's name so I decided to honor whomever it was and let that name stand. Not that the boy's father set the bar high, I still hoped whomever Gavin's namesake was that they were a better person than him.

"Gavin Michael McConnell," I said aloud as I wrote the name.

During our nightly phone call, Andy prodded me as to the name. "Why Michael?"

"It's my grandfather's first name and my father's first name" I replied as if he should know that.

"You introduced him as 'Pops' that Easter and, I'm sorry, I'm sure I should have remembered his full name from the funeral, but..."

I stopped Andy from further apologizing. "It's okay."

"I think that's the first time you've ever mentioned your dad."

"I guess that's also your way of asking why. There's no sorted story of him running off or anything. I don't talk about him because I never got to know him. He died in Vietnam, right before the war ended and right before I was born."

I continued, "I was conceived while he was stationed in Germany and my mother was doing a semester abroad. They met and fell in love and got married all in six weeks. The plan was that he would finish his stint in the army and come home. Every war bride's plan, right? Mom said it was funny she went all the way to Europe to find a boy from Lincoln County. 'For all I know I could have met him at a football game.' Their high schools played one another."

"Anyway, he was part of a medic team. After mom left, he got a promotion and was reassigned from hospital work to evac and transport. He helped on the medi-copter that flew the gravely wounded out of Vietnam and back to Germany. They were flying out one day and the Vietnamese had strung a guidewire between two mountains as a tactic to take down the enemy aircraft, and it worked. The chopper hit it. The helicopter he was on went down and there weren't any survivors. His name was Carroll Michael McConnell. It's on the Vietnam Wall and a marker at Arlington. Also, Carroll is my real first name."

"Have you ever been there?" Andy asked.

"Where?"

"Arlington."

"Ah. No, but I want to." I thought about how many times my mother promised to take me. "Mama always said we'd go one day, but she never got around to it."

"Millie said your mother took a job as a traveling nurse."

"Yeah, she went back to Germany. It's a civilian job, but she trains nurses at the base in Landstuhl. She's a regular Florence Nightingale."

"Maybe one day when she comes home we'll all go and take Gavin."

Two weeks later, the paperwork was all done, a social worker had visited my house, everything was complete. A hand on the doorknob of Millie's office, I took a deep breath. I wasn't Catholic, but I thought of making the sign of the cross over my head and across my chest. I didn't. I did say a prayer asking God to protect this child from all of the bad luck I'd had in my life. I asked him to let the days of my poor decision making be behind me so that I could be a good mother.

I was so nervous as I twisted the knob. I knew what waited inside. I saw Mrs. Hopewell's car in the line of those parked along the street in front of the office.

I felt the latch release and was just about to push forward, opening the door when a light honk came from a car horn behind me. A honking horn on the streets of downtown was nothing unusual, but it got my attention and I turned to look. It was a sight to behold, that 1980s yellow Mercedes. I couldn't say I'd never been so happy to see him because each time I saw Andy, I felt that way. My heart leapt, but this time I could swear it leapt a little higher.

"Hey!" Andy yelled from the car window. "Hold up a second!"

I waited and Andy and I entered the office together. We found Millie holding Gavin and showing him a stuffed fox one of her clients had given her.

"Look, it's Mommy," Millie said as they both laid eyes on me.

No one had ever referred to me as Mommy before and it caught in my throat, making me think of my girls for just a moment.

I held out my hands and Gavin came to me. He snuggled in and let me hug him close. I wasn't sure what Mrs. Hopewell used to bathe him, but he smelled fresh and clean, and still had that sweet smell that all babies have. I wasn't sure if it was the smell or the warmth of him against me, but the magic happened, the magic of when a mother first holds her child, the magic of instant love more powerful than anything you've ever felt before, the magic that makes you feel as if your heart is going to burst because it's so full. I might not have given birth to him, but

234

that magic happened for me and, in that instant, I knew he was mine.

Gavin was bashful around Andy.

"He's shy around men," Mrs. Hopewell explained, "but give him a minute and he'll warm right up."

Mrs. Hopewell teared up as she told him goodbye. "You be a sweet boy. Grandma loves you very much." She stroked his little head and kissed him on his forehead.

"I promise I'll take good care of him," I said and Andy concurred.

"We'll take great care of him," he added.

Mrs. Hopewell smiled and thanked us for taking him.

Gavin seemed slightly concerned that she was leaving, but wasn't fussy. Her leaving was almost too easy.

Mrs. Hopewell had been right about Gavin warming up to Andy. By the time we left Millie's office, Gavin had Andy as wrapped around his little finger as he did me.

The first week was a little rough with helping Gavin find a routine. One day he was especially fussy. He cried almost the entire day and I was on my last nerve, ready to cry too when Andy showed up.

"I've got this," he told me. "You go soak in the tub." And, perhaps before he realized what he'd said, Andy said, "Daddy's got this."

Andy and I hadn't defined what we were or what his role in Gavin's life might be. It was all so soon and I hadn't wanted to put any of this instant family stuff on Andy, but I didn't dare correct him or even acknowledge he'd said anything.

Later, when I emerged from the bath, I found Andy rocking Gavin in the swing. Gavin's head laid on Andy's shoulder with a fist full of one of my wash clothes stuffed in his mouth. Andy patted his bottom, that gentle pat that mimics a heart beath, and they floated back and forth. Gavin's eyes looked heavy and he was just about to give in to sleep.

"He's teething," Andy said. "A frozen washcloth will do the trick as good as any of those fancy teething rings."

I smiled and that fullness in my heart returned. I seemed to be having those moments over and over again lately. I don't think I'd ever seen anything more beautiful and amazing looking than Andy holding Gavin.

Time flew by. I learned fast that toddlers were quicker creatures than anyone gave them credit for. I learned what Andy said was true about white furniture. It was ushered out and leather, a fabric from which spaghetti sauce and condiments could easily be wiped. I also learned that Andy was a natural born expert at child rearing.

Months passed and one day it dawned on me that Andy lived with us. Digging side by side with Gavin in my little yellow rose garden, him slinging dirt more so than cultivating, I traced back to the day Andy actually moved in and couldn't specifically find one. There was no one set date where there was any declaration. As best I can figure, he stayed over the night Gavin came home with me and never stopped staying over. Little by little, a spot in the toothbrush holder in the bathroom, a drawer in the chest of drawers then the whole chest of drawers, part of the closet, and his side of the bed, this became our house.

Gavin and I spent weekends with Andy at the houseboat, but this was our home. There were photos of the three of us in the living room, candid shots hanging on the wall of us playing in the creek at Seven Springs, a photo of all three of us with the Easter Bunny because each time the two of us tried to step away, Gavin screamed bloody murder and a photo of Gavin jumping from the deck of the houseboat to Andy in the lake, arms out stretched and both smiling from ear to ear. There were more photos like those all around the house. This was our home and we were a family.

Initially, there was only one day per week that Gavin and I were on our own and that was Wednesdays. Andy spent the night in Milledgeville and had dinner with

Stephanie. Occasionally, he spent time with her on the weekends, but she was becoming more involved with her friends and cancelling with him more and more often.

After it dawned on me that we were our own little family, it also dawned on me that even though Andy seemed to tell me all about Steffi, as he called her, I'd never met her. Those thoughts occurred on a Thursday and over dinner Andy told me all about how their dinner had gone the night before.

"We ate pizza and wings at The Brick, the usual," he described.

Although I wasn't dissatisfied with it just being the three of us, it ate at me that he'd never even offered to introduce us and I asked him why.

Andy pushed back from the table, "I guess I never thought about it."

"How could you not think about introducing us?" I didn't want to point out it was as if he was living a double life, but did ask, "What exactly does she think you do with your time when you aren't with her?"

"She's fifteen, I don't think she thinks beyond herself," he admitted without realizing how that made her sound.

"And you don't think that's a problem?"

"I really hadn't given it much thought..."

I cut him off, "Really?"

Gavin was still playing with his chicken and more of his rice was on the tray of the high chair than in his stomach, but I let him be and took up mine and Andy's plates.

"I wasn't done," Andy protested, but I slung the contents of his plate in the trash.

"What has gotten into you?" he asked, mildly raising his voice.

"Did it occur to you that you are a part of our lives," I motioned between me and Gavin, "but right now I'm wondering if we are a part of yours."

237

"Oh, Jesus, are you kidding me?" Andy got up from the table and approached me.

I took two steps back, but heard the clanking of Gavin's baby spoon and fork hit the floor one after the other, and moved to pick them up. Andy met me on the other side of the high chair, helping to clean up the radius of food droppings and silverware around Gavin.

"I'm not kidding you. You go off to see her like she's some other woman." I quickly clarified my statement, "I know she's not, but you know what I mean."

"I'm not sure I do."

I placed the spoon and fork back on Gavin's tray and no sooner did I do that than Gavin throw them back down. It had become a familiar game for him.

"Maybe I'd like for you to want to include her in..." I stopped myself before I placed a label on what we had going on here. "Is it wrong that I'd like to meet her? We have dinner regularly with your brother and his wife and kids, but not Steffi. Does she even know about us?"

"Da-Da!" Gavin raised his hands in the air, signaling he wanted Andy to get him out of the high chair.

Andy answered, "Come here sport," and picked him up. "I missed you today!"

Watching their interactions, I just couldn't believe Steffi wasn't already a part of our lives and not just Andy's. I didn't let it go and the tension hung in the air the rest of the night.

"Okay, here's the thing," Andy started as we climbed into bed that night. "I haven't introduced you all because I don't want her opinion about you or to hear her repeat her mother's opinion or even deal with any negativity that might come from introducing you."

"Coward!" I said, pulling my covers up and cutting off my light.

"No, I just like what we have right now."

I came close to asking, "And what do we have?" but I refrained. "Why does it have to be negative?"

238

"Just trust me. She has her life and I have mine and everyone is..."

I sat bolt upright and cut the light back on. "You're a coward! Don't you want her to be more of a part of your life and don't you want to be more of a part of hers? You are walking a fine line of your daughter not knowing you and you don't seem to have a problem with that. It wasn't that long ago you were complaining about parenting from afar and missing her. What happened? If she's so easily replaced, it makes me wonder if..."

Andy didn't let me finish the question, "Now just hold on a moment. I haven't replaced anyone and I'm not planning to replace anyone. I do miss her, but, for God's sake woman, I'm happy now and I don't want that fucked with!" Andy was as adamant as I was in his tone.

I backed down in feistiness, but continued, "You're happy and you don't want to include your daughter?"

Andy lowered his voice too. "Well, when you put it like that..." He took a deep breath and said something I'd been wanting to hear for years. "I love you and if Steffi doesn't like you, I don't want to know it. I want her to love you too, but we can agree that's not how things usually go. She's still got some crazy hope that her mother and I will get back together. You and I know that's not happening and you and I know that you have nothing to do with that, but I'm not sure..."

I tried not to jump out of my skin and explode with excitement all over the room when he told me he loved me, but it was hard. I managed to stay on topic, but just barely.

"I understand, but what if she surprises you and is more mature than you think?" I asked, but didn't give him a chance to answer. "I would like to meet her and for her to be a part of this, but I will defer to you. And, Andy..." I stopped, making sure I had his eyes on me when I said it, "I love you, too."

Andy grinned from ear to ear. At forty years old, his teeth were still white and his smile was endearing. I really did love everything about him.

Chapter 20

Dinner at The Brick was scheduled within days of our argument. I was to get a sitter for Gavin and meet Steffi that Wednesday night. Andy was coming from work so we agreed to meet there. No sense in him driving an hour to Avera to pick me up and another to Milledgeville.

I made the trip there, wore heels and make up, and cruised by the college for nostalgia's sake. It looked exactly as I remembered. I could even picture me and Millie and Jay walking to class. I cruised by the building where we all lived. The Jefferson looked exactly the same, too. For a moment, I could see through the walls into the downstairs apartment. A yellow car passed by as I sat at the corner next to the building, not an old Mercedes, but for a moment, I saw me in the passenger's seat next to Andy and we were on our way to work at Port Honor.

After the trips down memory lane, I parked a block away, under a tree with low hanging branches along Hancock Street and had the misfortune of five Palmetto roaches falling in my hair. Sometimes I missed Milledgeville, but at that moment, as I jumped around swatting giant bugs from my hair, I didn't miss a thing.

I walked the block to The Brick and found Andy waiting on me outside. He held the door and, again, I felt like my twenty-year old self. I was excited to be back in town and so excited and nervous to meet Steffi.

"You look great!" Andy said, placing a hand on the small of my back and leading me to table.

The scent of garlic, pizza and wings was strong in the restaurant, but I could still smell Andy. I nuzzled up next to him. "You smell great."

We sat at a table along the right side of the room, past the bar. Steffi was supposed to be there at 6:30 p.m. Her mother was supposed to drop her off. The closer it got to time for her to arrive the more nervous I got. I almost ordered a drink to take the edge off, but knew that would definitely add fuel to the negative fire Andy was sure we were about to start.

By 7:00 p.m. we didn't have to worry about the impression I would make. Steffi was a no show. At 7:05 p.m. Andy tried phoning her mother.

I could hear her through the phone, "Yeah, she's not coming. She got a better offer."

"Excuse me? She got a better offer?" Andy struggled to control the volume of his response.

I diverted my eyes and took in the look of the new space. When I lived there, The Brick was located several store fronts down. It was classier looking now and comparing the new to the memory of the old only slightly distracted me. I could hear everything as if I was the one holding the phone to my ear.

"In case you haven't noticed, she's too old for these 'Daddy-daughter-date-nights. She has friends her own age that she wants to hang out with. You wouldn't know anything about that." Stacey seemed out to hurt him or at the very least to get a rise out of him.

His jaw clinched the entire time she was speaking, but loosened it just enough to respond through gritted teeth, "Couldn't you have called and let me know she wasn't coming?"

"I could have, but that would have been about as much fun as our divorce. If you wanted to know where she is at every moment and wanted to be with her more then you shouldn't have moved out."

"What the fuck?" Andy stood up and stormed out of the restaurant.

I paid for our drinks and followed. I arrived outside just in time to see him fling a tantrum as if he was going to throw his phone down and jump on top of it. I'd never seen him so pissed.

"What happened?" I asked, laying a hand on him to try to get him under control.

"Stacey knows the owner's wife." He threw a hand up, pointing to the sign above the door. "She was here and called and told Stacey I was here with a woman."

"Ah..." I sighed, patting his back. "Let's walk. Okay. You don't want anyone reporting back anything else."

I didn't know Stacey, but I didn't want her friend telling her that he had a full- blown melt down on the streets of Milledgeville.

Andy twisted away and started to walk. "See what I told you? The negativity. I knew it! I know her. As much as Steffi is..."

"A daddy's girl," I finished for him and cautiously took his hand.

"Yeah, her mother has a way of getting her claws in and it takes me months to get her sorted back out. Jesus Christ, if I could beat that woman's DNA out of the child, I would have already."

It took Andy a week to get Steffi to take his calls. It took him three weeks to get another date night in Milledgeville. I didn't say a word about going with him.

"You don't want to come?" he asked the day before.

"Nope. I've got plans of my own," I replied as if I didn't care.

"Really?"

"Yep. Gavin and I are going to the s'mores party at Seven Springs. The who's who of Avera are going to be there." That would sound like a bigger deal to those who didn't know the population of Avera, Georgia was somewhere around three hundred souls.

"Social event of the year, huh, and I'm missing it?"

I nodded. "You sure are, but no worries. Gavin will tell you all about it."

"I bet he will."

Soon after their dates went back to once per week and every other Saturday. I didn't bring up the subject, but one day, Andy did.

243

"Are you okay with the way things are?" he asked as he dried one of the plates from dinner.

Elbow deep in sudsy water and not having a clue what he was talking about, I gave him a curious side eye.

Andy put the plate in the cabinet and sat the dish towel on the counter. He turned to me. "The situation with Steffi. What are your thoughts?"

I kept washing and rinsing. "Ah, that. I really try not to have any thoughts about it." I handed him the next plate.

He took the plate and retrieved the towel. This time I was on the receiving end of the side eye.

"It's the beauty of Benzodiazepine," I replied.

"Ben-what?"

"Benzodiazepine. It's an anti-anxiety medication. It helps me not dwell on unpleasantries and staves off the nightmares."

The conversation that seemed like a nothing took a drastic turn when Andy responded. "My daughter is an unpleasantry that you have to take meds for?"

I pulled the drain on the sink. What was dirty stayed dirty and would have to wait.

"First of all," I began in a tone that came close to matching his, "I have been taking this medication since right after college. I stopped for a while, but you can imagine after the stories of my marriage that I had to go back on it. You know this. Secondly, unpleasantry? That's me describing them, not just her, but her and her mother, nicely. Yes, unpleasant is me putting it nicely."

"All because she wouldn't meet you?" His tone simmered down, but his confusion was real.

I snatched the dishtowel from him. "No, don't be ridiculous!" I snapped him in the leg with the towel and he flinched. "I think they might be two bitch peas in a pod for treating you the way they do. And, if you expect for me to feel any differently toward people who hurt those I love, then you have another think coming."

"Fair enough."

"What are your thoughts on the situation?"

Before Andy could answer, Gavin reminded us that we were not alone. A loud crash came from the living room followed by a blood curdling scream. Gavin wasn't steady on his feet and while toddling around the coffee table he fell, hit his head on the corner and split his right eyebrow open. Both Andy and I jumped into action.

I made it to Gavin first and scooped him up. "Mommy's here. I've got you."

Blood was running all down his little face and it was two shades of red, blood and screaming fright or fury. At the sight of this, Andy winced up, but then all of his color drained. I didn't think much of it because I was trying to sooth Gavin.

"Awe, baby, that's gonna need stitches. Shhhh. Shhhh. Mommy's gonna make it better."

Gavin continued to scream as if he was mortally wounded.

I started toward the kitchen with the intention of cleaning Gavin up, getting a better look at the cut, maybe grabbing some ice, and seeing if we needed to take him to the emergency room. Andy stood frozen, directly in my path to the kitchen and that's when I really noticed his face. He was white as a ghost.

"Shit!" I shrieked over Gavin's whales. "Don't you faint on me!"

With Gavin in one arm, I grabbed Andy with the other. "Put your head between your knees!"

Andy's head swirled, he grabbed for me, and down he went and, clonk, right on the opposite end of the coffee table. Praise Jesus, he lost his grip and I kept my footing. He almost took all three of us down.

"Oh, Jesus!" I said, bouncing Gavin soothingly and trying not to freak out over Andy.

Luckily, Andy popped up like a jack in the box and rubbed his head while stringing together a line of every curse word I'd ever heard, even hyphenating some.

Gavin stopped crying and looked on stunned as I was over the whole situation.

An hour and a half later and both of my boys had stitches in their heads courtesy of the Jefferson County Hospital in Louisville. Anna-Cat was on shift in the ER that night and she had been a sight for sore eyes when we arrived. Neither had a concussion, but one had four stitches and the other had three. It had taken me, Andy and a nurse to hold Gavin down even after the topical numbing cream in order for Anna-Cat to stitch him up. Andy held his feet and the nurse and I held Gavin up top, blocking Andy's view partially in fear that he might faint again.

"It will probably leave a little scar in his eyebrow, but he'll be fine," Anna-Cat said of Gavin and I was so relieved.

"The other one," she mentioned of Andy, "he can't stand the sight of blood so keep that in mind for future reference or I might be seeing y'all again."

"I love you," I smacked Andy on the shoulder as he sat at the end of the bed in the hospital, "but you better not ever scare me like that again!"

"I love you too, but same goes to little one here." Andy gave Gavin a playful tap on his shoulder.

That Sunday while Gavin was napping, Andy invited me to take a walk over to the playground.

"He'll be out for at least an hour. Bring the baby monitor," Andy insisted.

I wasn't sure why he wanted to walk over to the park, but I grabbed the monitor and headed out with him.

On the merry go round at the park in Avera, catty-cornered from the place I'd spent my childhood and where I'd built my own home, Andy Sheppard spun me. I went around and around.

"It's not fun until you fly off or puke!" He repeated something I'd said to him the first time I brought him over here.

246

My middle age equilibrium wasn't what it once was and throwing my head back, closing my eyes, and giggling were the only thing that kept the nausea at bay. I hung on tight because he'd really put his back into spinning me. To me Andy was everything he was when we were in our early twenties and I hadn't allowed myself to see back then. Now I wasn't scared of anything anymore, not even flying off of the old merry-go-round.

I spun and spun and expected to feel the jolt of his weight when he jumped on, but he never did. Finally, I opened my eyes and saw a startling sight.

Andy was on one knee. A hopeful grin as big as any kid you've ever seen on Christmas morning.

I passed by him, going too fast for my mind to register what was going on when I first saw him.

I let go of the bars and covered my mouth with my hands. I was coming around again and I threw down my feet. The momentum of the merry-go-round didn't take kindly to me trying to stop. I'd dug my shoes into the sand and my body went forward continuing with the spin, but my feet didn't. I hadn't flown off the thing or puked since I was ten years old. The flying off or puke line was supposed to be a joke. As I toppled off the seat, it was no longer funny and neither was what Andy appeared to be doing.

Andy scrambled and tried to catch me, but there was no hope. I'd been skipped like a rock and came to rest on my right hip and hands. I didn't have the wherewithal to be embarrassed or concerned about my physical state, I was too busy wondering what he was thinking.

"Um, that's not how I anticipated that going." Andy held out his hand to help me up. "Are you okay?"

I came close to refusing to let him help me, but thought better of it.

"I'm fine. Thanks," I said dusting myself off.

"So..." Andy started and paused. He tried to salvage the moment.

"Don't." I put an index finger to his lips.

Confounded and furrowed brow, Andy asked past my finger, "What? I mean, why?"

"I don't want to marry you." I put it as gently as I knew how.

His face went from confused to defeated in a flash. Andy threw out a heel to the bench on the merry-to-round, stopped it and took a seat, shoulders slumped and head bowed.

"I can't..." he started.

I dropped to my knees between his legs. God only knows what the driver in the car that passed by on the road behind us thought.

I took Andy's face in my hands. He was still the most beautiful man I'd ever seen and I'd never seen his eyes the color they were as tears started to fill them.

"I've loved you since I was twenty years old." I bit my bottom lip and waited for him to look at me. "You were the one. It was always you."

This confession did not help with Andy's confusion at all. "Then what..."

I gently shook my head as I spoke. "I hated being married."

"But, this time it's me and you."

"Right, it's me and you," I nodded in agreement. "I'll wear the ring or you can take it and get your money back. I'll love you with or without it. I'll wear it and love it because it came from you, but I don't need it and I'll never love anyone like I love you."

Andy smiled, but couldn't fully grasp what I was saying. "You won't marry me?"

I scooted in closer between his legs and draped my arms around his neck. "No, but I'll take my chances living in sin with you every single day for the rest of our lives if you will have me."

"Are you asking me to move in with you?" he asked, cocking his head to the side.

We both knew he already lived with me.

I pulled myself up to my full height while still on my knees and ran my hands down Andy's shoulders and around his back. I pulled him onto me and pressed my forehead to his and let the bridge of my nose caress his.

"I'm asking you to share your life with me."

Andy kissed me long and hard and I swooned into him. I was breathless when he finally released me.

"Is that a yes?" I leaned back and locked eyes with him.

"That's a definite yes."

I stood up and took him by the hand. We started walking back toward my house and about halfway there he asked, "Do you even want to see the ring?"

I leaned into him, "If it is what I think it is, I don't want you to give that to me."

"What?" he stopped.

"If that's your grandmother's ring in that box," I explained, "I want you to save that for Steffi. It should be hers, not mine."

"It should have been yours long before Steffi."

"Andy, we may wish to have back time that we lost, but I know you would never take back having her. I know it as sure as I know she is the love of your life and she deserves the ring."

"For a woman apt to burn in Hell for living in sin, you sure are a saint, Cara." Andy had a wry grin. "We both know I'm no saint, so hold out your hand."

Chapter 21

I wore the ring every single day, only taking it off to shower, wash dishes or dig in the rose garden. I even slept with it one. Time passed and living in sin with Andy and Gavin was strangely as close to Heaven on Earth as I'd ever known. Friendsgiving at Seven Springs, Thanksgiving with all of my extended family, seeing Gavin eyes bulge out of his head on Christmas morning when he saw what Santa brought him and, all the while, growing accustomed to sharing a little piece of Andy with those in Milledgeville, life was wasn't just great, it was amazing.

Gavin's third birthday came just days before Easter. He loved monkeys so I went with a Curious George theme. Balloons, cake, ice cream and more of our friends were in attendance than those Gavin had made at the Pleasant Grove Sunday school in which I'd enrolled him.

The party was scheduled for that Saturday afternoon and Andy had to make a quick run to Milledgeville that morning for a lunch date with Steffi. She asked him to come and he never cancelled on her.

"Can you believe he's going to be three?" I asked, tying the knot at the end of the balloon.

Andy blew up another one. "Can you believe he's been with us for over a year?"

"Time has flown by." I added strings and made the bouquet of monkey face balloons.

Andy did everything he could to help me get ready for the party the night before and early that morning.

"I'll be fine. I've got this," I assured him Saturday morning and I meant it. "Go on. You don't want to be late."

Andy kissed me. "I'll be back before you know it."

The party was at 2:00 p.m. and he promised to be back in plenty of time.

Jay and Peter arrived at 1:00 p.m. and Andy wasn't back yet, but I really didn't think much of it. By 1:

45 p.m. the rest of the guests started arriving and he still wasn't home.

"Where's Andy?" Millie asked.

"Oh, he had a lunch date with Steffi in Milledgeville. I'm sure he'll be back any moment," I explained.

At 2:00 p.m. everyone was there, but Andy. I was definitely concerned, but figured he'd just got caught up with Steffi and got a late start back. As we started the party without him, I kept telling myself he'd walk through the door any moment. He'd have some outlandish gift for Gavin, a four-wheeler or a canoe or something else equally ridiculous for a three-year-old.

As usual, Millie and Jay rivaled one another for the biggest gift. Millie gave him a stuffed monkey that was as tall as he was and Jay gave him a plush rocking horse.

"Ho-see!" Gavin clapped and jumped up and down at the sight of the rocking horse. "A ho-see, Mommy!"

"I see, Baby," I said, helping him climb on.

I really hated Andy was missing this, but I tried not to worry. Halfway through the party I couldn't take it anymore.

Jay was the closest person to me when I excused myself to the restroom.

"Can you watch him for a moment?" I asked him.

"Yeah, sure," Jay nodded, pleased as punch to be in charge of Gavin.

I snuck the phone in, shut the lid to the toilet, sat down and dialed Andy's cell phone. It went straight to his voicemail.

"Hey. Where are you? You're missing the party."

For the next thirty minutes, I sat with the phone clutched in my lap. By 3:00 p.m., Andy still hadn't shown up and he hadn't called back either.

At 3:30 all of my friends were cleaning up my house and I was doing my best to help. Gavin was wiped out and down for a nap and I still hadn't heard from Andy.

251

I was worried sick. The party was supposed to go until 4:00, but it dwindled early, folks seeing I wasn't in the party spirit. Gavin opened his presents and was pleasantly distracted.

Millie eased up next to me as I was picking up used Curious George cups from around the living room. "Okay, what's going on? Where's Andy?"

Tears filled my eyes. "I don't know."

I wiped them back and I explained everything.

"You still haven't met her?" Millie asked.

Jay over heard and joined the conversation. "Met who?"

"She hasn't met Andy's daughter," Millie replied.

Two minutes later and the whole room was a buzz about how I hadn't met Steffi and how odd that was.

"Thank God Stella sent regrets that she couldn't make it because I still hadn't gotten over the way she'd behaved to me the morning after Mrs. McDonald's funeral and seeing her gloat over me not meeting Steffi would be icing on the cake. I can't with her."

Jay shook his head. "Don't worry about her. She's been bitter even since the divorce from Travis."

"She's really a sweet person," Millie added. "She's just had a rough patch."

"Five years is a lifestyle, not a rough patch," Jay corrected Millie.

"The point is not that I haven't met his daughter. The point is that he was supposed to be back before the party started and he's not here. I tried calling him and he hasn't picked up," I screamed. "I've called him four fucking times! I'm starting to look like a stalker."

Peter stifled a snicker at the stalker remark and Jay elbowed him.

"He's going to turn up," said Millie.

"Or call," said Jay.

The group dwindled. Anna-Cat had to work the night shift at the ER so she changed into her scrubs in the hall bathroom before heading straight to work. Millie had to get home and make sure George-Ann fully understood what grounded meant. Jay and Peter had a room at Seven Springs and dinner plans there. Jay said they would stay with me until Andy got home, but not feeling a part of the core club, Peter left to pick up dinner.

At 4:15, Peter returned from picking up dinner at the inn, but I didn't feel like eating. He and Jay were starving as they hadn't eaten anything all day except the snacks at the party, but I wasn't hungry yet. I wasn't sure when I would be hungry again if I didn't hear from Andy.

"Do you know how to reach Steffi or her mother?" Jay looked to me as he cut his filet.

"No." I shook my head. "We settled in to living our lives here and I kind of pretended they didn't really exist."

"Okay, well, if he doesn't get here by 5:00, I'll call and get Stacey's number from Stella."

I nodded.

Peter took my hand. "I'm sure there's a perfectly good reason why he's not back. It's going to be okay."

The phone rang just after Peter got back. I snatched it up and answered, "Andy?"

It was Anna-Cat, "Is Jay still there?"

"Yes." I know I sounded put out.

"Can I speak to him?"

"Sure."

I passed the phone to Jay and within two seconds his face completely shifted and he handed Gavin to Peter. "Okay. We're on our way."

"What's wrong?" I asked before he'd even fully hung up the phone.

Jay didn't answer me directly. He spoke to Peter. "Can you stay here with him?"

Jay was already on his feet and looking for his keys as Peter agreed. "Cara, we've got to go. There's been an accident and I'll explain in the car."

My heart sank and my head swam. It just swam. "An accident?" The question raced through my mind like foreign words, but I don't know whether it exited my lips or not. I probably would have vomited had Jay not grabbed me by the hand and took me to his car.

Jay drove and we raced down Clarks Mill Road, the quickest route from Avera to Louisville. I'm sure he told me everything that Anna-Cat said, but it really sounded like he was yelling from the far end of a tunnel, a very long tunnel. I don't have a clue what he said, but it was bad. All of it was just plain bad. In fact, he could have stopped and just said, "Its bad. Super fucking bad," with no further details. The details didn't matter, not the why, not the how.

All the way to the hospital I twisted the ring on my finger. I hadn't taken it off since Andy gave it to me. All of a sudden it occurred to me, they don't take folks to Louisville in a trauma situation unless they can't get them stable enough to take them anywhere else.

We'd just crossed the bridge over the actual Clarks Mill Pond for which the road was named when Jay's phone rang.

"It's Anna-Cat," he said and this time I actually heard him clearly.

Jay started slowing the car. "She said they are life flighting him to Doctor's Hospital in Augusta."

"The burn unit?"

"She didn't say, but she said she's going to fly with him and we should head there."

One hand on the wheel, Jay started to turn into the next driveway.

"No, stay straight!" I stopped him.

Worried as I was, I knew the quicker way to Augusta than going back toward Avera was to make a left just ahead on Mennonite Church Road and link up with US 1 between Wrens and Louisville. Highway 1 would take us straight into Augusta.

When Anna-Cat hung up, Jay reached over and took my hand. He squeezed as he spoke. "She said they've got him stable enough to make the flight so that's something."

I sniffled and nodded. "I can't lose him."

We hadn't long turned on to Highway 1 toward Wrens and passed through what they called Captain's Curve when the helicopter flew over us. Red and white with one of those lines down it like on a heart monitor and flying at a rate faster than the 80 miles per hour Jay was pushing in his Acura.

"I wish we could catch it," I paused, fighting to find the words and knowing exactly what I wanted to say. "I want to see him when lands. I want him to know I'm there."

"I know, but..." Jay just trailed off.

I prayed as the helicopter faded into a little dot in the sky before us. It had disappeared completely as we passed the Wrens city limits sign.

Jay slowed just enough to keep us from looking like we were already running from the cops, but we got caught by the red light in the center of town. I could tell by the way Jay looked both ways, he contemplated running it. Instead, he noticed Millie's office building. He dialed her cell while we waited for the light to change.

"Hey. I'm on my way to Augusta with Cara." He proceeded to give her the facts as he knew them. "Andy was in an accident and..."

The tight quarters of the car allowed for me to hear both ends of the conversation.

"Peter called me and said you were on your way to Louisville."

"He's being flown to Doctor's Hospital as we speak."

"I'll meet you there."

"Millie, say some prayers, okay?" Jay asked her before they hung up.

I think I prayed all the way to the hospital in Augusta. By the time we arrived, the helicopter had come and gone so we had to assume Andy was there. Jay dropped me off at the front door and, while he parked the car, I went straight to the front desk and asked if a patient named Andy Sheppard had been admitted.

"Are you a family member?" the nurse at the front desk asked.

I shook my head. I had enough thought to lay my hand on the counter and flash the ring. "I'm his fiancé."

She pecked at the keys. "I can't find him. Are you sure he was admitted here?"

"He was being life flighted here from Jefferson County," I answered.

"Even if he was here, HIPPA regulations prevent me from giving you any information since you are not family." She smiled politely in that helpless way people do when they are just following the rules.

Jay, likely having heard the tail end of the conversation, approached the desk and waited like he was in line. I looked back at him wondering what was wrong with him.

"Hi, excuse me," he said as if he didn't know me and stepped past as if he was his turn.

I stepped to the side, out of his way.

He then greeted the nurse the same way. "Hi, I hate to bother you, but could you page Dr. Anna-Catherine Calloway?" He eased in and propped on the counter, looked at her name tag. "Tallulah, like after the gorge? Pretty name. Jay Calloway, he stuck out his hand."

Completely charmed, she actually took his hand.

"My sister's late for our lunch date. Ugh, doctors." He rolled his eyes. "I'm sure I'm not telling you anything new, but complete lack of consideration for anyone else's time. She's always late."

He leaned closer. "To tell the truth, I think she just likes for me to have to ask for her by her whole doctor name and all." He rolled his eyes and sighed, exhaustedly. "Pretentious much?"

Tallulah laughed and picked up the phone. Two seconds later, "Paging Dr. Anna-Catherine Calloway to the front desk. Dr. Calloway, please."

Taking her hand again, he kissed the back of it. "As far as I am concerned, you are the life saver."

She actually giggled and blushed. She looked old enough to be not quite his mother's age, but close to retirement.

I'd never seen Jay play it straight and shamelessly flirt like that before. Under other circumstances, I'm sure I would have laughed out loud.

"I'll just wait over there," he nodded toward a corner by the front door.

"Okay, sweetie." She was all eye lashes and dimples.

I sat right in front row of the waiting area facing the desk so she could see me. Here I've just told her my fiancé had been life flighted there and she wouldn't help me, but she probably creamed her shorts over the gay dude flirting with her. I was disgusted. I thought about reporting her when all of this was behind us, but decided against it. Perhaps I should be thanking her for taking my mind off of worrying about Andy for just a couple of seconds.

Anna-Cat appeared from a set of double doors. Clad in bloodied scrubs, she approached Jay. I felt that sinking sick feeling at the sight of the blood on her, no doubt Andy's blood.

Jay gave me a wait signal with his hand. I stayed put, but not because I wanted to. I really wanted to jump up and run to her, hysterically begging for her to tell me Andy was going to be okay.

Jay and Anna-Cat had a bit of a pow-wow before heading back toward the double doors. Discretely, Jay motioned again behind his back. He signaled me to follow and I did. Just past the doors, I found them waiting for me.

"He's in surgery now. I'm going to take you up to a waiting room for the ICU patients." Initially Anna-Cat spoke to both of us, but now she turned her attention

257

directly toward me. She took my hands before telling me, "It's not good, but if he makes it through this surgery..."

"Oh my God, if he makes it?" My hands went to my mouth and my knees buckled.

Jay caught me around my waist and saved me from becoming a heap on the floor. "He's going to be okay."

I looked to Anna-Cat for confirmation. Frowning, she shook her head side to side. "I can't make you any promises. It's in God's hands."

"How long do you think it will be before we know something?" Jay asked, still keeping a hold on me and propping me up.

"That depends on how much damage they find when they get in there and how he responds," Anna-Cat explained. "I did what I could and Dr. Lenon at Louisville did what he could, we got him this far, Cara, but by the grace of God."

Anna-Cat led us to a private waiting room on the third floor. They each took a seat beside me and held my hand. We sat there in silence, with the exception of my sniffles. I finally lost it and started to cry uncontrollably.

When I finally composed myself, I said, "I know you aren't supposed to tell me because of hippo regulations or something..."

"HIPPA regulations," Jay corrected me.

"Screw HIPPA," Anna-Cat said on the down low. "What do you want to know?"

"What happened?" I looked at her, blurry eyed through tears.

Chapter 22

There's a city named LaGrange in Georgia. It has a college and it's known for its antebellum homes. There's another speck on the map, not even really worthy of a dot, named Grange. Grange is about ten miles from Avera. It is basically a lone intersection where the four lane, Highway 88, crosses Highway 171, also known as Grange Road, between Sandersville and Wrens. It is along the route Andy took to and from Milledgeville.

Caution lights flash yellow and a stop lights flash red. There was only a caution light in each direction for Highway 88 and a stop light for Highway 171 at Grange. A caution light means slow down, but no one slows down for the caution light at Grange. I've traveled it many times and it's what I expect the Autobon to be like.

According to Anna-Cat, "Andy was running at least seventy miles per hour when one of the logging trucks crossing 88 on Grange Road didn't stop and pulled out in front of him."

Anna-Cat went on to tell that the driver said he didn't usually haul on Saturdays and he was new to the area. He was in a hurry to get home and thought it was a four-way stop. He saw Andy coming but thought Andy was going to stop. By the time he realized Andy wasn't stopping, and, even though he'd only just pulled out, he had the weight of the whole truck and the cargo of logs that pushed him forward as he braked.

"From what the EMTs said, the man was absolutely frantic and so apologetic at the scene. When they got there, they found the man holding Andy's hand, screaming for them to hurry and help him," Anna-Cat further detailed.

As Anna-Cat painted a picture the accident, tears rolled down my face.

"It took them a while to get him out of the truck and they didn't think he was going to make it from the scene." Anna-Cat then delivered a real blow that let us

259

know just how serious things were. "From what I gather, there's nothing left of the truck and the EMTs thought they were taking him to Louisville for the formality of having him pronounced."

She held back from saying, "pronounced dead," but we understood.

I gasped and threw my hands over my mouth. Again, Jay held onto me for support.

"Hey," Anna-Cat reached out and put her hands on my knees. "He's a fighter. By the time they got him to Louisville, he was rallying."

I was still crying and Anna-Cat and Jay were trying to comfort me when Jay's cell phone rang. He glanced at it.

"Millie," he informed us before answering and giving her instructions of where to find us in the hospital.

After Millie arrived, Anna-Cat explained, "One of the curious things is that Andy didn't have his wallet. The trucker, who mind you was uninjured thank God, found his cell phone. Until he arrived at the hospital, he was John Doe."

"How did they figure out who he was?" asked Millie.

"Luckily, his cellphone wasn't locked with a passcode or anything so they started by calling the last person he'd called," Anna-Cat shrugged.

"Oh my God," I shook my head. "They probably called his daughter Steffi."

"Right." Anna-Cat appeared about as displeased with the delivery of that news as she had been with the rest of the information she had shared.

"You didn't recognize him and let them know who he was?" Jay asked.

Anna-Cat winced at the question. "No. That's another thing. If he makes it through the surgery, you should prepare yourself for what he's going to look like."

She then went on to describe his actual injuries. "Although a seatbelt and airbag are meant for saving lives, there's only so much they can do with an impact at that speed. The locking up of the seatbelt caused internal injuries, the most serious being a laceration to his right kidney and the bottom portion of his right lung. The airbag caught his face and prevented further torso injuries with the steering wheel, but when the front end of the truck collapsed away as they are now designed to do, the cab of the truck met the steel portion of the trailer that held the logs. It stopped and didn't sheer into the cab, but the impact caused his head to jolt backward into the headrest. Headrests are not designed to take that impact. Picture not being hit with a baseball bat, but hit with a bat that was wrapped in a pool noodle except the pool noodle bat is still being swung by a major league player. The noodle takes some impact, but it's still a bat at a high rate of speed. That's what we call a closed head injury leading to a traumatic brain injury. There's bleeding and swelling on his brain and that's why they are doing surgery. They are going to remove a portion of his skull so they can drain off some of the blood and allow for the swelling. It sounds so bad, but it is a good thing. All the same, he will not be recognizable and you should prepare yourself."

That was a lot for us to take in, but all three of us, Millie, Jay and myself, looked at Anna-Cat in complete awe and shock. After a few minutes to answer questions and allow us to process, Anna-Cat excused herself to go and see if there was any news on how the surgery was progressing.

"You should also prepare yourself for Steffi and her mother to arrive here at any time," Millie said, supposing.

"Oh God!" The day just kept getting worse. "We're not married." I busted in to tears again. "He proposed and I refused." I looked side to side at Millie and Jay, not knowing what I was searching for in them, some answer as to what I would do. "Steffi's his next of kin and she's a minor so her mother gets the say as to his treatments? Oh shit! What have I done?"

261

I thought I was going to hyperventilate. I couldn't catch my breath. I huffed and huffed and Jay fanned me.

"Put your head between your knees!" Millie insisted.

Both of them had an arm around my back and we all three doubled over together. My heart was beating so fast and I couldn't breathe.

"His dad's still alive right?" Millie asked.

I shook my head feverishly as I huffed and puffed and tried to get a hold of myself with no luck.

"Then that makes his dad his next of kin since he and Stacey are divorced and Steffi is a minor. If Steffi was an adult, then it would be her."

That made me feel slightly better.

"Do you have his dad's number?" Jay asked.

I shook my head in the negative, still bent over and with my hair sweeping the floor.

Jay had a second question. "Have you ever met him?"

I shook my head again. "No."

"But you've met his brother," Millie said, sitting up.

I nodded. "Yes." I felt the slightest triumph. "I do have his number." I took a deep breath and worked my way back to an upright position.

Jay sat up too. "We should probably let them know anyway. I doubt with everything going on they dug deeper in Andy's phone and called anyone else." Jay held out his hand for my phone. "I'll make the call."

"No," Millie reached for my phone as I took it out of my purse. "I knew his brother in college. I'll make the call."

They both agreed I was in no condition to call.

"But I can dial the number from my contacts." I wiped back tears. It then occurred to me to remind Millie, "You know, his brother may not have his dad's number. The brother that I know is from his mother's second marriage."

Millie's hand remained outstretched for the phone. "We'll have to try." Millie took the phone and stepped into the hall leaving me along with Jay.

"I'm sure he's going to come through the surgery fine and he'll be his fine-looking self again before you know it." Jay smiled and tried to be encouraging.

Millie returned in about five minutes. "He's going to go get Andy's father and head this way."

I caught Millie by the hand and gave it a squeeze. "Thank you so much!" I looked from her to Jay. "I don't know what I would do without you."

Anna-Cat returned.

"Anything?" I asked, batting back more tears.

"No, but that's a good thing. They're still working on him so..." Anna-Cat tapered off as the looks on our faces confirmed our understanding. If he died on the table, they wouldn't be working on him still so he was alive.

We all sat together for a while in silence, each of us likely saying our own prayers for Andy. I certainly knew I was saying mine.

Time seemed to drag on forever and at some point Jay then excused himself to the hallway and called Peter to check in. He returned with news that Gabe and Gabby had dropped by my house to help with Gavin.

"It took the three of them taking turns rocking, but they finally got him down for the night. Apparently, he screamed for Mommy for a solid half hour."

I'd forgotten how late it was. It was going on 10:00 p.m. and according to Anna-Cat this was just the beginning of the waiting period.

The four of us still had the waiting room to ourselves. I'd snuggled into the corner of one of the couches and Millie sat at the other end. She'd pulled my legs up over hers and was rubbing my calves. Under normal circumstances, I don't think I would have let her sit there and rub my legs, but in this moment of wishing my mother was there and, knowing this was something my mother would do, I didn't protest.

263

Jay sat on the floor with his head leaned over, resting on the couch and I had a hand in his hair. It was so soft and I could smell his shampoo through my stuffiness. Maybe it was just because he was a man and had that man smell, a similar shampoo or maybe a similar cologne, but he made me think of Andy. The only thing they really had in common was the fact that, second only to my grandfather, they were the best men I'd ever known.

Anna-Cat was seated in a single chair by the entryway to the room. Although she had privileges and although she'd flown with Andy, Anna-Cat wasn't on shift at this hospital. She was no surgeon. She was a general practitioner. She did rotations in the ER at the Jefferson County Hospital, a tiny spot with little more action in a night than a broken bone and the occasional car wreck. Patients with traumatic injuries didn't really go to Louisville other than to be pronounced dead so a general practitioner in the ER wasn't a far stretch. Anna-Cat sat there in the waiting room as useless as the rest of us. She was still in her scrubs with Andy's blood on her which made it both hard for me to look at her and hard to look away.

Anna-Cat was the first one to her feet when a tall dark-haired girl entered the room followed by a woman of equal height. They were amazons and I immediately knew who they were.

Having just noticed me, the girl said over her shoulder to her mother, "What is she doing here?"

The woman, Stacey, glared at me. "I don't know."

Millie and Jay got to their feet, both stepping to each other's shoulder and blocking me. I stood just out of courtesy, one that clearly was not going to be reciprocated.

Anna-Cat extended her hand to the woman. "Hi. I'm Dr. Calloway."

It was interesting to hear Anna-Cat introduce herself so formally. It was interesting to see her become the point man in our group which was usually Millie's role.

With big sunglasses pushed on her head well past sundown, the woman took her sweet time shifting her coat and oversized purse from her right to her left hand. She looked Anna-Cat up and down, purposefully looking unimpressed, before extending her hand.

"I'm Mrs. Sheppard. We were told this was a private room for family," she held her head up and looked down her nose at Anna-Cat which was a feat since she and Anna-Cat were the same height, 5'10" each.

"Right," Anna-Cat gestured to the other couch and stepped aside.

"Mom," the girl motioned with her eyes between Millie and Jay to me.

"Private," the woman repeated a little more sternly to Anna-Cat.

Anna-Cat matched her tone and gestured to the couch again. "Exactly."

Neither Jay nor Millie moved an inch.

"Perhaps I should speak with someone at the nurse's station," the woman threatened.

"Perhaps you should. In fact, I'll show you where it is and introduce you to everyone," Anna-Cat offered and I thought how professional she sounded while challenging this woman to a duel of sorts.

Andy's ex-wife looked the part of a rich bitch, an extra-large Coach bag, Oakleys the size of something Jackie Onassis would have worn, each lens the size of the palm of my hand, cheetah print lettering on monogramed duck boots and matching cream colored cashmere sweater with the blue and navy Ralph Lauren logo tag on it. She looked real put together, but according to Andy, he'd been keeping her afloat with the child support he paid and taking over the mortgage payment on the house too just to keep them from losing the equity and keeping Steffi's life stable. In other words, she didn't have two cents of her own to rub together.

Steffi was everything that Andy had described. She was tall and filled out beyond most girls her age. In his

265

description, he watered down just how much like her mother she really was. It wasn't that she looked so much like her mother. From the glimpses I was getting just then, she appeared to me a mix of the both of them as far as looks, but her mannerisms and attitude were what appeared to be her mother made over.

Gathering she was defeated, Stacey took her daughter's hand and brushed past Anna-Cat and took a seat on the couch she'd been offered. She brushed off the couch, as if the swipe of her hand would clear any germs and then sat down

"Mom!" Steffi protested, refusing to sit as long as I was still there.

"Steffi, we're just going to have to endure."

"Endure," Jay scoffed and I smacked him on the shoulder.

Millie put on a forced smile and turned to them. "Sweetie," Millie said, "perhaps we should go ahead and clear the air because my friend here isn't going anywhere."

"Don't speak to my daughter," the woman stood and towered over Millie.

"Forgive me. I should have introduced myself." Millie smiled even more sweetly, completely fake. "I'm Attorney Amelia Anderson Hewitt, folks call me Millie. I'm sure you've heard of me. Andy and I have been friends since..." Millie appeared to ponder the length of time before snapping it out, "since before you were," she shifted her eyes at Steffi, "married. Now Dr. Calloway, a personal friend of the family..."

"Ha," Stacey scoffed, "a personal friend of the family? I've only just met the woman."

"Not your family," Millie continued very cordially,

Stacey threw up her hands, completely shocked, but Millie didn't stop.

"Andy's current family, that would be all of us you see here," she waved a hand toward all of us, "and some who couldn't make it and some who are on their way. So, as I was saying, Dr. Calloway, a personal friend of the family, will be glad to answer any questions you have about Andy's care and condition."

"Thanks," Stacey said tersely and stared to sit again.

Millie wasn't done. "I also wanted to let you know that his next of kin is on his way."

"Next of kin?" Stacey all but shrieked. "We," she emphasized, "are his next of kin."

"Um, no, not according to the Georgia Statutes." Millie paused and then apologized to Steffi, "I'm sorry, Miss?"

"Stephanie," she answered cautiously, like she didn't know if that was the right answer, but it was her name.

"Stephanie, since you are a minor, the laws of Georgia do not see you as his next of kin when it comes to the right to make medical decisions and govern your father's finances should there be a need."

"Of course, she isn't. That's my role as her guardian," Stacey interjected triumphantly, thinking she was correcting Millie.

"Well, that would be the case, if you were still married." Millie squinched her nose, that put-on air of sorry, not sorry.

The three of us watched, as amazed by Millie and her audacity as ever. She might have been a tiny framed woman, but she walked tall and carried a big stick of personality and legalese that she knew how to use. Watching her was better than any episode of Matlock, Perry Mason or Ally McBeal. Had we been there under any other circumstances, I would have cheered for her.

Millie clarified further, "In the eyes of the law, Andy's father is seen as his next of kin."

This was the second time Stacey's face dropped with defeat. She entered the room as if she was entitled to do something about our presence, but between Millie and Anna-Cat, she'd been set straight. She was not going to be the one in control here and we were not going anywhere.

267

Jay had lingered by my side the entire time. He was in just as much of a protective mode as Millie and Anna-Cat were. While Millie and Anna-Cat were interacting with Stacey, Jay took a moment to acknowledge Steffi. He managed to do it in a disarming way and managed to introduce me.

"Hi, my name is Jay and this is Cara. We've known your dad since we were in college. We're all praying he's going to be fine." Jay reached out and stroked her shoulder and she didn't back away. "I'm sure people tell you all the time, but you look so much like him. If you need anything tonight, you just let one of us know and we'll go get it."

She looked toward me and tried to smile.

"He left his wallet at the restaurant when we had lunch." It seemed odd considering how she acted when they first walked in, but she handed it to me. "One of my friend's older sisters works there and brought it to me."

I took it and thanked her.

"Don't thank me. His driver's license is in there and it says he's an organ doner. If it comes to it, I don't want my mom to have to make that decision, but you can live with it since he was on his way back to you when it happened."

"Wow," I said, shaking my head in disappointment at how she was nothing like Andy.

Jay intervened and stopped me from saying anything further. He whispered as she walked away, "Remember she's a child."

"A child that needs a spanking," I said under my breath.

Steffi took a seat on the couch that had been offered by Anna-Cat and her mother joined her shortly thereafter. Jay, Anna-Cat, Millie and I returned to our spots and we all waited.

It was nothing short of the wee hours of the morning when I awoke to the commotion in the room. Blurry eyed from crying, not from haven fallen asleep, I checked my watch. It was only fifteen minutes past the last time I'd checked. 4:18 a.m. I rubbed at my face and prepared myself for the news, thinking the older gentleman speaking with Anna-Cat and Millie was the surgeon. I thought he'd come to tell us about Andy. Instead, I heard a groggy Steffi rise from her seat and greet her grandfather.

Steffi cut between Millie and Anna-Cat and flung her arms around the silver fox version of her father. She was as tall as he was, but her body language was lanky and as immature as a five-year-old. Again, she was just as Andy had described.

Steffi broke from the hug, took him by the hand and attempted to lead him to her mother who sat waiting in the corner. Stacey appeared half gloating as he hadn't noticed me and half scared that he would. Steffi also strung together some version of what she'd heard of Andy's condition as if he hadn't heard that much before making the trip all the way to Augusta from Milledgeville. She showed more eagerness to gossip than concern for what was going on with her father.

Gently, her grandfather pulled away. "Why don't you leave all that to the adults, Sugga? And, you just go say some more prayers for your Daddy. You've been praying for him, haven't you?"

She acted like a five-year-old and he treated her like one, too.

Alex arrived just in time to introduce me and further thwarted any interaction with Mr. Sheppard and Stacey. Alex corralled Mr. Sheppard toward me as I stood up and my friends gathered around me.

"But, Granddaddy?" Steffi whined.

"Sugga, let the grown folks talk," he further dismissed her and the look on her face was priceless.

"This is Cara," Alex said

"Oh my goodness! I have heard so much about you!" The next thing I knew I was enveloped in a bear hug. Releasing me, he took a step back and said, "Don't you worry. We Sheppards are made of stern stuff. My boy's gonna be just fine and he's not gonna let you get away a second time."

Stacey cleared her throat, making her presence known, but Mr. Sheppard only gave her a side eye.

He lowered his voice as if sharing a secret, "It's a miracle he stayed with her as long as he did."

"He stayed for his daughter and that's a commendable thing to do," I smiled, holding back more tears.

"He was miserable and, well, no sense dwelling on that. It is what it is. He's not miserable anymore and how's that new grandson of mine? I've begged Andy to bring him to see me, but..." He cut his eyes toward Stacey and Steffi.

Alex added, "He's letting them have Milledgeville."

"And the house and everything else from the way it sounds," Millie interjected. "He should have had me do the divorce. I'd have got him set up a little better than whomever he used."

"Millie," I said softly, "his attorney did just what Andy wanted."

Mr. Sheppard smiled flatly, "He was trying to do better by his child than I did for him. I wish I'd been half the father he was."

"It's not too late," I took his hand and assured him. "I mean..."

"He's gonna be okay," Jay was quick to say.

"Hold that thought." Anna-Cat answered her cell phone. "Okay, I'm on my way," she said to the caller before turning back to all of us. "He's out of surgery. I'll be right back."

We all waited, testing just how long we could collectively hold our breaths.

Anna-Cat returned with the surgeon. He was a tiny man about the size of Millie in height and width. All of us made a move to greet him and hear what he had to say.

"This is Dr. Jude Williams. I could tell you he's an expert in neurology, but that would just make him blush some more. He was one of my favorite professors in medical school," Anna-Cat described before giving him the floor.

"I don't usually work on call anymore, but Dr. Calloway here called and reminded me that I had told my students if they ever needed anything to call so here I am. Now, I won't go into the graphic details, but Mr. Sheppard came through surgery like a champ. The next twenty-four hours will be critical, but if he makes it through those," he scrubbed at his head, "well, each hour thereafter makes things look more promising."

"So, he's going to be okay?" Steffi finally sounded genuinely concerned.

"I cannot say for sure, young lady, but he's on the right path at this moment," he answered.

"I have so many questions, but I just want to say thank you. Thank you so much!" I threw my arms around him and held on. "Thank you! Thank you! Thank you!"

"I'm not God. I'm just doing what I can to help," he said bashfully, giving me an awkward pat on my back as if he didn't know what to do when being hugged.

When I finally let go of Dr. Williams, I asked, "Can I see him?"

"He's going to be in recovery for a little while longer and then they are moving him to ICU. There are some strict regulations that Dr. Calloway will fill you in on. Traumatic brain injury patients cannot have any stimulation hence the restrictions."

Andy's father stepped forward. His face was streaked with tears of relief. He extended a shaky hand to Dr. Williams. "I can't thank you enough for what you've done for my son."

"It's nothing you wouldn't have done for mine if you could, right?" He clasped his hand over Mr. Sheppard's.

Dr. Williams was quite possibly the most-humble doctor I'd ever met. Anna-Cat was one of us and until tonight, I rarely saw her in doctor mode, but I knew she wore her education and position with a sense of pride no one could touch. Dr. Williams made it seem like what he had done or what he could do was nothing. He was just a guy helping another guy, like changing a tire on the side of the road for a stranger.

An hour later, and after Stacey required yet another reminder that she was not his wife anymore and Steffi was too young to see her father like this, Andy's father insisted on it being me that was allowed to go back to see Andy.

Anna-Cat escorted us to the nurse's desk in the ICU. It was in the center of a group of eight rooms, each had walls made of glass so the patients had an air of privacy, but the nurses could see them at all times and from all angles. Six of the rooms were occupied and Andy's name was written in Sharpie on a white board just outside of the door in the middle.

As we approached, I got a better view, but still couldn't see him.

"He looks... like... a... mummy," Mr. Sheppard said with fear quaking in his voice.

He had a point. There was white everywhere. White sheets and blanket and white wrapping all around his head so much so that we couldn't see his face from that distance.

"But it's him and he's in there, somewhere and he's going to come back to me." I straightened my back and steeled my nerves. I was going in there and telling him he couldn't leave me. I wouldn't allow it.

I inched the door open, making not one sound at all. I crept cautiously even though I knew I only had three minutes with him. The rules had been explained to me. Don't talk above a whisper. Don't touch anything. Don't turn on a light. Don't force him to think. Don't give into the shock of seeing him like this. Don't do all of this in three minutes. Yes, there was an actual timer and someone keeping that timer.

The closer I came, the more I realized how thankful I was for Anna-Cat and how she'd prepared me for what I was seeing. It didn't look like Andy laying there at all. It didn't look like anyone. He was so swollen. His head was wrapped in white bandages and, his face was exposed, but distorted beyond any recognition. In fact, his head looked about three times the size of normal, like a basketball in color and in size. He didn't really look like a human at all. I forced myself to keep in mind that my Andy, my man, was in there. What I felt for him wasn't about his looks, but Anna-Cat had promised that if he made it through the swelling would go away and he stood a good chance of looking like himself again.

There was a stool by the bed and I sat down, took Andy's hand, which was also double its normal size, and got on with what I'd come to say.

"I marry you. I marry you. I marry you," I said quoting my favorite movie.

I laid my head down on top of his hand, trying not to cry and failing miserably. "I'm sorry it took this for me to figure it out, but I want more than anything to be your wife. I love you more than you could ever know. You are my port in the storm, my true north, the place I'll always return to, my everything. It's always been you. Always. You know this." I sniffled and sucked back. "I can't do this without you. You can't leave me now. And, yes, I am that selfish. I want you for me, for Gavin, for your father, for Steffi."

"Yes, for Steffi," I continued. "She needs you in her life so badly. She needs your goodness and I don't know what will become of her without you. I know I shouldn't ask you for anything right now, but I'm asking, I'm begging you to come back to her and finish raising her. Make her a better person. Make her a person like you. Please come back to us."

His hand twitched beneath my forehead and I took it as a good sign. He'd heard me just as my three minutes expired and a nurse pointed to her watch on the other side of the glass door.

I crept out of the door as quietly as I'd come in, but as soon as the door shut behind me, I whisper screamed in Mr. Sheppard's ear as I jumped in his arms, "He moved his hand! He heard me! He's still in there!"

Anna-Cat later dashed my excitement. She explained, "Andy's in a medically induced coma so his brain can rest. There's no way he moved his hand. Not on purpose. It was probably just a muscle relaxing or something. I'm sorry, Cara."

I didn't care what she said. I knew he moved for me.

"He's in good hands here so I'm gonna head home so I can get back over here to meet with his doctors tomorrow. I plan on being the point person for you all, if that' okay?" Anna-Cat looked to Mr. Sheppard.

"Dr. Calloway, we call her Anna-Cat, is one of my best friends. She has a general practice in Wrens, one of the bigger towns in our county, and she works in the ER at our local hospital. She just happened to come on shift after Andy was brought in and flew on the helicopter with him here," I explained and Mr. Sheppard nodded along as I spoke.

"That's good enough for me," he agreed.

The three of us started back toward the waiting room. Mr. Sheppard held out his hand and offered for us to walk ahead. Anna-Cat hooked her arm in mine.

"It just occurred to me that I don't have a car here," she kind of laughed at herself.

"I've got to say here. I can't leave him, but we can get Jay or Mille to take you home."

Anna-Cat leaned in a little closer. "Someone needs to stay with you."

Chapter 23

It was nothing short of a miracle that Andy survived the night, but he did.

Little rest was had by anyone. Jay took Anna-Cat home and he went back to my house with the understanding that he would take care of Gavin as long as I needed him. Peter's job wasn't as flexible so he had to get back to Atlanta.

Millie stayed with me. She explained to Andy's dad that he needed to stay for the time being for any medical decision making, but she could have something drawn up to appoint me as Andy's medical power of attorney if he wanted. Mr. Sheppard wanted.

Mr. Sheppard discussed Millie's plan with Alex and they agreed.

"I think that's what Andy would want," Alex said.

Even though it was Sunday, Millie left to call her secretary and get the documents drawn up.

"What he would want? How would you know?" Stacey had been listening to our conversation and piped up just as Millie was out of earshot. "You never darkened our door when we were married, but suddenly you're an expert on him?"

"I didn't darken your door because I didn't want to make my brother's life worse since you never liked me and I didn't like you." Alex was just as direct as Stacey had been. "And, for your information, we had lunch twice a week while you were married. Tuesdays at Café South and Wednesdays at Brewers. When those closed, Tuesdays we started eating Chick-Fil-A and Thursdays we had burgers at Longhorns. He likes his medium rare with Texas Taters and sweet tea mixed with lemonade. That's his drink of choice, not whiskey sours or Sex on the Beach or vodka cranberries in 32 ounce cups from Racetrack while at his daughter's soccer games on Saturday mornings like you. So, yeah, I'm sort of an expert on my brother."

The entire time Alex spoke, Mr. Sheppard smiled, clearly enjoying the show.

"Look," I said.

"Who said you could talk?" she snapped at me.

"Your claws are showing," Mr. Sheppard chastised Stacey.

"As I was saying, there's no need for all of us to stay. I mentioned before that Dr. Calloway is a family friend. Her parents have a house about ten minutes from here. She called and said her mother would be glad to have any of us over who would like to get cleaned up, take a nap, and get something to eat."

"I'm not leaving!" Stacey barked.

"You really are a piece of work." Alex shook his head. "You know, one word and we can have you removed. You're not family anymore."

I put a hand on Alex's arm, calming him, but spoke to Stacey. "Perhaps you could think of your daughter."

Mr. Sheppard had sent Steffi to the vending machines with a five-dollar bill while we had our discussion. She'd be back at any moment.

"I AM thinking of my daughter," she said through her clinched jaw. "I am protecting her inheritance."

I didn't know until that moment that my hand had a mind of its own, but it did. In a split second, without thought at all, I found myself on the other side of having slapped that woman.

She screamed, completely stunned and holding the left side of her face. "You'll regret that."

"Say something else!" I dared her, coming to terms with what I'd just done.

"I didn't see a thing," Alex and Mr. Sheppard said in unison.

"You're just here in case he dies you can cash in? Get out! If your daughter wants to stay, she will stay under the care of her uncle or her grandfather, but you will leave of your own accord or I will have you physically removed. Don't try me!"

I caught my breath, but I wasn't done. She started to speak and I cut her off. "Just about the only thing in the world that I care about is laying in that hospital bed so I've got nothing to lose. Can you say the same?"

Alex meant what he said about having Stacey removed and she knew it. Also, I think she found the unity we had in our distain for her more than she wanted to deal with. After Steffi returned with her treasure trove from the vending machines, at which she must have spent the entire five dollars, Stacey told her, "Get your things. We're leaving."

They argued. Steffi wanted to stay. "I want to be here to see Daddy when he wakes up."

Stacey got sharp with her and we all thought she was about to snap and tell Steffi that her father wasn't going to wake up. She didn't, but she didn't tell Steffi we'd thrown her out either. Aiming to preserve the illusion of control and superiority, Stacey held her head high and told Steffi, "I'm leaving and you are coming with me. I'm not driving all the way back down here when you change your mind and want to come home."

Mr. Sheppard stepped forward and meekly interjected, "I'll take you home whenever you get ready."

"Thank you," Steffi said and with an air of her real age and stature, she then said to her mother, "I'm staying with Granddaddy."

Snatching up her purse and throwing her coat over her shoulders, Stacey flipped a hand, dismissing her daughter and calmly departed with the words, "She's yours now."

Millie passed Stacey on her way back and looked to us three remaining adults for confirmation. "She's leaving?"

We nodded in unison.

"Not just going to get coffee or something and coming back?" She knew as well as we did that Stacey leaving was almost too good to be true.

"She wasn't feeling well," Steffi said, covering for her mother.

Perhaps Steffi got more of Andy than just her looks after all.

Anna-Cat came back and Millie left, but Mr. Sheppard, Alex, Steffi and I stayed. Steffi stuck very close to Mr. Sheppard and continued to avoid me. Eventually having stayed up all night caught up with her and she took a nap with her head resting in his lap.

Once Steffi was asleep Anna-Cat gave us a run down on Andy's condition.

"The good news is there's brain activity and he's made it this far. The bad news is, the swelling hasn't gone down, but that is normal. It is going to take a little while. So we're going to keep praying, letting the staff here do what they do and letting his body heal itself," Anna-Cat explained.

"We just wait?" Alex asked.

I hadn't really introduced the two of them last night so I did. "This is Andy's younger brother, Alex."

"Funny, my husband's name is Alex, too," she pointed out.

"Yeah, I'm Andy's half-brother. We share the same mother," Alex shared.

"Ah, okay, so Mr. Sheppard isn't your dad?"

"No." Then, Alex mentioned, "In fact, other than bumping into him around town, this was the first time I'd spoken more than two words to him in all my life."

"He seems like a nice guy," I added.

"Yeah. He looks all put together right now, but when I went to get him yesterday and told him what had happened to Andy the man broke down. I was worried if he was going to be able to pull it together and come inside the hospital. He carries a lot of guilt over the way Andy was brought up and I heard all about it on the ride here."

Alex shifted from leg to leg as he spoke and yawned a number of times. Steffi wasn't the only one that was drained. His yawning was contagious. We were all feeling the need for a nap.

Anna-Cat checked in on a few other patients she had from Wrens while there. She was the only one who had purpose to take her out of the room, a room with walls that were closing in and seats that were filling. Another patient, a gunshot victim was brought to the ICU. His family filled the room, but only long enough for us to get a good look at how we could be at any moment should Andy not pull through. They also gave us a glimpse of how lucky we were to have come this far. We'd been in the room for a full eighteen hours and they only lasted an hour and a half.

Another family arrived to hold vigil for a mother who'd just given birth to twins and threw a blood clot. It wasn't like the nurses just came out and told us who was there or why they arrived, but it was easy to figure out when they came in fighting.

"You did this to her!" the woman I assumed to be the mother of the woman in ICU said to a younger man. "Knocked her up, you did, with twins and..."

The woman's eyes were red and furious with tears and the young man on the receiving in, hardly a day over twenty, cried tears of hurt. I felt his plight and was tempted to intervene, but held my seat and tried not to watch.

"Glinda, please," the older man on her arm, escorting her to a chair said. "It's not his fault Jenny got a blood clot. These things happen sometimes."

"If he'd kept his pants up. I mean, she didn't get herself pregnant!" she sneered at the young man who took a seat in the corner against the far wall. "You might as well go ahead and hand us those babies to avoid DFCS going to the trouble of taking them."

The boy got to his feet. "You'll get my children over my dead body."

279

"That can be arranged." She then reared back and with all her might she spit at him from halfway across the room.

The wad of nastiness, flew past Mr. Sheppard and landed at Steffi's feet. Steffi jerked her feet off the floor, grabbed her knees to her chest and screamed. Alex and I were on our feet before Steffi could finish her scream.

"Excuse me!" I said in protest. "Ma'am, we all understand that your family is clearly going through something traumatic, but..."

"Oh, mind your own business!" The woman snapped at me.

"Well," I started again in a calm yet threatening voice, "when it comes to someone nearly spitting on my fourteen-year-old stepdaughter, it is my business. Now, each and every one of us in this room right now is worried sick about a loved one. You are welcome to sit with us and we can all pray together or you can take your prayers to the chapel. I hear it is on one of the other floors. I'm sure one of the nurses could escort you there."

For a moment I thought I was going to have to slap another woman. I'd never slapped anyone before having slapped Stacey earlier. Now I felt my palm twitch and, had that woman said one cross thing to me about Steffi and spitting in her direction, I knew I was up for doling out another smack.

The woman, exasperated, whirled on her heels. "Gerald, I can't with these...people. I'm going to find someone who can tell me what's going on with Jenny." She left the room without another word.

I looked at Steffi, and figuring it wouldn't matter to her, but said it anyway. "I'm not normally this hostile, and you may not think of me as family, but like it or not, we are. And," I added, "no one is going to treat my family like that."

Steffi smiled. She smiled at me and I tried not to get my hopes up that the little ice princess was melting.

That night, Alex took Mr. Sheppard and Steffi home.

"I don't want to leave," Steffi protested. "What if he wakes up and I'm not here? He'll think I don't care."

"Cara is going to call us and I'll come get you and bring you straight here if he wakes up," Alex assured her.

"What if he doesn't wake up and I'm not here to say goodbye?" Steffi started to cry.

Again, unsure if she'd want to hear anything I had to say, I took a chance. "We aren't going to think about him not waking up. He knows how much we love him and he's not going to let us down."

Steffi didn't tell me to shut up and didn't act nasty.

"But he doesn't know how much I love him." She wiped her eyes on her sleeve. "I was ugly to him yesterday and we didn't leave on good terms. I wanted him to take me to get ice cream after lunch and he said he had to go. I made him cave and get ice cream. After we had ice cream, I wanted him to take me shopping, but he told me he had an appointment and he really had to go, but he'd come back later in the week and take me to dinner and shopping. I told him not to bother coming back if he couldn't take me then. He said I was acting spoiled. He wouldn't have gotten in the wreck if it wasn't for me."

Hearing her confession hurt, but she was only a child, a teenager, and Andy's wreck was not her fault.

"Trust me, he knows how much you love him, but even more importantly, you need to know how much he loves you and he loves you more than you could ever imagine."

She wasn't behaving like a five-year-old now, but she was crying like a child would in this moment.

Reaching out and gently taking her hand, I went on. "He was the adult and he could have chosen to eat lunch and end your outing then, but he loves you so much that he wanted to please you by taking you for ice cream. He hates when you are disappointed, but at the same time, he loves you enough to want you to be a good person so he reprimanded you about acting spoiled, right? If he didn't love you, he wouldn't care if you were spoiled or not. He wouldn't put forth the effort to try to make you a good person."

Steffi nodded and Alex and Mr. Sheppard agreed with me about how much Andy loved her and that he knew she loved him. Reluctantly, Steffi left with Alex and Mr. Sheppard.

The next day, Anna-Cat tried to get me to go home to see Gavin and rest, but I refused to leave. I called and checked on Gavin. I missed him terribly, but Jay had things under control.

I agreed to leave long enough to meet Millie at Anna-Cat's parents' house. Anna-Cat drove and we met Millie who'd brought my car. While there, I showered, changed and looked over the documents she'd prepared. We'd talked about it on Saturday night and agreed Mr. Sheppard would appoint me as his Power of Attorney for making any medical decision for Andy in his absence.

"I really hope it doesn't come to this," looking up from the end of the page, I said to Millie.

"Better safe than sorry," she replied.

"If I would have just married him when he asked, we could have avoided all of this." I shook my head, still disgusted with myself.

"Should-a-would-a-could-a. You'll do better next time," she teased me, trying to lighten my mood.

"I just pray there is a next time."

"There will be a next time," she assured me.

Mrs. Calloway made me a plate of roast beef, carrots and mashed potatoes. It smelled heavenly. The hospital food smelled good too, but it tasted like lukewarm nothingness.

"They only let me see him at 11:30 a.m. and 3:30 p.m. and not again until 7:30 p.m. I only get ten minutes with him," I explained, reluctant to sit and eat. "You need to eat." Mrs. Calloway pushed the plate of food in front of me.

"You're no good to anyone if you don't take care of yourself," she added and Mille concurred.

I conceded and ate at breakneck pace, but didn't get back to the hospital with the speed I had intended. Traffic was terrible coming from the hill section of Augusta where the Calloway's lived back to the hospital. I got stopped by every single redlight and barely arrived in time for the 3:30 opening.

Although I'd been in the room to see him four times now, it didn't get any easier. I still had to take their word that it was indeed Andy in the bed. It didn't look like him at all. It didn't really look like a human at all.

Without a sound, I pulled the stool over and sat down. His hand was in the exact spot where I'd placed it the last time I was in the room, two inches between his pinky finger and the edge of the bed, palm down. His hand was probably the only thing that wasn't swollen and still looked like a normal hand. I eased my left hand under his and slowly raised it to meet my lips.

"I miss you," I said, tears creeping in. "I miss everything about you. Anna-Cat and your doctors swear this is temporary. Soon you'll wake up and see me sitting here and all of this will just be a little blip in our lives. You'll be fine."

I turned his hand over, tracing his life line. "See, it's long. Do you feel that? You're going to live to be 80 and, right here," I stopped my index finger at the half-way mark, "that's where you are now." I started to trace the line again. "And you have all of this to go. So, see, that's how I know you're going to be fine."

I didn't believe in all of the palm-reader/lifeline stuff, but I couldn't think of anything else to say. I spent all of the other times I'd been in there begging him to come back to me, telling him who all had been there or called to check on him and I'd told him all about how Gavin was missing him. I was running out of ways to hold up a one-sided conversation.

Monday slowly turned to Tuesday and Tuesday slowly turned to Wednesday.

I kept in touch with Alex and Mr. Sheppard who both swore they relayed my messages to Steffi. On Wednesday afternoon, I spoke with Alex and told him the latest.

"Do you think I should bring Steffi yet? She is hounding me to come back. I know she still feels terrible about how she left things with him."

"I don't know. I don't want her to be upset like I am keeping him from her, but I can't help thinking she's still a child and whether she should see him like this?" I had been pondering that question since the day she and her mother showed up at the hospital.

"We could always let her mother decide. If Stacey lets Steffi come, fine, that's on her. If she doesn't, fine, that's on her too."

"Good idea. Make her mother be the parent."

"Yeah, that too."

"One more thing, they talked about his hip again. They told me before they had been holding off on doing anything with it because..."

"Oh my God," Alex gasped. "He isn't going to be paralyzed, is he?"

"Ah, no. I mean, they didn't say that. It's just dislocated and they hadn't dealt with it due to the more pressing matters with his brain."

"Thank God! I thought you were about to say..."

"I'm so sorry. I didn't mean to scare you. I think with him making it this far they are starting to talk about his other injuries and what is coming next."

"So, that's hopeful?" Alex was getting the picture now.

"I think so."

I hadn't gone home since the day I arrived. I held vigil for Andy, wanting to be there if he woke up and scared he'd die if I left. I missed Gavin, but most of all, I missed our life together with Andy. Anna-Cat didn't usually come to the hospitals in Augusta or the one in Louisville or Thompson every day, but she'd made the trip to Doctor's Hospital every single day to check on Andy and to check on me. She'd basically been the medical terminology translator between Andy's doctors and myself. She made the big, ten syllable medical terms not so scary and helped me so I could keep Mr. Sheppard and Alex informed. She also wrote me a prescription for a little extra strength version of my keep the nightmares at bay meds. I'm not sure what I would have done without Anna-Cat.

Each of my friends had been a Godsend that week. Until this week, I hadn't felt so helpless since the nights David locked me in the closet. Sitting alone in the waiting room gave me time to think of a million little things. I wondered what my life would have been like if I had just reached out to my friends for help when I was married to David.

Friday night, I was right on time for our 7:30 appointment. I had no place else to be and I was living for the few moments I got to spend with Andy each day, still unsure if he'd recover and how many more moments I'd have with him.

"Ms. McConnell," Dr. Williams, the doctor who'd saved Andy the night he was brought in said gently prodding.

The ICU had been busy the night before and I hadn't had the waiting room to myself as I'd had some of the night's I'd been there. I hadn't been able to stretch out on one of the couches, but I'd managed to score one of the arm chairs in the corner of the room. It wasn't the most comfortable, nothing about that room was, but I'd managed to get a couple of hours sleep. I was asleep when Dr. Williams sat down in the chair next to me.

"Ms. McConnell," he said again.

I blinked, slowly opening my eyes, but noticing who it was saying my name, I snapped to full wakefulness. Terror flew through me.

"Is he okay?"

"Oh, yes, Mr. Sheppard's coming along nicely. I was just in there with him." Dr. Williams, in a manner much like that of Anna-Cat began detailing what I could expect next with Andy.

I slumped back in the chair, sighing with relief. "Thank God."

"So," he started again after giving me a moment to catch my breath. "I want you to go home, get some rest and be with your son."

I looked at him completely befuddled.

"I know you want to be here when he wakes up and I know you don't want him to be here alone, but perhaps we haven't been clear with you. It could take weeks or months for someone who's had the kind of injury he's had and the craniectomy, the surgery," he looked me directly in the eye. "It's a long recovery and he may not wake up for..."

"Weeks?" I asked. Resolve flew through me to stay as long as it took. "I can't leave him."

He nodded. "You're not doing him any good sitting out here and it's not good for you either. I'm sure he wouldn't want this for you."

The way he spoke to me reminded me of my grandfather. He delivered knowledge and comfort in just the way I needed.

"We're going to call you if there's the slightest change. Your friend, Dr. Calloway is also going to keep in direct contact with me and, you trust us to give him the best possible care, right?"

I inclined my head. "Yes, sir."

"Then trust me to take care of you. I promise I'll personally let you know when you need to be here and trust me to take care of him in your absence."

"I don't want to be absent. I want to be here."

"You can still visit, but you can't live here for weeks or months," he frowned. "You have a child that needs you too. He can't lose both of his parents, right?"

I understood he wasn't kicking me out and that he was sincere in putting things into perspective for me. Not that I hadn't thought of Gavin the whole time I was there, I just hadn't thought of him the way Dr. Williams made me think of him then.

Thursday morning I said my goodbyes to Andy, hoping he could hear me say how much I loved him and hoping he couldn't hear me say I was leaving. I cried all the way to the car and all through the drive home.

Once in my driveway, I sat in the car working up the courage to go inside. My wrist resting on the steering wheel, I buried my face in my left arm and just bawled. I still could not believe this had happened to us. Finally, I wiped my face and did my best to hide the tears. I didn't want Gavin to see me like this, a complete puddle of a woman.

Chapter 24

I assured Jay of something I wasn't even sure of myself. "We'll be alright. You can go home." I swore I would call him if I needed him.

I held back tears as Gavin and I waved goodbye to Jay from the front porch. I didn't want him to leave us, but I couldn't keep him any longer. He'd been so gracious to stay this long.

I let out a long roll of air as I shut the front door behind us. "It's just you and me for a while now, Buddy," I said, cuddling Gavin close.

He leaned back and in his little voice he said, "I want Daddy."

"I want Daddy too." I hugged him again.

I hadn't ever been in the house alone with Gavin. From the day he came to live with me, so did Andy. We just blended into a little family and there wasn't an inch of the house that Andy hadn't touched somehow.

The first night home was the worst. I'd slept in that bed for over a year before Andy came back into my life. I'd slept there alone, all stretched out in the middle with it enveloping me like a giant pillow. Now, I stood on my side staring down, wondering how I was going to get in it alone. I could hardly bring myself to look at Andy's side. Finally, I shook myself back to reality, grabbed my pillow and went to camp out in the twin bed in Gavin's room opposite of his crib. I awoke stiff and swearing off the twin bed.

The second night home, I put Gavin in my bed with me. I laid there stroking his hair and singing "Jerimiah Was a Bullfrog" and "Day Dream Believer", the only songs I really knew all of the words to. He drifted off to sleep in Andy's spot while sucking his thumb. I drifted off to sleep crying into my pillow.

I went back and forth to the hospital every couple of days and ladies from the church took turns hanging out with Gavin while I was gone.

"It still doesn't look like him," I whined to Anna-Cat.

It wasn't like just the portion of his head where they'd done surgery or where the headrest had impacted him that was swollen. He didn't just grow something like a cone. His entire head, face and all, was swollen and distorted. Yes, the swelling was going down ever so slightly and he still didn't look like himself. He looked like an old, fat, Cabbage Patch Kid or a sumo wrestler, little slant mouth and eyes, puffy cheeks and a whole lot more forehead than was normal.

"It's going to take time," she said, "but every day is a good day because it is a day more than I thought he was going to have when I got on that helicopter with him. He gets stronger every day. Hang in there."

Three weeks passed like a river of molasses flowing up hill. I'd started to notice a difference in the swelling. There wasn't so much of it. I could almost recognize him. Finally, the call came.

"They are weening him off of the medication. They're going to wake him up." Anna-Cat's voice was filled with excitement. "This is great news, Cara!"

"Can I be there? What do I need to do?" I was already packing my purse and thinking of who to call to stay with Gavin while I went back to the hospital.

"No, just wait," she told me.

"Wait? I've been waiting!"

"No, it's going to be a process. He's not just going to wake up from being asleep and wonder where you are and where he is. It doesn't work quite like that."

I stopped short of putting a toothbrush and toothpaste in my purse and sat down on the edge of the tub in my bathroom.

Anna-Cat went on, "They are going to scale back on the meds which will allow him to start waking up. They'll see how he reacts to pain..."

"Can they give him something for that?" I was so simple minded. I thought he was feeling all of his injuries,

289

like a massive headache or the pain from the breaks in his leg.

"No, they'll do a test on him."

Anna-Cat tried to put it in layman's terms, but I'm sure I still looked confused.

"They'll pinched him and if he twitches, great. Nothing complex and they are keeping his actual pain controlled with other meds."

"Ahh, okay," I understood that. I must have seemed really dense, but between the lack of sleep and the all-consuming, worry for Andy, I was not thinking straight. It had been almost a month since the accident and since then I hadn't slept more than a couple of hours at a time.

"Later in the morning they'll tested him again," Anna-Cat went on. "They'll give him a little shake see if he comes to a bit more, like opening his eyes. If all goes well, by tonight, he could be responding to sound."

"So, he might be able to hear me?" I could hardly contain myself.

I'd hoped he'd heard me all along, heard me begging him to come back to me, to Gavin, to Steffi and to everyone that loved him.

"Possibly." I could hear the hope in her voice.

After I got off of the phone with Anna-Cat, I didn't even move from my spot on the edge of the tub before I dialed Alex.

"They're waking him up!" I said before he had time to say "Hello."

"What?" Alex screeched. "I'll get Steffi and Mr. Sheppard and head that way!"

"No! Wait!" I cautioned. "It's not fast like you know, waking up in the morning or from a nap. It's going to be a bit before, or even if, I mean, just plan on...well, I don't know. They are just going to try and then run some tests. If it all goes well, then he should be responding to sound by tonight so..."

"Ah, okay. Tomorrow!" I could almost see him fist pumping.

"Just pray it all goes well. I'm trying so hard not to get my hopes up too high."

"I know," Alex consoled, "but, he's going to wake up and..."

"We're going to be there!"

I paused, considering Steffi. "Y'all are welcome stay here if you don't want to drive all the way back to Milledgeville. I mean, I'd give anything if you could help me with some small headway toward Steffi not hating me. Maybe if she saw that we had room for her in our house, in our lives? I don't know."

"I'll do what I can, but ever since Andy moved out her mother's been getting her claws in deeper. Just focus on Andy getting better, first things first, okay?"

"Okay, I know. I guess I just want him to wake up with his world better than he left it."

"He hasn't left it yet," Alex corrected me.

I made the trip to the hospital that night, leaving Millie's youngest daughter, George-Anne in charge of Gavin.

The lights were dim and the room still smelled like the love child of some sweetness I couldn't quite place and bleach. Andy was right where I left him two days before, bundled up to his chest.

I rolled the stool over to the bedside and took a seat. The swelling had gone down just a little more and I could see more than a hint of his face had returned. Still, I tried to picture him in his prime, a sight in my mind that always made my mouth water. I picked up his hand, turned it over and laid my cheek in his palm.

Feeling the softness of his touch, I asked, "Do you know what I love about you?"

His fingers curled and the tips brushed against my face. I might as well have been hit by a bolt of lightning. I snapped my head up, straightened all of me and looked his way.

291

"Did you just move your hand?"

His eyes, squinted by the puffiness that remained in his cheeks, were open, but fixed.

"Can you do it again?"

Nothing.

"Please. I know you can do it."

Nothing. Not one wiggle.

Disappointment drained through me. I waited. Knowing I felt him move and it wasn't just a muscle reflex as it was the whole hand lightly moving, a slight stroke of my cheek. I wondered was it a response to my question, but not my request. I leaned my face into his hand and I asked my initial question again. Perhaps the question prompted the response.

"Do you know what I love about you?"

It worked. He squeezed ever so slightly and his thumb moved across to meet the inside of his hand near his index finger, a caress.

Eager to answer, I just barely firmed my hand over his. "I love everything about you. Everything! Come back to me."

I gave Alex the Cliff Notes version of the call from Dr. Williams that morning. "Dr. Williams is putting the skull piece back on tomorrow morning."

"So soon?" Alex asked.

"I'm so nervous, but he said its time." I held the phone in one hand to my ear and with the other, I rubbed two fingers from the bridge of my nose up my forehead. "He said the longer they wait the less viable the bone is."

I felt a slight headache coming on due to the stress of worrying, but didn't dare complain considering what Andy's head must have felt like for the last month.

Alex listened as I went on. "I didn't quite understand all of it, even with Anna-Cat dumbing it down for me. Something about bacteria getting to the bone and, if that happened, they'd have to use some alternative."

"So, he might have a steel plate in his head?"

"I guess." Even though he couldn't see me, I shrugged. "Anyway, Andy's not talking, but he's definitely in there and ready to come out they have told me and after the other night, I know he heard me. I know he did!"

"I assume you're going to be there? Do you want me to come and wait with you?"

"Dr. Williams swore to me the worst part was over as far as fatality risk during surgery. He almost made like this was a formality. I guess he's a professional doing it every day so it may be just a formality for him, but jacking around with Andy's skull and brain is no formality to me. I won't turn down the company, but he made like this was a nonevent."

"I'm with you about brain surgery not being a formality. What time's the surgery?"

"7:00 a.m." I then added. "You're welcome to come tonight and stay here."

"I'll have to talk to Jenny, but I don't think she'll have a problem with it."

Alex arrived that night around 8:00 p.m. and he brought someone with him, Steffi and Mr. Sheppard.

"I hope you don't mind," he said, stepping aside so I could see who was with him at the door.

I hesitated due to the surprise of seeing them.

Steffi stepped forward first. "Uncle Alex said you wouldn't mind if I came, too."

I wanted to open my arms to hug her, but I was holding Gavin, plus I wasn't sure if that would be pressing my luck. I quickly replied, "I don't mind at all. You're welcome here any time."

Steffi held her posture like a normal fifteen-year-old girl as she entered the house. She didn't seem like the spoiled child she'd been at the hospital that first night.

"I'm so glad to see you." I shifted Gavin to free one of my arms. Using the free one, I took Mr. Sheppard by the hand and led him inside. "I wish it was under better circumstances."

"Mommy," Gavin said sleepily, "who's dis?"

293

"I'm Granddaddy," Mr. Sheppard said, holding out his arms to Gavin.

I cut my eyes to Steffi as Mr. Sheppard referred to himself. I guess I was lucky she was preoccupied helping Alex bring in their luggage.

Skeptical as ever, Gavin clung to me and nuzzled his face into my neck. He shied away from Mr. Sheppard.

"Please don't take it personally. Give him a few minutes and he'll warm right up," I pleaded.

"Not to worry, my dear. Andy told me quite a bit about him. I'd be shocked if the boy wasn't shy of strangers." He then spoke to Gavin, lovingly giving him a little stroke down the back of his head. "We've got plenty of time to get to know each other, don't we sport?"

Gavin peered at him from under his brows, still clinging.

Gavin had met Alex a couple of times and went to him straight away. Alex tossed Gavin in the air just like Andy would do to him and Gavin squealed with delight.

"Now he's never going to go to sleep," I shook my head, teasing Alex for getting Gavin riled up.

"I used to toss you in the air and you would giggle and scream to go higher," Alex said, including Steffi.

While Alex had Gavin, I showed Mr. Sheppard the room that I considered my grandparents. It had never been slept in since I built the house. After getting him settled, I returned and showed Steffi to her room.

"I hope I'm not pressing my luck by telling you this, but your dad decorated this room just for you." I opened the door to the bedroom off of the kitchen.

Steffi hesitated in the doorway. "You'll never be my mother," she said, but not snidely, just matter of fact, kind of warning me not to get my hopes up.

"I know, but if you will let me, I can be your friend. 'Mothers and daughters can't be friends,' is what my mother always said. I'm not your mother, but the friend part is up to you."

She glanced around the room, taking it all in, before letting her eyes land on me. "You're not going to go away, are you?"

I shook my head, "No."

She drew up to her full height. "You should know, I won't ever do more than tolerate you."

I stood firm, chin up and showing no intimidation by her height which was a solid six inches above mine. "Fair enough. At least I know where I stand."

She turned to put her duffle bag on the bed.

"I wasn't done," I called her attention back to me. "You should know that I will love you despite yourself for the sake of how much I love your father."

She eyes me with skepticism. "Fair enough."

The four of us waited for word on the surgery. It went well.

"Can I see him?" Steffi looked to all three of us.

I spoke for the group. "If they let any of us see him, then sure. You can come too."

The look on her face gave away her thoughts. Triumph of getting her way turned to fright of what she might see from one breath to the next.

"He's going to have bandages and look like he's asleep," Alex assured her.

"It won't look like you remember him, but he's in there and he's getting better," I added.

Eventually, we were invited back to see him. The rules were a little looser for our visits now, but not by much. Dim lights, no talking much higher than a whisper, and one at a time with the exception of Steffi who was allowed back only with the supervision of an adult. Mr. Sheppard went with her.

"I thought I could handle it," Alex wiped back tears as he waited with me while Mr. Sheppard and Steffi were in with Andy. "It's not like you hadn't warned us all. I mean, I just told Steffi what to expect, but when I saw him." Alex paused, trying to find the words.

"It's okay." I put my arm around him and we sat there in the waiting room with three other families. It was a busy day in the ICU.

"It's not okay. All I could think is that's my big brother. We've talked this situation to death," he paused again, realizing what he'd said. "Sorry. You know what I mean. It's just that he's always been invincible."

"I know exactly how you feel. You know how big he is compared to me. Those broad shoulders and his chest. Let's face it, he's shaped like Superman."

Alex let out a laugh. "Superman, so that's the draw for the ladies?"

"It's the draw for me." My thoughts shifted back to what I saw now. "Now he's so frail looking and that's so foreign to me, but I know he's in there. He'll bounce back."

"What if he doesn't?"

"I'll love him anyway."

"I knew you were going to say that, but come on? What if he's never the same?"

"Then I'll figure it out, but I don't want to think about that. I want to stay positive and hope for the best for him."

As Alex and I sat there waiting on Steffi and Mr. Sheppard to return, Anna-Cat arrived.

"They are going to keep him on steroids to give him time to heal from this and then they will wean him off of that," she told us. "He's making remarkable progress."

"Remarkable" must have meant "slow" in Anna-Cat's medical dictionary.

Four days later, Andy was coming around. He felt the pinch. He felt the shake. He heard sounds. He opened his eyes and started to move them around as if he was really looking at things. All of that was a definite. He wasn't fully aware yet, but he was getting there.

At the five-day post-surgery mark, I was there and he squeezed my hand. On day six, through a very raspy dry voice, he spoke. The first thing he said was, "I want to see my children."

296

I was so thrilled he used the plural. He wanted to see Gavin, too. I had hoped his first words would be, "I love you," but this was better. I thought his first request might be for food, a cheeseburger. He loved cheeseburgers from Longhorn's Steakhouse, but this was the best.

I picked up the phone and called Alex. "Bring Steffi as soon as you can. Andy's awake and asking for her and Gavin."

Even better, in Anna-Cat's opinion was that he was aware of his surroundings, knew who we were, that he had children and all of the tidbits that made up his life seemed to be there.

Exam after exam after exam and, finally, Anna-Cat gave the assurances all of us had been hoping for. "We won't know immediately the extent of any damage, but if there is any, it looks like it will be minor or the type that, given time, will heal. I think he's doing great!"

She explained he'd need physical therapy to get him walking and occupational therapy to help with motor skills, but he'd probably catch back on quickly.

Chapter 25

Six months post-accident, I stood over Andy and picked through his hair. "You can hardly see a scar. It really is remarkable."

"How is it that it itches and it's numb at the same time? Such a..." Andy trailed off searching for the word.

"Contradiction," I said, filling in the blank and barely scratching with the ends of my fingers, but not my nails.

Dr. Williams said his loss of words was normal, but, initially, it happened so frequently it frustrated Andy, now not so much.

A lot frustrated him early on. When he first got home, he was frustrated by the complete and total exhaustion he felt. He had to learn how to walk again and the cane was more of a hindrance to his pride and virility than it was an aid to his mobility. Next, he became frustrated that he couldn't pick up anything heavier than five pounds. Between the exhaustion, the weight restrictions and the utter refusal to be seen with the cane, meant I had to wait on him hand and foot.

A physical therapist came three times per week and that frustrated him as well.

"I'll fucking walk when I'm ready! I don't need a paid cheerleader!" He screamed at both of us one afternoon in the middle of a grueling session.

"I'm sorry," I apologized on his behalf. "He's not usually like this."

"Don't apologize for me. I meant what I said. I'm a grown ass man and I don't need this shit!"

"I'll see you again on Tuesday," the therapist said cheerily as she packed up her paperwork.

Andy scowled.

"I'll walk you out." I showed her through the foyer and back to the front door.

"He's got to get up and start moving. The old saying, 'Move it or lose it,' it's a real thing and he needs to get with the program before he loses it," she said clutching her paperwork to her chest.

"It's just that..." I started.

"Let me stop you right there. If you love him and want to help him, you won't make excuses for him." She looked all of twenty-five, but was clearly wise beyond her years. "March yourself back in there and tell him you expect better and since he's a grown ass man he'll do better. Now, chin up, you've got this."

"Okay," I squeaked out having been nearly stunned silent.

"I've seen it all. Men with limbs missing from landmines in Iraq. If they can get up and get on with it, prosthetics and all, he can sure 'nuff do it. I'll see you Tuesday."

After she left, I did march back in the living room where I found Andy kicked back with his feet on the coffee table.

"Well, you just embarrassed yourself royally. You know she works with wounded soldiers, yeah, guys who've had their legs blown off in Iraq and they get off their asses and work to get back on ...their new feet. Your feet and legs aren't the problem and your mind isn't the problem either."

I wasn't done yet, but Andy rolled his eyes right on cue.

"That's right. It is your attitude that is your problem. You know I still have that medical power of attorney from your father, right? If you won't help yourself while here, I'll have Anna-Cat fill out a referral for you to go to a rehab center."

Andy sat up. "You wouldn't?"

"Wouldn't I? I'll make you help yourself one way or another." I thought for a second and then hit him where he lived, right in his pride. "You hate that cane so much you don't want people to think you are frail. What will they think if they hear you are in a rehab center? And, just to be clear, rehab center is the nice, modern term for nursing home. You wanna go to a nursing home?"

"You can't do that!" Andy screamed.

I screamed back. "Try me!"

His attitude toward therapy did not become markedly better, but Andy did try and wasn't such an asshole to the therapist anymore. He was sore after each session and complained.

"That just means its working," I told him with a smile.

Two weeks after begin home, he forgot he wasn't supposed to lift anything and, when Gavin ran toward arm stretched wide and jumped into his arms, Andy snatched him up. Gavin weighed nearly thirty pounds and Andy immediately realized he'd made a mistake.

I heard the crash from where I was in the office and came running. I broke the threshold of the foyer to the living room to find Andy laying on the floor. I also heard the scream of broken curses coming from Andy. One of the words that were lost to him in that moment were 'America' and 'fucker.'

The string of curses that jumped from his mouth were intended to protect Gavin's ears, but when he couldn't recall the word 'America' it went downhill fast.

"God bless ..." He gritted his teeth. "Mother.... Oh, just God Dammit! Dammit! Dammit! DAMN IT!!!"

Unsteady on his feet and the blinding pain from the pressure of lifting a thirty-pound child, Andy's knees buckled and he went down like a shot barely having sense enough to lean back, placing himself between Gavin and the hardwood floor. Having hit the floor on his back, his chest softened the blow for Gavin, he loosened his grip and Gavin crawled away, terrified. Andy's hands had made their way to his head and he laid flat on the living room floor holding himself.

"Are you okay, baby?" I was talking to Gavin, having found him cowering by the end of the couch.

Andy answered, "No! I feel like my head is about to blow off the ... from above the ... joints that attach my bloomin' arms."

Gavin whimpered and pointed to Andy, "Hurt Daddy."

"It's okay, Sweetie, Daddy's okay."

"I am not okay!" Andy reigned in the volume as not to scare Gavin further, but still insisted on letting me know.

The frustration compounded three weeks after that when Andy had enough strength to make it up the stairs and moved back into our bedroom. I never closed the door to the bathroom, other than if I was using the toilet, and I never thought twice about getting undressed in front of him. That particular night, I stripped down starting in the bedroom and continuing to the bathroom in preparation for getting in the shower. All the while talking to Andy.

"Gavin has pre-school at the church tomorrow. Do you think you can stay put while I run him up there or would you like to ride with me?" I asked, slipping off my bra and panties in front of the bathroom sink and mirror.

Andy didn't answer.

"Hey," I called to him as I stepped in the shower. "Did you hear me?"

His hearing hadn't been a problem and it wasn't the problem then. Over the sound of the running water, I heard him, but it wasn't an answer to my question and I do not believe his statement was meant for my ears.

"I might as well have just died! I can't even get hard now!" His brain remembered the words and the concept just fine, but apparently his dick didn't and he sounded pissed.

I scrubbed up and pretended I didn't hear him. For a while, I took care not to flaunt myself in front of him. Of course, he noticed and wasn't please by that either.

One night I settled Andy into bed and proceeded to get undressed in the bathroom, leaving the door

301

cracked so I could hear him, but he couldn't see me. I thought I was being courteous, but it just served to fuel more of his frustration.

"I've about had it! I can't hardly taste food, but that's coming back. I can barely get up the stairs without needing a nap. I can't lift my kid without feeling like my head's going to explode. I can't half think. Now, I can't even look at you? Why didn't you just let me die?"

I stepped from the shower, not bothering with a towel and stormed back into the room, dripping water everywhere.

"Excuse me?" I glared at him, fiery eyed and fuming. "Did you just ask me why I didn't let you die?"

"Might as well have. This is no quality of life!"

"How dare you!"

I snatched a book from the shelf right outside of the bathroom door and threw it at Andy as hard as I could. He ducked and it crashed into the wall. He whipped his head around seeing the dent in the sheet rock left by the book and back to me.

"I'm tired of you sitting around here feeling sorry for yourself!" I yelled at him. "If you don't know why I didn't let you die then you really have got brain damage. And, just so you know, you find your words just fine when you are airing your grievances about having lived and how you're not satisfied with your predicament."

"I don't want to live like this!" He got to his feet and screamed at me.

I grabbed another book and hurled it toward him. I missed on purpose each time, but he didn't know that. "Then do something about it!" I screamed back as I let the third book fly.

Andy rounded the bed and I held my ground, only inching back to grab another book from the shelf.

"Throw another one and see what happens to you?" He dared me.

"Why? What are you going to do?" I goaded him and threw Pride and Prejudice. I still hadn't finished reading that book.

I aimed for just over his right shoulder, but this time I didn't miss. I intended to miss, but he was moving this time. I hit him square in the shoulder and it took him back a step.

"You hit me!" he protested.

I lied. "I meant to!"

Moving faster than he had since the accident, he darted toward me. I scrambled back feeling for another book, but apparently my bedroom library left a lot to be desired. The shelf was empty.

Andy grabbed me by both shoulders and shook me.

"Are you going to hit me?" I jerked and he tightened his grip. "Go on then! At least we'll both know there's still some fight left in you!"

A look of complete shock flew across his face.

I stretched my chin up toward him daring him to hit me and reminded him of something he'd once said on the drive home when I'd taken him to Easter with my family back in college. "Where is that guy that didn't want anyone to feel sorry for him especially not me?"

Andy let go of me and took a slinking step back.

Still in a fury, I went for him, aiming to slap him or punch him in his chest or strike him in some manner to snap him out of the self-pity and while screaming, "I want that guy back now!"

In the midst of my swing at him, I slipped in the water I'd dripped on the hardwood floor. Naked as a jay bird, I tried to recover my footing, but there was no recovering. I slipped with one foot, scrambled with the other and slipped with it. I threw out my hands, flailing about until my feet went totally out from under me and I squeaked, "Shit!" as I gave into the fall.

I definitely had Andy's attention and he stood there and laughed. Realizing how ungraceful that had just been, there was nothing for me to do but laugh as well.

I leaned up on my elbows starting to get up when Andy stooped to the floor to help me. He offered his hand, but I grabbed a fist full of his t-shirt instead and pulled him toward me. My legs went wide and I fell back to the floor.

"Remember the night on the floor in the foyer?" I asked him as I pulled him to me, wrapping my thighs around his hips and locking my ankles.

I pulled his t-shirt over his head and he let me.

"Let me remind you," I whispered into his neck as I planted kisses.

I could feel his arms tremble, straining to support his weight. He was thinner now, but not so thin as when I first brought him home from the hospital.

"I love you and I could never let you go," I said to him, using my legs to pull him closer to me, grinding his pajama pants into me.

Andy didn't draw back and there was a hint that all was not lost as he'd previously suspected.

"It may not be tonight," I bucked my hips into him, "and, if it's never, I'll love you just the same."

He might not have been able to find his words all the time or use his dick to his full intention, but he used his hands and found all of the right spots that night. It seemed like a lifetime since he'd touched me and it didn't take much.

"What if that's all I'm ever able to do for you?" he asked when I climbed into bed.

"You know our life is about more than sex, right?" I cuddled into his outstretched arm.

"I know, but..."

I cut him off. "Would you not love me anymore if I could never get you off again? Would you leave? Would you... what? What would you do?"

Andy didn't have an answer.

"I'm sure you'd be pissed and we'd see every doctor around if that's what you wanted to do, but would it change how you feel about me?"

He shook his head, "No." He thought for a moment. "It changes how I feel about myself."

"I know." My fingers were laced with his and I pulled his hand to my mouth and kissed it. "I think you just need to take the time to heal and not put so much pressure on yourself. You're not going anywhere and neither am I so just relax."

I scooched down and laid my head on his chest. "The fact that you are here at all is enough for me so no more talk of letting you die and you've got to get over feeling sorry for yourself. It really is the least sexy thing about you."

Andy stroked my hair. "I'll do what I can."

I fell asleep on his chest.

Weeks passed and Andy inched toward his former self. Alex, Steffi and Mr. Sheppard called frequently to check. Alex brought Steffi to visit every other weekend and Mr. Sheppard made several visits as well. Andy's boss from Port Honor also visited. They were holding his job for him.

The more time passed, the better things got.

"What are you doing?" I said through a yawn.

At first, I thought I was dreaming. I had the most real sensation of a tongue grazing my ear lobe and a slow, firm hand inching down my thigh. It wouldn't have been the first dream of this sort I'd had in the last few months, but it wasn't a dream.

"I need you," through the darkness of the bedroom, Andy's voice came in a heated whisper on my ear.

This was real. This was happening. I could feel him hard against my ass. I rolled in his arms to face him. Potentially afraid that his time was limited or in the throes of madness from pent up frustrations, Andy tore off my pajamas with the speed of a teenager needing to get their rocks off before the parents returned.

"I don't think I can go slow," he growled deeply.

"That's okay," I panted, "I've been wet for you for weeks."

Unsure of how much energy he could exert, I rolled him to his back and climbed on top of him.

"Oh, God, yes!" He said with enthusiasm.

The street light at the corner shined threw the window, giving just enough light for my eyes to adjust and they raked across Andy as we moved together. I didn't have to close them and imagine what he once was. His face wasn't gaunt anymore and the natural bulk in the tone of his pecks was returning. I could see them and feel them as my palms rested on his chest. He wasn't so frail anymore and he wasn't helpless.

Andy had never been a "two pump chump" as Jay had described some of his past lovers, but this time he came fast.

"Shit!" He breathed raggedly as he came and quaked out the words, "I'm so sorry."

I leaned over and laid my chest on his, letting my hands glide over his arms and into his. I locked our fingers together. "Don't worry about it. I had to think of dead puppies to keep from coming when you did that thing you do to my nipple."

Andy shifted me onto my back, "I can do it again, if you like."

I nodded, biting my lower lip in anticipation. I wanted him back inside me and his mouth and hands all over me. I wasn't ready for this to end.

Andy had a talent with his tongue which answered the question of whether a woman could orgasm from just nipple action. That night, I learned the answer. It was yes. I couldn't put into words what exactly he did, but it blazed a trail straight to my G-spot.

One morning, while Gavin was at the church school, I coaxed Andy to walk with me across to the park.

He'd been out of the house several times for doctor's appointments, but down the street and across to the park was the farthest he'd walked at that point. His strength was recovering nicely, but he was slightly winded when we made it to the merry-go-round and he took a seat to rest.

"You're dying to spin me, aren't you?" He asked breathing a little heavier than the average person for such a short walk and glancing up at me.

"You know me too well," I grinned, resting a hand on the bar as if I was going to give it a whirl. "I won't, but you know I want to."

I wouldn't dare spin him. I couldn't imagine what that might do to him. The headaches tapered off at about the one-month mark, but he still got them. He described them as 9 to 10 of 10 on the pain scale and I wasn't about to risk setting one off. They came on about twice a week in the afternoons and wiped him out for the rest of the day.

I waited a minute, letting him catch his breath before I got to the point of our stroll. As he leaned his head back, closed his eyes and concentrated on breathing, I dropped to my knee in front of him.

Andy opened his eyes, checking to see what I was doing and found me kneeling. "What are you doing?"

"Remember the last time we were here and what you asked me?" I watched his for his expression, expecting he'd know what I was talking about.

Andy remembered everything up until the day of the accident. He didn't remember much of the day before the wreck and things were foggy from the time he woke up in the ICU until about ten days after that. I was certain he would remember the day he asked me to marry him, but his expression didn't waiver.

I reminded him, "You asked me..." I wanted him to figure it out without me having to completely spell it out.

"Right here," I pointed to the bench where he was sitting and back to where I was standing. "But I was sitting and you were here."

307

I knelt there and Andy let me linger, actually wondering what he was thinking.

"Perhaps, we could revisit..."

Before I could finish, Andy looked away, pensive, as the tiny pebbles mixed about the sand, dug into my knees. The glass cutting feeling mixed with the wait was causing considerable discomfort.

"Well?" I questioned.

I hadn't asked out right, but he knew the question and his sense of inference hadn't been lost in the accident. He knew exactly what I was getting at and was letting me stew. Maybe I deserved it after giving the answer I gave when he asked.

"Oh, I don't know." He didn't meet my eyes.

"You don't know?" I got to my feet, indignancy resonating more so than the heartbreak.

"See, I was thinking, perhaps I need another near-death experience so you can be certain about this." His right brow arched a bit and the corner of his mouth twitched up. That was his tell. He was teasing me.

"Don't joke about such things!" I demanded hotly.

"I'm not the man I was," he cautioned.

I turned in frustration even though I was aware he was likely toying with me.

"I'm pretty high maintenance now and, I dare say, I'm more of a head case than you."

Andy had regained his strength so grabbing my hand, whirling me around and catching my off-balance fall into his lap was a successful move for him. We didn't topple over and make a complete repeat of our last trip to the park.

Andy kissed me, slow deep and hard.

I drew away barely, using my cheek to caress his and ask, "What are you doing this Saturday?"

His hands still in my hair and holding me pressed to his chest, for the first time in ages, I relaxed in his arms. The rise and fall of his muscles with each breath moved

308

me concurrently as we seemed to float together on the merry-go-round.

"Saturday, two days from now?"

A car passed on the street and, with my peripheral vision, I saw the driver wave. I didn't wave back. I couldn't think past planning a wedding with Andy.

"Yes. This Saturday. Around 2:00 p.m." I placed soft kisses and nibbled at his ear lobe.

"Probably sitting on the front porch, counting the cars that stop at the four-way."

I cocked my head and Andy snapped back matching my move.

Facing me, he said with all kidding aside. "I have a feeling I'm getting married that afternoon."

"I think you are."

"What if our friends and family already have plans?"

"Do you plan to marry them?" I asked, this time messing with him.

"No, but don't you want them to be there."

"Of course, but I don't need anyone but you to be there." I emphasized the word "need."

So, here we were six months after the accident ignoring the old superstition about seeing the bride before the wedding. We were living on faith that the bad luck was behind us.

Andy sat on the toilet lid and I stood over him, combing his hair. I couldn't see the scar at all unless I really searched for it. "It really is remarkable. You know, Dr. Williams is coming today."

Andy stood. "Turn around. I'll help you with your dress." He fumbled with the buttons on my dress. "It'll be good to see him."

"Yeah," I said lifting my hair as he inched up the back.

My dress was so different from the one I'd worn in my first wedding. First of all, the color was candlelight and not white. This time the dress wasn't the fairytale, the wedding was.

Finished with the buttons, Andy wrapped his arms around me and rested his chin on the top of my head. He was already in his shoes and I was still barefooted. He looked over my head at our reflection in the bathroom mirror. "You are so beautiful."

"This old thing?" I questioned, referencing the dress.

I'd found the dress in my grandmother's house when I was cleaning it out before the demo and reconstruction. It was in a giant Ziploc bag inside a box on a shelf where it has sat since the invention of Ziploc bags. As soon as Andy got out of the hospital, I had it dry cleaned and tailored to fit me. I also had it altered, removed the sleeves and dropped the neckline. Now it wasn't so conservative as it was when she wore it as a World War II bride.

I turned in his arms and admiring his smile. I fingered the collar of his shirt, unbuttoned and casual under a black tuxedo jacket. "I would have helped you with your tie."

"I'm not gonna wear one."

"Oh really?"

"Nope."

I stood on my toes. "You're perfect just the way you are." I kissed him.

Another superstition is that rain on your wedding day brings good luck. It didn't just rain on our wedding day, it poured buckets. Chairs sat empty in the side yard, short of the puddles that filled the seats. The roughly two dozen guests including our mutual friends Millie, Gabe and their daughters, Jay and Peter, Daniel and Jerry, Anna-Cat, Alex and Auggie, Mr. McDonald, Millie's Aunt Gayle, my cousin Grace and her mother, Andy's brother Alex and his wife and children, Mr. Sheppard and Andy's step-mother and lastly Gavin and Steffi came. Stella sent her regrets.

As many as could fit peered through the windows of the kitchen to the side porch where Millie, not only a local attorney, but a Justice of the Peace, readied herself to marry us. The side porch was lined with yellow roses and each bud had opened overnight. They had taken a beating by the rain, but they were shining as bright as the sun.

Nervously killing time waiting for Millie, Andy glanced around and, noticing the fullness of the bushes with all of their blooms, Andy took my hands and commented, "It's as if she's giving her blessing."

"Your grandmother?" I assumed aloud.

Tears formed in the inside of his eyes. "I wish she was here."

"I wish she was too. I would like to thank her."

"For what?"

"For making you into the fine man you became. I hope I can do as well with Gavin."

That afternoon, Jay was the most amazing bridesmaid ever and Andy's brother served as best man. They huddled with us and our children as Millie guided us through our vows and pronounced us man and wife. Steffi was even a good sport and held my flowers while Jay held Gavin.

The reception followed where our guests toasted us with glasses of Old Fashioned and Port.

Thank you for reading.

Other Books by T.S. Dawson

The Port Honor Series
Port Honor
In Search of Honor
The Price of Honor

The Wrightsboro Hunt Series
When I Was Green
A Horse of a Different Color

The Senator Series
My Summer With the Senator
The Road to the White House

The New Normal

Available for purchase on Amazon.com for Kindle and in
paperback format as well as From Books on Broad, an
independent book store in Louisville, Georgia.